THE FIFTH VICTIM

Beverly Barton

ZEBRA BOOKS
KENSINGTON PUBLISHING CORP.

http://www.kensingtonbooks.com

THE NEXT TO DIE

"What is it?" Genny asked. "What did Teri tell you about me?"

"Teri has searched through every bit of information she could find about the fifth victim in each series of murders," Dallas said. "Linc Hughes believes that all the other victims, the first four in each case, might have simply been chosen at random, but the fifth victim was somehow different."

"Different in what way?"

"Through some intensive research, Teri has found something that all four of the fifth victims had in common," Dallas said. "Barbara James, who was the fifth victim in Mobile, had a rare talent. According to her family, she was clairvoyant."

Genny closed her eyes.

"The first fifth victim, Kim Johnson, entertained her friends with telekinetic tricks. Daphne Alaire worked part-time as a medium. Lori Wright was telepathic. Apparently the friends and families of the fifth victims hadn't bothered mentioning their unique talents because they hadn't thought that information had anything to do with their murders."

"I'm the reason he's come to Cherokee County," Genny said, certainty in her voice. "He intends for me to be his fifth victim. . . ."

Books by Beverly Barton

AFTER DARK

EVERY MOVE SHE MAKES

WHAT SHE DOESN'T KNOW

THE FIFTH VICTIM

THE LAST TO DIE

AS GOOD AS DEAD

KILLING HER SOFTLY

CLOSE ENOUGH TO KILL

✓ MOST LIKELY TO DIE

THE DYING GAME

THE MURDER GAME

Published by Zebra Books

To my precious niece, Ja'Net Horton, who is as beautiful inside as she is outside. I remember the first time I saw her when she was a little beauty of eight and I was dating her uncle. I knew then that I wanted a little girl who looked like her—blond curls, blue eyes, and sweet smile.

Prologue

Dark. Cold. Predawn quiet. Wind whipped through the tall, ancient trees in the forest. Soon the sun would ascend over Scotsman's Bluff. He was prepared, ready to strike the moment the morning light hit the altar. Once the deed was done, once he had sacrificed the first victim, the ritual would begin anew. As soon as he tasted her sweet life's blood, he would no longer feel the winter's cold. Her blood would warm him, empower him, prepare him for the others who would lead him to the most important transposition of his life. All these years he had diligently searched for perfection, for the most powerful, all the while building his strength, bit by bit, with lesser mortals.

He gazed down at the naked girl tied to the wooden altar, her long blond hair flowing about her angelic face as the frigid wind caressed her luscious body. Her eyelids fluttered. Good. That meant the drug he'd given her was wearing off and she would be awake for the ceremony. He loved to see the look on their faces—the shock and horror—when they realized what was about to happen to them.

Flinging back his dark cape, he smiled. There was no need to hurry. He could take his time afterward, savor the kill for as long as he liked. No one in their right mind would be out in the woods at dawn in January. Only he and the girl.

He laid the ornately carved wooden case atop the girl's trembling body, opened it and removed the heavy sword, then placed the case on the ground. Gazing up at the sky, he waited.

She whimpered, but the gag in her mouth kept her from doing more. He glanced down at her, ran his hand over her naked breasts and lifted the sword toward the heavens.

A pale pink blush spread out over Scotsman's Bluff, only a hint of color in the dark sky.

"Soon, my little lamb. Soon."

Languidly, with tendrils of light reaching farther and farther into the sky, the sun welcomed the dawn of a new day. He jerked the gag from her mouth. She screamed. He brandished the sword and spoke the sacred words in an ancient tongue.

From the depths of hell, hear me and do my bidding. Let this sacrifice please thee. I bid thee to accomplish my will and desire.

He brought the sword down, down, down. From throat to navel, he split her open. Her sightless eyes stared up at the towering treetops overhead.

He wiped the sword with a soft cloth and returned the weapon to its bed, then stuffed the bloodstained cloth into a plastic bag and dumped the bag into the case. With her blood still warm, he lowered his head until his lips touched the gaping wound. He licked, then sucked, filling his mouth with her blood and energizing himself with her life force before it escaped.

Genevieve Madoc woke with a start, sweat drenching her body, soaking her flannel gown. Her heart beat at a dangerously accelerated pace as she shot straight up in bed.

"Oh, God! Oh, God!" she moaned as she recalled her dream, a shadowy, terrifying vision of death.

Uncontrollable tremors racked her body. She hated these moments directly following a revelation, when she was weak and vulnerable. Drained of all energy, barely able to move. She fell backward; her head hit the pillow. She would call Jazzy for help once she regained enough strength to reach out to the nightstand for the telephone. But for now she would lie still and wait. And pray the images would not return. Sometimes *the sight* came to her in dreams, but just as often she experienced it while wide awake.

Rising from the handwoven rug in front of the fireplace, Drudwyn's keen eyes searched the darkness, seeking his mistress. He uttered a concerned whimper.

"I'll be all right," she told him, her voice a delicate whisper. Then she spoke to him telepathically, assuring him that she was in no danger. The big, mixed-breed animal lumbered to the side of the bed, then slumped to the wooden floor. She sensed his mood and knew his protective instincts had automatically kicked in. The dog she had raised from a mongrel puppy considered himself her bodyguard. Like she, Drudwyn's heritage—the results of a wolf having mated with a German shepherd/Lab-mix mutt—made him unique. Her ancestry, comprised of Scots-Irish, English, and Cherokee might not be all that uncommon in these parts, but the gift of sight she had inherited from her grandmother was.

As she lay in bed, waiting for her strength to renew, she couldn't help thinking of the vision she'd had. Out there somewhere, a young woman had been murdered. Genny knew it as surely as she knew her own name. She had not seen the girl's face, only her flawless naked body and the huge sword that had sliced her open as if she were a ripe melon. Bile rose from Genny's stomach and burned a path up her esophagus to her throat.

No, please, I can't be sick. Not now. I don't have the strength to crawl out of bed. She willed the nausea under control.

Who could have committed such a heinous crime? What sort of monster would sacrifice a human being?

Her cousin Jacob had mentioned that there had been several animal sacrifices in the area—four since Thanksgiving. Had those been nothing more than a precursor to the killing of a human?

After she called Jazzy for help, she would call Jacob. It would be too late for him to do anything to help the woman, but as the county sheriff, it would be his job to investigate the murder.

What will you tell him? Genny asked herself. *If you explain that you've had another vision, only this one far more gruesome than any you've had before, he'll understand. He's your blood-kin. He won't dismiss your vision as nothing more than a dream.*

Fifteen minutes later, Genny forced herself to ease to the edge of the bed. She lifted the telephone receiver and dialed Jazzy's number. The phone rang five times before a harsh voice answered.

"Who the hell's calling at this ungodly hour?"

"Jazzy?"

"Genny, is that you?"

"Yes. Please—"

"I'm on my way. Just stay put."

"Thank you."

The moment she heard the dial tone, Genny punched in Jacob's home phone number. He picked up on the second ring. Always an early riser, as was she, her cousin was probably in the middle of preparing his breakfast.

"Butler here," he said, his voice gruff and deeply baritone.

"Jacob, it's Genny. Please, come to my house . . . now."

"What's wrong?"

"I've had a dream . . . one of my visions."

"Are you all right?"

"No, but I will be. I've called Jazzy. She'll be here soon. But I must tell you . . ." Her voice suddenly failed her.

"Tell me what?"

She cleared her throat. "Someone has been murdered. A young woman. I'm sure you'll find her body in Cedar Tree Forest, not far from here. I saw . . . through the killer's eyes

. . . I saw—'' She sucked in a deep breath. ''He watched the sunrise over Scotsman's Bluff.''

''Are you sure, Genny? Are you positive it wasn't just a nightmare?''

''I'm positive. It's too late to save her, but you can find her body and perhaps find some evidence of who killed her—if you can get there soon. I think I can guide you to the exact spot.''

''Ah, shit . . .'' Jacob murmured under his breath.

''Jacob?''

''Hmm?''

''He tied her to an altar of some sort and sacrificed her. I—I think he drank her blood.''

''God damn son of a bitch!''

Chapter 1

FBI Special Agent Teri Nash glanced at the fax in her hand. A letter and a photograph. While waiting for Dallas to shower and shave, she'd sat down at his cluttered desk in the corner of the living room. The fax had come in while she'd been relaxing with a gin-and-tonic. Dallas and she hadn't dated in several years, and she was actually involved with a profiler at the Bureau, but she still considered Dallas a good friend. Since his niece's death eight months ago, she'd tried to keep tabs on her old lover. Although he'd handled Brooke's brutal murder as he did everything else—with little emotion and iron control—she'd seen past his steely facade to the pain beneath. Once he'd returned to FBI headquarters in D.C. after Brooke's funeral, he'd begun a personal search for any information that might lead him to his niece's killer. Using the Bureau's vast resources for unofficial use had become a bone of contention between Dallas and the assistant director of the Criminal Investigation Division. Although Dallas and Tom Rutherford disliked each other personally, Tom had allowed Dallas a lot of slack. Teri wondered for how much longer?

She read the fax for the third time. The message was in

response to a letter Dallas had sent out to local law enforcement officials nationwide. This was the seventh such response in the past few months, but she had a sinking feeling that this was the one he'd been waiting for ever since Brooke's murder. Teri didn't want to look at the faxed photo again. Once had been more than enough. It wouldn't be easy forgetting the sight of the young blond girl with her body sliced wide open. Teri shivered.

The sheriff of Cherokee County, Tennessee, had reported what appeared to be a sacrificial killing in his county early this morning. The details of her death were practically identical to those of Brooke's horrific murder in Mobile, Alabama, in May of last year.

As Teri finished scanning the information again, she shook her head and sighed. The minute Dallas saw this fax, he'd be off and running. On some sentimental, protective level, she wished she could just dump the fax in the garbage and pretend it didn't exist. Even though her love affair with her fellow agent had been short-lived and had ended three years ago, she still had strong feelings for him. The poor guy had been through enough, had followed too many dead-end leads these past few months. She hated to see him go off on another wild-goose chase, searching for an elusive serial killer. That is, if there was a serial killer. Dallas had come up with his own theory that there was a barbaric serial killer on the loose. Besides, she wasn't sure how many more vacation days he could take before he used them all up. Or how much longer Rutherford would put up with Dallas's absenteeism.

Dallas Sloan, his dark blond hair damp from his shower, emerged from the bathroom adjacent to the small bedroom in his three-room efficiency apartment. Teri sucked in a deep breath. Damn, the guy still took her breath away. Wearing nothing but his white briefs, he exposed his tall, lean body for her perusal. A dusting of brown hair covered his legs and arms and created a V over the center of his muscular chest. Teri forced her gaze from his body to his face. He grinned at her. Wickedly.

class at the junior college last fall, you done gone and got all uppity on me.''

"Me uppity?" With large, expressive black eyes, Ludie glared at Sally. "You're the one who's been acting like rich folks ever since Jazzy had that white siding put on the outside of this shack of yours.''

"Are you calling my house a shack? What do you call that place of yours—a palace?''

"I call it a cottage," Ludie replied. "That's what I call it. A cottage. Like one of them pretty little places you see on calendars and in the movies about the English countryside before World War Two.''

"Now what would an old Cherokee squaw from the hills of Tennessee know about the English countryside? Besides, your house ain't no cottage. It's a four-room, wooden share-cropper's shack, the same as mine.''

"Well, Miss Know-It-All, I know as much about the English countryside as you do. And who are you? Just a crazy old white heifer from the Tennessee hills.''

Jazzy Talbot stood in the doorway that separated her aunt Sally's kitchen from the living room where Sally and her best friend Ludie stood arguing together as they'd done as far back as Jazzy could remember. Any outsiders listening to the two old women would swear they hated each other, when in actuality the exact opposite was true. Ludie and Sally had been friends all their lives, but neither would ever admit how much they truly loved each other. Their favorite form of entertainment seemed to be debating a wide variety of subjects—everything from the weather to the proper way to cook collard greens.

Jazzy cleared her throat. Both women hushed immediately and turned to face her. Rawboned, with big hands and feet, Sally stood nearly six feet tall, possessed a shock of short white hair and ice blue eyes. With black eyes and steel gray hair, Ludie, on the other hand, was barely five feet tall and round as a butterball. Jazzy had no idea exactly how old either woman was, but her best guess would be that her aunt and Ludie had both passed their seventieth birthday.

"How long you been here?" Sally asked, a broad smile on her face.

"Just got here. Didn't you hear the Jeep?"

"She was too busy caterwauling," Ludie said. "She thinks it's gonna snow, but the weatherman said plainly that—"

"It's going to sleet and ice over first, then snow," Jazzy said.

Both women stared at her with round eyes and wrinkled brows.

"How do you—you've seen Genny today, haven't you?" Sally lifted another piece of wood, then stuffed it into the stove. After shutting the door and trapping the fire inside, she wiped her hands off on her faded jeans.

"Did Genny say it's going to snow?" Ludie asked.

Jazzy nodded. "I heard her tell Jacob that they'd better go over the crime scene with a fine-tooth comb now because of the bad weather we'll get tonight. She thinks it'll be really rough."

"Then we'd better get ready for it," Sally said. "That gal ain't never wrong about the weather. She's just like her granny. Melva Mae had *the sight,* too."

"Ain't it awful about that poor little Susie Richards." Ludie shook her head. "What kind of person would do such a thing to anybody, least of all a seventeen-year-old girl?"

"Why were you up at Genny's?" Sally asked. "Did she have another spell?"

Jazzy nodded. "She saw the Richards girl being killed. But that information is not to be broadcast by either of you."

Ludie keened. "Lord have mercy!"

"She called Jacob and told him where he could find Susie's body. Now, he's got a murder case to solve and a county filled with scared people."

"Jacob ain't got the manpower or the up-to-date equipment to handle a crime scene investigation." Sally headed toward the kitchen. "You staying for supper, gal, or you heading back to your place before the weather turns bad on us?"

"Guess I'll head home," Jazzy replied. "I just stopped by to see if you needed anything. With you out here so far away from town, you might not be able to make it in to Cherokee Pointe for several days if there's ice under the snow."

"Got all I need." Sally called from the kitchen. "Want a cup of coffee before you leave?"

"Coffee and a piece of that custard pie I saw on the counter." Jazzy winked at Ludie, knowing full well that Ludie had baked the pie and brought it over. Sally wasn't much of a cook—never had been. If it hadn't been for Ludie's good cooking, Jazzy figured she'd have grown up on nothing but cornbread, fried potatoes, and whatever greens were in season. Ludie had a real talent for cooking and worked at Jazzy's restaurant in town. Last year, she'd cut back from full-time to only a few days a week.

When Jazzy and Ludie joined Sally in the kitchen, Sally had already sliced the pie and set three plates and forks on the table. She lifted an old metal coffeepot from the stove and poured steaming black coffee into mismatched earthenware mugs.

As the three sat around the yellow oilcloth-topped table, Sally and Ludie got awfully quiet. Jazzy had an uneasy feeling that there was something wrong. Something other than the fact that there had been a murder in Cherokee County yesterday.

"Business good?" Sally asked.

"As good as it usually is in January," Jazzy replied. "We've got a handful of tourists staying in the cabins and a few more stopping by the restaurant on their way to Pigeon Forge and Gatlinburg."

"It'll pick up in the spring," Ludie said. "Always does."

"I'm ready for spring, myself." Sally sipped on her coffee.

"Me too." Ludie sighed. "Nothing like spring birds chirping and buttercups and tulips blooming."

Jazzy caught her aunt and Ludie exchanging peculiar glances. "All right, what's going on?"

"Don't know what you're talking about." Sally stared up at the bead-board ceiling.

"Might as well tell her," Ludie said. "I'm surprised she hasn't already heard."

"Heard what?" A tight knot formed in the pit of Jazzy's stomach.

"Just 'cause he's back don't mean you gotta have anything to do with him." Sally skewered Jazzy with a warning glare. "If he comes sniffing around, send him packing. That's what you'll do if you're smart. He ain't no good. Never was."

"Who are you talking about—my God! You don't mean that—"

"Heard it in town this morning, before the news about the Richards gal got out," Ludie said. "Jamie Upton showed up at the farm two days ago, and his granddaddy done brought out the fatted calf to celebrate the prodigal's return."

"Tell her the rest," Sally said.

Ludie hung her head and avoided eye contact with Jazzy. "He's brought home a woman with him."

"A wife?" Jazzy asked.

"A fiancée," Ludie replied.

"He's been engaged before," Jazzy said. "That doesn't mean anything. You know how Jamie is."

"I know he ain't worth shooting." Sally finished off her coffee, then rose and poured herself another cup.

Jazzy toyed with the piece of pie. She loved Ludie's pies but knew that if she took a bite now it would taste like cardboard in her mouth. It wasn't that she was still in love with Jamie. Actually she wasn't sure she'd ever loved him. But she'd wanted him. God, how she'd wanted him. He'd been her first, back when she'd been young and foolish enough to think Big Jim Upton's only grandson would marry the likes of her, a white-trash bastard raised by a poor, eccentric old woman half the town thought was crazy.

Jazzy rose to her feet. "I'd better be heading into town. Can I give you a ride home, Ludie?"

"Goodness no. You know my place ain't a quarter of a mile from here."

"But with a killer on the loose—"

"Got my revolver in my coat pocket, as always," Ludie said. "You know I don't go nowhere without it."

Ludie carried an old Smith & Wesson that had belonged to her father; and Sally toted a shotgun. A couple of old kooks, that was what most folks thought.

Jazzy hugged Ludie, then turned to her aunt. "Keep your doors locked."

"I intend to," Sally assured her. "I've got my shotgun, and I'll bring Peter and Paul in before nightfall, like I always do in the dead of winter. Them dogs ain't gonna let nothing slip up on me."

Five minutes later Jazzy headed her Jeep down the mountain toward Cherokee Pointe, all the while her mind swirling with memories of Jamie Upton. His smile. His laughter. The way he called her darlin'. The little presents he'd given her over the years—ever since she'd been sixteen and had given him her virginity. Expensive trinkets. Payments for services rendered? He'd told her at least a hundred times that he loved her. Every time he left town for months, even for years, he came home expecting her to be there waiting for him, with arms wide open. Actually, a better expression would be with legs spread apart. Why was it that every time he came back, she found herself unable to resist him?

Because, idiot, every time he comes back into your life, he convinces you that he loves you, wants you, and someday you'll have a future together. Even when he'd brought home a fiancée, on two other occasions, he'd come to her for sex. How could she have been so damn stupid?

Well, this time Mr. Jamie Upton could find himself another whore. That's the way he made her feel—like the whore people thought she was.

Just as she rounded the next corner, the county roads intersected. She halted at the four-way stop and glanced to her left at the arched gates and long driveway that led up to the biggest farm in Cherokee County—the Upton farm.

Half a mile up the private drive sat a typical Southern mansion, fashioned after old antebellum homes and built over a hundred years ago for Big Jim Upton's grandmother, who'd been a Mason from Virginia.

Once, long ago, Jazzy had dreamed of marrying Jamie and living in that big white house, with hot and cold running servants. All her life she'd wanted more, needed more than four walls and a roof. Something inside her yearned to be a lady, and to her that meant being wealthy.

Jazzy swallowed the emotions lodged in her throat, laughed out loud, then gunned the motor and raced through the intersection. Maybe this time Jamie wouldn't come looking for her. But if he did, maybe this time she'd find the strength to turn him away.

Jacob Butler zipped up his brown leather jacket, positioned his brown Stetson on his head and headed out of his office. He hadn't had a bite to eat since he'd wolfed down a scrambled egg sandwich at seven this morning while he'd been heading toward Scotsman's Bluff. It had been a long, tiring day. He was now facing his first murder case since he'd been elected sheriff.

Deputy Bobby Joe Harte called out as Jacob passed by his desk, "That FBI guy just called. He said to tell you he's in Knoxville and has rented a car. Said he was heading out soon and wanted to talk to you tonight when he gets in."

"Did you tell him it was going to snow tonight?" Jacob asked.

"No sir. I figure the guy had checked the weather."

"I'm not going by what the weathermen are predicting. Genny said heavy snowfall tonight."

"Funny how she's always right about things like that." Bobby Joe grinned.

"Look, if he shows up—this Sloan guy—before I get back, tell him I'm over at Jasmine's eating supper."

"Just curious, Jacob, but what interest do the Feds have in a local murder case?"

"The Feds don't have an interest," Jacob replied. "It's a personal matter with Sloan. He had a niece who was killed the same way Susie Richards was—slaughtered like a sacrificial lamb."

"Ah, man, that's gotta be rough."

Jacob left the Sheriff's Department, located on the first floor of the south side of the Cherokee County courthouse, closed the door behind him, and walked out onto the street. A frigid evening wind whizzed around him, blowing tiny new-fallen snowflakes up from the sidewalk. When he looked at the dark sky, he saw snow dancing downward in the glow from the nearby streetlight.

As he walked up Main, he thought about the young girl who'd died at the hands of a monster early this morning. Pete Holt, the coroner and owner of Holt's Funeral Home, had said she probably hadn't been dead more than a couple of hours when he'd examined her at the site. He and Pete had done their best to make sure proper procedures were followed, that all the evidence was gathered, and nothing was left undone. He'd called in Roddy Watson for advice. Roddy had been the chief of police in Cherokee Pointe for the past fifteen years, and what he lacked in brains he partly made up for with experience. Roddy had told Jacob that with a case like this, they'd have to send all the evidence over to Knoxville to the crime lab there.

Jacob rounded the corner onto Florence Avenue and headed straight for Jasmine's, the best restaurant in town. As he drew near the front entrance to the renovated two-story building, he sensed he was being followed. When he glanced over his shoulder, he didn't see anyone, but he couldn't shake the notion that someone was watching him.

Damn, Butler, get a hold of yourself. Just because there was a gruesome murder in your county this morning doesn't mean there are boogeymen lurking in the shadows.

He stood across the street and watched the sheriff as he entered Jasmine's.

Jacob Butler. Got elected by a landslide. Local boy done good. Jacob had left Cherokee Pointe when he'd been eighteen and joined the navy. The big guy—he stood six-five and had to weigh in at no less than two seventy five— had become a SEAL, been decorated for bravery, and got wounded bad enough on his last assignment to end his career at the ripe old age of thirty-five. Despite his quarter-breed heritage, he'd been welcomed home by the whole town and talked into running for office six months after his return.

He knew all about Jacob, which would make everything so much easier. Knowing one's enemy was wise. What was the old saying about keep your friends close, but keep your enemies closer. He intended to know every move Jacob made concerning the Susie Richards case.

There was no reason for anyone to ever suspect him. His reputation was above reproach. So when the next murder occurred, the local authorities would be stumped again, unable to figure out who and why. All he had to do was the same as he'd done countless times before—be diligent and patient and careful. With each death, his strength increased. But this time it would be different. This time he had found the perfect fifth victim.

Chapter 2

Genny had spent the day recuperating, and now she was restless. A winter storm was brewing—an unexpected storm. By morning there would be several inches of ice beneath a thick layer of newly fallen snow. There were things she needed to do to prepare for the isolation that lay ahead for her here in the mountains. Although she hadn't regained all her strength after her dream vision, she had recovered enough to care for herself without any assistance. Jacob had called to check on her twice, and Jazzy had even driven up Cherokee Mountain late in the afternoon to see about her for the second time today. Jacob and Jazzy were the only two people to whom she could turn in moments of crisis, especially if the crisis was a result of her inherited *second sight*.

Having shared a childhood bond with Jacob, who was like a brother to her, and with Jazzy, with whom she'd been best friends since they were in diapers, she trusted them both implicitly. They understood she was different—Jazzy said she was special—and each stood by her, supported her, and loved her. They might not understand fully what she went through, but they understood better than anyone else ever had . . . anyone except Granny.

Some people didn't believe in a sixth sense of any kind, and half of those who did believe in it were afraid of anyone they thought might have it. During her twenty-eight years, she'd been called some terrible names, as her maternal grandmother before her had been. Granny Butler had been ridiculed by those who didn't understand she had little or no control over her psychic gifts. The ability to see things, to know things that should be impossible for her to see or know had been a mixed blessing, even a curse sometimes. Narrow-minded folks in Cherokee County had called her grandmother "the witch woman," and many had been deathly afraid of her. But just as many had come to Granny, seeking her out for her special powers. And now those same people, as well as their children and grandchildren, often came to her. Sometimes she could help them; other times she either frightened them or sent them away without the help they'd been seeking.

She thanked the good Lord every day of her life that she'd had Granny to teach her, guide her, advise her, and protect her for so many years. Granny's death six years ago had left a huge hole in Genny's heart. She'd been two and Jacob eight when her mother had died in the same car wreck that had killed Jacob's mother, leaving both children motherless. And since her own father had deserted her pregnant mother before Genny's birth, Jacob's father, Uncle Marcus, had been the only father she'd ever known.

During her years at Cherokee County High School, she'd tried to hide her abilities, had tried to fit in and be just one of the gang. But everyone had known about her grandmother. People had whispered behind her back, saying that Granny and she were witches. Jacob had gotten into numerous fistfights defending their honor. How did you explain to people that you weren't a witch, that you didn't practice any type of magic, black or white?

The blood of a Cherokee shaman and a Celtic Druid princess had run in Granny Butler's veins.

"Both my grandmothers had *the sight*. It skipped over your mother and your uncle Marcus and came right to you, just as it skipped over my mother and her siblings and came directly to me.'' Granny had explained her unique inheritance to Genny when at six she had experienced her first vision.

Never a gregarious person and always one who enjoyed being alone, Genny had gravitated more and more to living a solitary life here in the massive old house where she and Jacob had grown up in Granny's loving care.

Taking her heavy winter coat from the rack on the enclosed back porch, Genny headed for the door. The evening wind whistled around the corner of the cabin and cut into her skin like a thousand frigid little blades. She slipped into the coat hurriedly, grabbled in the pockets until she found her hat and gloves, then put them on. The moment she stepped into the backyard, Drudwyn came racing out of the woods that lay all around the half acre clearing where her great-grandfather had built a home for his family.

''Been visiting your lady friend again?'' Genny asked as she reached down to stroke the huge dog's head and back.

He gazed up at her with the eyes of a wolf, with his father's eyes. She knew that someday he would leave her to run wild with the wolf pack that lived high in the mountains. She hadn't seen Drudwyn's leaving her in a vision, but she had sensed it several times lately when they spoke to each other. One of her several abilities was the rare gift of being able to communicate with animals. It wasn't that she actually talked to animals and they replied; it was simply that she sensed what they thought and felt, and they in turn seemed able to do the same.

''I have to check the generators,'' Genny said. ''The electricity will likely go out tonight and I can't have the greenhouses without power.''

Drudwyn followed at her side as she went through the routine of checking the generator and the greenhouses. Her livelihood depended upon those greenhouses, where she grew specialty flowers and various herbs that were sold locally and by mail-order throughout the country. She hadn't expanded her nursery of shrubs and trees to her mail-order business, but had hopes of adding it in the near future. During the winter she and Wallace were able to handle everything, but come spring every year she hired a dozen part-time workers.

Wallace drove up from Cherokee Pointe every day except Sunday and Monday. He hadn't made the drive today since today was Monday. Wallace was a hand-me-down employee from Granny. The old man had worked in the nursery for as long as Genny could remember. People in and around the area had been as unkind and cruel to Wallace because he was ''slow-witted'' as they had been to Granny because she was ''fey.'' It didn't matter that Wallace was Farlan MacKinnon's younger brother and the MacKinnons were one of the two wealthiest families in the county. Long ago Mr. Farlan had ceased trying to control his mentally impaired brother and simply let him do as he pleased. It had always pleased Wallace to work for Melva Mae Butler.

Genny lifted an armful of wood from the huge stack at the back of the house and carried it inside to the box on the back porch. When the electricity went out—and it would; it always did in really bad weather—she would have to rely on the fireplaces and the wood stoves to keep the place warm. The generators were for the greenhouses only.

Suddenly, just as she eased one arm from the sleeve of her coat, she felt an overwhelming sense of foreboding. And then she sensed the presence of another. A man. A tall, fair-haired man. She shook her head, trying to dislodge the strange thoughts. Was she trying to visualize the killer, the man who had murdered poor little Susie Richards?

Standing there on her back porch, Drudwyn nuzzling the side of her thigh in a show of concern, Genny closed her eyes and allowed the vision to come to her, full force, surrounded by bright light and not dark shadows the way the vision had been this morning. Clear, white light. That always meant goodness, not evil. A tall, blond man trudged through the snow and came toward her cabin. He was angry. No, not angry. He was aggravated. He came closer and closer.

Her heart raced wildly. Not out of fear, but from excitement. He was coming toward her. Coming for her.

No, no, that's not right. It can't be. Why would he be coming for her? He wasn't the killer. She sensed no evil in him, only an enormous sadness.

As quickly as the phantom appeared, he disappeared. Genny shook from head to toe, then reached out and laid her hands flat against the wall to brace herself. Weakness crept through every muscle in her body.

He's coming, an inner voice told her. *He's coming to you tonight.*

Drudwyn whimpered. Genny took several deep, calming breaths, looked the wolf-dog in the eyes, then removed her coat and hung it on the rack there on the porch.

"I don't know who he is," Genny said to Drudwyn as they entered the kitchen. "But whoever he is, he'll be here tonight. And I believe he's a good man, one we can trust."

Genny hoped she was right about the stranger. Only occasionally could she judge a person with her sixth-sense ability. Most people cloaked their true selves from everyone around them, even from psychics. But for some odd reason, she'd gotten past this man's defenses, even if for only a few moments. Just long enough to sense his sorrow.

"Jamie Upton, you devil you." Cindy Todd playfully swatted the young prince of the Upton family on the chest. "You know I'm a happily married woman."

"I know nothing of the sort," he said as he shoved her up against the wall at the far end of the hallway, near the powder room. "Jerry Lee's sexual prowess can't have improved that much since the last time I was in town. I distinctly remember—"

Cindy gently slapped the palm of her hand over Jamie's mouth. He licked the moist, salty surface. She shivered, jerked her hand away, and glared at him. "You've got a new fiancée who should be keeping you satisfied. And . . . and I've got somebody else, too."

"Somebody besides Jerry Lee, huh? Who is he? Do I know him?"

"No, you don't know him. He's new in town." *And he's the best thing that ever happened to me.*

Jamie ran his hand between their bodies and cupped her left breast. "Does he make you feel the way I do? Is he as good in the sack?"

"Dammit, is that what this is all about? You heard something, didn't you? Somebody hinted to you that I was involved with Dillon and your ego couldn't stand it because I haven't been pining away for you the way Jazzy Talbot has."

Jamie grinned. "You didn't answer my questions."

"And I'm not going to. I don't owe you any explanations. What we had was a wild fling . . . a couple of wild flings."

After releasing her breast, Jamie eased back, putting some space between their bodies. "No problem. Just thought I'd give you first dibs before I call Jazzy. I figured you'd be easier. Jazzy always puts up such a fuss before she gives in."

"If she's half as smart as I think she is, she won't give in to you this time," Cindy told him. "You know she's dated Jacob Butler several times since he came back to Cherokee Pointe."

"Jacob Butler? The old witch woman's grandson? I thought he joined the army or something. When did he come home?"

"Last year. He's the new sheriff and all the women have a thing for him, even Jazzy."

"He's not her type. Jazzy likes her men rich—like me. She wouldn't seriously waste her time on a quarter-breed with nothing more than a county sheriff's salary."

"People change," Cindy said. "You've been gone three years this time. Jazzy's grown older and wiser. Besides, like I told you, she hasn't been pining away for you any more than I have."

Jamie laughed. The sound rippled through Cindy in sensual waves. Everything about Jamie Upton reeked with sex appeal. He was prettier than any man had a right to be, with his wavy brown hair and hypnotic hazel eyes. He wasn't a big man, but every inch of his five-foot-ten-inch frame was honed to sleek, muscular perfection. He was handsome, rich, and could be charming when it suited him. And he knew how to please a woman in bed—if it suited him.

"I need to get back to the others," Cindy said. "Jerry Lee's going to wonder what's taking me so long in the ladies' room."

Jamie stepped aside. Cindy released a relieved sigh, then hurried up the hall, walking only a bit faster than her usual pace. Even though her flight-or-fight instinct urged her to run, she didn't. She wouldn't give Jamie the satisfaction of knowing how desperately she wanted to get away before she succumbed to her wicked desire for him. Until she'd had her first fling with him, she hadn't understood why Jazzy Talbot repeatedly made a fool of herself over the man. But she understood now. There was something irresistible about the black-hearted bastard. But she doubted Jamie had ever loved anyone in his entire life—anyone other than himself, that is.

When Cindy reached the huge front parlor, she paused, licked her lips, smoothed her hands down either side of her clinging silk dress, and squared her shoulders. *Back into the fray,* she thought. Forcing a false smile, she entered the room where the Uptons were entertaining a variety of local society. Although the dinner party had been planned weeks ago, before Jamie's return, the event had turned into a welcome home for the Uptons' only grandchild. Miss Reba had quickly added a dozen more to the guest list, including Jerry Lee and Cindy, and changed the sit-down dinner into a buffet.

When she entered the room, Jerry Lee didn't even notice her; he was deep in conversation with Big Jim Upton, the patriarch of the Upton family. Jerry Lee's daddy had been friends with Big Jim, who had used his influence and wealth to help get Jerry Lee elected mayor of Cherokee Pointe for two terms, the second of which had just begun.

Big Jim stood six-four and probably tipped the scales at close to three hundred pounds. He possessed a shock of thick white hair and sported a dapper white mustache. The Upton family owned Upton Farms, which still provided dairy products to most of northeastern Tennessee. They were semi–old money. Four generations of wealth. And each Upton son had married class, making each successive generation a bit more refined than the previous one. But something had gone wrong with the only heir. Jamie Upton might be well-bred, but he was a worthless, heartless son of a bitch.

"Cindy, there you are," Reba Upton called. "Come here, dear, and meet the Stowes."

Cindy forced a smile and went directly toward Miss Reba, Big Jim's petite blond wife. Her unlined face and sleek, slender body belied the fact that she was seventy years old. A visit to a skilled surgeon every six years or so kept the old biddy's face as smooth as a baby's butt, and daily workouts with her own personal trainer kept her body in shape.

Reba laced her arm through Cindy's, her mauve lips spread wide in a hostess smile. "Cindy, this is Reverend and Mrs. Stowe. They're new in Cherokee Pointe. The reverend has been assigned to the Congregational Church." Reba patted Cindy's hand. "And this dear girl is our mayor's wife, Cindy Todd."

The minister, a tall, slender man with thinning brown hair and washed-out blue eyes nodded. "Pleased to meet you, Mrs. Todd. It would be an honor to have you and the mayor attend services with us this Sunday."

Mrs. Stowe, though dressed conservatively in a simple beige linen dress, eluded an aura of sexiness—maybe it was the long, straight, platinum blond hair or the huge brown eyes framed by thick black lashes. She stood at her husband's side, quiet and obedient, a bored expression on her face.

Cindy turned her attention to Mr. Stowe. "We certainly appreciate the invitation, but Jerry Lee and I are staunch Baptists."

Before the minister could reply, Reba tugged on Cindy's arm and said to the Stowes, "Y'all will excuse us, won't you? I see Dr. and Mrs. MacNair over there all alone. I'll just take Cindy over to meet them. Do mix and mingle. Enjoy yourselves. So glad y'all could come tonight."

Reba rushed Cindy away, and when they were out of earshot of the Stowes, she said, "They're the oddest people, don't you think? She's years younger than he is. I'd say no more than thirty, if that. And she acts as if she's deaf and dumb. The woman hasn't said a word since they arrived."

"Maybe she's shy," Cindy said.

"Shy? I doubt it."

Reba led Cindy toward a young couple standing off by themselves in the crowded room. The man had a stocky build, ruddy complexion, and a receding hairline, although he was probably in his early thirties. His wife was as tall as he, around five-nine, and was as willowy thin as he was stout. Although not really pretty, the strawberry blonde had a pleasant face. Cindy liked her instantly.

"Hello, there," Reba called to the secluded twosome. Reaching them, she said to Cindy, "You must meet these lovely people. This is Dr. Galvin MacNair and Mrs. MacNair." Reba stared at the wife. "What is your given name, dear?"

"Nina," the young woman replied, a hint of a smile on her lips.

"Galvin has taken over Dr. Webster's practice at the clinic," Reba said. "He's fresh from his residency in— where was it now? What city?"

"Bowling Green," Galvin replied.

Cindy chatted with the MacNairs for several minutes after Reba moved on to charm more of her guests. She liked the young couple, the wife more than the husband, who seemed oddly quiet. She even made a date with Nina MacNair for lunch at the country club on Thursday.

Checking her watch, Cindy noted that it was nearly nine. She'd promised Dillon she would find a way to meet him tonight, even if only for an hour. When she'd made that promise she thought she would be able to fake a headache and stay home from the party, but Jerry Lee had seen through her ploy immediately.

"Get yourself dressed and be ready to go to the Uptons in twenty minutes," Jerry Lee had told her, his round face red with rage. "If you aren't ready by then, I'll dress you myself—after I prove to you once again who's the boss around here."

Jerry Lee could be violent if pushed, and on several occasions he'd gotten rough with her. He'd never broken any of her bones, but he'd left her bruised and sore at least half a dozen times in the past four years. She thought about leaving him, dreamed of some other man whisking her away, but no one had come along to rescue her. Not until now. Not until Dillon. They'd been sleeping together for a month, ever since she'd joined the little theater group. He had moved to Cherokee Pointe late last summer after being hired by the city to oversee the local theater that produced plays to draw in the tourist trade.

What would Jerry Lee do if she went to him now and told him she had a splitting headache and needed to go home? He wouldn't want to leave the party. Whenever either the Uptons or MacKinnons threw a party, Jerry Lee Todd was one of the first to arrive and the last to leave. Her dear husband knew how to suck up better than anyone she'd ever known. He was a brownnoser par excellence.

As she strolled out into the foyer, seeking relief from the incessant chatter that had reached a deafening roar in the parlor, Cindy noticed Dr. MacNair and his wife accepting their coats from the maid. They were leaving early.

Before she realized what she was doing, Cindy rushed toward Nina MacNair. "Would y'all mind giving me a lift into town? I have a dreadful headache and I don't want to bother Jerry Lee. He loves these parties so."

"Yes, certainly." Nina reached out and patted Cindy's arm. "We'd be happy to drop you off at your house. And if you'd like, Galvin can give you something for your headache."

"Oh no, really, that won't be necessary. I have something

at home I can take." She turned to the maid. "Would you get my coat, please? And once I'm gone, tell Mr. Todd that I wasn't feeling well and caught a ride home with Dr. and Mrs. MacNair."

"Yes, ma'am," the maid said and hurried to get Cindy's coat.

Half an hour later, Cindy stood outside Dillon's apartment. She'd walked there in the freezing rain, the three blocks from her house on Chestnut Street to the two-story apartment building on Baker's Lane. Drenched to the skin and out of breath from running up the stairs to the second floor, she punched the doorbell repeatedly. She had an hour at most. An hour to find comfort and caring before she'd have to rush home and feign sleep when Jerry Lee returned from the Uptons. With luck the party would go on until at least eleven, even if this was a Monday night.

Dillon threw open the door and surveyed her from head to toe. "My God, sugar, come on in and get out of those wet clothes."

Dillon wasn't a handsome man, but there was an inexplicable sexiness about him. He stood about six-one. Curly dark hair tumbled about his broad shoulders. And when he did nothing more than grin at her, her pussy moistened.

Smiling, she moved past him and into his cluttered living room. Many creative people were known for being messy and disorganized. Dillon was certainly both. Newspapers and magazines lay strewn about, an empty cup rested on the edge of the coffee table, and two pairs of sneakers and dirty socks lay discarded on either end of the sofa.

"You're earlier than I thought," Dillon said as he helped her off with her damp coat. "Did Jerry Lee go to sleep early tonight?"

Cindy ran her hands up and down her arms in an effort to warm herself. "We had to go to that party at the Uptons'."

"So that's why you're wearing such a fancy dress—why you look exceptionally pretty tonight."

"Oh, God, don't lie to me," she told him. "I look like a drowned rat and we both know it."

"You're beautiful, even soaking wet and with your makeup smudged." He ran the back of his hand across her cheek. "Why don't you go in the bedroom and strip off all those wet things."

She grabbed his hand. "Come with me. I don't have long. I don't know for sure what time he'll get home tonight."

Dillon turned her hand over and kissed the center of her palm. "You go ahead and I'll be right there. I'll pour us a couple of drinks. Some Jack Daniels should warm you up pretty quick."

She didn't want the whiskey; she wanted him. But she did as he'd requested and scurried off to his bedroom, which was as cluttered as the living room. Clothes were strewn hither and yon. A laundry basket filled with what she assumed were washed but not folded towels and underwear perched atop the chest of drawers in the corner. An unmade bed lay before her, the comforter sloping halfway onto the carpeted floor. She doubted the sheets had been changed in weeks, but she didn't care. She'd rather share a dirty bed with Dillon than sleep on satin sheets with Jerry Lee.

Hurriedly she stripped off her dress, then kicked off her shoes and removed her pantyhose and bra. She was in the process of sliding her panties down her legs when Dillon came into the bedroom. She let the black bikini panties drop around her ankles as she faced him.

He stared at her appreciatively for several minutes. Heat rose up from within her as her body clenched and unclenched. She knew she looked all right naked. She wasn't that old. Thirty-three. Never having gone through childbirth, her breasts were small but perky, her stomach flat, and by exercising like a maniac she'd been able to keep the cellulite at bay and her muscles toned.

Dillon came across the room toward her, his movements lazy and deliberate, like a dancer in slow motion. He held out a half-filled tumbler. Her gaze met his, the two joining together for endless moments. After lifting one foot and then the other, she kicked her panties aside and took the glass of whiskey from him.

"Not knowing when your hubby will get home, you're taking a terrible risk coming here this way." Sipping on the liquor, he eyed her over the rim of his glass.

Why had he reminded her? Didn't he want her here? Had he decided having an affair with the mayor's wife was too dangerous?

"Being with you is worth the risk." With shaky hands she lifted the tumbler and tasted the whiskey. A hot blaze zipped down her throat and hit her belly like a ball of fire. She coughed a couple of times, but never took her eyes off him. "I thought you felt the same way."

Dillon gulped a couple of swigs from the glass, blew out a warm breath, and set the tumbler aside. Before she knew what was happening, he reached out and grabbed her. She gasped when her naked breasts crushed against his bulky knit sweater.

"I'll show you how I feel." He took the glass from her and set it alongside his atop a discarded pair of jeans on the chest at the foot of the bed.

Her heartbeat accelerated the moment his hands cupped her hips and pressed her against his erection. With frenzied motions, she ran her hands up under his sweater to touch his sleek chest. Together they quickly divested him of his clothing, all the while kissing and touching. Moments later, he tossed her onto the bed and took her without any real foreplay. He rammed himself up inside and began pumping her like mad. Luckily she was already dripping wet and pulsating with need. They went at it like a couple of animals and both came within a few minutes.

Later—five minutes or ten, Cindy wasn't sure—she eased out of his arms and off the bed. She went to the bathroom, cleaned herself, and came back into the bedroom to gather her clothes. Dillon scooted up in the bed, leaned his back against the headboard and watched her perform a reverse striptease.

Her clothes were damp and clammy, but it couldn't be helped. She didn't dare stay long enough for them to dry.

"Dillon?"

"Hmm?"

"If I leave Jerry Lee, will you . . . would you be here for me?"

Dillon stared at her, his eyes wide with surprise. "You've told me yourself that he'd never let you leave him. That he'd kill you first."

"Not if I had someone to protect me."

"Is that what you want? You want me to protect you from your husband?"

"Yes, that's exactly what I want. I want someone who cares enough about me to take me away from Jerry Lee and keep me safe."

"Sugar, I'm not sure I'm that man. I care about you, but—"

"But not that much."

Before she embarrassed herself even more, Cindy ran from the room. She picked up her coat off the sofa in the living room, slipped into it, and rushed out into the hallway. Taking several deep breaths, she forced herself not to scream; but she could do nothing to prevent the tears from cascading down her cheeks.

When she walked out onto the sidewalk, she realized it was snowing to beat the band. Heavy snow, so thick she couldn't see ten feet away. God, she'd freeze to death before she made it home on foot.

Suddenly she saw the headlights of a vehicle creeping down the street. Maybe she could hitch a ride. In a town this small there was a good chance she'd know whoever was driving.

The vehicle slowed and then stopped. The passenger door swung open.

"Cindy, is that you?" he asked.

She sighed with relief. "Yes, it's me."

"What are you doing out on foot on a night like this?"

"Visiting a friend," she replied. "Hey, would you mind giving me a ride home?"

"I don't mind at all," he said. "As a matter of fact, it would be my pleasure."

Chapter 3

Jacob sat in a booth at the back of the empty room in the restaurant part of Jasmine Talbot's two businesses on Loden Street. Jasmine's was a nice family restaurant that catered to locals and tourists alike. Jazzy's Joint, in the adjoining building at the end of the street, was an old-fashioned bar/juke joint. Appealing to vastly different clienteles, the establishments had separate entrances and thick, double brick walls separating the two. When he was off duty, sometimes he'd mosey on over to the wilder side, but tonight, he wasn't looking for excitement. Just a decent meal and some time to collect his thoughts.

He was facing his first murder case since being elected sheriff of Cherokee County, and it wasn't just an ordinary killing—a gunshot wound or a stabbing. The victim hadn't been involved in drugs, a domestic quarrel, or a revenge scheme. Susie Richards had been barely seventeen years old. A good kid from a good family, according to everything he'd learned about her. A straight-A student, president of the junior class at Cherokee Pointe High, and liked by everyone who knew her.

Just as Jacob finished off the last bite of apple pie and

shoved the plate aside, Jazzy appeared beside him, a full pot of fresh coffee in her hand. He glanced up and smiled. She was a sight for sore eyes. A good-looking woman could always improve any bad situation. And Jasmine Talbot was about as good-looking as they came. Tall, long-legged, and big-boobed, she was definitely built like the proverbial brick shithouse. She had a short, unruly mane of fiery red hair, the color so striking he knew it came out of a bottle, and a pair of cat-green eyes that seemed to possess the ability to look right through a man.

They had dated a few times, shared a few kisses and gropes, but hadn't crossed over the line from friends to sex partners. And he was glad. They genuinely liked each other, but the sexual chemistry just wasn't right between them. If they had screwed around, it would have been harder to remain buddies.

"More coffee?" Jazzy asked, but before he could reply she filled his cup, placed the pot on the table and sat down on the other side of the booth directly across from him.

"Thanks." He lifted the cup to his lips.

"It's decaf," she told him.

He frowned. "I don't drink decaf."

"You do tonight. I figure you're pretty wired already, what with all you've had to handle today. And my guess is that you've been swigging down high-octane coffee all day. The stuff has probably replaced the blood in your veins."

"You know me too well."

"You should go home and get a good night's sleep. You look like hell."

He grinned. "That's one of the many things I like about you—your brutal honesty."

"Good thing you've got a place in town," Jazzy said. "That snowstorm Genny predicted has already started. There are probably a couple inches of ice under the three or four inches of snow that's already fallen, and it's only ten-thirty."

Jacob nodded. "I doubt I'll sleep much tonight."

"Yeah, I don't suppose I would either after getting a good look at Susie Richards." Jazzy turned over a clean empty cup on the table and poured herself some coffee. "Rumors are flying like crazy around town. I know you can't tell me anything much, but . . . you can't put off making another statement to the press much longer. Brian MacKinnon's going to make a big deal out of this murder. It'll be headline news in the *Cherokee Pointe Herald* for weeks, especially if you don't nab the killer soon. He'd like nothing better than to find reasons to put you in a bad light."

"Brian's a prick." Jacob grunted. "He's another one who thinks money can buy him anything he wants." He looked Jazzy square in the eyes.

"Yeah, I know Jamie's back in town. Sally and Ludie told me. And no, I have no intention of getting involved with him again."

"Your life. Your decision," Jacob said. "Jamie's not my problem, but Brian, on the other hand, is. He doesn't like me because I don't approve of him sniffing around Genny. He's too old for her and she's too good for him, and I told him so. More than once."

Jazzy laughed, then lifted the cup to her lips and sipped on the hot coffee. "Brutal honesty. A trait we have in common."

"Something about Brian bothers me. Always has, even when I was a kid. He's too slick, too smooth. What you see is not what you get with him. I think Genny senses it, too, and that's why she hasn't encouraged him."

"A guy like Brian doesn't need much encouragement. He's used to getting what he wants, and believe me, he wants our Genny real bad."

"Yeah, well, he's got some competition now with that Pierpont guy after her, too. Can't say he'd be my choice for Genny, but he's an improvement over MacKinnon."

"Royce Pierpoint seems nice enough." Jazzy topped off both their cups. "He is more Genny's type. Gentle. Sensitive. Soft-spoken."

"Maybe he is. But we don't know much about him. How long has it been since he came to town and opened that antique store of his? Three or four months?"

"Back before Thanksgiving sometime."

Jacob took another swig of coffee, then stood, pulled his wallet from his pants pocket, and took out several bills. He handed the money to Jazzy. "I think I'll stop back by the office before I head home."

Jazzy stood up beside him and wrapped her arm around his waist. "You'll solve this crime. I have every confidence in you." She stood on tiptoe and kissed his cheek.

He gave her a quick hug, then lumbered out of the restaurant and into the frigid night. Damn, he could barely see the streetlight in front of Jazzy's Joint. It was snowing so hard he couldn't see much of anything. He flipped up the collar on his jacket and stomped through the snow, making his way back to his office a few blocks away.

The streets were deserted, making Cherokee Pointe look like a frozen ghost town.

Dallas Sloan cursed loudly! How the hell had this happened? Nobody had said anything about a winter storm. All the weather forecasters had mentioned was some freezing rain and sleet. A trip that should have taken him about an hour had taken him three times that long. Of course making a wrong turn fifty miles back hadn't helped any. He wasn't even sure he was on the right road now. Cherokee Pointe was located in a valley in the foothills of the Smoky Mountains, so being on a road on the side of a mountain seemed logical to him. What didn't seem logical was the fact that he'd wound up in a ditch. He wasn't the type to take wrong turns or lose control of a vehicle. Everything that could go wrong had gone wrong ever since he'd stepped off the plane in Knoxville.

He was slightly distracted, his mind mired in the details of Brooke's murder and the similarities between her brutal killing and the slaying of a seventeen-year-old named Susie Richards. Brooke had been fifteen, the oldest of his sister's three children. She'd been the first grandchild in the family and everyone had doted on her, even her Uncle Dallas.

He had found out quickly that when a case was personal, you couldn't handle it with the same cool detachment you managed to use to your advantage when the victim was a stranger. It hadn't been easy doing his job the past eight months, but he'd tried. And he had succeeded, at least part of the time. He'd been following a lot of leads that led nowhere, but he had a gut feeling about this one. Okay, so he'd already used almost all his vacation and sick-leave days and called in favors from everyone he knew at the Bureau. So what? No one questioned his right to act the way he did. After all, anyone else in his shoes might have gone ballistic and become totally obsessed with finding their niece's killer. Sometimes it was difficult to maintain control, to make sure he didn't move beyond determination into obsession. But Dallas prided himself on being in firm control. He'd never been a man to allow emotions to overrule common sense. If he was going to find Brooke's killer, he couldn't allow sentiment to get in the way.

Dallas punched in the sheriff's number on his cell phone. No reception. Was he out of range of a tower or was the crappy weather messing up signals? So what should he do now? He couldn't call for help, and he might freeze to death if he stayed in the car all night. But what was the alternative? If he got out and went in search of help, he'd probably get lost in this damn storm. Okay, maybe he could figure out a way to get the rented Saturn out of the ditch and back on the road.

The moment he opened the car door, the fierce wind bombarded him with a stinging mixture of sleet and snow. Blinking several times to clear the moisture from his eyes, he got out, slammed the door behind him and scanned the vehicle from hood to trunk. The right half of the car rested in the deep roadside ditch, with the left half perched on the shoulder of the winding mountain road. As he stomped toward the rear of the car, his feet slid out from underneath him. Reaching out, he grabbed the left rear bumper, but his gloved hands slipped and he completely lost his balance.

His backside hit the ground, sending a cloud of newly fallen snow flying into the air all around him.

Dallas cursed a blue streak. He should have known a dangerous blanket of ice lay beneath the innocent-looking snow. After getting to his feet, he glanced at the road, first in the direction from which he'd come to see if he'd missed any sign of a house, and then he looked ahead, searching through the blinding snow. He wiped his face, blinked, and zeroed his focus on one specific spot. Was that a light he saw shining through the darkness? It couldn't be the moon or a star, not in this kind of weather. It had to be a man-made light. Another car? Or was it a house out here in the middle of nowhere?

Cautiously Dallas climbed out of the ditch, his leather shoes slipping and sliding. He grabbed hold of a low branch on a small tree growing by the roadside, then hoisted himself up and onto the road. He moved carefully down the road, continuously wiping the snow from his eyes so that he could see. After going no more than thirty feet, he caught a glimpse of the house sitting high above the road. The porch light burned brightly, like a beacon in the night. Within minutes he reached the driveway leading up to the big white clapboard farmhouse. Damn, but it was a steep climb. How the hell could he climb an iced-over drive that appeared to go straight up? Suddenly he noticed the bright red mailbox a good eight or nine feet from the drive.

Steps! Stone steps led from the mailbox upward, hopefully all the way to the front yard. If he had to, he would crawl up those steps. When his feet touched the first stone-covered niche, he saw the long iron railing that ran the length of the primitive stairway. Hallelujah!

Good thing he was in prime physical condition, otherwise he would have been huffing like a steam engine by the time he reached the expansive front yard. He couldn't remember when anything had looked as welcoming as that porch light. But why would anyone have a light on this late at night, unless they were expecting someone or unless they were gone? He sure hoped the people who lived here were at home; if not, he'd have no choice but to do something illegal—break in.

The moment he set foot on the porch, he shook the snow from his head and brushed it off his overcoat. After a couple of seconds searching for a doorbell, he realized there was none, so he lifted his hand and knocked. Instantly the sound of deep, rumbling growls alerted him that there was a dog in residence. From the sound of its powerful bark, a very large dog.

The door swung wide open. His gaze bounced back and forth from the massive dog, who vaguely resembled a wolf, to the small, black-eyed woman standing beside the animal, one hand tenderly stroking the fierce beast's head. The howling wind blocked out soft sounds, so when the woman spoke to him he couldn't quite make out what she was saying.

He leaned forward. The dog bristled and bared his sharp teeth. The woman soothed the animal with words Dallas couldn't understand.

She motioned to Dallas to come inside, which he did immediately, entering to the woman's left, since her pet stood guard on her right.

"Thank you, ma'am," Dallas said as he waited just inside the doorway. "My car skidded off the road not far from here and my cell phone isn't working, so—"

She slammed the door closed, bent down and whispered something to the dog, then turned and looked directly at Dallas. "Please, come into the living room by the fire and warm yourself."

Dallas stared at her, into the darkest, most hypnotic eyes he'd ever seen. Eyes the color of rich, black earth. Why was this woman not afraid of him? Did she think her dog could protect her from any and all harm? Surely she knew there was a killer on the loose in Cherokee County. Perhaps he should identify himself and put her totally at ease, just in case she had any qualms about having a perfect stranger in her house.

"I'm Special Agent Dallas Sloan, with the Federal Bureau of Investigation." He unbuttoned his overcoat and reached inside his sports jacket for his ID and badge, then held it up so she could inspect it.

She glanced at his ID, then smiled. "You're the agent who called Jacob, aren't you?"

"Jacob?"

"Sheriff Jacob Butler."

"Yeah, I'm the one who called him. You know the sheriff?" He supposed in a rural area like Cherokee County everybody knew everybody else.

"Jacob is my cousin, but we're more like brother and sister."

She smiled. A warm, soft expression that radiated gentleness. Dallas studied her, from her long, free-flowing black hair, down her small, delicate body covered in denim jeans and a red plaid flannel shirt, to her booted feet. She was an exotically beautiful creature, with skin the color of rich café au lait. Full, naturally pink lips, slender nose, and almond-shaped eyes completed the package.

When he realized he was gawking at her, he looked away abruptly. "Is your phone working?" he asked gruffly, aggravated at himself for allowing her extraordinary beauty to affect him. "I can call a wrecker service or maybe a taxi—"

She giggled, the sound like tingling wind chimes. "I'm sorry," she said. "I'm not laughing at you. My phone is still working, for the moment. But no one will venture up the mountain on a night like this. Besides, I'm afraid Cherokee Pointe has no taxi service. Old John Berryman ran the only taxi in town, and when he died, no one took over his business. Just not enough calls for a taxi in these parts."

Huffing, Dallas ran his hand over his face and found his beard stubble rough against his palm. "Are you saying I'm stuck here?"

"Yes. At least until the storm passes and the roads clear. The county will send out a crew in the morning and begin clearing the roads."

"Would I be imposing if I—"

"You're welcome to stay here," she said without a

moment's hesitation. "I have plenty of room. It's just Drud-wyn and me in this big old house."

"Ma'am, you shouldn't tell a stranger who has invaded your home that you live alone." She simply looked at him and smiled. "I'll be out of here first thing tomorrow. Just as soon as I can get a—"

"Not tomorrow morning," she said. "The plows won't make it out this far before afternoon. You should be able to get into Cherokee Pointe by sometime late tomorrow. That is, if the storm lets up by morning, and I believe it will."

"But I can't stay here that long. I have to talk to Sheriff Butler as soon as possible."

She reached out and placed her hand on his. Every nerve in his body reacted to the touch of her small hand atop his. He felt as if he were on fire.

"Call Jacob and let him know you're here, with me. You can discuss whatever you need to discuss with him over the phone."

"How's he going to feel about a man neither of you know spending the night here with you?"

"He'll no doubt warn you to behave yourself, but he won't really worry about me. He knows I can take care of myself. And he knows Drudwyn would kill anyone who tried to harm me."

As if understanding his mistress's words, the huge dog growled menacingly.

Dallas held up his hands in a "stop" gesture. "All right, boy, I get the picture. I'm not here to harm her."

"I've told him," she said. "He knows you mean me no harm, but I'm afraid he's a bit jealous. You see he thinks of himself as the alpha male around here and he senses that you, too, are an alpha male, one who is trespassing on his territory."

"I won't have to worry about him ripping out my throat while I sleep tonight, will I?" Dallas asked, only halfway joking.

"Please, may I take your coat and gloves?" she asked. "I'll hang your coat up and it should be dry in a few hours."

He shed his overcoat, ripped off his gloves, and handed both to her. "Thanks."

She took the garments, then waved an outstretched hand toward the room to the left. "Go on into the living room and take a seat by the fireplace. I'll put these away and bring you some tea, and if you'd like, a sandwich, too."

"I don't want to put you to any trouble." Talk about Southern hospitality. This woman would win first prize in the perfect hostess contest.

"No trouble," she replied and disappeared down the hallway. Thankfully, Drudwyn followed her. Then she called out, "There's a telephone in the living room. Feel free to call Jacob. Try the Sheriff's Department and if he's not there, I can give you his home number."

"Okay, thanks. I'll give him a call."

Dallas glanced around the room and suddenly felt as if he'd stepped back in time. He doubted there was anything in here that wasn't at least fifty years old, most of it probably a lot older. The walls were paneled halfway up in an aged wood that looked like pine to him, mellowed to a rich patina that glistened in the soft lighting from the two table lamps flanking the sofa and from the firelight. The furniture looked like museum pieces, except it had a well-used appearance that came only from generations of continuous service. The floor beneath his feet consisted of wide planks, spotlessly clean and waxed to a glossy finish.

The modern portable telephone on the open antique secretary caught Dallas's eye. Thank goodness something in this place was up-to-date. He picked up the phone, then sat down in one of the two wing chairs near the fireplace. The warmth seeped through his damp clothing. He sighed. He had driven here in a damn storm and might have been forced to stay in his stranded vehicle had it not been for fate. Fate had sent him into a warm, inviting home.

As he made himself comfortable, he pulled out a small black notepad and flipped it open. He repeated aloud the number he'd scrawled down before leaving D.C. earlier this evening. He'd caught the first available flight, which had taken him into Knoxville, instead of waiting for a morning flight that would have taken him to Cherokee Pointe's small airport. In retrospect, he realized he'd have been better off to have taken the morning flight.

He punched the ON button and dialed the number for the Sheriff's Department. On the second ring, a male voice answered.

"This is Special Agent Dallas Sloan," he told the man who had identified himself as Deputy Bobby Joe Harte. "Is Sheriff Butler around?"

"Just so happens he is. Hold on and I'll get him for you. I know he was expecting you in tonight."

"I got held up," Dallas said. "I won't be able to make it into town until tomorrow."

Dallas waited for a reply. None came. Then he realized the phone was dead. Damn. Now he wouldn't get a chance to speak to Butler tonight.

"Did you get Jacob?" the woman asked as she entered the living room carrying a silver tray.

Dallas came to his feet instantly and went to her. He took the tray from her and carried it across the room, then placed it on the table to the left of the fireplace where she indicated with a wave of her open palm.

"I got hold of a Deputy Harte, but the line went dead before I could speak to the sheriff."

She motioned for him to take a seat, which he did.

"Well, that means the ice has gotten heavy on some of the phone lines and snapped them." She lifted a silver teapot and poured a reddish-brown liquid into a china cup. "I fixed you a chicken salad sandwich. Is that all right?"

"Are you always so accommodating to strangers stranded on your mountain?" He accepted the cup of tea she held out to him. "If so, then I'm surprised your cousin Jacob hasn't cautioned you to be more careful. Even with Drudwyn around"—he scanned the room—"by the way, where is your companion?"

She sat across from Dallas and removed a linen napkin from atop a china plate with roses on it, revealing a large, thick sandwich. Dallas's mouth watered. He hadn't had a bite to eat since lunch, which had been over ten hours ago.

"He stayed in the kitchen," she replied.

"By choice?"

"By mutual agreement."

She stared at him unabashedly. An odd sensation hit him square in the gut. "Please, Dallas, go ahead and eat."

His named rolled off her tongue as if coated in honey. A sweet Southern drawl. A tight fist clutched at his insides. Something was definitely wrong here. He didn't go around reacting this way to women. Not ever.

"I don't know your name." He forced a smile. Hell, he didn't feel like smiling; he felt like running scared out of this house and away from this strange yet oddly appealing woman.

"Genevieve Madoc. But people call me Genny."

Genevieve. The name suited her. And yet so did Genny. Old-fashioned, even a bit romantic.

"I appreciate your hospitality, Genny."

"You're quite welcome."

Once again she reached out and touched his hand, but this time she closed her eyes. What the hell was she doing? Suddenly, she jerked her hand away.

"Are you all right?" he asked.

"Your pain is very great," she told him. "Almost more than you can bear. It wasn't your fault that she died. And it isn't your fault that you haven't found her killer. But you will. And soon."

Dallas dropped the cup; it crashed into pieces as it hit the hard wooden floor. Hot tea spread out across the shiny surface. He sat there staring at Genny for several minutes. Moments out of time.

"I'm sorry about the cup," he said as he reached down to pick up the pieces. "If you'll get me a mop, I'll—"

"Don't worry about it. I'll take care of it. Here—" she

took her cup, filled it with tea, and handed it to him. "Drink, eat, relax. Let me take care of you."

Before he could reply, she rose to her feet and hurried from the room. Dallas stared after her, stunned by her words. *Let me take care of you.*

"How did you know about my niece?" he asked.

"I'm sure Jacob must have mentioned it," she replied as she paused in the doorway.

He couldn't quite put his finger on it, but there was something peculiar about Genny, something that didn't quite add up. *Get real, Sloan,* he chastised himself. *You're tired, you're stressed, and you haven't gotten laid in six months. You're overreacting to simple human kindness.*

Maybe so, but he couldn't shake the unnerving feeling that Genevieve Madoc was going to change his life forever.

He laid her limp body in the middle of the bed, gazed down at her, and smiled.

The second victim had fallen into his arms as easily as the first had. Providence always provided. He never had to choose the first four—they always came to him. He simply waited for them. Sometimes it took only days. Other times it might take weeks. But they were essential. Their blood sustained him, strengthened him, prepared him for the fifth victim.

She would remain unconscious for several hours. Long enough for him to remove her clothes and pleasure himself. With the weather so nasty, he didn't believe an outdoor setting was wise. Where could he find an appropriate place to make the sacrifice? Only two things were necessary for him to accomplish the deed: an altar and complete privacy.

He couldn't keep her here for very long. Not without risking being found out. No, he'd have to choose a place quickly, somewhere close by, since traveling very far would be out of the question in this winter storm. Before daybreak he would place her on the altar, speak the solemn, sacred words he'd been taught as a boy, then, when dawn broke over the eastern horizon, he would make the sacrifice.

One sacrifice had already been made and there were three more to make before he could take her, the one who would give him more power than all the other fifth victims combined. Just the thought of taking her, consuming her, aroused him unbearably.

While a drugged Cindy Todd lay on the cot in the basement, he unzipped his slacks, eased his penis free and jerked off. Within moments his cum spewed out over her naked belly.

Chapter 4

Big Jim Upton poured himself a brandy and tried his best to shut out the sound of his wife's droning voice. It wasn't that he didn't love Reba. He did. She was a good woman, but not an endearing one. He'd married her on the rebound over fifty-five years ago, when the love of his life married another man. He didn't regret marrying her—at least not until recently. Reba had given him a son and a daughter; and together they had survived the loss of both children. For years they had clung to the hope that their only grandchild would eventually mature into a decent, responsible human being. Jamie was thirty now and it was past time for him to settle down, but Jim didn't see any evidence of that happening anytime soon.

"Where on earth could he be?" Reba whined as she paced the floor in the living room. "How could he leave his own welcome-home party without so much as a by-your-leave?"

Jim glanced across the room at Jamie's most recent fiancée. Laura Willis sat on the sofa, her eyes downcast and her hands folded in her lap. The girl was a great improvement over some of the other women the boy had brought home—two other fiancées during the past eight years. Jamie wouldn't marry this girl, just as he hadn't married the ones that had come before her, but she probably didn't realize it—not yet. But she would. Possibly tonight. Jim had a pretty good idea where Jamie had gone. Once he was back in Cherokee County, not even a winter storm could keep him away from Jazzy Talbot.

"Do you suppose he had car trouble and that's why he hasn't returned?" Laura lifted her head but didn't make eye contact with either Jim or Reba.

"He could have called," Reba said. "The phone is not out of order. I checked myself only a few minutes ago."

"What's the point of our staying up any longer?" Jim asked. "Jamie will come home when he comes home. That boy doesn't have a responsible, reliable bone in his body."

"Jim, really!" Reba's voice screeched. "What will dear Laura think, hearing you speak about your own grandson in such a manner?"

Dear Laura? Jim chuckled inwardly as his lips twitched in an effort to refrain from smiling. The minute Reba had found out that Laura's parents were part of the horse-breeding set, the Willis family from Lexington, Kentucky, she'd taken the girl to her bosom. More than anything, Reba wanted Jamie to make a good marriage; and to Reba that meant marrying the right sort of girl from a proper family. She'd certainly seen to it that their son, Jim Jr., and their daughter, Melanie, had married the right sort.

He supposed Jim Jr. and his wife had been moderately happy, especially after Jamie's birth, but Melanie had been miserable with her state senator husband, the son of one of Reba's college sorority sisters. Poor little Melanie. The sweetest child. The most devoted of daughters. On her fourth wedding anniversary she'd left her husband; and it had been a dozen years later before anyone had heard from her. Actually, they hadn't heard from her, only about her. The police in Memphis had phoned to inform them that their daughter was dead. A drug overdose.

"I'm going to call Sheriff Butler." Reba headed out of the living room.

"Wait up," Jim called. "You and I both know where that boy is. There's no use bothering Jacob Butler at this time of night. It's nearly one o'clock. Besides, by now the roads are probably a holy mess, so Jamie wouldn't even try to come home tonight."

"You know where he is?" Laura's sparkling blue eyes dared a head-on meeting with Jim's dark gaze.

"No, no, he doesn't know. He's just guessing." Reba turned back into the living room and scurried over to the sofa. She sat beside Laura, then gave Jim a condemning look.

"Hell, Reba, the girl might as well know the truth. She'll find out soon enough."

"Shut up, Jim," Reba snapped shrilly.

"What—what is it that you don't want me to know? Is there another woman?"

"Yes!" Jim said.

"No!" Reba said simultaneously.

Jim felt sorry for Laura. The girl was so young, probably not a day over twenty-two, and seemed to be madly in love with Jamie. Of course, they all were, every poor fool he'd ever asked to marry him. Most women easily fell under Jamie's spell, even Jazzy Talbot. Now there was a woman for you! Too bad she didn't possess a suitable pedigree. If she did, Reba might approve of her. If any woman could ever get Jamie to the altar, it would be Jazzy.

"Jamie has some good friends here in Cherokee County," Jim said. "One friend in particular. And he usually pays this friend a visit the minute he gets home. That's probably where he is right now."

"Is this friend a woman?" Laura asked, her voice a mere whisper.

"Of course not," Reba said. "It's just an old high school buddy. The boys played football together."

Grunting with disgust, Jim rolled his eyes heavenward. Let Reba lie for the boy; he wouldn't. "You ladies stay up as long as you'd like. I'm going to bed."

"Jim, please, phone Jamie's friend and make sure he's

there and safe." Reba looked at him pleadingly. "He could have had a wreck or—"

"You two go on up and get ready for bed," Jim said. "I'll call Jaz—Jay and see if Jamie's there."

"Come along, dear." Reba stood and waited for Laura to rise to her feet, then she laced her arm through the younger woman's and led her out of the living room, into the foyer, and toward the grand staircase.

After the ladies made it to the landing, Jim meandered into his study. Switching on the banker's lamp atop his massive oak desk, he sat down in the leather swivel chair and flipped through his Rolodex. He had promised himself the last time Jamie came home after one of his long absences that he wouldn't keep tabs on the boy. He'd done everything he could to rein the boy in, to make a man of him, and all to no avail. As much as Jim hated to admit it, Jamie was a total failure as a human being. He blamed himself and Reba. They had spoiled him rotten. Given him anything and everything he'd ever wanted. But nothing had been enough; nothing made him happy for very long.

The only thing he'd ever wanted that they hadn't allowed him to have was a life with Jazzy Talbot. At twenty he'd wanted to marry the girl, but Reba'd had one conniption after another just at the thought.

"She's nothing but a little white-trash whore," Reba had said. "And that aunt of hers is as crazy as a Betsy-bug."

Jim didn't kid himself into thinking that if they'd let Jamie marry Jazzy, things might have turned out differently. The marriage wouldn't have lasted. Nothing was permanent in Jamie's life. He wanted variety, excitement, and challenges. But most of all he wanted what he couldn't have. That's why he still wanted Jazzy so damn much. He'd put that poor gal through hell more than once.

Jim lifted the receiver from the phone on his desk, dialed the number, and waited.

She answered on the fifth ring, her voice groggy with sleep. "Yeah?"

"Jazzy, this is Jim Upton."

"What do you want?"

"Reba's concerned because Jamie left his welcome-home party and hasn't returned. By any chance is he there with you?"

Jazzy laughed. "I assume the new fiancée is not in the room with you."

"No, she and Reba have retired for the night."

"Jamie's not here."

"Do you have any idea where he is?"

"I might."

"Would you mind telling me?"

Jazzy sighed. "He came by to see me at Jazzy's Joint. We talked. I told him to get lost. And Jamie being Jamie, he didn't take it well, so he latched on to the nearest woman he could find to make me jealous."

"He picked up someone in the bar?"

"That's right."

"Do you know—"

"I think her name was April or Amber. She's been in a few times, but I don't know her personally. I'd say he's probably with her."

"Thank you, Jazzy. And . . . I'm sorry."

"Sorry for waking me?"

"Yes, that, too, but mostly sorry that Jamie never had the backbone to stand up to his grandmother and marry you despite her protests."

Jazzy was silent for several minutes. "Tell that new fiancée of his to run as far and as fast as she can."

The dial tone buzzed in Big Jim Upton's ear.

Jacob had sacked out on the cot in his office at the courthouse instead of going home. After tossing and turning for nearly an hour, he'd finally fallen asleep sometime after midnight. When the ruckus outside his office door woke him, he punched the button on his digital watch to light the face. Four-twelve.

"I want to see Jacob right now!" a man's voice shouted.

"But he's sleeping," Deputy Tewanda Hardy informed the irate man. "He's worn to a frazzle."

"Dammit, woman, get out of my way. I need to talk to Jacob."

Jacob lifted himself into a sitting position on the edge of the cot, ran his hand over his face, yawned heavily, and rose to his feet. He'd recognized the man's voice. Mayor Jerry Lee Todd. What the hell had put Jerry Lee into such a panic?

By the time Jacob took a couple of steps, the office door swung open and Jerry Lee stormed into the room, Tewanda hot on his heels.

"Sorry, Jacob," Tewanda said, "but the mayor insisted on seeing you immediately."

"It's all right," he told his deputy. Tewanda was his only female deputy and one of the best, if not the best, he had. She was taking courses at UTC in Knoxville to get her degree, so he arranged her schedule so she could work nights. Her dream was to become a lawyer, and Jacob had no doubt she'd make a good one. Already she knew as much about the law as he did. Maybe more.

"You've got to help me," Jerry Lee said.

"What's wrong?" When Tewanda flipped on the overhead light in Jacob's office, he took a good look at the mayor. The guy looked like death warmed over. Drenched to the skin, his face red from exposure to the frigid temperatures and his hair plastered to his balding head, he was a sorry sight, downright pathetic. Jacob glanced past Jerry Lee to Tewanda, who lifted her hand to her lips repeatedly in a gesture that told him she believed the mayor was drunk.

"Have you been drinking?" Jacob asked.

"Yes, I've been drinking," he replied. "I was out at Big Jim's for a welcome-home party for Jamie tonight and I had a couple of glasses of champagne. And then I had a few sips of Scotch at the house, to warm myself up. But I'm not drunk." He whirled around and glared at Tewanda. "I'm upset, dammit, not drunk."

"Whatever you say, Mayor Todd." Tewanda rolled her eyes toward the ceiling.

"Would you mind leaving us? I need to speak to Jacob alone," Jerry Lee said.

Without another word, Tewanda turned and exited the office, but she left the door open. Jerry Lee kicked the door closed behind her.

"Women shouldn't be deputies," Jerry Lee said.

"Want to tell me what's going on?" Jacob crossed his arms over his chest. "It's four o'clock in the morning. What couldn't wait until a decent hour?"

"Cindy's missing."

"What?"

Jerry Lee rubbed his closed eyelids with his fingertips. "She left the party early. Caught a ride with the new doctor and his wife." He opened his eyes and stared toward Jacob, but his gaze was unfocused as he continued explaining. "I've talked to them. They said they dropped her off on their way home, around nine forty-five. I got home a little after eleven and she wasn't there."

"Any reason why she would have left you?" Jacob asked, knowing full well that half the town had heard about Cindy and Jerry Lee's marital brawls.

"She didn't leave me. All her stuff is still at the house. Whenever she takes off for a few days, she always packs a couple of bags. Nothing's missing."

"Maybe she spent the night with a friend." Jacob purposely didn't mention the friend's gender. Cindy had a reputation for sleeping around and had cheated on Jerry Lee with at least half a dozen men—maybe more—during their six-year marriage.

"She never stays out all night with any of her friends. She's always home by this time of the morning." Jerry Lee slumped down in one of the two chairs facing Jacob's desk. The man aged ten years right before Jacob's eyes. "I know what you're thinking. You believe she's gone off with some man, but I tell you she hasn't."

Jacob walked over and placed his hand on Jerry Lee's shoulder. "How can you be so sure?"

"Her latest is that Carson guy. You know, the wannabe

actor/director who's in charge of the town's little theater.''
Jerry Lee entwined his fingers and popped his knuckles. "I
called him and he wouldn't talk to me, so I went over to
his apartment. He finally admitted that she'd been there last
night, but swore she'd left before eleven.''

Jacob wanted to feel sorry for Jerry Lee, but he couldn't.
He'd brought a lot of this misery on himself. He'd married
the wrong woman, refused to let her go, then had taken out
his misery on her and everyone else around him.

"Give me a list of her friends," Jacob said. "Around six
I'll make a few phone calls.''

"She's not with any of her friends. I'm telling you, she's
in trouble. I feel it''—he punched his stomach with his
closed fist—"in here. We've got ourselves a killer running
loose in Cherokee County—''

"Don't go jumping to conclusions. Cindy's probably just
fine and she'll show up at home in a few hours.''

"Do you really think so?''

Jacob nodded.

"I want to fill out a missing person's report," Jerry Lee
said. "And if she doesn't come home, I want you to—''

"If she isn't home by noon today, call Roddy Watson.
You live in town, remember? You'll need to file a report
with the Cherokee Pointe police.''

"Yes, yes. I know. It's just I trust you to find Cindy for
me. You know about our past history and all. Roddy and I
play golf together, we belong to the country club, our moth-
ers are bridge partners. You understand.''

Yeah, Jacob understood all too well. Jerry Lee didn't want
to involve his friend, the chief of police, a man the mayor
considered his social equal. He could admit to Jacob that
he'd confronted Cindy's most recent lover, but he could
never be that honest with a friend.

"Why don't you go home, try to get some rest, and if
Cindy doesn't show up by noon, give me a call and we'll
go from there.''

With his shoulders slumped and weariness etched on his

features, Jerry Lee rose from the chair, held out his hand, and said, "Thanks," as he shook Jacob's hand.

The minute the mayor left, Tewanda brought two cups of coffee into Jacob's office and handed one to him. He looked up from where he sat behind his desk and smiled at her as he accepted the coffee.

"He's a real piece of work, isn't he?" Tewanda said.

"Why, Ms. Hardy, saying something like that makes me think you don't like our mayor."

"Like him?" Tewanda harrumphed. "The man's a bigot, a wife beater and a—"

"Don't hold back, tell me what you really think of him."

"I hope Cindy Todd has run off with somebody and stays gone for good."

"If she has run off with some guy, I wish she'd left Jerry Lee a note or something. As it is, he's going to run us crazy if she doesn't come home." Jacob sipped on the hot coffee and sighed with pleasure when he realized it was fresh. "You made a fresh pot. Thanks."

"As soon as Jasmine's opens for breakfast at six, I'll run out and get us some sausage biscuits," Tewanda said. "Until then, I've got peanut butter and crackers if you want some."

"Nah, thanks." He held up the orange UTC mug. "This will tide me over for the time being."

Tewanda glanced down at the photographs spread out on Jacob's desk. Crime-scene photos of Susie Richards's mutilated body.

"Makes me sick at my stomach just to look at those," she said.

Jacob gathered up the photographs, slid them into a folder, and laid them aside. "We did everything we were supposed to do, but I doubt it will be enough to catch this guy. He didn't leave us much to go on. He covered his tracks like a pro, which tells me he's done this sort of thing before."

Tewanda shivered. "Are you saying what I think you are?"

"Yeah. If he's done it before, he'll do it again. I just hope we find him before another innocent person is killed."

* * *

After a restless night, Jazzy woke at dawn. She had slept
an hour, woke, and thought about Jamie. Then she'd slept
another couple of hours, woke, and thought about Jamie.
The pattern had repeated itself all night—except for when
Big Jim's telephone call woke her around one-thirty.

Had she seen Jamie? Hell, yes! He'd come by Jazzy's
Joint around ten-thirty. One look at him and her stomach
had tied in knots. Even now she wasn't sure whether the
reaction had been lust or fear. Perhaps both.

He'd been so damn sure of her that she'd derived a great
deal of pleasure from telling him to leave her the hell alone.
He had pressed her; she'd retreated.

"I'm over you," she'd told him. "I've moved on. So
don't think you can walk back into my life and crawl back
into my bed. Never again!"

Half the patrons in Jazzy's Joint had heard her screaming
at him. She didn't care. The whole damn town knew their
sordid history, knew she'd gotten pregnant with Jamie's
baby when she was seventeen, knew his grandmother had
forbidden him to marry her. Most folks thought she'd had
an abortion and she'd never told them any different. Only
a handful of people knew the truth—Aunt Sally, Ludie,
Genny, and Jacob. She'd miscarried at three and a half
months. A part of her heart had died with that sweet little
baby.

As she climbed out of bed, the chill in her bedroom
encompassed her. She reached out and lifted her robe off
the foot of the bed, then slipped into it as she headed for
the bathroom. After relieving herself, she went to the tiny
kitchen in her second-story apartment over Jasmine's and
hurriedly prepared the coffeemaker.

She glanced out the window facing the east and saw the
first faint glimmer of dawn. Was Jamie asleep at home with
his latest fiancée, or was he in bed with the woman named
April or Amber or something that started with an A and had
a cutesy sound to it? He was with one or the other, Jazzy

thought. He'd made love to one of those women, held her, kissed her, and whispered sweet nothings in her ear. That woman could have been her. All she'd had to do was welcome him back into her life. He'd be with her now and every night for as long as he was in town, if only she'd said yes.

Her body ached for his.

Jazzy opened the refrigerator, took out a carton of orange juice, and drank straight out of the carton.

Was it Jamie her body ached for or was it just a man? Any man? She hadn't been with anyone in a long time. Despite what people thought—that she was a slut—Jazzy took sex seriously. Over the years, there had been a few men other than Jamie, but not many. And she'd cared about each of them, had hoped for a future with each of them, and had been disappointed by each of them.

A part of her might always love Jamie, but she wasn't in love with him anymore. He was poison to her. Every time he breezed into town, he came to her and renewed her hope for something real and lasting between them. But not this time. Not ever again. She'd cried her last tear over Jamie Upton!

Dallas woke instantly when he heard the woman's screams. He shot straight up in bed. For a moment he didn't remember where he was. *You're in Genny Madoc's home in Tennessee, in the mountains,* he reminded himself. Good God, had that been Genny screaming? He jumped out of bed, slid into the slacks he'd tossed across the cedar chest at the foot of the bed last night, and then eased his Smith & Wesson semiautomatic from his hip holster and raced out into the dark hallway.

"Genny?"

Silence.

"Genny?" he called again as he rushed toward her bedroom.

He knocked on the door. No response. He knocked again. Drudwyn growled. And then he heard a soft, weak voice.

"Help me," she said.

He flung open the door, not knowing what to expect. A kerosene lamp's dim glow shimmered over the room, illuminating the mantel on which it rested and casting shadows across the wooden floor and over the flowery wallpaper. Genny lay in the middle of the bed, unmoving, rigid, her gaze focused on him as he made his way to her.

Drudwyn growled when he approached the bed.

Genny closed her eyes and instantly the dog quieted. If he hadn't known better, he would have sworn the animal had read Genny's mind.

As he leaned over her, his gaze fixed to hers, he asked, "What's wrong? Are you sick? Are you in pain?"

She nodded, then whispered, "Yes."

Okay, he knew a little first aid, enough to get by in a pinch, but if there was something seriously wrong with Genny, then they were in big trouble.

"Can you tell me what's wrong?" he asked. "And what can I do to help you?"

"Stay with me." She glanced at the edge of the bed.

"Do you need me to help you to the bathroom?" Maybe she had a stomach virus or food poisoning.

"No, I'm not sick." Her voice was breathless, as if she'd run a race and was now exhausted.

"Then what's wrong?"

"Is the telephone working?" She looked at the extension on the bedside table.

Dallas lifted the receiver to his ear. Dead. "No. It's still out."

"Try my cell phone."

"Where is it?"

"In the drawer in the nightstand."

He opened the drawer, removed her small phone, and looked to her for instructions.

"Call Jacob." She recited the number.

"Damn," Dallas said. "Still no reception."

Tears flooded Genny's eyes. "It doesn't matter. He'd be too late to save her even if we could get in touch with him."

Dallas tossed the cell phone back into the drawer, then sat down on the bed beside Genny. "What are you talking about? Who couldn't Jacob save?"

"The woman he's going to kill."

"I don't understand—"

"I had another dream. Another vision. He's going to kill again. He may already have sacrificed her."

Dallas grabbed Genny and jerked her into a sitting position. With his hands clutching her slender shoulders, he glared into her mesmerizing black eyes.

"What the hell are you talking about?"

"I saw her on the altar. Windows with light. Colors. Stained-glass windows maybe. And the sword. He was excited. Waiting. Waiting for the right moment."

What the hell was going on? What sort of crazy dream had Genny had? "You must have had a nightmare," Dallas said. "With a killer on the loose, your imagination kicked into overdrive."

"It wasn't just a dream . . . it was . . ." her voice faded.

Suddenly Genny fainted. She fell into Dallas's arms. Delicate. Fragile. Helpless. Dallas cursed loudly.

Chapter 5

For a split second Dallas couldn't think straight. All he could do was react to the feeling of having this beautiful woman in his arms. Although she was small and slender, her body rounded in all the right places. At the present moment her high, full breasts were pressing into his naked chest. And her long, silky black hair draped over his shoulder. He took a deep breath, eased Genny off him, and laid her gently back on the bed.

She'd said that it wasn't just a dream. What did that mean? Some maniac had cut a young girl wide open out in the woods in the county where Genny lived. Her cousin was the sheriff and had probably told her more than he should have about the gruesome murder. Undoubtedly she'd had the recent killing on her mind when she'd gone to bed, and her subconscious had created a hideous nightmare.

He could still hear the panicked scream that had awakened him. Genny had been terrified. But once she'd fully awakened and realized she was not only safe, but also not alone, she should have recovered quickly. She hadn't. She'd fainted dead away, as if for some reason she was totally exhausted.

While she lay there, her eyes closed, her breathing slow

and steady, he studied her face. The face of an angel. His gaze traveled downward and came to a screeching halt where her breasts rose and fell with each breath she took. Her nipples were tight, peaking against the soft cotton material of her long-sleeved pajama top.

Dallas swallowed hard. Now was not the time to get all hot and bothered over a fine piece of ass. Two seconds after the thought flashed through his mind, he grimaced. Why the hell had he done that—reduced his attraction to this woman as nothing more than lust? It had become a fatal flaw with him. Whenever he found himself more than mildly interested in a woman, he convinced himself that there was nothing emotional about it, simply normal male libido.

Genny groaned softly. Her eyelids fluttered.

Dallas caressed her cheek.

She opened her eyes and looked up at him. The fear he'd noticed only moments ago was gone, replaced by weariness.

"Are you all right?" he asked.

"Tired. Very tired."

"I don't understand. Why would a nightmare drain you this way?"

"They always leave me very weak."

She tried to lift her hand, to reach out for him. When he realized how difficult the effort was for her, he grabbed her hand in his and held it against his chest.

He still didn't understand. It had to be highly unusual for a nightmare to devastate a person the way it had Genny.

"What can I do to help you?"

"Stay with me. Please. Until I recover."

"This has happened to you before?"

She nodded. "Many times."

"How long will it—"

"Several hours."

"Rest. I'll stay right here."

"Dallas?"

"Yes?"

"From time to time, try the phones. Jacob needs to know."

"About your dream?"

She nodded. "About the second sacrifice."

Again, the blood ran cold through Dallas's veins. Damn! Half a dozen wild thoughts went through his head. The second sacrifice . . . the second sacrifice.

"Genny?"

When she didn't respond, he glanced down at her and realized she had fallen asleep. He lowered her arm down beside her, then eased off the bed and paced around the bedroom. Drudwyn's keen eyes followed his every move.

"What's going on with her, boy?" he asked the dog.

Drudwyn rose, came forward, and halted at Dallas's side. Two concerned gazes met, locked, and exchanged an odd sense of understanding. Both would protect Genevieve Madoc to the death.

"Hell," Dallas cursed under his breath. Protect this woman to the death? Where had that thought come from? What was wrong with him? He barely knew her, had met her only hours ago.

Dallas shoved back the lace curtains at the long, narrow windows and gazed outside at the dawn light creeping up and across the horizon, spreading a pale pink glow over the dark gray sky. The snowstorm must have ended sometime during the night, but as best he could make out in the semi-darkness, a blanket of white covered everything in sight.

Letting the curtain fall back into place, Dallas closed his eyes and tried to think straight. He had allowed this situation—being marooned for a night with a good-looking woman who somehow had very quickly put the hoodoo on him—to muddle his thought processes. If he didn't know better, he'd think Genny was a witch who had cast a spell over him.

Dallas chuckled. Yeah, sure. A witch? He didn't believe in anything he couldn't experience with his five senses. If he couldn't see it, hear it, touch it, taste it, or feel it, then it didn't exist. In the real world in which he lived, there were no witches, no faith healers, no ghosts, no psychics, no guardian angels. That sort of stuff was for saps, for the poor misguided souls who couldn't cope with reality.

He glanced around the room. Feminine, but not frilly. Antique furniture. Lace curtains. Pale pastel colors blended with white. When he spied a large, comfortable-looking chair in the corner, he went over and sat, then lifted his big feet onto the round ottoman. A chill rippled through him, reminding him he was bare from the waist up. He dragged the white crocheted afghan off the back of the chair and wrapped it around him.

As soon as the phones were working, he'd put in a call to a wrecker service and get his rental car hauled out of the ditch, then he'd thank Genny for her hospitality and get the hell out of here as fast as he could. His business was with Sheriff Butler, not Butler's bewitching cousin.

He needed to make a definite connection between Susie Richards's murder and Brooke's murder. Over the past eight months, since his young niece had been brutally killed, he had spent every minute he wasn't working to try to unearth any evidence that might point to her killer. Sacrificial killing was not unheard of; in fact there had been more in the United States than Dallas had suspected. Many had been connected to some sort of pagan devil worship, but certainly not all. Over the past eight years there had been twenty-four unsolved cases involving murders that were very similar to Brooke's. And the oddest thing about twenty of these murders was that they appeared to have taken place in sets of five.

With Teri's and Linc's assistance these past few months, Dallas had put together a startling hypothesis: someone sacrificed five women living in the same area over a period that averaged between three to six weeks, then disappeared only to show up in another region a year or two later and repeat the same scenario. All these facts had come together only a couple of weeks ago, and Dallas hadn't had the chance to personally travel to each area and go over all the evidence.

But if his supposition was correct, and if Susie Richards was the first victim, then that meant four women in Cherokee County were in danger. And it also meant that Brooke's murderer was here.

* * *

Deputy Bobby Joe Harte knocked on Jacob's office door, then poked his head in and said, "Chief Watson just called. He said for you to meet him over at the Congregational Church ASAP. They got a dead body in the church and it looks like the same MO as the Susie Richards' case."

"What?"

"That's all he said. Just told me to tell you to get your ass over there pronto."

"Damn! What's going on around here? We haven't had a murder in Cherokee Pointe in years and now we have two in the county in forty-eight hours."

Jacob strapped on his hip holster, put on his leather jacket, and yanked his Stetson off the hook by the door, then headed through the outer office. Once outside, he moved carefully over the icy sidewalk until he reached his truck. His booted feet made large, deep impressions in the snow piled up along the edge of the street. He unlocked his black Dodge Ram, climbed inside and started the engine. While sitting there, letting the engine idle and warm, he allowed his mind to wander, allowed himself to question his decision to run for sheriff this past year.

He'd been born and raised in Cherokee County, a poor boy, a quarter-breed, a young hellion who'd joined the navy at eighteen. Ten months ago, when he'd left the service, put his years as a SEAL behind him and come home, he'd been hailed as a hero. When Farlan MacKinnon had approached him about running for sheriff, he hadn't seriously considered the offer of his backing. But Farlan had been insistent. And what Farlan wanted, he usually got. One of the two richest men in the county, and the most influential man in his political party, Farlan had promised Jacob that if he ran for office, he'd win. The old man had been right. Now Jacob wondered why the hell he'd let Farlan and his cohorts talk him into this job.

A horn honking behind him brought Jacob back to the present moment. He glanced through his partially defrosted back window and saw Royce Pierpont, in his silver Lexus sedan, throw up a hand and wave at him. Jacob returned the wave. Why was Royce bothering to open up his antique shop today? Jacob wondered. There wouldn't be any tourists in town with weather like this, and probably not many locals either.

Jacob shifted the gear into reverse, backed up, and headed down the street, going slow and easy over the thin sheet of ice still clinging to the asphalt.

A large brick structure that had been built in the early twentieth century and modernized from time to time, the Congregational Church was on the corner of Monroe and Highland. Jacob parked his truck, got out, and headed up the sidewalk. Policemen swarmed like bees inside and out. Looked like the entire Cherokee Pointe police department was here.

Chief Watson met Jacob in the vestibule the minute he entered the building. "Glad you're here," he said. "It's a bloody mess in there."

"Bobby Joe said you mentioned that this murder was similar to Susie Richards'—"

"Another sacrificial killing," Watson said. "I saw the pictures of Susie Richards your department took, but I'm telling you that unless you see it for real, you can't imagine how bad it is."

"Mind if I take a look?" Jacob steeled himself to view another horrific crime scene.

Chief Watson led Jacob into the sanctuary. Morning sunlight flooded through the stained-glass windows, casting bright rainbows over the wooden pews with their red velvet seats.

"She's up here, on the altar," Watson said.

"Hmm."

Several members of the forensic crew busied themselves gathering evidence. Jacob moved closer, took a quick look, and glanced away.

"Cindy Todd."

The mayor's wife lay naked atop the altar, her calves and

feet hanging off the end, a gaping wound from breasts to pubic area glistening with blood and exposed entrails.

"It's enough to turn a man's stomach," Watson said, his face pale and sweaty.

"Has anyone contacted Jerry Lee?" Jacob asked.

"I called him right before I called you. Told him to come down to the police department, but I didn't give him any specifics. Just told him it was important."

"He came by my office early this morning looking for her."

"You don't reckon Jerry Lee could have—"

"Not his style," Jacob said. "He'd have either shot her or beat the hell out of her. Besides, this has all the earmarks of being identical to Susie Richards' murder."

"You think we got ourselves a serial killer here in Cherokee Pointe?"

Jacob shook his head. "Too soon to make that kind of judgment. Could be some sort of cult thing."

"You mean one of them devil-worshiping cults?"

"Just a possibility." Jacob glanced around and quickly spotted the church's new minister and his wife huddled together toward the back of the sanctuary, a police officer speaking to them. "Who found the body?"

"Reverend Stowe," Watson said. "The guy's pretty shook up, but then who wouldn't be?"

"What's his wife doing here?"

"After he called us from his office down the hall there"—Watson indicated the location of the office with a nod of his head—"he went back home and waited for us. He and Mrs. Stowe came back over here together."

Jacob studied the Stowes for a moment before turning his attention to the chief. "I think we probably need some help. Neither your department nor mine is equipped to handle this sort of crime, especially not now that there have been two identical murders."

"Don't go putting us down," Watson said. "I've got no intention of calling in outside help. Not yet."

"Do you think your department can handle this case if it turns out we're dealing with a serial killer?"

"Hellfire, Jacob, I thought you said it was probably a devil-worshiping cult."

"I don't know for sure. And that's the problem. I'm new at this job, and my experience in matters like this is nil. The resources of the Cherokee County Sheriff's Department is limited. And I'm not too proud to ask for help when I need it."

"Then, boy, you go ahead and call for help. I don't need any. I've been police chief for fifteen years. I know my way around a murder investigation."

Jacob knew better than to argue with Roddy Watson, the stubborn, narrow-minded, ignorant son of a bitch. "Whatever you say."

Just as Jacob turned to leave, Jerry Lee Todd came storming into the church. When several policemen tried to stop him, he shoved them aside and when they moved to overpower him, Chief Watson motioned for them to leave the mayor alone. Jerry Lee ran toward the altar.

"Hold up there," Watson called. "You don't want to do this."

"Is it her?" Jerry Lee asked. "Is it my Cindy?"

"Yeah, it's Cindy," Watson replied. "Believe me, Jerry Lee, you do not want to—"

"What happened? Is she really dead?" Jerry Lee barreled past the forensic team, taking no heed of their requests for him not to disturb the scene.

Jerry Lee skidded to a halt when he saw his wife's mutilated body. "Cindy! Oh, God, Cindy!"

"Hell," Watson murmured.

Jacob rushed forward and grabbed Jerry Lee's shoulder, stopping him from getting any closer to Cindy's body. Jerry Lee spun around, grief and fury in his eyes. "Let me go, damn you. I've got to see her, talk to her, touch her."

"No," Jacob said. "What you've got to do is let the police do their job so they can find the person responsible."

"You can't stop me. That's my wife." Jerry Lee jerked away from Jacob. "I have every right to—"

Jacob drew back his fist and clipped Jerry Lee on the temple. The mayor dropped like dead weight tossed into the river. Turning to Chief Watson, Jacob said, "Get a couple of your boys to take him home and stay with him until he calms down."

"He's going to be mad as hell when he comes to," Watson said. "But you did what you had to do."

Jacob nodded. "You know where to reach me if you need me."

He left the murder scene, left behind the cocky, stupid police chief, and took a lot of unanswered questions with him.

Esther Stowe held her husband's hands tightly in hers as they stood at the back of the sanctuary. They had answered questions repeatedly for the past hour and still they weren't allowed to leave. They'd been told the chief would want to verify a few things. Esther wasn't sure how much longer Haden could hold himself together. Her husband wasn't emotionally strong. If not for her strength, he wouldn't be the man he was today.

Sometimes she regretted having married such a weakling and longed for a man who was her equal. No one would ever guess, seeing Haden and her together, that she was the dominant partner. To the world they presented a rather amusing facade, the old-fashioned married couple, with the husband as head of the household. Haden Stowe didn't have the balls to be the man of the house, but it served her purpose to allow him to playact the part.

Haden whispered, "What if they find—"

"They won't!"

"But what if—"

"Shut up. There's no way they'll find it. It's not here in the church. It's in our house, and there's no reason for them to search our house."

"How could this have happened? Why here? Why in my church?" He looked at her accusingly. "You didn't—"

"Don't be absurd. Of course I didn't."

"But she was sacrificed, just like the other one."

"We were not involved with either. You know that."

Haden nodded.

Esther kept her gaze fixed on the sheriff as he left the building. Chief Watson she could handle. The man was an idiot. But Jacob Butler was another matter. The sheriff could prove dangerous to her. He needed to be watched. Watched closely.

Chapter 6

Genny woke slowly, languidly, feeling safe and secure. Several moments passed before she remembered what had happened. When she did remember, a deep, profound sadness overwhelmed her. She'd had another vision. One yesterday around dawn and then a second one this morning at daybreak. Both times she had sensed what the killer was going to do. Yesterday she'd actually witnessed his crime. Today she had seen only the woman's body lying on the altar and felt the man's anticipation. Oh, God, the poor woman was probably already dead by now. Genny had received a forewarning this time, but it had come to her far too late to help save this second victim.

Morning sunshine brightened the bedroom, telling Genny she had slept for hours. Glancing around the room, she caught sight of Dallas Sloan asleep in the corner chair, Drudwyn curled on the rug beside him. Odd how her wildly protective dog had accepted this man, as if he, too, sensed a trustworthiness in Dallas. When she rose from the bed and dropped her bare feet to the floor, Drudwyn lifted his head and stared at her. She placed a finger to her lips. Drudwyn rumbled an aborted yowl. Dallas's eyelids flew open and his gaze connected with Genny's.

"Good morning," she said as she reached down for her robe at the foot of the bed.

As Dallas sat up straight, the white cotton afghan slipped off his shoulders and down to his waist, revealing his muscular chest.

"Are you all right now?" he asked.

She nodded, belting the long pink chenille robe and tightening the sash around her waist.

After tossing the afghan aside, Dallas stood and stretched. "I didn't mean to fall asleep. I must have been beat."

"Then you haven't checked the phones, have you?"

He shook his head. "Afraid not."

Genny lifted the receiver from the telephone base on her nightstand and placed it to her ear. "Still no dial tone." She walked over to the window, pulled back the curtain and secured it on a clip behind the window frame. After glancing out, she said, "It's a beautiful day. The sun might melt away some of the snow. We should be able to get into town this afternoon, if the snowplows make it up this far."

Without waiting for a comment from Dallas, she motioned to Drudwyn. "Time to go out, boy." Her gaze fell on Dallas. "How do pancakes with maple syrup for breakfast sound to you?"

"Delicious," he replied. "But please don't go to any trouble for me. I usually just grab a quick cup of coffee before I head out in the morning."

"Why don't you take a shower while I let Drudwyn out and start breakfast? I have a gas hot-water heater, so even with the electricity out, you'll have plenty of hot water."

"Sounds good to me."

"I'm sorry I don't have anything for you to change into, but I don't think anything of mine would work, and when Jacob moved into town last year, he didn't leave any of his clothes behind."

"I'll be fine."

"All right. When you finish your shower, you'll find me in the kitchen."

Although a powerful magnetism drew her to Dallas, she forcefully pulled herself away from him. As she went through the house toward the kitchen, Drudwyn at her heels, she thought about the peculiar feelings Dallas Sloan evoked in her. From the first moment she opened the door to him last night, she'd known he was destined to become important to her. As a friend? As a lover? Or simply as an instrument of change in her life? She wasn't sure. She knew only that her fate was intertwined with the big, blond stranger's.

When she opened the back door, Drudwyn bounded onto the porch and out into the snow. Shivering, she closed the door quickly. Two sets of high double windows on the outside walls let light flood into the kitchen. Genny flipped the switch to check for electricity. Just as she had suspected, the power was still out. She set about preparing the coffee in an old metal pot, then placed it atop the gas cookstove. While the coffee brewed, she prepared the batter for their pancakes. As she kept herself occupied, she tried not to think about this morning's vision, but her mind kept replaying the scene over and over in her mind.

Another young woman dead. She'd been able to tell that the woman was fairly young because her breasts had been firm, her body supple. Who had been killed this time? And where? The first victim had been slaughtered on a makeshift altar in the woods. But this time the altar had been more elaborate, similar to ones used in churches.

Oh, God! Multicolored light. Stained glass. A decoratively carved altar. Had he murdered this woman in a church? In a church in Cherokee Pointe?

Genny's hands trembled. A fresh egg fell from her fingers to the floor and splattered its sticky contents across the wide planks. She hurried to clean up the mess and get on with preparing the pancakes. There was absolutely nothing she could do for the second victim, just as there had been nothing she could do for Susie Richards. *Why, Lord? Why give me this incredible gift and not allow it to be used to save lives?*

Fifteen minutes later, Dallas joined her at the kitchen table. His thick, unruly hair was still damp, and a day's growth of brown beard stubble added a rather rakish quality to his ruggedly handsome appearance. His dark slacks and white shirt were wrinkled, but his slightly disheveled appearance didn't seem to bother him at all. And oddly enough, Genny thought it made him all the more appealing.

"Something sure smells good," he said.

"Please, sit down. Everything is ready."

They sat across from each other at the big, round table and ate in relative silence, occasionally exchanging glances. While she picked at her food, he ate heartily and asked for seconds.

"Would you like another cup of coffee?" she asked as she rose from her seat.

"Stay there," he told her. "I should be waiting on you. After all, you cooked for us."

"I have to get up anyway. Drudwyn and the others need to be fed."

"The others?"

"The squirrels, raccoons, birds, and other wild creatures that depend on me in weather like this."

"You must have quite a feed bill if you're providing food for all the animals out there in those woods."

"I have more than enough money for my needs, so I share my bounty with others."

Dallas finished his breakfast, downed his fourth cup of coffee, then gathered up their dishes and placed them in the sink. He glanced out the window and saw Drudwyn racing around in the snow, playful and exuberant despite the desperate cold. Then he caught a glimpse of Genny. She wore a heavy, black wool coat over her pajamas and robe, thick rubber boots on her feet, and a black knit cap pulled down over her ears. She stood in the middle of the backyard and was surrounded by a variety of animals. Squirrels. Raccoons.

Possums. A couple of foxes. A deer. A silver-gray wolf. And birds perched on her shoulder and outstretched arm.

Dallas blinked to clear his vision, thinking he had imagined the scene before him. Not his imagination. It was real. Genny Madoc had charmed the wild animals in the forest. They came to her like babes to their mother. He'd never seen anything like it. And although he was seeing it now with his own two eyes, he found it incomprehensible.

An odd feeling hit him in the pit of his stomach. He'd humorously considered her a witch who had cast a spell over him last night. Seeing her now, in this setting, with a host of spellbound animals circling her, Dallas didn't find the thought of Genny possessing some sort of unearthly power quite as amusing.

Get a grip, Sloan, he told himself. *Genny isn't a witch, because there is no such thing as witches. She hasn't cast a spell over you or those animals. You find her sexually appealing. And as for the animals—she's probably been feeding them for years.* Yeah, that was it. Those explanations made sense to him. They were logical.

Suddenly the birds flew away and the animals scattered. Genny turned her head and looked toward the front of the house. That's when Dallas heard the drone of motors in the distance.

Genny came running into the house, stripping off her coat and hat as she flew into the kitchen. "The snowplows are coming up the mountain," she said breathlessly. "We'll be able to get into town soon."

"We?" Dallas asked.

"Your car is still in the ditch, so we'll take mine. We can send a wrecker back for yours. We both want to see Jacob as soon as possible, don't we?"

"Why do you want to see—"

"To tell him about the second victim," she replied. "But it's possible he already knows. I feel fairly certain she was killed in a church, probably one of the fancier churches in town. None of the country churches have stained-glass windows."

"What are you talking about? You're actually going to bother the sheriff with that crazy dream you had? You don't honestly think it was real, that what you dreamed really happened."

Genny stared at him quizzically, as if he'd spoken to her in an alien language. "You don't understand, do you? No, of course not." She tossed her coat and hat on the table, then kicked off her boots. "I'll freshen up and get dressed. We should be able to head down to Cherokee Pointe very soon."

As she raced past him, Dallas reached out and grabbed her arm. She halted, glanced over her shoulder and looked directly at him, as if to ask *What?*

"You're right, I don't understand," he said. "How about explaining it to me?"

She tugged against his grip. He released her immediately. "Everybody in these parts knows about me. My grandmother and both of her grandmothers before her were . . . different. And so am I. I'm able to sense things, see things, feel things that other people don't."

Dallas glared at her. Hell, what was she trying to tell him? Whatever it was, he already didn't believe her.

"Before you start trying to convince me that you're some sort of soothsayer or psychic or whatever the hell all the phonies call themselves, don't bother," Dallas said sternly. "If I can't experience it through my five senses, then I don't believe it."

"Ah." Her mouth formed a soft oval. Moisture glistened in her black eyes.

"Ah, what? You act like I'm the crazy one for not believing you."

"No one knows except Jacob and my friend Jazzy—and probably Sally and Ludie—about my recent vision. If you stay in these parts for a while, you'll meet Sally and Ludie." Genny shook her head. "That's neither here nor there, of course. The truth is that whether you believe me or not, it doesn't matter. Jacob believes me. He knows."

Genny rushed out of the kitchen, leaving Dallas with his mouth hanging open. *Well, she told you, didn't she?*

After a few minutes, he followed her, not willing to leave things as they were between them. When he caught up with her in her bedroom, he walked in on her just as she jerked her pajama top over her head and threw it on the bed atop her robe. Holy shit! Hurriedly, she removed the bottoms, which left her completely naked. He stood frozen to the spot, looking at her, devouring her perfect body with his gaze, unable to move or speak.

When she tossed her pajama bottoms on the bed, she must have sensed his presence. She turned, then gasped. Her eyes rounded in surprise.

"Sorry," he said, lying through his teeth. To his dying day, he'd never regret this moment. Genny Madoc might be a certifiable nutcase, but he didn't care. Her beauty took his breath away.

She didn't scream or try to cover her nakedness. She simply stood there, allowing him to drink his fill. After a couple of minutes, he realized how totally inappropriate his actions were.

"Genny . . . I-I'll wait for you in the living room." He turned and practically ran down the hall.

When he reached the living room, he pounded his fist against the wall. "Idiot!" The sight of Genny in all her naked glory flashed through his mind repeatedly. She was small and slender, delicately made. Her skin, the color of light honey, was flawless. Tiny waist. High, round breasts, peaked with dusty peach nipples. Full, tapering hips. A tight, lush butt. And a triangle of jet black hair nestled between her trim thighs.

Dallas swallowed, then cursed under his breath. He had the hard-on from hell.

Jim Upton caught his grandson trying to sneak up the back stairs. The boy had been out all night doing only God knew what. Jim hadn't slept much, worrying about Jamie, wondering just what the hell kind of mischief he'd been up to. Some of his usual nonsense, no doubt. Screwing some two-bit floozie. Drinking himself into oblivion. Gambling away money he'd never earned. Getting into a fight and landing himself in jail or winding up in County General's ER. Seeing Jamie all in one piece, with no black eyes or broken bones, allowed Jim some momentary relief. More than once these past few years he'd been on the verge of writing the boy off as a lost cause. But Reba would champion their only grandchild to her dying day, no matter what he did.

Jim walked across the big, modernized kitchen and stopped at the foot of the stairs. "Glad to see you finally made it home."

Jamie stopped dead in his tracks. He squared his shoulders and turned to face his grandfather, a silly, aw-shucks grin on his handsome young face.

"Morning, Big Daddy." Jamie made his way back down the stairs. "Looks like it's going to be a right pretty day, despite the foot of snow we got last night."

"Got caught in town, did you?" Jim asked.

Jamie shrugged. His cocky grin widened. "Yeah, something like that."

"You could have called. Your grandmother was worried sick about you. And Laura was none too happy that you'd deserted her."

"I'll smooth things over with my ladies. Don't worry. They'll forgive me."

"Reba will forgive you for anything, but I won't. You'd better keep that in mind. Sooner or later, you'll cross the line as far as I'm concerned."

Jamie reached over and grabbed Jim's shoulder. "We're both men of the world. You know how it is. A man's gotta do what a man's gotta do."

Jim glowered at his grandson. "Exactly what is it that you do, boy, other than spend my money and raise hell?"

Jamie laughed, an infectious, lighthearted chuckle that personified his shallow, flippant personality. "Don't tell me you don't understand what it's like to need a little variety. Laura is a sweetie. Really she is. But every once in a while I need something a bit spicier. You adore Big Mama, but that doesn't mean you don't dip your quill in other inkwells and we both know it.''

Anger heated Jim's face. The unmitigated gall of the boy! ''We aren't discussing my behavior.''

''Don't get all huffy.'' Jamie patted Jim on the chest. ''You're liable to give yourself a heart attack and we don't want that. I didn't mean any offense. I was just stating a fact. You've kept something on the side for as long as I remember, so don't go getting all righteous on me just because I—''

Jim slapped Jamie soundly across the cheek, the force of the blow sending the boy reeling backward. Jamie caught hold of the counter behind him, then lifted his hand to his stinging cheek.

Jamie glared at his grandfather. ''What's the matter? Can't stand to hear the truth, old man?''

''Your grandmother wants to see you married to Laura, so if you know what's good for you, you won't do anything to run that girl off the way you did the other two you brought home.'' Jim swallowed, then took several deep, calming breaths. ''If Laura finds out that you spent the night with—''

''I didn't spend the night with Jazzy, if that's what you're thinking.''

Jim cocked his eyebrows inquisitively.

''Jazzy was just punishing me by sending me away,'' Jamie said. ''She'll give me a hard time for a week or two, then she'll come around. She always does.''

''Then who were you with?'' Jazzy had mentioned she thought Jamie had left her place with a woman named April or Amber.

''What difference does it make?'' Jamie's eyes widened with speculation. ''Are you afraid I might have been diddling your latest lady love?'' Jamie laughed right in Jim's face. ''Hell, unless your mistress hangs out at Jazzy's Joint, I didn't screw her last night.''

Damn fool boy! He didn't know the first thing about keeping a mistress faithful. He thought most women were sluts who would spread their legs for any man. Jim knew better. If a man chose wisely and kept the lady content, she didn't go to other men for satisfaction.

"Get your ass upstairs, take a shower and change clothes, then come back downstairs for breakfast with the family," Jim said. "You tell your grandmother and Laura that you went into town to see one of your old high school buddies and got caught by the snowstorm. Tell them that you're sorry you worried them, but by the time you realized you couldn't get home, it was too late to call and wake everyone."

Jamie grinned. "Yes sir. Whatever you say. And may I compliment you on your ability to weave a convincing tale."

Jim grunted. With his stupid grin in place, Jamie turned and bounded up the stairs. Before he made it halfway up, he started whistling.

Jim heaved a deep sigh. That good-for-nothing boy was his legacy to the world. A sad and sorry thought. He'd wanted more children, but Reba had been unable to conceive again after Melanie's birth. A cruel trick of fate had taken away the son he'd been so proud of and the daughter he'd loved to distraction. How was it that Jamie was so different from Jim Jr.? Had he inherited some weak genes from his mother? Or had Reba and he simply ruined the boy by overindulging him all his life? But they'd spoiled Jim Jr., hadn't they? Yet he'd been a credit to his family.

Enough of this, Jim told himself. *Can't change a damn thing. A man makes do with the hand he's dealt. Concentrate on the positive things.*

He poured himself a cup of coffee from the pot the housekeeper had prepared earlier, before she'd gone back to her quarters to get ready for the day. Mug in hand, he made his way down the hall and into his study. He closed the door securely behind him, crossed the room, and sat down behind his massive mahogany desk. After taking several sips of black coffee, he placed it on the leather coaster in front of him and lifted the telephone. He dialed her number and waited.

"Hello," the sultry feminine voice said.

"How'd you make it through last night's storm?" he asked.

"Just fine. But I'd have enjoyed being cooped up here a lot better if you'd been with me."

"I probably won't be able to make it out there today."

"I figured you wouldn't."

"I wish you had come to the party last night," Jim said. "You got your invitation, didn't you?"

"I got it. But I didn't think I'd enjoy seeing you with your wife. I'm quite jealous of her, you know."

A warm feeling came to life in his gut. "You got everything you need out there to see you through a few days until the roads clear up?"

"I've got everything I need . . . except you."

"You've got me. Got me wrapped around your little finger."

"If only that were true."

"Be careful, will you? I don't like the idea of you being out there all alone with a killer on the loose."

"I have the gun you gave me," she said. "And I know how to use it."

"Just be careful. And don't let anyone inside the house you don't know and trust."

"Come see me just as soon as you can. I miss you."

Jim's penis twitched. She had a way of bringing him to life with just the sound of her voice. "I miss you, too . . . but I've got to go. I'll call you this evening."

The dial tone hummed in his ear. He was a damn old fool and he knew it. Erin Mercer was twenty-five years his junior, a fine-looking woman, and really didn't need him to support her. He'd met her several years ago when she'd first moved to the area. And he'd known the minute he saw her that he wanted her. She was no whore, so paying her for her services had been out of the question. He'd figured he didn't stand a chance with her. He'd been wrong. She had been the one who'd chased him, lured him into her bed and kept him coming back, begging for more. It couldn't last. His affairs never did. He'd never wanted anything permanent from any of his mistresses. But Erin was different. He was halfway in love with her, and if he was ten years younger, he'd ask Reba for a divorce.

But he was seventy-five. He was able to keep Erin sexually satisfied because he kept a supply of Viagra on hand. But how many more good years could he possibly have—four or five? He was physically fit for a man his age, but even a healthy, tan, muscular body couldn't stop the ravages of time.

Jim ran his open palms over his face and rubbed his eyes. If only he could be Jamie's age again, he wouldn't waste his life the way his grandson was doing. If he had it to do all over again . . . what would he do differently?

Everything! Starting with not marrying Reba.

Chapter 7

Dallas manned the wheel of Genny's Chevy Trailblazer, taking it slow and easy on the freshly cleared road into town. He had deliberately kept quiet, uncertain how to deal with this woman whose beauty attracted him, but whose admission of having *visions* disturbed him. Knowing he'd gotten all hot and bothered over a woman who was probably the town kook didn't sit well with him. Teri would laugh herself silly if she knew that the stoic Dallas Sloan was tied in knots over somebody like Genny. In the past he'd scoffed at people claiming to possess any type of sixth sense. Sure, there had been a couple of times when he'd come close to believing, when he'd been part of an investigation where a so-called psychic had been brought in and appeared to have helped trap the assailant. But in each of those cases, he'd been able to figure out a logical reason behind the person's foreknowledge.

"Turn left where the road forks," Genny said. "The right turn will take us back up the mountain."

Grunting, Dallas nodded and kept a lookout for their turn. Within minutes, he saw the divided roadway and carefully veered to the left. Despite having been cleared and sanded, the pavement was still slick in a lot of places, and muddy slush covered the shoulders on each side of the road and filled the numerous potholes.

Up ahead on the left he noticed massive wrought-iron gates heralding the entrance to a country estate. Far in the distance, a good half mile, he saw a large mansion with towering white columns spanning the front of the house.

"That's impressive," Dallas said.

"That's the Upton Farm," Genny replied. "The Uptons are one of the wealthiest families in Cherokee County."

"Old money?" Dallas asked.

"Not too old. Theirs is post–Civil War money."

"You said they're one of the richest. Anybody richer?"

"The MacKinnons are probably just as wealthy, maybe more so. They made their fortune post–Civil War, too. There's quite a rivalry between the two families. They're divided on just about everything, from politics to religion. The MacKinnons are Democrats and Methodists. The Uptons are Republicans and Congregationalists."

"Don't tell me—the son of one family fell in love with the daughter of the other family and they had a tragic Romeo and Juliet romance."

Genny smiled. "Not exactly. When they were just boys, Big Jim Upton and Farlan MacKinnon, both now in their midseventies, fell in love with a young woman named Melva Mae Nelson, whose family was quite poor and lived up in the mountains."

"And they've hated each other ever since," Dallas said. "So, which man won Miss Melva Mae? Upton or MacKinnon?"

"Neither. Melva Mae married the love of her life, a half-breed Cherokee like herself. Jacob Butler."

"Jacob . . . any relation to your cousin Jacob?"

"Jacob was our grandfather."

"Then Melva Mae was—"

"Our grandmother."

"The one who was—"

"Special," Genny said.

"Quite a story. The two richest men in town in love with a girl everyone thought was crazy. And she proved them right when she chose a poor boy over either wealthy man."

"You're a cynic," Genny remarked as if the realization had just come to her.

"If you were truly psychic, you'd have known that already."

"That's where you're wrong. People who possess any type of sixth sense aren't all-knowing or all-powerful. And most of us have a very difficult time controlling our special gifts, whatever they may be."

"I've heard that explanation before. It gets people like you off the hook when they're wrong."

"People like me? People who possess a sixth sense?"

Dallas snorted. "People who claim to have a sixth sense."

"Yes, of course. We only claim to be gifted, but none of us really are. Is that your take on it?"

"That's what I know to be a fact." He stole a quick glance at her, then returned his full attention to the road ahead.

"So you've known others like me?"

"A few who claimed to be psychic, telepathic, precognitive, whatever the hell you want to label it." He paused for a couple of seconds, then said, "But none of them were anything like you, Genevieve Madoc."

"Who was it that closed your mind to the possibilities that there's more to life than what we can perceive through our five senses?"

Dallas huffed. "There's no point in our discussing this. We'll just go around and around in circles. How about we simply agree to disagree?"

"All right, then. For now."

He didn't like the sound of that. He figured Genny believed she could change his mind. She couldn't. Not unless she turned out to be exactly what she claimed to be. And that was highly unlikely.

Several minutes later they drove into Cherokee Pointe, population 10,483. He instantly got the feeling he was entering Mayberry, U.S.A. Moderate traffic flowed along the slushy streets, but only a handful of people trudged up and down the sidewalks. They drove past a remodeled hotel that had probably been built in the early part of the twentieth century. A myriad of little shops lined Sixth Street.

"Take a right at the next red light. We'll go past my friend Jazzy's restaurant and bar on the way. Then take a left off Loden Street and go two blocks. You can't miss the courthouse on Main Street. It's a big white building with huge white columns."

"Your friend Jazzy, who believes you're psychic, is a local restaurateur?"

"Jazzy's a local businesswoman. She owns Jasmine's, the best restaurant in town, as well as Jazzy's Joint, which is Cherokee Pointe's version of a cross between a pub and a roadhouse. And she's part-owner of Cherokee Cabin Rentals."

"Hmm . . ."

Dallas turned right, drove past the two establishments owned by Genny's friend Jazzy, went two blocks and then took a left on Loden. He could see the courthouse up the street. A three-story brick structure painted white, with a bell-tower dome and impressive Ionic columns on three sides. The building sat in the middle of the block, flanked by the local fire and police departments.

"You can park in the rear," Genny said. "Everybody knows my truck, so we won't get a ticket."

"Being the sheriff's cousin gets you preferential treatment, huh?" Dallas said jokingly.

Genny laughed.

Dallas parked the Trailblazer alongside a department vehicle in the shaded parking lot at the rear of the courthouse. He killed the engine and turned to Genny. "I want to thank you again for taking in a stranded traveler last night. If you hadn't been so gracious, I'd have been forced to sleep in my car."

"You would have frozen to death," she told him. "Anyway, you're quite welcome."

Dallas opened his door, stepped down, rounded the hood, and was standing by the passenger door by the time Genny opened it. He held out his hand, which she took, and helped her onto the icy pavement. He held her hand for a fraction longer than necessary, then released her abruptly.

"In case I don't see you again after today . . . thanks, and . . . well, just thanks."

"You've already said that."

"So I have."

She placed her hand on his upper arm. Damn! He actually thought he could feel her body heat through his shirt, jacket, and overcoat. Logic told him what he thought he felt was impossible, but his senses insisted it was true. The warmth in her palm spread up and down his arm. He stared into the depths of her black eyes and found himself unable to speak.

As if sensing his unease, Genny lifted her hand from his arm and said, "Let's go talk to Jacob."

Dallas simply nodded, then allowed Genny to lead the way into the courthouse. He followed behind her as she went inside the back door, down a marble-floored corridor, and to a rotunda with curving staircases that led upward to a second-story mezzanine and downward to the lower level.

"The Sheriff's Department is this way," Genny said. "It's not far."

Within minutes, they entered the outer office, where a clean-cut young redhead with a freckled face and a welcoming smile hopped up from behind one of the three desks and came rushing toward Genny.

"Hey there, Miss Genny." The obviously smitten deputy grinned like an idiot. "What brings you into town in weather like this?"

"I came to talk to Jacob," Genny said, then turned to Dallas. "Special Agent Sloan, this is Deputy Bobby Joe Harte." She smiled at the boy. "We need to see Jacob right away. Is he in his office?"

"Yes ma'am." Bobby Joe surveyed Dallas from head to toe, then swallowed hard. "But I guess since there's been a second murder—"

"There's been a second murder?" Dallas asked.

"Yes sir. Didn't you know?"

"Another sacrificial murder?" Dallas's heartbeat hummed loudly inside his head.

Genny grasped Dallas's arm. "Let's talk to Jacob. He can tell you what you need to know."

"He's on the phone with the crime lab in Knoxville," Bobby Joe said. "Just knock before you go in."

Genny smiled warmly, and Bobby Joe Harte melted like an ice-cream cone dropped on a red-hot sidewalk in July. Dallas felt sorry for the deputy because he understood all too well the lady's spellbinding appeal.

Outside the sheriff's office door, Genny lifted her hand and knocked softly several times. Dallas stood tensely at her side, wondering just how forthcoming Butler would be to an agent on unofficial business.

"May we come in?" Genny asked. "I have Agent Sloan with me."

In two seconds flat, the door opened all the way, and standing there was one of the most intimidating-looking men Dallas had ever seen. Jacob Butler had to be at least six-five. With shoulders that spanned the width of the door and arms and legs like tree trunks, his weight would probably tip the scales somewhere between two-fifty and three hundred. Add to his impressive size a pair of slanting green eyes set in a leather-tan face that looked like it had been chiseled from granite, and shoulder-length jet black hair pulled back in a ponytail, and you had a man whose mere presence cautioned others to tread lightly.

"Genny." Jacob's deep baritone voice sounded like sandpaper being scraped over metal. His face softened ever so slightly. "Are you all right? What are you doing in town, with the roads in such bad shape?"

Before she could reply, Jacob glanced over her shoulder at Dallas. His eyes narrowed speculatively and his brow furrowed.

"Jacob, this is Dallas Sloan, the FBI agent you spoke to on the phone last night before—"

"Where did you stay last night?" Jacob asked.

"He stayed at my house," Genny replied. "His car skidded off in a ditch and he couldn't get into town last night, so he stayed in one of the guest rooms."

Dallas could swear he heard a feral growl coming from the sheriff. Hell, this was no way to start things off, having Butler go all protective about his cousin's honor.

Genny leaned over and kissed Jacob's cheek. He cleared his throat. "Bobby Joe said there's been a second murder. Can you tell us what happened?"

"Come on in and sit down." Jacob stood aside until Genny and Dallas came into the office and took the chairs in front of his desk. He closed the door.

Jacob braced his hips on the edge of his desk, crossed his massive arms, and laid them over his chest. "That new minister over at the Congregational Church discovered a woman's body strapped across the altar when he arrived there this morning. He called us immediately."

"That church has stained-glass windows, doesn't it?" Genny asked.

"Yeah, why? Did you have another . . ." He glanced at Dallas.

"Dallas knows. He was there at the house when I woke screaming at dawn this morning. I told him what I saw."

"What did you see?" Jacob asked.

"A young woman's naked body on a fancy altar. The early morning sun. Multicolored lights. And—and the sword."

"Did you see the guy's face?"

Genny shook her head. A lone tear trickled down her cheek.

"Are you all right? Did you rest afterward?"

"Dallas was there. He was very kind."

Dallas listened to the conversation as if he weren't there. He heard what was said, but somehow he couldn't get past how easily Jacob Butler believed every word Genny told him. How could he deal with a lawman who believed in all this hocus-pocus stuff? Then again, how the hell could

Genny have known the second victim was murdered in a church?

Jacob eased off the edge of the desk, reached out, and took both of Genny's hands in his. *"I gi do . . ."*

Dallas sensed the tension hit Genny the moment her cousin spoke to her in a language Dallas didn't understand. What had he said to her?

"When you call me sister, I know what you have to say is very serious." Genny looked Jacob square in the eyes.

"The victim was Cindy Todd."

"Ooh . . ." The word rushed out of Genny on a released breath. "Poor Cindy."

"You knew the victim?" Dallas asked as he inexplicably leaned toward Genny.

She shook her head. "We were acquaintances. Friendly acquaintances. She was such an unhappy soul."

"You shouldn't be here," Jacob said. "Why don't you head home before it gets dark? Or better yet, spend the night in town with Jazzy."

"I plan to see Jazzy while I'm in town, but I'll go on home tonight."

"I don't like the idea of your traveling up the mountain alone at night. Not with a killer on the loose. I'll follow you home when you get ready to go."

Genny nodded agreement. "There's nothing I can tell you that will help you, except . . . this man, he enjoys what he does. It excites him."

"Sexually?" Jacob asked.

"Yes."

"Son of a bitch."

"He has no conscience. I felt no conflict within him, no sense of right and wrong."

Dallas watched her closely as she spoke, wishing the hard knot in his stomach would dissolve. He forced his attention away from her to the sheriff.

"Were both victims raped?" Dallas asked.

Jacob eyed him quizzically. "You're not here in any official capacity, Agent Sloan, and that information is—"

"Tell him," Genny said. "He can help you."

Dallas clenched his teeth. He was torn between wanting to thank Genny and telling her to stop this idiotic psychic nonsense.

Jacob eased back and sat on the side of his desk. He grasped the edge with both hands. "According to Pete Holt, our coroner, Susie Richards and Cindy Todd were sexually assaulted."

Dallas glanced at Genny. "You hesitated to share this information with me, and I'm a federal agent, but you don't have any problem sharing it with your cousin?"

"Genny has helped the Sheriff's Department and the local police on more than one occasion," Jacob said. "Let's just say she's an honorary deputy."

"I see. Then I can speak freely in front of *Deputy* Madoc?" Dallas asked, a hint of sarcasm in his voice.

Jacob nodded agreement, but narrowed his gaze disapprovingly.

"The two victims were sexually abused, tied to an altar of some kind, and slit open from breasts to pubic bone with a sharp sword," Dallas said. "Both victims were female between the ages of fifteen and forty, and they lived within a fifty-mile radius of each other, but other than that the two had nothing in common."

"You mentioned on the phone that you'd been involved in another case where the killer had a similar MO," Jacob said. "A series of sacrificial killings in Mobile, Alabama, sometime last year."

Dallas steeled himself against the pain before he responded. "Five women were murdered over a six-week period, each one sexually abused, cut open with a sword while tied to an altar or something that was used as an altar."

"How were the Feds involved?" Jacob asked.

"They weren't."

"Then how were you—"

"The fourth victim was my niece." Dallas ached with

the agony, unable to forget his sister's grief over the cruel death of her eldest child.

"Great. Just great." Jacob tightened his hold on the edge of the desk until his knuckles turned white. "Why don't you go back to D.C. and stay there? I don't need some guy poking his nose into my business when he's motivated by a personal vendetta."

"She's right, you know." Dallas inclined his head toward Genny, but didn't look at her. "I can help you."

"How's that?"

"I can tell you that there will be three more victims, that they'll all be women who live in and around this area, that they'll be chosen at random, and that there's something special about the fifth victim."

"And that would be?" Jacob asked.

"He'll cut out her heart and take it with him."

Genny gasped.

"You've lost me," Jacob admitted. "You're basing this theory on a series of five murders that took place last year in Mobile, the fourth victim your niece. What makes you so sure that, even given the similarities, the killer's the same man who murdered Susie and Cindy? And what makes you think there will be a total of five victims here in my county?"

"Because since my niece's death eight months ago, I've gotten some unofficial help from friends at the Bureau, and we know that during the past eight years there have been four almost identical cases—twenty murders in all. In Mobile, Alabama; Hilton Head, South Carolina; Lafayette, Louisiana; and Breckenridge, Texas. And in each case there were exactly five victims. And in each case the killer removed the fifth victim's heart."

"And there is no connection between the five victims? Nothing that linked them together in any other way?" Jacob asked.

"Nothing the local law enforcement agencies could figure out." Dallas wondered just how honest he should be with Jacob Butler. "These four sets of murders I mentioned . . . I'm the one who figured out that they were identical and that there's only one killer—a serial killer who moves around on a fairly regular basis.''

"Could be you're grasping at straws," Jacob said. "You want to find your niece's killer so you've built a case on the evidence you've unearthed. You can't be certain that we're dealing with the same man who killed your niece."

"And you can't be certain that we aren't," Dallas told him. "If we are, there are three more women out there—in your county—who are going to die a really gruesome death. Unless we work together to stop him."

Chapter 8

Brian MacKinnon slapped the newspaper down on top of his desk and smiled. Today's issue of the *Cherokee Pointe Herald,* owned and operated by his family for four generations, would hit the stands in a couple of hours. The article he had personally written about the two brutal murders in the area, yesterday morning and this morning, made both Chief Watson and Sheriff Butler look like bumbling fools. He'd known for years that Watson was a joke, remaining in office only because Big Jim Upton's power and influence kept him there. Everybody knew that Big Jim had Watson in his hip pocket. Butler was a different matter altogether. The sheriff was an elected official, put in office by the people of the county. It galled Brian that his own father was such a staunch Butler supporter, which certainly hadn't hurt the guy during last year's election. Despite his mixed heritage, Jacob Butler was well liked by just about everyone who knew him. His background in the navy had made him a local hero. Rumors abounded about his exploits as a navy SEAL.

Brian had tried hard to make Butler like him. For Genny's sake. But for some reason the man had taken an instant dislike to him, which certainly didn't help his cause to woo and win the fair Genevieve. He wasn't quite sure when he realized he was in love with the beautiful young woman. It had happened so gradually that it had taken him by surprise. She wasn't the type he usually found attractive; nothing like his ex-wife Phyllis, who'd been worldly and sophisticated. Genny mesmerized him with her beauty, her gentleness, her kind heart. He'd never known anyone like her. Of course he'd heard the rumors—that she was like her Granny Butler, whom the town had called a witch. But how could anyone who knew Genny believe there was anything evil about such an angelic creature?

He had worked longer and harder to win Genny's friendship than he ever had to finagle any other woman into his bed. She had never encouraged him, never given him the slightest hope that their relationship could evolve into a romantic relationship, but he felt certain that sooner or later he would wear her down. All he needed was patience. Several months ago, just when he'd decided he would soon be able to ask Genny to marry him, another man had come between them: Royce Pierpont, the effeminate jackass. The man had driven into town in his shiny silver Lexus, opened an antique shop on Main Street, and zeroed in on Genny almost immediately. She had succumbed to his good looks and charm, as had several other ladies in town.

The very thought of Pierpont or any other man touching Genny enraged Brian to the point of near madness. She'd allowed him to kiss her, but nothing more. He suspected that Pierpont had gotten no further. His Genny was pure. A true innocent when it came to men. There was no doubt in his mind that she was a virgin. He wanted her to remain unsullied, to come to him undefiled on their wedding night.

A repetitive knock on the outer door snapped Brian away from the delicious thoughts of Genny.

He stayed seated, conveniently concealing his state of arousal. Whenever he thought about making love to Genny, he got hard.

"Yes?"

The door opened and his secretary, Glenda, poked her head in and said, "Your Uncle Wallace is here."

Hell! What was that fruitcake doing coming to see him at the office? His father's younger brother was the family disgrace, a mentally retarded old fart who should have been shipped off to an asylum years ago. But, like his parents before him, Brian's father refused to even consider the possibility of locking Wallace away. Instead, they pampered him, humored him, and let him roam around town as if he were normal. As luck would have it, Genny had a soft spot in her heart for Wallace. Her grandmother had hired Wallace to come to work for her when he was twenty. And after the old woman's death, Genny had kept his now seventy-year-old uncle on at full salary, although he wasn't worth half what she paid him.

Brian had realized early on in his relationship with Genny that he could use her fondness for Wallace to his advantage.

"Tell Uncle Wallace to come on in. And, Glenda, bring us a couple of Dr. Peppers. Uncle Wallace especially likes them."

Glenda lifted her eyebrows in a gesture of surprise, but wisely kept any comments to herself. Brian knew he had a reputation for being a real asshole. But he'd found that if you were too lenient with employees, they took advantage of you. And nobody took advantage of Brian MacKinnon.

Like a clumsy grizzly bear, Wallace lumbered into the office. His uncle stood six-three, possessed a rounded potbelly, and wore overalls and a baseball cap. A shock of thick gray hair stuck out on either side of the cap. He kept his face clean-shaven, thanks to daily grooming at a local barbershop, paid for by the MacKinnon family. Wallace squandered away his own meager salary with donations to the county's animal shelter and by giving handouts to every Tom, Dick, and Harry with a sob story.

"What can I do for you?" Brian remained sitting.

"Have you heard from Genny today?" Wallace asked as he removed his baseball cap and scratched his head.

"I've tried contacting her, but her phone's out of order,"

Brian replied. "The ice from last night's storm downed power and telephone lines out that way."

"I been up there. Got a ride with Bill Davis. I been all the way up to Genny's house to make sure she was doing okay. And she wasn't there," Wallace said breathlessly, the words tumbling from him in a rush.

"She wasn't at home? Did you check everywhere?"

"Her truck was gone, too."

"Then maybe she's in town. I'll call—"

"Yeah, that's it. Why didn't I think of that? Genny's come into town." Wallace reached out, grabbed Brian's arm, and shook his hand, pumping it repeatedly. "I've been so worried about Genny. You know there's a bad person out there killing people. I don't want any bad person hurting Genny."

Brian managed to jerk his hand free from his uncle's tenacious grip. "If you'd like, I'll call Jazzy. I'm sure if Genny's in town, Jazzy will know where she is." He would prefer not to speak to Jasmine Talbot, but if necessary he would. Like Jacob, Genny's best friend, Jazzy, didn't seem to care for him at all. No doubt she, too, had tried to convince Genny not to date him.

"That's all right," Wallace said. "I can just go over to Miss Jazzy's place and ask her myself."

"All right. You do that." Brian stood, finally free from his embarrassing erection. "And when you find Genny, ask her to give me a call. Tell her I've been concerned . . . worried about her."

"You like Genny, too, don't you?" Wallace grinned, which made him look even more simpleminded than he was.

"Yes, I'm very fond of Genny."

Glenda stopped at the open door, two frosty bottles of Dr. Pepper in her hands. "Want these now?"

Brian motioned to her. "Sure we do. Come on in."

Glenda handed a bottle to Brian, then to Wallace. She smiled at Wallace and said, "How are you today, Mr. MacKinnon?"

Wallace chuckled. "I'm not Mr. MacKinnon. That's my brother, Farlan. I'm just Wallace."

"Well, how are you, Wallace?" Glenda rephrased her question.

"I'm just fine, thank you, ma'am."

Brian cleared his throat. Glenda fled the office.

"People say you're not a very nice man, but they're wrong." Wallace lifted the bottle to his mouth and downed half the cola in one long swig. He grinned at Brian. "You've changed from the way you used to be. It's because of Genny, isn't it?"

Brian hated being given the third degree by his crazy uncle, but he could hardly admit the only reason he bothered giving Wallace the time of day was to impress Genny.

"Yeah, it's because of Genny. She's a very special lady."

"You love her."

Brian sucked in his cheeks, then released them. "I want to keep that a secret for now, just between the two of us. I'm not quite ready to tell Genny how I feel."

"She loves you, too."

Brian's heartbeat thundered in his ears. "What?"

"Genny loves you and she loves me. Genny loves everybody."

Brian forced himself to pat Wallace on the back. "Yes, of course she does. Now, you run along to Jazzy's and ask her about Genny."

"All right." Wallace headed toward the open office door.

Brian did love Genny. Loved her to distraction. And someday soon she would love him, too. But not the way Wallace meant. Genny would love him passionately, the way a woman loves a man. When she was his wife, he would tutor her in the ways to please him.

Feeling a renewed arousal, Brian plopped down in his chair behind his desk, then called to his uncle, "Don't forget to tell Genny that I've been worried about her."

* * *

"Why don't I go over to Jasmine's and get Gertie to fix supper for us," Genny said. "I know you two have a great deal to discuss and probably don't want me around."

"It's not that I don't want you around," Jacob said. "It's just—"

"You and Dallas need time to figure out if you trust each other and if you can actually work together. And if I'm here, neither of you can be brutally honest."

"Get Gertie to put together some soup and sandwiches and bring them back over here," Jacob said. "Then, after supper, I'll follow you home."

Genny left Dallas with Jacob, knowing before she walked out the door that Jacob wouldn't be the one following her home tonight. Already Dallas had decided he would save the sheriff the trip. She sensed how hard Dallas was fighting his attraction to her, but knew that in the end, he would lose that particular battle. He had come to Cherokee County on a personal quest, not to find romance with a woman who claimed to possess psychic abilities he didn't believe existed. She understood why he didn't want anything sidetracking him from his mission. He resented being distracted by anything or anyone who might interfere with him capturing the man who'd killed his niece. And right now, the biggest question in both Dallas's and Jacob's minds was whether or not the man who had murdered Dallas's niece was the same person who had sacrificed Susie Richards and Cindy Todd.

As Genny made her way up the street toward Jasmine's, she thought about the last time she'd seen Cindy. The mayor's wife had driven up the mountain to talk to her about a month ago, right before Christmas. As a general rule, Genny didn't do "readings." But for a select few who desperately needed help, Genny used her special powers. If ever someone had needed help, it was Cindy. An abused child who'd gotten pregnant by her boyfriend at sixteen, given up a baby for adoption at seventeen, and then had gotten hooked on drugs, Cindy's young life had been a horror story. When Jerry Lee Todd had vacationed in Florida six years ago, he'd swept

Cindy off her feet in a whirlwind romance and brought her home to Cherokee Pointe with him. He'd given her a fictitious personal history and tried to pass her off as what he referred to as *quality*. But in their private lives, Jerry Lee had gradually become abusive. Emotionally abusive at first, then, in the past year, physically abusive as well. Even in the very first year of her marriage, Cindy had turned to other men for comfort, reverting to the bad habits of a lifetime.

Genny had seen unhappiness ahead for Cindy and advised her to leave Jerry Lee. She had thought the tragedy she'd sensed in Cindy's future could be averted if she escaped from her abusive husband. But now it seemed that the tragedy Genny foresaw hadn't had anything to do with Cindy's marriage.

Stopping outside the restaurant, Genny kicked the snow off her boots and opened one of the double doors. When she entered the restaurant, the comfy indoor warmth surrounded her. It took a couple of minutes for her eyesight to adjust from the brightness outside to the dimmer lighting inside. After taking off her coat and draping it over her arm, she moved past the entrance and headed toward the kitchen. As she glanced around, she noticed there was only a handful of customers seated at various tables and booths. Since it was early for the supper crowd, she was surprised the place wasn't empty. Before she reached the kitchen doors, Misty Harte called out to her.

"Hey there, Genny."

Genny paused and turned to face the woman who'd been chasing after Jacob for quite some time. Misty was Deputy Bobby Joe Harte's older sister. Thirty-five. Twice divorced. No children.

"Hi, Misty. How are you?"

"Doing just fine. How about you?" Genny casually scanned the woman from head to toe. Bleached blond hair, pulled back in a ponytail. Bright red lipstick and nail polish. A pair of huge gold hoops in her ears. And her waitress uniform of dark slacks and white blouse hugged her slender, long-legged figure.

"I'm okay. I need to see Jazzy. I want to put in an order for supper to go."

"She's not in the kitchen," Misty said. "She's in her office."

"Thanks. I'll place my order, then pop in Jazzy's office for a few minutes."

Genny started to turn away, but before she could take a step, Misty asked, "Are you getting supper for Jacob?"

Genny let out a quiet sigh. "That's right."

"I guess he's working late tonight, what with those two murders and all. Damn shame about Cindy Todd and Susie Richards. Who'd ever believe something like that could happen around here."

"Yes, Jacob's working very late, and I plan to have supper with him before I go home."

"Tell him Misty said hi."

"I'll do that." Genny forced a smile. It wasn't that she didn't like Misty, it was simply that she didn't think Misty was the right woman for Jacob. And Misty wasn't the type to give up easily.

After giving her supper order to Gertie Walker, the cook at Jasmine's, who had been trained by Miss Ludie, Genny made her way down the back hallway toward Jazzy's office. Before reaching the partially open door, she heard Jazzy's voice.

"Don't bother trying to see me again," Jazzy said. "I told you last night that I don't want to have anything to do with you. Not ever again."

Genny knocked on the door to alert Jazzy of her presence. Otherwise she would have felt no better than an eavesdropper even though Jazzy would no doubt tell her everything. The two had no secrets from each another. They'd shared their innermost thoughts and feelings since childhood.

"Leave me the hell alone!" Jazzy slammed down the receiver, then shoved back her chair and stood. She glanced toward the door and said, "Come on in."

"Let me guess who that was on the phone." Genny entered the office and closed the door behind her.

"He thinks if he keeps after me, I'll eventually give in to him." Jazzy came over and hugged Genny. "What are you doing in town? I've tried several times today to call you, without any luck. I figured the phone lines were down."

"I brought someone into town to see Jacob."

Jazzy starred at Genny questioningly.

"His name is Dallas Sloan. He's an FBI agent whose car skidded off into a ditch not far from my house last night."

"The Feds are involved?"

"Not officially."

"You're confusing me."

"Dallas's niece was murdered in a fashion similar to the way Susie Richards and Cindy Todd were killed. Nearly a year ago in Mobile."

Jazzy rubbed her hands up and down her arms. "This whole business of a guy out there using women in Cherokee County as sacrificial lambs scares the bejesus out of me." Jazzy studied Genny for a moment, then said, "You called this guy 'Dallas.' How'd you get on a first-name basis so quickly? And just where did he spend the night last night?"

Genny couldn't stop her lips from twitching in an almost-smile. "He stayed at my house, in a guest room. And it's strange, but . . . I feel as if I know him, as if I've always known him."

"Uh-oh. Let me guess—he's tall, dark, dangerous, and devastatingly good-looking."

Genny laughed. "He's tall, blond, devastatingly good-looking, and"—her expression became somber—"in a great deal of emotional pain."

"You've got a thing for him, don't you?" Jazzy grabbed Genny's shoulders and shook her playfully. "Was it love at first sight?"

"Don't be ridiculous. No one's in love. We're simply attracted to each other," Genny admitted. "Besides, I'm pretty sure he has a problem with my, er, my sixth sense."

"He knows that you're—"

"I had another vision . . . a premonition about Cindy's death. Only I didn't know it was Cindy."

"Oh, God, Gen, how'd you make it there all alone—oh, you weren't alone, were you? This Dallas guy was there with you."

"He was very kind, but he didn't understand why I was so exhausted or why I was saying the things I said. I think he believes I'm either crazy or a phony."

"And he's attracted to you anyway?"

"I don't know." Genny shook her head. "Probably not by choice. Besides, this is the wrong time for him to get involved romantically with anyone. He's come here looking for answers. He's searching for his niece's killer."

"And he thinks the person who killed Susie and Cindy is the same guy who killed his niece?"

"He thinks it's possible."

"What does Jacob think?"

"He's undecided, but he has an open mind on the matter."

The phone rang. Jazzy eyed the Caller ID.

"Jamie again?" Genny asked.

"He's called half a dozen times today."

"Want me to answer it?"

"Just let it ring." Jazzy grasped Genny's arm. "Come on, let's go get some coffee and pie."

"I've put in an order for soup and sandwiches with Gertie. I thought I'd have supper with Jacob and Dallas before I head home."

"Why don't you come stay with me until this killer is caught? I hear there's safety in numbers." They exited Jazzy's office, leaving behind the telephone's insistent ringing.

"I'll be all right. I have Drudwyn. And I can usually sense when someone is coming."

Before they reached the dining room, Misty Harte rushed toward them. "That crazy old retard, Wallace MacKinnon, is here and he's making a scene. He wants to see Genny. I had no idea when he asked if she was here that he'd go nuts. He says he has a message for her from Brian."

Jazzy laughed. "Come home, Gen. You'd better soothe the savage beast. Poor old Wallace has probably been frantic if he tried to contact you and couldn't.'' She turned to Misty and said, ''Go tell Wallace that Genny is coming out to see him right away. And, Misty, never again refer to Wallace as a retard.''

When Misty hurried off in a huff, Jazzy said to Genny, ''Wallace appointed himself your guardian angel when you were a kid, and he takes his job of protecting you seriously. I swear, I don't know what it is about you that makes men idolize you and want to take care of you. All they want to do is fuck me.''

Genny grinned. ''Jazzy, you're outrageous! You want everyone to think you're really bad. You've cultivated your bad-girl image and won't let anyone see through the facade to the real you.''

''You see through.''

''Yes, but I've known you since we were in diapers.''

''And you know better than anyone that being a bad girl is only partly a facade. I'm not lily white and we both know it. I've done more than my share of stupid things. Case in point—Jamie Upton.''

''You loved Jamie. He's the one who's stupid for not appreciating what a wonderful person you are.''

The sound of Wallace's nearly hysterical voice echoed down the hallway.

''You'd better get him quieted down before he scares off what few customers I have out there,'' Jazzy said.

Genny hurried into the dining room. Wallace was going from table to table, searching for Genny, shouting her name.

''Wallace,'' she called to him in a gentle yet loud voice.

He stopped halfway across the room, turned, and smiled broadly. Wallace had the sweetest, kindest smile. Like the smile of a small child. And in many ways, that was exactly what he was. A small, loving child living in the body of a large, physically strong man of seventy.

He came barreling toward her, grinning, chuckling to himself, with his arms open wide. When he reached her, he lifted her off her feet in a bear hug, knocking her coat off her arm.

"I was so worried about you. I went out to your house and you weren't home."

"I came into town today," she told him.

"That's what Brian said. He said Genny's probably in town. Go over to Jazzy's and ask her. She'll know."

"Put me down, Wallace," Genny said, keeping her voice even and calm.

He did as she requested, then picked up her coat off the floor and handed it to her. "Brian has been worried about you, too. He said to tell you so."

"It was very sweet of you and Brian to worry about me, but as you can see, I'm fine."

"Brian likes you."

"I like Brian, too."

Wallace's smile widened. "He's a good man. Not like he used to be. He's always nice to me now. He even talks to me."

"That's nice." Genny laced her arm through Wallace's. "Why don't I take you home? It's nearly suppertime and I'm sure Miss Veda will send Mr. Farlan out looking for you if you aren't home by dark."

Jazzy whistled to get Genny's attention. "Take him home in my Jeep. It's parked out back." Jazzy reached into the pocket of her jeans, pulled out a set of keys, and tossed them to Genny, who caught them in midair.

"Are we really going to ride in Jazzy's red Jeep?" Wallace asked.

"Yes, we are." Genny led Wallace through the kitchen, out the back door, and into the alley where Jazzy's sleek late-model Jeep Liberty awaited them.

"Care for some coffee?" Jacob asked. "I can make a fresh pot."

"No, thanks," Dallas replied. "Look, I realize there's no reason for you to cooperate with me, but if I'm right and this killer is the same one who has been committing a series of five murders in various states these past eight years, then

I probably know more about him than anyone. And just between us''—Dallas looked right into Jacob's eyes, taking a chance on trusting him—''I have an FBI profiler who is working up a profile of this guy for me.''

''Unofficially?''

Dallas nodded.

What could he say or do that would convince Sheriff Butler to confide in him, to agree for them to work together? He'd had no luck with some local lawmen he had approached, while others had bent over backwards to be accommodating because he was a Fed. But none of the other new cases he'd looked into privately had turned out to have enough similarities to Brooke's to warrant further investigation. The two Cherokee County murders were different. So far, everything about the deaths of these two women matched the MO of the guy who'd killed Brooke.

''Put yourself in my place,'' Dallas said. ''What if someone you loved was one of this fiend's victims? Wouldn't you do everything in your power to track him down and bring him to justice?''

Jacob nodded.

''Then let me work with you on these cases. You help me and I'll help you.''

''I checked you out, you know,'' Jacob said.

''I figured you would.''

''You've got quite an impressive résumé. But even before your niece's murder, you didn't always play by the book. And since then you've acquired a reputation as a bit of a rogue agent.''

''I do my job. What I do on my own time is my business.''

''Are you willing to risk your job to see this thing through to the end?''

''If that's what it takes.''

''Genny seems to think you're trustworthy, and I trust Genny's instincts, despite the fact that she has a tendency to like everyone. So all right.''

''All right what?''

"I'll give our working together a try, but if you cross the line, you'll answer to me."

Dallas figured that, for most men, answering to Jacob Butler was a fate to be dreaded, a fate worse than death. Dallas was no fool. He'd rather not cross swords with the sheriff, now or in the future. But Butler didn't intimidate him. He couldn't remember the last time anyone had.

But one particular woman intimidated the hell out of him. Genevieve Madoc.

"Susie's body is in Knoxville for an autopsy," Jacob said. "Cindy's body is on its way there. I've asked for a rush job on both, even though our local coroner, Pete Holt, was able to give me a preliminary report."

"Let me guess." Dallas leaned over, dropped his hands between his spread thighs, and tapped his fingertips together. "Your local guy found semen between the breasts and on the belly of both victims."

Jacob narrowed his gaze until his eyes were mere slits. "Is this part of the MO for the killer you're looking for?"

"Am I right?" Dallas demanded.

"You're right."

"If the Knoxville medical examiner does a thorough job, he'll discover another gruesome fact."

"And that would be?"

"He'll find human saliva mixed with the victim's blood up and down the sides of the incision."

Jacob frowned, creating creases in his forehead and above the bridge of his nose. "Are you saying this guy—"

"Drinks some of his victim's blood and then licks them."

"Holy hell." Jacob shot out of his chair and walked over to the windows overlooking the snow-covered ground outside. "Once this guy is apprehended, there should be more than enough DNA evidence to put him on death row."

"More than enough," Dallas said. "But all the DNA evidence in the world is worthless without a suspect."

Chapter 9

Dallas treaded up the street, over the icy patches and slushy snow, making his way to Jasmine's. Butler had thought it was taking Genny an awfully long time to pick up soup and sandwiches and had been about to phone the restaurant when he'd received a call from Roddy Watson, Cherokee Pointe's chief of police.

"I'll walk over to the restaurant and check on her," Dallas had offered.

Butler had put the police chief on hold long enough to give Dallas directions—and pierce him with a warning glare. That evil-eyed glower made Dallas wonder if Butler had picked up on the chemistry between Genny and him. But why would he? Neither of them had said or done anything that would make him suspicious. Maybe the sheriff put out protective, big-brother signals to any man who came in contact with Genny. If she were his to protect, he knew he'd sure as hell do the same.

Dallas paused in front of Jasmine's. Nothing fancy on the outside. Just a renovated old building with a green canopy over the entrance and the name of the restaurant etched in gold letters across the front door. The name appeared again on a simple square metal sign hanging between the first and second floor of the establishment.

Once he was inside, the warmth of the interior assailed him, forcing him to remove his overcoat and drape it over his arm. Business wasn't great, he noted. Only about half the tables and booths were filled. A combination of the winter season, bad weather, and a Tuesday evening was probably the cause.

He scanned the room for any sight of Genny. When he saw her, an involuntary smile formed on his lips. But suddenly he noticed she was sitting at a table across from a slim, brown-haired man impeccably dressed in navy trousers, a light blue shirt, and a tweed sports coat. Genny's face was alight with warmth and friendliness as she chatted with *Mr. Beau Brummell*. Perhaps she was being a little too friendly. She laughed at something the guy said. Dallas's stomach muscles tightened.

"Smoking or nonsmoking?"

Dallas snapped his head around and stared at the hostess, who held a menu in her hand. She was a good-looking redhead, with cat green eyes and an aura of world-weariness that only a fellow battle-scarred-from-life casualty would instantly recognize.

"Neither, thanks. I'm here to pick up Genny Madoc." His gaze zeroed in on Genny as she continued chitchatting with the man Dallas could see only in profile.

The redhead sized Dallas up, then grinned. "You must be FBI Special Agent Sloan."

Dallas's attention focused on the hostess. "And how would you know that?"

"I'm Jazzy Talbot. Genny's my best friend. We don't have any secrets from each other." Jazzy nodded toward the table where Genny sat. "That's Royce Pierpont. He and Genny are just friends, although he'd like for them to be more."

"Ms. Madoc's personal life is none of my business. If she told you who I am, then she told you why I'm in Cherokee Pointe."

Jazzy nodded. "She also told me that you spent the night at her house last night." Once again she surveyed him from head to toe. "She described you perfectly."

"Would you mind telling her that I'm here?" Dallas asked. "I don't want to interrupt, but Sheriff Butler was concerned because it seemed to be taking her too long to pick up supper."

"Mm . . . Jacob does worry about Genny. I guess we all do. She's an extraordinary person, you know. Very trusting and caring."

Jazzy waited as if she expected some sort of response from Dallas, but he didn't know what she thought he should say. Barely knowing Genny, he had nothing to go on but first impressions, which seemed to corroborate Jazzy's assessment.

Dallas simply nodded in agreement.

"Jacob keeps close tabs on the men in her life," Jazzy continued. "Always has. Not that there have been very many. Lately there's Royce over there. He's new in town and Genny likes him, but she hasn't fallen in love with him. Then there's Brian MacKinnon. He's rich and powerful and Jacob dislikes him. Can't say I think much of Mr. Moneybags myself. But Genny believes he's redeemable."

"Ms. Talbot, why are you—?"

"Genny has a way of seeing the best in people. That's one of her gifts. She sees the best in you, Dallas Sloan. I'd hate to think you might disappoint her."

"Look, I don't know what she told you about me, but—"

"She told me that you were very kind to her this morning after she came out of . . . after her vision. She's always totally wiped out afterward and needs someone nearby. I'm glad she wasn't there alone."

Dallas glanced down and studied the tips of his damp shoes. Apparently those closest to Genny actually believed she had visions, that she possessed some sort of sixth-sense ability. He supposed it was easier to fool the people who loved you.

Before Dallas could think of a reply, Jazzy walked over to where Genny sat and spoke quietly to her. Genny lifted her gaze and looked right at Dallas. Her mouth widened into a broad smile. She threw up her hand and waved at him. Royce Pierpont pivoted slowly, only enough to glance over his shoulder at Dallas. A set of crystal blue eyes raked over Dallas with curiosity. And jealousy? Genny said something to Pierpont, leaned over to kiss his cheek, then picked up a box sitting on the table and walked toward Dallas.

He met her halfway and took the box from her. "The sheriff was worried about you," he said.

"I'm sorry if Jacob was concerned," Genny replied. "I got delayed by—"

"By your boyfriend? Or should I say one of your boyfriends?"

Genny looked at him in bewilderment, then sighed. "I see Jazzy's been talking to you."

Dallas grunted. "Where's your coat?"

"Oh, my, I forgot and left it—"

Pierpont walked up behind Genny and draped her coat around her shoulders. He allowed his hands to linger on her just a tad longer than Dallas liked, but Dallas forced himself not to stare at the man's possessive touch.

"You don't want to forget this," Pierpont said. "Can't have you getting chilled."

"Thank you, Royce." Genny offered him another brilliant smile.

Looking directly at Dallas, the man held out his hand. "I'm Royce Pierpont, one of Genny's gentlemen callers."

Was this guy kidding? Gentlemen callers? No one had used that archaic term in at least four generations.

"Special Agent Sloan." Dallas shook hands with Pierpont. The guy's handshake was soft and mild. And cordial. No machismo show of strength. Apparently he didn't see Dallas as a rival.

"Genny says you're going to be working with Jacob on these murder cases," Pierpont said. "I had no idea the FBI would be interested in a couple of deaths here in Cherokee County.''

''The FBI is interested in illegal activities everywhere. And we always do what we can to help local law enforcement agencies.''

''I see.''

Dallas reached out, grabbed Genny's arm, and asked, ''Ready to go?''

She nodded. ''Enjoy your dinner,'' she said to Pierpont, then glanced at Jazzy. ''I'll call you later, if the phones are working.''

''If they're not working, she won't be staying alone tonight.'' The minute Dallas had thought the words, they'd flown out of his mouth.

Pierpont frowned. Jazzy smiled. Genny's soft, pink lips formed a silent gasp of surprise.

At seven-thirty Dallas Sloan left Jacob's office with Genny. The three had shared the delicious vegetable soup and hardy roast beef sandwiches prepared by Gertie. And they'd topped off the meal with bowls of the absolutely best blackberry cobbler in the world, made from Miss Ludie's recipe, with the wild blackberries that grew in the Tennessee hills.

Although she'd known that Dallas and not Jacob would see her home tonight, she felt an amazing sense of anticipation as he pulled his new rental car up behind her Trailblazer in the partially icy driveway at the side of her house. Exactly what did she expect to happen? She didn't really know. But something was transpiring between her and the FBI agent who had entered her life less than twenty-four hours ago. Something unusual. Something extraordinary. If asked, he would probably deny it, but he would simply be lying to himself. He could postpone the inevitable, delay it for a while; but in the end there would be no denying the truth.

By the time she unlocked her door and got out, Dallas had exited the car and stood at her side. ''I'll go in with you and check things out before I leave. If your phones aren't working, I'm taking you back into town.''

"I'll be perfectly safe right here,'' she insisted.

He grabbed her arm and gently tugged her into motion. Together they made their way carefully over the patchy blanket of snow-covered ice still coating the ground.

When he headed her toward the front of the house, she balked. "Let's go in at the back. There aren't any slick steps to climb if we go in that way.''

"All right.''

After swinging open the screen door to the back porch, she headed straight for the kitchen door. Holding the decorative silver chain laden with keys, she inserted the key into the lock of the door and turned it. She opened the door and Dallas followed her into the kitchen. Genny flipped a switch and the room filled with light. Drudwyn rose from his bed in the corner and came charging toward them. Kneeling, Genny grabbed Drudwyn around the neck and hugged him.

"I'll bet you need to go out, don't you, boy?''

She watched while he galloped past Dallas and out onto the porch. He shoved open the screen door and disappeared into the darkness.

"The electricity is back on,'' Genny said. "I'll try the phone.''

"Yeah, you do that.''

As she lifted the phone from the base mounted on the wall, Dallas waited, his gaze fixed on her. The moment she put the receiver to her ear, she heard a dial tone.

"The phone's working.''

"Good.'' He stood near the door, still bundled in his overcoat, scarf, and leather gloves.

"Would you like to stay for a while?'' she asked as she removed her gloves, hat, and coat and tossed them onto a kitchen chair. "I can fix decaf coffee or tea.''

"I should probably head on back.'' His gaze kept shifting from her face to various angles of the room, as if being alone with her made him uncomfortable. "I need to check in at the rental place and then find my cabin before it gets too late.''

''Jazzy said one of the cabins close to town was available, so you shouldn't have any problem finding it.'' Genny finger-combed her waist-length hair, knowing it must be a mess after being trapped under her knit hat.

''Your friend Jazzy is quite the entrepreneur, isn't she? She owns a restaurant, a bar, and rental cabins.''

''She's a partner with a couple of other people in Cherokee Cabin Rentals,'' Genny explained. ''But you're right— Jazzy is a remarkable lady.''

''She said something similar about you.''

''Did she?''

''She and your cousin Jacob actually believe you possess some sort of special powers, don't they?''

Genny heard the skepticism in his voice. He had told her he was a logical man who didn't believe in anything he couldn't experience with his five senses. Did that mean he thought himself incapable of real love? Love wasn't always logical. And although physical love could be experienced through the senses of taste, touch, sight, hearing, and smell, a spiritual love—one that bonded two souls for eternity— could not.

''You don't believe,'' she said. *But you will. Someday soon, you will.*

''If it was anyone other than you, I'd call you a phony, but . . . Undoubtedly you've somehow convinced yourself that your dreams—your nightmares—are visions. Maybe it's because of your grandmother's influence. If she thought she was a witch—''

''She didn't think she was a witch,'' Genny said. ''Some people called her a witch woman because of her powers. Granny had *the sight,* that's all.''

''Do you know how preposterous that sounds? In this day and age, sane people don't believe in hocus-pocus. But there are thousands who want to believe in magic, want to believe there are easy solutions to their problems. There are so many damn charlatans out there preying on emotionally vulnerable people. You wouldn't believe the phonies I've run into in my job.''

''And what about the psychics who aren't phonies?''

''There is no such animal.''

Dallas's statement was more than a proclamation. It was a protective shield, guarding him from her. Perhaps he didn't know it; but she did.

''I see.'' She saw beyond the surface, deep inside this big, lonely man with the wounded heart and tormented soul.

She turned and busied herself preparing decaf coffee while Dallas stood near the door. After a few silent moments, he slipped off his gloves and stuck them in his overcoat pocket, then he removed his coat and laid it across the back of a wooden kitchen chair.

''Anything I can do to help?'' he asked.

''Just listen for Drudwyn when he scratches at the back door.''

''Sure.''

Genny removed two Blue Willow cups and saucers from an upper cabinet and placed them on the table. She remembered that Dallas took his coffee black, as did she, so there was no need to provide cream and sugar. The silence between them lingered. The coffee brewed. The clock in the hall struck eight-fifteen.

''Would you tell me about your niece?'' Genny asked, sensing that Dallas had never truly shared his grief with anyone. He wasn't the type of man to open a vein and emotionally bleed all over the place.

''What do you want to know?''

''Anything you'd like to tell me.'' Genny lifted the glass pot from the coffeemaker, walked over to the table, and filled both cups to the brim, then returned the pot to the warmer.

Dallas pulled out her chair and seated her before he sat across from her and lifted the decorative cup to his lips. He took a sip. ''Brooke was fifteen. Her birthday was a few weeks after. . . . She was a beautiful girl. Blond, blue-eyed. The all-American type. And she was smart and sweet and . . .'' He took another sip of coffee, then held his cup between both hands.

"And you loved her dearly," Genny said.

Dallas glared at Genny, fighting his need to admit how deeply affected he'd been by Brooke's death. He set his cup on the saucer and looked down at the table. "She was my sister's first child. We all adored her. She was a great kid."

Genny reached across the table and laid her hand over his. He tensed immediately, as if he found her touch unbearable. She grasped his hand and squeezed. Their gazes clashed, and he quickly looked away, then withdrew his hand.

"I should get going." He scooted back his chair and stood. "Be sure to lock up when I leave. And please be extra careful."

Genny stood, then followed him to the back door and onto the porch. Drudwyn bounded out of the woods. The pale moonlight reflected off the white snow and illuminated the yard.

"Dallas?"

He paused, glanced over his shoulder, and looked right at her. "Yeah?"

"Good luck finding what you're looking for."

"I want this killer caught and stopped," Dallas said. "I don't want any more families to have to go through the hell we went through when we lost Brooke."

Genny sensed that what Dallas really wanted was to kill Brooke's murderer with his bare hands, to strangle the life out of him, slowly, cruelly. She shuddered at the thought of Dallas's big, strong hands committing murder.

But was retribution really murder?

Genny nodded. "Drive carefully."

"I will," he replied. "Now take Drudwyn and go back inside and lock the door before I leave."

She did as he asked, then rushed through the house to the windows in the living room where she had a sideways view of the drive. She stood there and watched Dallas back out onto the road, not moving until his rental car disappeared into the darkness.

Jazzy stepped into the bubbling water in the Jacuzzi tub in her bathroom. As she eased her naked body beneath the warm water, she sighed aloud. Today had been a long day, as had yesterday. Two murders in twenty-four hours. The whole town was tense and nervous, not knowing what was going on and wondering if or when another victim would be chosen. Last night's winter storm had left many county residents without power or telephone service—just what people didn't need to happen with a murderer on the loose. Business at Jasmine's and Jazzy's Joint had been down these past two nights. Even though there wasn't much tourist trade during the winter, she could usually count on a healthy local clientele to keep both establishments financially in the black.

She supposed she thought about, worried about, and concentrated too much on money. But she'd grown up without any money. Poor as church mice was the way Aunt Sally had described them. Being poor never seemed to bother Sally Talbot, but Jazzy was different. From an early age, she'd yearned for all the things money could buy. As a teenager, she'd wanted the nice house, the fancy car, the pretty clothes. But more than all the material things money could buy, she had longed for the respect it seemed to bring with it. God, how she'd envied the MacKinnons and the Uptons. She supposed that was the reason she'd been attracted to Jamie in the first place. Not so much because he was handsome and charming, but because he was rich. She had thought marrying Jamie and becoming an Upton could make all her dreams come true.

She'd given her virginity to Jamie when she was sixteen. He had professed his undying love, so she'd been certain that when she told him she was pregnant with his child, he would marry her.

Jazzy lifted the loofah sponge and ran it over each arm

and then each leg. At twenty-nine she still possessed a flaw-less body, unmarred by childbirth.

A deep sadness clutched at her heart, but she forced it away, refusing to relive that painful part of her life.

You'd better remember, she told herself. *Only by learning from your mistakes will you be able to protect yourself.* She had forgiven Jamie time and again, had fooled herself into believing that he could change and become the man she needed. But each time, in the end, she and she alone paid the price of her foolishness.

Jamie had come into her life and gone away so many times during the past ten years that she couldn't keep track. His current fiancée was the third and would, no doubt, go the way of his previous conquests. Once they discovered what Jamie was all about, they fled home to Mommy and Daddy and the protection of their wealthy families. And whenever Jamie came back to Cherokee County, with or without a woman in tow, he always sought out Jazzy. She supposed that in his own way he was as addicted to her as she was to him. They were in each other's blood, like some insidious poison.

But this time she wouldn't give in to him. The only way she could survive was to find a way to rid herself of the slow-acting poison that would eventually kill her. She didn't think she could live through loving Jamie again, knowing it was only a matter of time before he broke her heart.

Jazzy soaked in the tub until the water became barely lukewarm, then she rose, got out, and dried herself. Just as she wrapped her quilted satin robe around her, she heard the doorbell ring. *Who the hell?* But she knew. Before she made her way through her bedroom and into the living room of her apartment above Jasmine's, she knew who waited for her on the other side of the door.

Standing at the door, she took a deep breath, then asked, ''Who is it?''

''Let me in, lover,'' Jamie said, his voice slightly slurred. He'd been drinking. One of his many vices.

''Go away,'' she told him.

He pounded on the door. "I'm not leaving."

"If you don't go, I'll call Jacob."

Jamie snorted. "What is it with you and Butler? You like fucking that big, ugly Indian?"

"Damn you, Jamie. Leave me alone."

He continued pounding on the door and began saying her name repeatedly. "Jazzy . . . Jazzy . . . Jazzy . . ."

She unlocked and then opened the door, her heart beating ninety-to-nothing. He stood there, one arm braced on the doorjamb as he swayed forward and grinned.

"I've missed you, lover," Jamie said. "I've missed you something awful."

A familiar stirring came to life in her belly. "I haven't missed you," she told him truthfully. She hadn't missed him. Her life was so much better without him. As far as she was concerned, he could drop off the face of the earth.

He took an unsteady step toward her. She held her breath. He lowered his face down to hers until only an inch separated their lips.

"I don't love you. I don't want you. I don't need you." Jazzy wasn't sure who she was trying to convince—Jamie or herself.

He tugged on her belt, loosening it enough to enable him to slip one hand inside and sneak it around her waist. She gasped when he splayed his hand over her naked hip and drew her up against him. His breath was warm and drenched with whiskey. He rubbed his nose against her neck and whispered her name in her ear.

"Has Butler been servicing you, honey? Keeping you all primed and ready for me?"

Jazzy's body went rigid.

"He's a big man," Jamie said. "He hasn't stretched you out of shape, has he? You know I like my pussy hot and wet . . . and tight. Real tight."

Jazzy lifted her hand to slap him, but he caught her wrist midair. "Now, don't be that way. I don't mind if you've kept in practice. Lord knows I have. Actually, I've learned a few new tricks I'd like to teach you."

"I've learned all the tricks from you I want to learn."
Although some sick, pitiful part of her still cared about
Jamie, the strong, smart part of her hated his damn guts.
"I've got nothing for you, Jamie. Go home to your fiancée.
Teach her those new tricks."

His eyes glimmered with determination. He jerked Jazzy's
robe apart, revealing her naked body. When she tried to pull
the lapels together, he grabbed her, yanked the robe off her
shoulders, and shoved her naked body up against the wall.
Realizing his intentions, she fought him. For several minutes
his superior strength overpowered her. His mouth covered
hers while his hands manacled her wrists above her head.
She tried to avoid his wet kisses, but gave up and allowed
him to assault her mouth. When he freed one of his hands
to unzip his pants and ease his body a few inches from hers,
she took advantage of the opportunity to attack him. She
kneed him in the groin and just as he doubled over in pain,
she socked him in the nose. While he groaned and writhed,
Jazzy ran into her bedroom, yanked open her nightstand
drawer and removed the loaded .25-caliber Beretta she kept
there.

Jamie stood in the doorway, rage etched on his features.
"I'm going to make you sorry you did that."

She waited until he was only a couple of feet away from
her, then pulled the gun out from behind her back and pointed
it directly at him. "Come one inch closer and you'll be
singing soprano the rest of your life."

Jamie glanced from her face to the gun she held, then
back up to her face. "You'd really shoot me, wouldn't
you?"

"You got that damn straight."

"What happened to my Jazzy?" he asked. "What did
you do with the girl who loved me?"

"You destroyed her, bit by bit, piece by piece." She held
the gun in a steady hand, determined to show no sign of
weakness. She wasn't a hundred percent sure she could shoot
Jamie, but he didn't know that. All she had to do was

convince him that she had no qualms about blowing off his
balls.

"You win this round, lover." His grin was more shaky
than cocky.

She stood in the bedroom, unmoving, barely breathing,
until she heard the front door slam. Holding the gun in front
of her, she rushed into the living room, checking in every
direction to make sure Jamie wasn't waiting to jump out on
her. With quick, sure moves, she swung open the kitchen
door, flipped on the light, and made certain the room was
empty; then she hurried back into the living room to lock
and double-bolt the front door.

Suddenly she started trembling. A shuddering tremor
racked her from head to toe. Slumping down onto the nearest
chair, she dropped the gun to the floor. As tears streamed
down her cheeks, she jerked the knitted afghan from the
back of the chair and wrapped it around her naked body.

Bone-weary and in desperate need of a good night's sleep,
Jacob arrived home at eleven-fifteen. Just as he turned his
truck into the parking area in front of his apartment, he
noticed the bright yellow Vega. The windows were steamed
up and the engine was idling. *What the hell was she doing
here?* He didn't think he could deal with Misty tonight. He
was exhausted and frustrated. The last thing he needed was
having to deal with a woman. Any woman.

He got out, locked the car, and pocketed his keys, then
walked across the parking area and pecked on the passenger-
side window of the Vega. Immediately Misty killed the
motor, jumped out of her car, and rushed over to him.

"Hi, there, sugar," she cooed.

Misty's red lips widened in what she thought was a seductive smile. Even in this frigid weather, she wore a miniskirt,
with textured stockings and flashy yellow boots. Her only
real concession to the freezing temperature was the fake-
fur jacket she had on.

"What are you doing here?" he asked, trying his best to keep his tone civil.

"Is that any way to treat a woman who's here to give you a little TLC?"

"Is that what they're calling it now?"

Misty laughed, the sound like a shrill siren screaming through the night air. "I'm freezing my butt off out here. What do you say we go inside where it's warm?"

"Look, Misty, I'm pretty beat. Maybe you'd better—"

"All you have to do is lie back and enjoy," she told him as she hooked her arm through his. "I'll do all the dirty work."

Jacob's penis responded to her blatant offer. Apparently the old boy wasn't as tired as he was. His body instantly reminded him that he hadn't been with a woman in quite some time. Not since the last time he'd had a date with Misty—over five months ago. Of course, she had no way of knowing that, since she and most of the townsfolk assumed he and Jazzy had slept together when they dated.

"I appreciate the offer, but—"

"You aren't still hung up on Jazzy, are you? I thought you two were over, finis, caput."

"We are, except as friends."

"I've just been waiting for you two to end things, which I knew would happen sooner or later."

What the hell! It wasn't as if Misty expected anything more than sex. He'd made it perfectly clear to her when they went to bed together on their first date over a year ago, right after her second divorce, that he wasn't interested in a commitment of any kind.

Arm in arm, they made it up the stairs to his apartment on the second floor of the two-story building that housed eight apartments. He unlocked the door, escorted her inside, and didn't even bother to switch on a light. He kicked the door closed with his booted foot, lifted Misty off her feet, and carried her straight to his bedroom.

When he set her on her feet at the edge of his bed, she

ran her hand over the fly of his jeans. "You are glad to see me, aren't you?"

"Part of me is," he admitted.

She laughed again, and before the sound could turn him off completely, he kissed her. A rough, tongue-thrusting kiss that silenced her. Misty wasn't the most beautiful woman in Cherokee County or the smartest, but she had her talents. She knew how to kiss. And she knew how to fuck.

They tore at each other's clothes and within minutes Jacob had tossed her flat on her back in the middle of his bed. He made a hasty detour into the bathroom for his stash of condoms, then removed his briefs and tossed them aside on his way back to the bed. Standing over her, he slid a condom into place.

Wriggling seductively on the bed, Misty said, "Come on, big boy, give me what I want."

"I thought you said you were going to do all the dirty work."

She held open her arms to him. "Come down here and I'll show you what I'll do."

He covered her body with his, sliding his erect penis over her belly before settling between her legs. When he lowered his head and licked first one pebble-hard nipple and then the other, she bit his shoulder. He barely felt the pain.

"Let's change places," Misty suggested. "I'm in the mood for a good, hard ride."

Before the words were barely out of her mouth, he flipped her up and over him. She straddled his hips. He reached up to tease her nipples.

"I always get my cookies off when I'm on top."

She lifted herself up enough to reach between them and circle his erection. While he lay beneath, his body taut with need, she guided him up and inside her. She slid down over him like a slick, hot glove covering a hand.

She rode him, slowly at first, building the tension, but soon she increased the pace as she lowered her breasts to his lips. He could feel his climax approaching, knew it was only a matter of seconds before he exploded. Wildly, panting like mad, Misty pumped him harder and faster. She screamed when she came, but Jacob was able to silence her with a kiss just as his orgasm ripped him apart.

That slut Misty Harte was in the sheriff's apartment fucking his brains out right now. He knew her type so well. But was she really any different from all other women? Most were good for only one thing. Except for the few who possessed a special essence. But those special women were rare and when found were far more precious to him than anything else in the world.

He stood in the corridor outside Jacob Butler's apartment, wondering if Misty would spend the night or leave before dawn. He'd go back downstairs and wait in Misty's car. The damn fool bitch hadn't bothered to lock her doors.

If she left the sheriff's bed before morning, then it would be a sign that she was destined to become the third victim.

Chapter 10

The early morning sunshine brightening the blue sky overhead was deceptive. The temperature hovered only a few degrees above freezing, just enough to continue the thaw that had begun yesterday. Dallas hesitated before getting out of his rental car. His hand settled over the cell phone attached to his belt. He couldn't remember the last time he'd felt such an overwhelming urge to call a woman. But he was not going to telephone Genny Madoc, no matter how much he wanted to. He had repeatedly pointed out to himself that she didn't need him to act as her protector. Her cousin, the sheriff, played the role of big brother quite well. She also had friends like Jazzy Talbot. And a couple of boyfriends.

Yeah, Sloan, don't forget the boyfriends.

Dallas's stomach rumbled, reminding him he was hungry. He got out of the car, locked the door and made his way down the street to Jasmine's. When he'd checked in with Cherokee Cabin Rentals last night, the clerk had told him the best place in town for a hot, home-style breakfast was Jasmine's.

The minute he entered the restaurant, he smelled the aroma of freshly brewed coffee and sizzling bacon. The proprietress was nowhere to be seen. But that didn't surprise Dallas. He'd pegged Jazzy for a late sleeper.

A young waitress with frizzy brown hair and a welcoming smile came up to him. "Smoking or nonsmoking?" she asked.

"Nonsmoking," he replied as he removed his overcoat and slung it over his arm.

"Follow me, please."

As she led the way to a back booth, Dallas caught a glimpse of Sheriff Butler sitting alone, a large stack of half-eaten pancakes in front of him.

Butler nodded, then spoke. "Join me?"

"Sure." Dallas accepted a menu from the waitress. He tossed his coat onto the far side of the seat and slid into the booth, placing himself directly across from the sheriff.

"Coffee?" the waitress asked.

"Black," he told her. "And a large glass of orange juice."

"Be right back." Whistling to herself, the young woman hurried off.

Dallas wanted to ask Butler if he'd checked on Genny this morning, but managed to stop himself from mentioning the sheriff's cousin.

"There's something I'd like to know," Dallas said.

"Such as?" Jacob sliced the pancakes with his fork, then speared a chunk and brought it to his mouth.

"Have you made a list of suspects?"

Jacob chewed and swallowed, then lifted his mug and glanced at Dallas over the rim. He grunted. After taking a swig of coffee, he replied, "We don't have any suspects. Not yet."

"Sure you do. Just figure out who's new in town—say, in the past six months."

"We have tourists in and out of here all the time."

"This guy will be someone who has moved here. He's been getting to know the area and the people . . . and perhaps deciding on his victims, choosing the women he wants for whatever his perverse reasons are."

"You're basing this theory on what? Why the six-month time frame?"

"Because the fifth murder in Mobile last year was seven and a half months ago. After he killed my niece, he murdered one other woman ten days later."

The waitress returned and placed a mug of steaming coffee and a tall glass of frosty orange juice in front of Dallas. "Have you decided what you'd like?" she asked.

"Bacon, scrambled eggs, and biscuits," he told her. "I figure they're on the menu. Right?" He held out the closed menu to her.

She took the menu from him. "Right. I'll go place your order." When she smiled at him again, he noted her name tag read Tiffany.

As soon as Tiffany left them alone again, Butler finished off his pancakes and shoved his empty plate aside. "You're assuming the man who killed Susie Richards and Cindy Todd is the same one who murdered five women in Mobile last year. That's a major assumption. You have no proof to actually connect the murders."

"If I had any substantial proof, you would know we're dealing with a serial killer," Dallas said. "Right now, all I have are a few facts that link several series of five murders, each in various parts of the country over the past eight years. But I'm telling you that my gut instincts tell me it's the same guy."

"I realize you've probably got some damn good instincts," Butler said. "But—"

"I told you yesterday that he kills in groups of five. You're going to wind up with three more victims if we can't figure out who this nutcase is and stop him dead in his tracks."

"Okay, let's say I buy your theory. Where do we start? Have you figured out why there are five victims and not four or six?"

Dallas shook his head. "The only thing I know for sure is that he sexually assaults each woman and when he sacrifices the first four, he drinks some of their blood. But the fifth victim is different in one distinct way—he removes her heart. My guess is he eats it.''

''He eats the fifth victim's heart?''

The waitress returned carrying a coffeepot and quickly refilled both men's mugs. ''Did I hear you right? Did this killer eat Cindy's heart?''

''Forget you heard that,'' Butler said. ''Agent Sloan wasn't talking about Susie or Cindy. He was telling me about another case in another city.''

Tiffany let out a long sigh. ''Thank goodness. It's bad enough we've got a killer on the loose. If he was eating his victim's hearts . . .'' She shuddered, then scurried off when she saw a new customer enter the restaurant.

Butler's keen gaze fixed on the restaurant entrance where a broad-shouldered guy, about six feet tall, waited for Tiffany. The man removed his expensive overcoat and handed it to the waitress, which clued Dallas to the fact that the man was probably used to servants being at his beck and call. All the other customers had either hung their coats on the rack just inside the front door or had taken their coats with them to their tables and booths. Dallas speculated on the new customer's occupation. Lawyer maybe. Wealthy. No doubt about it. He wore his graying brown hair conservatively short; and he walked with an air of command.

Dallas glanced at Butler and noted the way his slanted eyes narrowed to slits and his facial expression darkened. The sheriff didn't like Mr. I'm-Somebody-Important.

Tiffany led the man to the smoking section on the other side of the restaurant. She fluttered around him, practically bowing before she rushed off, his coat over her arm.

''Who's that guy?'' Dallas asked.

''Brian MacKinnon,'' Butler replied.

Jazzy's voice echoed inside Dallas's head. *He's rich and powerful and Jacob dislikes him. But Genny believes he's redeemable.*

''Why do you dislike him?''

''What?'' Jacob Butler stared straight at Dallas.

"Jazzy told me yesterday afternoon that the guy's got a thing for Genny and that you don't like him."

Butler harrumphed. "Let's just say that Mr. MacKinnon and I don't see eye to eye on several things."

"Including his relationship with Genny?"

Butler studied Dallas closely. "I think he's obsessed with her. That bothers me."

"What does Genny think?"

"Maybe you should ask Genny." Butler lifted his coffee mug.

Before Dallas could comment, Tiffany brought his breakfast, laid his bill on the table, and hurried to take Brian MacKinnon his first cup of coffee.

Butler stood. He lifted his brown leather jacket from the seat, slipped into it, then picked up his Stetson and placed it on his head. "When you finish up here, come on over to the office and we'll compile a list of all the men who have moved into Cherokee County in the past six or seven months." Removing his wallet from his pocket, Butler took out three dollars and laid them on the table for a tip, then picked up his bill.

"Yeah, okay." With a smart sheriff like Butler in charge, maybe they had a chance to catch the killer. Dallas had Butler pegged as one of the good guys—someone he could trust.

Before Butler reached the cashier, who did double duty as one of the waitresses, he paused and called out to Dallas. "I checked on Genny this morning. She's fine. And she said to tell you hello."

Dallas tried not to react. He nodded to acknowledge he'd heard Butler, who glanced across the restaurant at Brian MacKinnon, then looked away, paid his bill, and headed out the door. Dallas's gaze made contact with MacKinnon's. Instantly he felt the hatred seething inside the man. Had Butler made the comment about Genny to rile MacKinnon? If he had, his ploy had worked.

When Tiffany came to his table to refill his mug, Dallas asked, "Exactly who is Mr. MacKinnon?"

''Brian MacKinnon is the owner of the *Cherokee Pointe Herald* and our local TV station, WMMK,'' she said. ''And his daddy is Mr. Farlan MacKinnon, one of the richest men in these parts. They live in that big old Victorian mansion over on Bethel Street.''

''I see. Thanks.'' Dallas finished his breakfast, left Tiffany a nice tip, paid his bill, and avoided making eye contact with MacKinnon as he left the restaurant.

He didn't know Brian MacKinnon from Adam, but if Sheriff Butler thought the guy was obsessed with Genny, that alone was reason for Dallas to dislike him. Obsession was a dangerous thing. He should know. He'd come damn close to becoming obsessed with finding Brooke's killer. Only by sheer will, coupled with his years of training and experience as a federal agent, had he been able to stop himself from crossing the line between ruthless determination and obsession. If MacKinnon wanted Genny and he had crossed the line from wanting her to being obsessed with having her, then he could become dangerous.

He had waited in her Vega all night and had given up hope that she would leave the sheriff's place before dawn; but just when he'd started to leave, she came sneaking down the stairs. The morning sun had been rising in the eastern sky. Too late to sacrifice her today. He had experienced several moments of indecision. Should he let her go or should he take her? He never chose his first four victims. He allowed Fate to make those choices. It had seemed to him that Fate had placed Misty Harte directly into his hands; and he wasn't a man to go against Fate. He'd learned at an early age the importance of the unexpected and the unexplainable, and the power of the cosmic forces that ruled the universe.

After tying and gagging Misty and depositing her in the basement, he had disposed of her little yellow car, parking it behind an abandoned service station less than half a mile from town. It had been an easy walk back into Cherokee

Pointe; and not one single soul had seen him, because he'd been very careful. He was always careful.

The basement was the perfect place to keep her. No one ever came down here. He could keep her for several days, if he wanted to prolong his enjoyment. He had found from past experience that when he kept a woman for more than a few hours, it was best to drug her heavily. Sedated, they didn't put up a fight. He didn't want any telltale scratches on his arms or face.

Using the towel he had taken with him on his second trip to visit his captive, he wiped his penis, then pulled up his briefs and pants. He glanced down at the naked woman tied to the cot and smiled when he saw his semen glistening on her belly.

He would shower, shave, and dress a little later, before beginning his day. Around noon he'd have to come back down here and give Misty another injection. Although she was gagged and securely tied, he didn't want to take any chances. Over the years, while he'd been seeking his ultimate goal, not one law enforcement agency in any state had even come close to catching him. He had outsmarted them all. And he'd do it again. Jacob Butler was an intelligent man, but he was nothing more than an inexperienced sheriff in a backwoods Tennessee county. He'd have no better luck than the others had in discovering the killer of five local women.

But what about the FBI agent? What the hell was he doing in Cherokee Pointe? The Bureau didn't get involved in cases like this unless the locals requested assistance. And even then Bureau involvement was restricted to providing investigative resources. Had Butler called in the Feds?

He would have to be very careful. No mistakes. He couldn't afford for anything to go wrong. After all these years of searching, he had finally found her. The one who could give him what he desired most in this world.

Dropped off at Genny's house by the MacKinnons' chauffeur, Wallace had arrived at Cherokee Nurseries a little late.

It had taken Genny a good ten minutes to assure Wallace she wasn't upset with him. Sweet Wallace. If everyone were as kind and gentle as he, the world would be a far better place. The old man had been a part of her life as far back as she could remember, having worked for Granny Butler since his youth. He was extraordinarily fond of Genny, as she was of him. She thought of Wallace as family. Over the years she'd had occasion to meet the other members of the MacKinnon family, although their social circles seldom mixed. Mr. Farlan was a nice enough man, if you liked the old-fashioned, ruler-of-all-I-survey type. Miss Veda was never friendly, but neither was she rude. The few times Genny had actually been in the grande dame's presence, she had sensed a terrible sadness in the woman. Genny suspected that Veda MacKinnon had never been truly happy a day in her life.

And then there was Brian, the only son, the heir apparent. He was much older than Genny, and their paths had seldom crossed until a few years ago. When Wallace had broken a leg and been hospitalized, Farlan had sent Brian to handle the situation. And that's where she'd actually met Brian for the first time. Although they'd never met before, she'd always known who he was—and that he had a reputation for being a heartless bastard.

For some reason, Brian had become smitten with her, and she had to admit that at first she'd been flattered by his attention. It wasn't as if she hadn't been pursued before. She had. But never with such dogged determination. Even the rumors about her being a witch like her grandmother hadn't scared Brian away.

She certainly didn't love him, and there were times she didn't like him. But she sensed how desperately he needed her. Even Wallace had commented on what a good influence she was on his nephew. So how could she turn Brian away completely? But she had never lied to him—had never given him any false hopes.

"I want us to be friends," she'd told him as he'd held her hand.

He'd brought her hand to his lips and kissed it tenderly. "I want that, too. I want us to become good friends. I'm a patient man, Genevieve. I can wait for you as long as it takes."

Genny shook her head, dislodging thoughts of Brian. Lately he had begun to unnerve her with his relentless attention, but Jacob had spoken to him and that seemed to have cooled his ardor. At least temporarily. She suspected that Jacob, in his own strong, unemotional way, had threatened Brian. Jacob was not a man for subtleties.

"What's the matter, Genny?" Wallace asked as he carried their lunchtime dishes from the table and placed them in the sink.

Genny glanced at him and smiled. "Nothing's wrong. I was just thinking."

"About what?"

"About Jacob."

"I like Jacob. He's a good man."

Genny lifted her hand and laid it on Wallace's shoulder. "He has a very difficult job, you know. With two murders to solve and no suspects."

"Why would anybody hurt those women?" Wallace asked guilelessly.

Genny squeezed his shoulder. "I don't know. But I do know that there is great evil involved in those deaths."

"Couldn't you have one of your visions and see who the killer is?"

Genny sighed. "I wish it was that simple." She rinsed off the dishes and began placing them in the dishwasher. "I have no control over my visions."

Wallace patted her back. "It's all right. It's not your fault you can't see who the killer is. Melva Mae always said her visions were a curse more than a blessing."

"Granny was right about that." Genny finished stacking the dishes in the dishwasher, then added detergent and closed the door. "Come on. We need to get those herbs shipped out today. We'll finish packing them, and you can take them by the FedEx office in town on your way home."

"I thought you were going to check the drying shed first," Wallace said. "Isn't Miss Sally coming by later to help with the packing?"

"You're right," Genny replied. "Why don't you go ahead and get the boxes ready in the shipping room while I check out the drying sheds? But we won't wait on Sally. She's liable to show up any minute now or not show up at all. You know how she is."

Wallace chuckled. "I think Miss Sally's funny. She makes me laugh."

"You're right. Sally can be a real hoot."

Genny washed and dried her hands, then headed toward the back porch. Drudwyn, who'd been sleeping peacefully by the screen door, lifted his head and looked up at Genny.

"Come on, boy, if you want to go out and run around for a while."

The minute she opened the screen door, Drudwyn bounded outside. The sun shone high overhead like a glossy yellow-orange ball. The weather forecasters were predicting a slight warm-up, with the high temperatures today hovering around forty-five. Over half the snow had melted yesterday, leaving patches of icy white dotted about everywhere. Genny grabbed her heavy coat from the rack on the back porch and retrieved her gloves and hat from the pockets. She slipped on her gloves, then her hat and coat.

"I'll meet you in the shipping room," Genny called out as she left Wallace on the back porch.

She had enlarged the drying shed a few years ago when she had expanded her business. Organically grown herbs were a top item in today's market, and nearly a third of her profits came from the sale of medicinal herbs. Her list of herbs was quite extensive, everything from anise to yarrow. Some of the herbs grew quite nicely in the greenhouses, others she cultivated in warm weather in her gardens; but several were wild specimens found in the surrounding woods. She had learned everything she knew about medicinal herbs from Granny, who had learned the art of healing with herbs from her two grandmothers, one a full-blooded

Cherokee and the other a descendant of Celtic Druids. She had been taught that both her Native American ancestors and her Scots-Irish ancestors shared a respect for nature. The Cherokees, as did most other tribes, lived in harmony with nature and used herbs as a means of drawing healing powers from the universe.

The drying shed, situated behind the greenhouses, was built of wood and glass, with forced-air drying. Granny and Wallace had made a simple solar hot-air device from a length of dryer hose, but she had replaced the homemade system with a propane forced-air heater. Propane was a better choice than electricity because it was more efficient and reliable.

Genny opened the shed door, then closed it behind her quickly. Her gaze scanned the interior of the five-hundred-square-foot area. She had used rafters, screens, and racks to make full use of the space. In one area she had also used a "raised" floor, which was a framework of beams covered with permeable sisal cloth.

After making her way through the room, visually checking the dried herbs, Genny made a note of what needed to be processed soon. She always kept a personal supply of processed herbs to share with family and close friends. From time to time various Cherokee County residents came to her for potions, remedies, and such like.

Dried herbs could not be kept indefinitely, of course, not without losing their healing properties. Granny had taught her that medicinal plants could be kept only as long as their growing cycle. If a flower blooms every year, it can be stored for only a year. And if an herb seed matures in two years, then the seeds cannot be kept longer than two years.

Just as Genny emerged from the drying shed, she saw Sally standing near the back porch. Sally and Wallace were deep in conversation. The two were of a similar age and seemed to have a great deal in common. Wallace was known as the town idiot and Sally the town eccentric. Both possessed hearts of gold.

Perhaps what this world needs is more idiots and eccentrics.

Sally had brought along Peter and Paul, her bloodhounds. The two red dogs, each weighing well over a hundred pounds, frolicked in the sunshine with Drudwyn. The animals were old friends, too.

Sally threw up a hand and waved when she saw Genny, then called out to her, "Have you talked to Jazzy today?"

Genny shook her head. When she approached Sally and Wallace, she asked, "Why did you ask about Jazzy? Is something wrong?"

"Don't know for sure." Sally lifted a container of snuff from her pocket, flipped the lid, and, using a small stick, packed the finely ground tobacco in the hollow between gum and jaw. "I tried calling her a couple of times and didn't get no answer at her apartment, and the folks at the restaurant said she had called them to say she wouldn't be in this morning."

"That doesn't sound like Jazzy, does it? Did you try her cell phone? Maybe she went out of town for some reason?"

"No answer on her cell phone," Sally said. "Besides, that gal don't leave Cherokee County without telling me. She knows I'm a worrier."

"Did whoever you spoke to at the restaurant say Jazzy was sick?"

"I talked to Tiffany. She was the one who talked to Jazzy, and she told me Jazzy didn't give her a reason."

"I hope Miss Jazzy isn't sick," Wallace said. "Genny, maybe you should take her some of our medicine."

"I'll try to get in touch with her this afternoon, and if I can't contact her, I'll drive into town this evening," Genny said.

"You know Jamie Upton is back in town." Sally spit out a dark brown liquid on the ground, then wiped her mouth with the back of her hand. "I wish he'd stay away." Sally grunted. "Hell, I wish he'd drop dead. Mark my words, one of these days somebody'll kill that no-good rascal."

"Do you think Jazzy's with Jamie?" Genny hoped and prayed not. Jamie had given Jazzy nothing but grief for as long as they'd known each other, which was just about all their lives.

"She swore to me that she wouldn't have nothing to do with him this time. I sure do hate that things didn't work out with her and Jacob. That's what my gal needs—a good man who'd treat her right."

"Why don't you and Wallace go on into the shipping room and I'll give Jazzy a call before I join you?" Genny offered Sally a forced smile, then hurried into the house.

She lifted the receiver from the wall phone and dialed Jazzy's home number. The phone rang repeatedly, then the answering machine picked up. Genny tried the cell phone. Voice mail. After that she tried the restaurant.

"Tiffany, this is Genny Madoc. Has Jazzy come in yet?"

"Yes, ma'am, she just showed up. I don't know what's going on, but we're having an epidemic of no-shows. First Jazzy didn't come in, then Lois called to say one of her kids was sick and Misty hasn't shown up for the afternoon shift."

"Sorry y'all are having a problem," Genny said. "Would you mind putting me through to the business line in Jazzy's office?"

"Sure thing."

Jazzy picked up on the third ring. "Jasmine Talbot. How may I help you?"

"Next time you decide not to answer your phone or show up for work, you'd better call Sally so she won't worry about you."

"God, Genny, tell her I'm sorry. But . . . well, I—"

"What's wrong?"

"I need to see you. I want you to give me a reading."

"What's happened? Is it Jamie?"

"He came to see me last night."

"Did you—"

"No. I made him leave. At gunpoint."

A cold shiver danced along Genny's nerve endings. "Come out around five-thirty. I'll make sure Sally and Wallace are gone for the day."

"Genny?"

"What?"

"I'm scared."

"Of Jamie?"

"Yes, of Jamie. And of myself. I believe I could have actually shot him last night. I—I wanted him dead."

Brian MacKinnon had put in a phone call to Senator Everett first thing that morning. He needed to know what Dallas Sloan was doing in Cherokee Pointe. If he'd been on better terms with Jacob Butler, he would have asked him about the FBI agent. The two seemed damn chummy at breakfast this morning. Jacob had been especially reluctant to talk to the press about the two recent murders. But murder in their relatively crime-free county was big news. And two sacrificial murders was front-page headline news.

Had Jacob asked for FBI assistance? The *Cherokee Pointe Herald* readers had a right to know, didn't they? And hundreds of WMMK viewers had been calling the "Have Your Say" hotline since the morning of the first murder.

Besides, he had a burning need to find out everything he could about the man who was interested in Genny. Having Pierpont as a rival was bad enough, but where Pierpont was merely a minor thorn in his side, Agent Sloan might prove to be real competition.

Chapter 11

While Jacob was out of the office tending to business earlier in the day, Dallas had made a phone call to Teri Nash. He'd given her an update on the second murder and asked her if Linc Hughes had finished with the profile he'd promised to compose from the information Dallas had given him on the murders in Mobile.

"Fax me whatever Sheriff Butler will share with you and I'll get it to Linc and he can compare the murders in Mobile to the ones in Cherokee Pointe," Teri had told him. "Rutherford's got him working night and day on another case right now."

Rutherford had given Dallas about as much leeway as he was going to. The guy could be a real prick sometimes, a real stickler for rules and regulations. Rutherford had given him a couple of verbal reprimands and threatened him with suspension for a few weeks or even months. Dallas figured that he'd have to take a leave of absence to avoid getting suspended.

Although they would have to be careful not to risk their jobs, Dallas knew Teri and Linc wouldn't let him down. They understood how much finding this killer meant to him personally—and they also realized that if he was right about Brooke's murderer being a serial killer, other women's lives could depend on narrowing down the suspects with a top-notch profile done by an FBI expert. But with only a handful of profilers on staff, the Bureau kept them busy all the time.

Because none of the local or state law enforcement agencies in Alabama, Texas, South Carolina, or Louisiana had requested federal help, the FBI hadn't been involved in the four other cases where a series of five sacrificial murders had been committed. The Bureau seldom looked into cases involving a lone criminal. If the killer had continued murdering women in the same area and the crimes had been suspected as the work of a serial killer, there was no doubt that the locals would have looked to the Feds for help. The fact that there were similarities in the four sets of murders in various southern states came to light only because Dallas had started digging for information.

Teri had been the one who'd helped him comb the files collected by the UCR—the Uniform Crime Reporting Program—for the information about reported homicides that had anything relevant in common with Brooke's murder. And when they'd found those cases, Dallas had made phone calls to each local law enforcement authority to request all the information they had on each case. As late as the day he'd left D.C., more documents arrived from the similar case prior to Mobile, in Hilton Head, South Carolina.

Dallas had also made another call while Jacob had been gone—to the FBI field office in Knoxville. Chet Morris, who headed up the office as the special agent in charge, was an old friend and had agreed to cooperate with Sheriff Butler by using the FBI's labs to conduct examinations of evidence. All Dallas had to do was get Butler to put in a call to Chet.

Jacob entered his office, where Dallas sat behind his desk studying every tidbit of information on the two Cherokee Pointe murders. When Dallas glanced up, Jacob nodded as he shucked off his coat and removed his hat, then hung them on the rack in the corner.

"Sorry about being gone so long, but I've been following

every lead, responding personally to every phone call about anything suspicious.'' Jacob headed for the coffeemaker on the small table braced against the side wall. ''Half a dozen people are convinced that the animal sacrifices we had back before Christmas are somehow connected to Cindy's and Susie's murders.''

Dallas rose from the chair and rounded the desk to join Jacob at the coffeemaker. He'd been so busy studying the files that he hadn't even stopped for lunch.

''What do you think? Is there a connection?'' Dallas asked.

''I don't know what to think, but if you're asking me what my gut instincts tell me, I'd say there probably isn't a connection.''

''I tend to agree. Animal sacrifices aren't all that uncommon, but human sacrifices are.''

Jacob poured coffee into a clean mug and handed it to Dallas, who said, ''Thanks,'' then asked ''Were there any reports about animal sacrifices prior to the human sacrifices in any of the other cases? In the series of murders in Mobile?''

Dallas shook his head. ''Nope.''

''Did you talk to your people at the Bureau today?''

''No profile on my killer. Not yet. But soon.''

Jacob eased his hips down on the edge of his desk and lifted the orange UT mug to his lips. He took a couple of sips, then set the mug on his desk. ''I'm going to be totally honest with you—I think I'm not experienced enough to handle this case properly, and it doesn't help that our chief of police is a numbskull. I'm considering asking for some help.''

''Call Chet Morris at the Knoxville field office and ask for some official assistance from the Bureau so that your department can have access to all our resources. Chet's an all-right kind of guy, and he's not going to bellyache about my looking over your shoulder. And if you're willing to let me, I'll work with you in an unofficial capacity. I've got the law enforcement experience you lack.''

"I need to talk to Roddy Watson first. The damn man is determined for us to handle these murders ourselves. He's going to put up a fuss."

"You've got jurisdiction over the Susie Richards case. Call Chet about using the Bureau's resources just for that case and you really won't leave Watson a choice in the matter. And you might want to consider asking Chet to send some people here to join your task force."

"Yeah, it sounds like a good idea." Jacob chuckled. "That's damn sneaky, going behind Roddy's back, but it's probably the best way to handle him."

Dallas downed several large gulps of coffee, then set his cup on the floor. He dragged a chair up to the side of Jacob's desk and picked up a notepad and pen.

"Have you got time for us to compile that list of suspects now?"

"You mean the list of newcomers to our area?"

Dallas nodded.

Jacob rubbed his chin. "To begin with, there's Reverend and Mrs. Stowe over at the Congregational Church. They've been here only a few months. They came after old Reverend Thomas retired."

"Isn't Reverend Stowe the one who found Cindy Todd's body?"

"That's him."

"What's the preacher's first name?"

"Haden," Jacob replied. "And his wife is Esther."

Dallas printed the names on the notepad. "Who else?"

"Dr. MacNair is new. Been here a couple of months. Galvin MacNair's a general practitioner. His wife's name is Nina."

Dallas added MacNair's name to the list.

"A minister and a doctor," Jacob said. "Not exactly your criminal types."

"A serial killer can hide behind any facade," Dallas told him. "I'll see if Teri can check them out for us, or, if you get Chet on the case soon, he can run a check on our suspects list. We need to find a man who moves around quite a bit or at least travels a lot.''

''Jamie Upton.''

''Who?''

''Forget it.'' Jacob finished off his coffee and walked across the room for another cup.

''Why forget it? Who's Jamie Upton?''

''A spoiled brat who grew up to be a sorry bastard. He travels a lot. He comes back to Cherokee Pointe every so often. He just came back into town less than a week ago.''

''Right before Susie Richards was murdered?''

''Yeah, about that time. But forget Jamie. His name just popped into my mind. I'm afraid I'm prejudiced where he's concerned.''

''I take it that along with Brian MacKinnon, this Jamie guy is high on your shit list.''

The corners of Jacob's mouth lifted ever so slightly. A hint of a smile. ''Yeah, I have some issues with rich guys who think their money can buy them out of trouble or get them whatever they want.''

Dallas jotted Jamie's name down on his list.

''If you're adding Jamie's name, you might as well add MacKinnon, too. He travels quite a bit. Wouldn't hurt to check him out.''

Dallas grinned as he wrote Brian MacKinnon on the list. ''Who else has been living in Cherokee County six months or less, or travels a lot?''

''Dillon Carson runs the little theater in town. He's new, and a real ladies' man. And there's Genny's friend, Royce Pierpont. The guy's a wimp and a bit of a weirdo if you ask me, but Genny likes him. He owns an antique shop here in town. He hasn't been here more than six months.''

''Anybody else?''

''I can't think of anyone off the top of my head. Isn't that list long enough? How many names do you have?''

''Six.'' Dallas quickly scanned the names. ''It's a place to start.''

''Do you want to wait until I contact Chet Morris or do

you want to ask your friend Teri to start the ball rolling with that list of names?''

"I'll call Teri. We don't need to waste any time. But when you talk to Chet and ask him for assistance, tell him that I've got a friend doing me a favor at the Bureau, just so we don't work at cross purposes. And don't mention Teri's name.''

"If our killer is the same man as the one who committed the crimes in Mobile, how long do you think we have before he strikes again?'' Jacob asked. "He's already killed two women only twenty-four hours apart.''

"He has no specific time frame. Some of the murders were committed twenty-four hours apart, others three weeks apart. There seems to be no rhyme or reason to it. But there's one thing all the murders have in common, timewise.''

Jacob narrowed his gaze. "And that would be?''

"They've all occurred early in the morning, probably at dawn.''

"The more I learn about this serial killer of yours, the freakier the whole scenario becomes. If our man is the same as yours, then we're dealing with a very sick mind.'' Jacob cursed softly under his breath. "Hell, what am I saying? Even if they're two different guys, our killer is a real sicko. He's gutted two innocent women.''

"And if he's my killer, and I'm sure he is, he's already on the hunt for his third victim.''

Genny put the kettle on so that when Jazzy arrived, they could have chamomile tea. Something soothing. Jazzy was deeply troubled and needed a calm, caring friend—a shoulder to lean on. Genny seldom wished ill to any of God's creatures, not even bottom-feeders like Jamie Upton. But if she possessed the power to intervene in people's lives, she would remove Jamie from Jazzy's life. Permanently. Oh, no, she wouldn't have him die, but she would have him leave Cherokee County and never return.

After removing the container of chamomile from the cupboard, Genny measured the correct amount and placed it in the teapot on the counter. Granny had cultivated the Roman chamomile plant with double flowers because it possessed the strongest healing properties.

The sound of a car entering the driveway alerted Genny to the arrival of a guest. By the time she made her way to the front door, Jazzy was on the porch. Genny flung open the door and held out her arms. Jazzy rushed into Genny's embrace.

"I've been going nuts ever since it happened." Jazzy lifted her head from Genny's shoulder. "You don't know how close I came to killing that son of a bitch."

Genny grasped Jazzy's hand and led her into the house. After closing the door, she escorted Jazzy into the kitchen.

"Come with me," she told her friend. "I'll pour us up some tea and we'll talk."

Jazzy followed like an obedient child. And anyone who knew Jazzy knew she wasn't the type to be obedient or submissive. But she trusted Genny as she trusted no one else on earth, and Genny felt the same way about her. True friends.

While Jazzy sat at the kitchen table, Genny prepared their tea, then handed Jazzy a cup and sat across from her.

"Start at the beginning and tell me everything."

Jazzy sighed loudly. "I've told you that he's been pestering me, just as I knew he would." Jazzy searched Genny's face, apparently seeking some sign of understanding. "I'm finished with him. I can't keep doing this to myself over and over again. I want him out of my life permanently. But"—Jazzy took a deep breath—"I don't want him dead. I swear I don't."

"Drink your tea, then tell me exactly what happened last night."

Jazzy lifted the cup to her lips and sipped the hot liquid. She shivered. "I hate this stuff."

"It's good for you," Genny told her. "Drink up."

Jazzy took several more sips. "He'd been drinking. He

threatened to make a ruckus if I didn't let him in. Stupid me, I thought I could handle him, talk sense to him.''

"You should have called Jacob.''

"I threatened to, but all he did was accuse me of screwing Jacob.''

"Jacob wouldn't have cared what he said. He'd have put him in jail overnight. You know Jacob isn't afraid of Big Jim Upton.''

"He—he would have raped me.''

Genny opened her mouth in a silent gasp.

Jazzy spoke slowly, softly. So softly that a couple of times, Genny could barely hear her. But she didn't interrupt as Jazzy told her about her unnerving experience with Jamie.

"And that's when I threatened to blow his balls off. He knew I meant it.'' Tears gathered in Jazzy's luminous green eyes. "But it's not over. He won't let it be. He'll come back again . . . and I'm not sure what I'll do.''

Genny reached across the table and took Jazzy's hands into hers. "Come stay with me until he leaves town.''

"I can't do that. I have three businesses in town.'' A tentative smile played at the edges of Jazzy's lips. "Besides, I won't give that bastard the satisfaction of thinking he has me running scared.''

"We'll call Jacob and ask him to have a little talk with Jamie.''

"Jacob has his hands full right now with those murder cases.''

"He can make time for a two-minute talk with Jamie.''

"Two minutes, huh?'' Jazzy's lips widened into a full smile. "Yeah, you're right. Jacob could put the fear of God into just about anybody in two minutes.''

"Stay and have supper with me and Drudwyn, then I'll call Jacob.'' When Jazzy hesitated, Genny said, "I promise I won't make you drink any more chamomile tea.''

Jazzy laughed. "I'll stay, but you don't have to call Jacob. I'll go by and see him when I drive back into town.'' Jazzy glanced down at the tablecloth and began straightening invisible wrinkles in the material. "Genny . . . I . . . would you . . ."

Genny looked her friend directly in the eyes. "What do you want?"

"You know."

"Are you sure?"

Jazzy nodded. "In all these years, I've never asked you to do it for me, but . . . Is it wrong of me to want to know?"

"Wanting to know the future is neither right nor wrong, but sometimes it's . . . dangerous."

"I need to know about Jamie. That's all. Nothing else."

"You know it doesn't work that way. Once I look into your future, I can't control what I see."

Jazzy grasped Genny's hands. "Just do it, will you? Please."

Genny pulled away and stood. "Let's go into Granny's room. It's quiet and dark in there. And the candles are already set up."

Jazzy followed Genny upstairs and into Melva Mae Butler's room, which lay in darkness, the curtains closed, the unmistakable scent of roses in the air. Granny had always smelled of roses because she used rose-scented powder. An antique four-poster dominated the fourteen-foot-square area. Genny went about the room and lit the white candles that were strategically placed throughout, then she sat in one of two chairs by a small, antique table. Jazzy took a deep breath and sat in the other chair. She laid her hands palms up on top of the table.

Genny closed her eyes and repeated the name "Jasmine" several times. With her eyes still shut, she reached out, ran her open palms over Jazzy's and let them remain there.

Silence. The whispering moan of the winter wind. Steady breathing. Two hearts beating.

Genny did "readings" for only a few people, those she knew truly believed in her abilities. She never took money, never asked for anything in return. Usually people came to her for a reading only when everything else had failed. Most people feared the future; few were brave enough—or foolish enough—to actually want to know what lay ahead for them.

The readings weren't like the visions. She had no control over the visions, and they were devastatingly real, almost like watching through the lens of a video camera. But that camera was held in someone else's hands. When she did a reading, she didn't get clear pictures. Or at least not often. She got feelings, sensed things, sometimes heard a voice inside her head whispering to her.

"Sadness. Terrible sadness. A death. Not yours, but someone you know, someone—" Genny gasped. "A man is going to die."

"Is it Jamie? Do I kill him?" Jazzy's voice quivered with apprehension.

Genny squeezed Jazzy's hands, then opened her palms and rested them atop Jazzy's once again. "I don't know who he is. But you are not responsible for his death. He will die soon. In a few months. His death harms you in some way." Genny shivered.

"In what way? How?"

"I don't know."

"Is that all you see?"

Genny didn't respond. She simply sat very still, very quiet, and waited. If there was more to be told, it would come to her. She saw the shadow of a man, his image blurred. Genny felt a gentleness in him, a tender love toward Jazzy. And that's when she knew.

"Thank you, God," Genny whispered.

"What? What?"

"There is a man—not Jamie and not Jacob—who will make you happy. He will be good to you."

"Will I be free of Jamie once and for all?"

Genny hesitated. "Yes. Yes, you will be free of him." The darkness consumed her momentarily. A black, swirling reality that threatened to pull her in and trap her. Genny understood and backed away from its power. Evil, not good. She opened her eyes. Her body went limp.

Jazzy jumped up. "Are you all right?"

Genny nodded. "I'll be fine. I just need to rest for a few moments."

"Thank you so much." Jazzy hugged Genny. "All I needed to know is that I don't kill Jamie, but that I'll be free of him. Finding out there will be a good man in my future who'll treat me right was a bonus."

Two hours later, just as Jazzy cleared away the supper dishes, Drudwyn's ears perked up and he growled.

"It's all right, boy." Genny reached down to where he sat beside her and scratched his head. "I hear it, too. Someone just drove up."

"Were you expecting anybody?" Jazzy asked.

Genny shook her head. "No, not really."

"What does that mean?"

"It means I wasn't expecting anyone, but I was sort of hoping that . . . well, that Dallas Sloan might—"

The loud pounding at the front door stopped Genny midsentence.

"Whoever it is wants your immediate attention," Jazzy said. "You sit still and rest. I'll see who it is."

Sessions such as the one she'd shared with Jazzy taxed her energy, but she usually recovered quickly, unlike when she experienced the visions over which she had no control. At least with the readings she could back away at any point.

Genny rose from the chair, and with Drudwyn at her side, walked out of the kitchen. When she entered the hallway, she heard voices.

"Come right on in. I think Genny was expecting you," Jazzy said. "I was just leaving. I need to get back into town and tend to business."

"Don't rush off on my account," Dallas said. "I came by to ask for Genny's help."

"What sort of help? You haven't come for a reading, have you? Because if that's why you're here—"

"Hush up!" Genny called out. "You're saying too much."

She had to make Jazzy stop talking. Dallas Sloan didn't believe in psychics, didn't think people possessed a real sixth sense. She didn't want to scare him off before he got to know her. He needed a chance to fully connect with her, to trust her, before he would be able to believe in her.

Dallas and Jazzy turned around and stared at Genny.

"I'm sure Dallas didn't come here for that. He's not interested in anything vaguely connected to sixth-sense abilities." Genny rushed down the hallway, but the quick movement made her dizzy. She staggered, then reached out and placed her hand on the wall to steady herself.

"Are you all right?" Jazzy asked.

Dallas bolted past Jazzy, straight to Genny. His big hands came down on her shoulders. "What's wrong? You look like you're going to faint."

She gazed up into his blue, blue eyes and smiled. "I was dizzy there for a moment. I'm fine now."

"You haven't had another one of those visions, have you?" he asked.

She shook her head. He eased his hands across her shoulders, down her arms, and to her wrists, then released her.

Jazzy cleared her throat. "I'm going to get my coat and head out."

"Promise me you'll talk to Jacob," Genny reminded her.

"I promise."

Genny turned to Dallas. "Would you care for something to eat? I have plenty left over from supper."

"No, thanks. I've eaten already. At Jasmine's."

"Best place in town," Jazzy called out, then closed the front door behind her.

Genny laughed. Dallas smiled.

"Why are you here?" she asked.

"I need your help."

"In what way can I help you?"

"You can help me find a serial killer before he kills again."

Chapter 12

What the hell was he doing here? Dallas asked himself as he removed his hands from Genny's slender shoulders and backed away from her. He'd tried his best to talk himself out of coming here, but, heaven help him, he'd been drawn back to this woman in a way that made absolutely no sense to him. For all he knew, she was a total crackpot. *Dammit, you idiot, she believes she's psychic. The woman has visions. And her friends and relatives actually believe she possesses these weird powers.* But he knew better. She was a fraud— she had to be—just like all the other phonies who professed to be blessed with unusual talents like ESP.

Genny stood there, her black eyes staring at him, as if penetrating far beyond what the normal human eye could see. Dallas glanced away from her and cleared his throat.

"It's all right," she told him.

"What are you talking about?" *She hasn't read your mind,* he told himself. *She simply made an assumption and guessed right.*

"You can be as skeptical as you'd like, and it doesn't change anything."

"It's no secret that I don't believe in your hocus-pocus

stuff.'' Dallas shoved his hands into the pockets of his overcoat. ''Look, it was probably a mistake my coming here. I
just thought that maybe ...'' Reaching up with his right
hand, he raked his fingers through his thick blond hair,
grumbled incoherently under his breath, then said, ''Hell, I
don't know why I'm here.''

''Yes, you do. You told me yourself. You want my help
to find the serial killer who murdered your niece.''

''I know what I said, but I don't see how you can help
me. Not really. Just chalk this visit up to a guy having the
hots for you.''

''Do you have the hots for me, Special Agent Sloan?''

His gaze collided with hers. She was smiling.

Dallas grinned. ''You don't seem surprised. Don't tell me
you saw, in your crystal ball, my coming here tonight and
acting like a fool.''

Genny's smile wavered slightly. ''I don't use a crystal
ball.''

''What is it about you, lady? We have absolutely nothing
in common. My life is a holy mess. I have only one goal
and that's to find Brooke's killer. So unless I'm just in bad
need of getting laid, there's no reason for my being here
tonight.''

Genny's smile disappeared. ''Are you in bad need of
getting laid?''

Had he actually said that to her? Damn! Shrugging, Dallas
grunted. ''I didn't mean it as an insult. It's just that you
need to know I'm not the kind of guy who makes commit-
ments, who gets involved. I'm not a man you can count on
for the long haul.''

''Are you warning me off?''

''Do you always ask so many questions?''

''Yes, when the answers are important.''

''We'd mix like oil and water, you know.''

Say good night and leave, he told himself. *You aren't
getting any pussy from Genny Madoc. She's not the one-
night-stand type. You knew that before you showed up on
her doorstep.*

"Oil and water, huh?" She took a tentative step toward him. "I was thinking more along the lines of a stick of dynamite and a lit match."

Dallas drew in a deep breath as images flashed through his mind of Genny lying beneath him, her long, black hair spread out over a white pillow and her slender limbs wrapped around him.

"Lady, you know how to hurt a guy."

She took another step toward him. He didn't move, although his brain warned him to run. If she came any closer, he'd probably grab her and yank her into his arms.

She halted. "How about some apple pie and coffee?"

"Huh?" Her hospitable offer took him as much by surprise as the subject change.

"Don't go," she told him. "And it doesn't take a sixth sense to figure out that you're on the verge of running from me. Stay, have some pie and coffee, and we'll talk. About the serial killer. About Brooke. About whatever you need to talk about. I have a feeling you need someone to listen to you, to talk things over with, to care about what you care about, far more than you need to get laid."

She was right. He did need someone to talk to, someone to listen. Teri had been a real friend during the past eight months, and he'd relied on her to be his sounding board after Brooke's murder. But he'd soon realized he was taking advantage of the feelings she still had for him. He'd backed off. She deserved better. He'd wanted her to have her chance with Linc, and as long as she thought he needed her, she wouldn't move on. He'd allowed her to help him with his unofficial investigation and to drag Linc into the mix because he was desperate for help. But he'd quickly severed the emotional bond Teri had tried to rebuild between them.

Now here was Genny offering to be a shoulder to cry on, and he was damn tempted to accept her offer.

"I appreciate your offering to be my confidante. And you're right about my needing somebody to listen and to care. But you're sadly mistaken if you think a little hand-holding will satisfy me more than our fucking would."

Genny gasped. "Are you deliberately trying to scare me off?"

"Is that what you think I'm doing?"

She nodded. "Yes, but it isn't working." She motioned for him to follow her. "Come on into the living room while I get the coffee and pie."

"You know I want to take you to bed and you're still inviting me to stay?"

"Yes, I want you to stay. You need me." She turned and walked away from him. When he followed her, she paused and glanced over her shoulder. "You won't be taking me to bed. Not tonight."

Coming as a total surprise, the innuendo in her comment sucker-punched him. She hadn't said not ever, no way, no how. She'd said not tonight.

"I'll settle for coffee, pie, and talk. For tonight."

Jazzy's Joint had a wild side, but it wasn't showing that boisterous, rowdy side tonight. Since it was a weeknight in midwinter, only a couple of the usual crowd were at the bar, and a few more were scattered at various tables throughout the establishment. Jazzy had learned it didn't pay to hire a live band during the winter months, except on weekends. But the loyal patrons kept the old jukebox she'd found several years ago at an antique fair in Knoxville blasting out the oldies. The drone of half a dozen drinkers talking and two guys shooting pool did little to interfere with the loud music. Fats Domino's rendition of "Blueberry Hill" pumped out a steady beat.

When she'd bought this building and turned the downstairs into a bar, she had wanted a place with a little atmosphere. Something more than just loud music, liquor flowing like water, and a smoke-clouded interior. Although the place possessed those three qualities in abundance, the decor combined sleek modern with a hint of country. The bar, tables, and chairs had a clean-cut line, with chrome neatly edging the light wood and glass. The refinished hardwood flooring was beginning to show some wear and tear. A pair of large chrome light fixtures hung over a couple of pool tables placed at the back of the room. Cherokee Indian artifacts—including ceremonial pipes, handmade pottery and baskets, and carved masks—graced the walls, as did Native American pictures. Three fascinating paintings hung along the entrance wall, one being a portrait of Austenaco, a Cherokee chief in the eighteenth century; another being Robert Lindneux's rendering of Sequoyah, who had created the Cherokee alphabet; and the third a portrait of George Lowery, a prominent Cherokee leader of mixed blood who had been a delegate to the 1827 Constitutional Convention.

With Cherokee Pointe situated so close to the Smoky Mountains, and the Cherokee lands held by the natives who had escaped the Trail of Tears, anything Native American appealed to the tourists. In order to make sure that nothing she did was offensive to Genny and Jacob, who were both a quarter Cherokee, Jazzy had asked Genny to help her decorate the place.

Jazzy entered from the back of the bar. Her office at Jasmine's had a door that opened up to the storeroom of Jazzy's Joint, making it easy for her to go back and forth and keep a check on both of her establishments. She nodded to her bartender, Lacy Fallon, a middle-aged brunette with a smoker's gravelly voice and deep lines in her face. Lacy motioned for Jazzy to approach.

As Jazzy eased up on a bar stool, she asked, "What's up, Lacy?"

"Bert didn't show up tonight," Lacy said.

"Did he bother to call?"

Lacy shook her head. "This is the fourth time since Christmas that he's missed work without calling or without a halfway decent excuse when he does show up. I'd say it's time you found yourself a new bouncer."

Jazzy let out an exasperated huff. "This hasn't been a good day for my employees. First Misty is a no-show over at Jasmine's and now Bert. I'll give Misty another chance since she doesn't make a habit of laying out, although today makes twice for her this month. But Bert's paycheck will be waiting for him when he does show up.''

"Let's hope we don't have any problems tonight.''

Jazzy glanced around at the slim crowd. "Looks pretty tame to me. But any decent honky-tonk needs a good bouncer. I'll call the *Cherokee Pointe Herald* tomorrow and put an ad in the paper.'' As Jazzy continued scanning the evening's clientele, her gaze stopped at the pool table where Dillon Carson, the guy who ran the little theater, and a stranger were engrossed in their game.

Dillon was a regular. He liked Crown Royal and Coke. And he enjoyed a game of pool almost as much as he loved picking up any willing woman who'd walk out of the place with him. It really hadn't been a secret—at least not to her or the Jazzy's Joint regulars—that Dillon had been screwing Cindy Todd. But Cindy had been only one of many. Dillon wasn't choosy, as long as the woman was under fifty and willing.

She didn't really know much about the former actor turned amateur director and producer. He'd told her one night, after he'd had several drinks, that he had tried Hollywood and Broadway when he was in his twenties. After his going-nowhere career had hit the skids when he was in his early thirties, he'd taken a job directing a little theater somewhere out in Texas. He'd been moving from job to job ever since. She figured winding up in Cherokee Pointe had to be pretty damn close to the bottom of the barrel for a director or actor.

"Dillon's sure not crying in his beer over Cindy, is he?'' Clicking her tongue, Lacy shook her head. "I'll tell you right now that knowing somebody out there is grabbing women and then killing them as if they were gutting a hog has got me double-checking my locks at night.''

"Yeah, I know what you mean. When Misty didn't show up for work today and didn't call, I started wondering if I should contact the police.''

"Did you?''

"I called the Sheriff's Department and talked to Bobby

Joe. He had no idea why she'd lay out, so he's going to stop by her place this evening to make sure she's all right.''

"She's probably okay, just overslept or something. Misty's quite a night owl, what with her carousing, so she could have still been asleep at noon. Or she could have gotten sick and just didn't think about letting you know."

"That's what I figured. I told Bobby Joe to give me a call later."

Boisterous laughter from the back of the room gained everyone's attention. Jazzy and Lacy turned their heads in time to see a chuckling Dillon slap his opponent on the back, then pull out his wallet and hand over several bills.

"This guy must be really good," Lacy said. "I've never seen Dillon lose a game since he's been coming in here."

"At least he's not a sore loser."

While Dillon picked up a nearly empty glass of whiskey and Coke and headed toward the bar, Jazzy studied the man who racked the balls and hung up the cues. She'd never seen him before anywhere in Cherokee Pointe; and she didn't miss many travelers, since she owned a bar, a restaurant, and was part-owner in a cabin rental outfit. *He's probably new in town,* she thought as she surveyed him from the top of his shaggy brown hair that touched the collar of his black shirt to the tips of his scuffed, black leather boots.

He was tall—about six-two would be her guess—with a lean, muscular build that would attract any female with red blood in her veins, and a swagger that proclaimed his self-confidence without being cocky. He was dressed all in black. Inexpensive attire. Jeans. Black flannel shirt with a white T-shirt visible at the neckline. But she'd lay odds those boots had cost him a pretty penny.

She watched him as he walked across the room to a table near the back. He had an easy, in-no-hurry stride, like a self-assured big cat, knowing he was king of the jungle. He dropped into a chair where a black leather jacket hung, then picked up the bottle of beer, finished off its warm contents, and set the bottle down. He turned halfway around and glanced over his shoulder, obviously searching for the bartender.

When Lacy started to come out from behind the bar, Jazzy said, ''I'll see what he wants.''

She sauntered over to his table, taking her time, allowing him several minutes to watch her, to study her as she had studied him. When she reached his table, he smiled.

''What'll it be?'' she asked.

''Another of the same.'' He glanced at the beer bottle. ''And how about some conversation?''

''While I go get your beer, be thinking of an interesting topic.''

His smile widened, and for a split second it held her mesmerized. He wasn't movie-star good-looking, not a pretty-boy the way Jamie was, but he was stunningly attractive in a totally masculine way. His eyes were a rich whiskey brown with golden highlights. And his dark brown hair displayed the same honeyed tones.

''Hurry back,'' he said, his voice a deep rumble.

Jazzy returned to the bar and asked Lacy for a Budweiser.

''Looks sort of dangerous to me,'' Lacy said.

''Maybe.'' Jazzy grasped the beer bottle. ''But when has danger ever scared me off?''

Lacy chuckled.

After Jazzy handed the stranger his beer, she sat in the chair across from him. ''You're new in town.''

''Been here a few days.'' He lifted the cold beer to his lips and took a hefty swig, then wiped his mouth with the back of his hand.

''Where are you staying?''

''Motel out on three twenty-one.''

''You should rent one of my cabins,'' she told him. ''We've got winter rates.''

''You own some cabins?''

She nodded. ''And this bar and the restaurant next door.''

He whistled softly. ''Rich lady.''

Jazzy laughed. ''Far from rich. Just a hardworking girl who knows how to manage her money.''

"Then you must be Jazzy. Or is it Jasmine?" He took a couple more sips from the bottle.

"Jasmine Talbot," she replied. "But my friends call me Jazzy."

"May I call you Jazzy?"

"Do you think we're going to be friends?"

His smile disappeared. "I'm not the type who makes a good friend. So how about we just remain good acquaintances . . . Jasmine."

There was something about the way he said her name that sent sensual shivers through her. A soft, caressing tone that a man would use in bed, after the loving.

"Works for me," she said. "So, my *good acquaintance,* what's your name?"

"Caleb McCord."

It suited him. It was a strong name. Her gut instincts told her that Caleb was a good man, albeit perhaps a dangerous one. And there was no doubt in her mind that he was one strong, tough son of a gun. Without realizing it, he exuded a warning not to mess with him.

"Where are you from, Caleb?"

"Memphis."

"Mm—hmm. What are you doing in Cherokee Pointe?"

"Visiting."

"Then you have friends or relatives in Cherokee County?"

He shook his head. "Just visiting the area."

"Planning on staying long?"

"Maybe."

"You're not much of a conversationalist, are you?"

"My talents lie elsewhere."

A fire ignited deep inside Jazzy and quickly spread through her body. A picture of the two of them naked and wrapped in each other's arms flashed through her mind. She'd never felt such a strong attraction to a man—not since she'd been sixteen and had fallen hard for Jamie Upton. But in retrospect she figured she'd fallen more for who Jamie was than the boy himself. This man was different. She sized him up to be a drifter, no ties, no roots—and little or no money. So what was it about him that excited her?

"You're blunt-spoken, too, I see." Jazzy stared directly into his eyes and saw a reflection of her own desire.

"I've found that being totally honest and up front from the very beginning is the best policy." He took another swig from the beer bottle. "If anything happens between us, it won't be anything more than body heat. You scratch my itch, I'll scratch yours. No emotional entanglements."

"If anything happens between us, a purely physical relationship suits me just fine."

Jazzy scooted back her chair and stood. Caleb stared up at her.

"Leaving me already?" he asked.

She grinned. "I'm here almost every night about this time. If you show up again, I'll take it as a sign you're interested. If not . . ." She shrugged.

"I'm interested. Tonight. Right now."

"Put on the brakes. We just met. I don't even kiss on a first date."

"Was this our first date?"

"Could be our only date."

Before she succumbed to Caleb's lethal magnetism, Jazzy turned and walked away. When she got halfway to the bar, she took a deep breath, then let it out slowly. Just as she headed toward the back storage room, planning to escape into her office, the front door of Jazzy's Joint opened, letting in a swish of frigid night air. She paused a moment, glanced back, and then groaned. Jamie Upton marched into the bar; and when his gaze connected with hers, he smiled as he came toward her. Same old sexy, overconfident swagger. Damn his black soul to hell!

"Jazzy, honey, don't run off," Jamie called to her.

Putting a stoic expression on her face and squaring her shoulders for battle, she turned to face him.

His smile widened as he scanned her from head to toe, his gaze lingering at her breasts. "You sure do look good tonight. Good enough to eat."

Jazzy glanced around the room. Every eye in the place focused on her. Except Caleb McCord. He glared at Jamie, studying him as if he were a specimen under a microscope.

The three-inch heels on her calf-length boots clip-clipped sharply on the wooden floor as she made a beeline to Jamie.

"What do you want?" She kept her voice low, not wanting to share any more of her private life with her customers than she already had.

Jamie reached for her, but she sidestepped him. He laughed. "You know what I want. I want you. Same as always."

"It's not going to be the same as always," she told him. "Not ever again."

"Ah, honey, why do you want to act this way when you know that sooner or later you're going to surrender and give us both what we want."

"I want you to leave." She pointed to the door. "Get out of here. Go away and stay away."

"I'll leave if you'll go with me." He cast his gaze toward the ceiling. "Invite me upstairs. Come on, Jazzy, baby, you know you want to."

This time when he reached for her, he outmaneuvered her so that she wasn't able to avoid his clutches. He grabbed her and hauled her up against him. She smelled liquor on his breath. Jamie was always at his most conniving and his most charming when he'd had a few drinks.

"Let go of me," she demanded. "Leave me alone."

"No way, baby. I'm staying right here and keeping you close until you come to your senses."

"If you don't let go of me, I'll—"

"You'll do what?"

Jamie tried to kiss her. She struggled against him. Why had Bert chosen tonight, of all nights, not to show up? If ever she needed somebody to toss Jamie out of Jazzy's Joint on his ass, it was tonight.

Suddenly a big hand clamped down on Jamie's shoulder and jerked him away from Jazzy. She almost lost her balance when he released her so unexpectedly. After taking a deep breath and steadying herself, she saw Caleb McCord man-handling Jamie. He had one hand on Jamie's shoulder and the other gripping the back of his neck. Jamie squirmed and grumbled. Caleb held fast.

"What the hell?" Jamie tried to free himself, but to no avail. "If you know what's good for you, you'll release me this instant."

"And if you know what's good for you, you'll do as the lady asked and leave."

Caleb began marching Jamie toward the door. Jamie's feet skidded on the wood in an effort to halt his departure.

"Do you know who I am?" Jamie asked, his voice tinged with anger and fear.

Jazzy wasn't sure she'd ever heard fear in Jamie's voice.

"I don't give a damn who you are," Caleb said. "You're leaving here and not coming back. If I find out you've bothered Jasmine again, I'll take it personally."

Caleb escorted an uncooperative Jamie out the front door, onto the sidewalk, and to his car. As if drawn by an invisible force, Jazzy followed them, as did all the customers in the bar. And even Lacy came over and stood behind the others in the open front door.

Caleb bent Jamie over the hood of his fancy little Mercedes parked in a no-parking zone directly in front of Jazzy's Joint. Caleb leaned over and whispered something in Jamie's ear.

Jazzy held her breath.

Caleb released his hold on Jamie and took several backward steps. Jamie straightened to his full height, turned around, and glowered at Caleb. But he avoided even glancing at anyone else.

"You'll be seeing me again," Jamie said.

"Bring it on," Caleb replied. "Anytime. Any place."

Jamie jerked the keys from his pocket, unlocked his car, got in and revved the motor. When he drove off down the street, a resounding cheer rose from the small crowd standing behind Jazzy. The minute Caleb walked toward her, the others scattered and returned to the bar.

Standing there on the sidewalk, the bitterly cold winter wind whistling around the street corners, Jazzy waited for Caleb.

"Thanks," she said. "Not many people in Cherokee Pointe would stand up against Jamie Upton."

Caleb's eyebrows lifted. "Jamie Upton, huh? I take it he's not used to being told no."

"What did you say to him? When you had him bent over his car, what did you say?"

Caleb laced Jazzy's arm through his and led her toward the front entrance to the bar. "What I said to him is between me and him. Besides, it isn't something fit for a lady's ears."

Jazzy felt as if the wind had been knocked out of her. Nobody had ever called her a lady. And only a few had ever treated her like one.

"Come on inside and let me buy you a drink," she said. "And, call me Jazzy. I think we are going to be friends after all."

Chapter 13

Genny sensed that Dallas wanted to stay longer, even if that need went against his better judgment. He'd gotten up to leave a couple of times, but kept lingering. He didn't understand why, of course, but she did. Everything in life happened for a reason. And despite any evidence otherwise, she knew there was a rhyme and reason to events, even those that seemed inexplicable. She had been waiting a lifetime for him, perhaps more than one lifetime. Waiting for the man destined to be her mate. Naturally, she'd known from the beginning that Brian MacKinnon wasn't the man for her; and even though she'd been drawn to Royce Pierpont, she'd never felt "the connection."

Granny Butler had told her once, long ago, she had known the moment she met Papa Butler that he was the one. She'd known because of the strong spiritual connection. Granny had tried to explain it to Genny, but until Genny had sensed Dallas Sloan's presence—even before he appeared on her doorstep—she'd had no idea how powerful the connection would be. And as Dallas and she spent more time together, the bond between them strengthened. He felt it, but dismissed it as mere physical attraction. He didn't believe in anything beyond the five senses, so it would take a while for him to come to terms with what was happening to him.

"You're awfully quiet," Dallas said. "Have I put you to sleep? I've been talking nonstop." He shrugged. "It's not like me to talk so much. But there's something about you that makes me want to tell you everything."

"I've been told that I'm a good listener."

"You must be. I've never talked so much in my entire life."

"It's been good for you to tell me about your family, about your two sisters. I love the way your mother chose her children's names. Savannah, Alexandria, and Dallas."

"She and Dad moved around quite a bit in the early years of their marriage. Wherever they lived when one of us was born, that's what she named that particular kid."

"Thank goodness you weren't born in New Orleans or Los Angeles or Salt Lake City."

"Yeah, and I'd hate to be the one named Savannah." Dallas chuckled. "Things were pretty good for us growing up. Until Mom died. After that, Dad was never quite the same. And unfortunately, his second marriage hasn't been a happy one."

Genny reached out and laid her hand on his. Instantly he stiffened. "Don't be afraid of me," she said.

He eyed her skeptically. "What are you talking about? Why would I be afraid of—"

She leaned closer to him on the sofa and placed her index finger over his lips to silence his denial. "I would never hurt you. Don't you know that?"

He grasped her wrist and pulled her hand away from his face. "It's not you that I'm afraid of. It's myself. And you're the one who could wind up getting hurt. My track record with women isn't all that good."

"Are you trying to tell me that you've left a string of broken hearts behind you?"

Dallas let go of her wrist and took her hand in his. "I'm trying to tell you that I'm the wrong man for you, even for a brief affair. You and I aren't on the same page, so to speak. Hell, we aren't even in the same book. I'm a cynical bastard. I've spent twelve years with the Bureau and seen the world's underbelly, and it's not a pretty sight. I've had a couple of short-lived, semi-serious relationships, but for the most part, I'm a loner.'' He released her hand and eased backward, putting some distance between them.

"I'm a loner, too,'' she said. "I've had several romantic relationships, but none of them progressed to the serious stage. And although I tend to be an optimist, I've seen the dark side of life, too. In my visions.''

"Dammit, Genny, that's another thing.'' Dallas shot to his feet. Standing over her, he focused on her face. "You have dreams and nightmares, and you call them visions. It's your subconscious or simply your imagination. Nothing more. Somebody did a number on you, convincing you that you possess some sort of psychic talents. I guess that grandmother of yours put the hoodoo on the people around these parts and—''

"Granny had powerful abilities,'' Genny told him. "She didn't put the hoodoo on anybody.''

"Would you just listen to yourself? You honest-to-God think you're psychic! Do you have any idea how crazy that is?''

Why was it that when the man destined for her and her alone finally came into her life, he had to be such a stubborn jackass? "I am psychic. I do have visions. I can see into the future. I often know things before they happen. And I'm not crazy. I'm gifted. Or I'm cursed. Take your pick. There are times when I'd give anything to be normal. To be just like everyone else.''

Dallas reached down, grabbed her by the shoulders, and yanked her to her feet. "I can't buy into that garbage. Believing shit like that goes against my basic nature.'' After releasing her abruptly, he turned and paced the floor; then he stopped dead still and settled his gaze on her again. "I'll admit that you're unlike any woman I've ever met. There's something special about you, but . . . Let's just forget it, okay? I was a fool to come here tonight and a bigger fool for thinking . . .''

Halting midsentence, he gave her a hard look, then walked out of the room. Genny took a deep breath. Give him time, she told herself. He's fighting his feelings because he doesn't understand them.

He doesn't understand me!

When Genny followed Dallas, she found him in the foyer, putting on his overcoat. As she approached him, he kept his back to her and reached for the doorknob.

''Don't leave this way,'' she said.

She sensed him tense and knew he was running from her, trying to get away while he still could. What he didn't comprehend was the fact that he could never escape from her. Not now that they had actually met. Their lives would forever be intertwined.

''I didn't count on this . . . this thing between us,'' he admitted. ''I don't want it, don't have time for it.''

''You can run, but you can't escape.''

He snapped his head around and glared at her. ''I can sure as hell try.''

When he opened the door and walked out of her house, slamming the door behind him, Genny stood in the foyer for several minutes and listened to the sound of his car as he drove away. She pulled the edges of her cardigan sweater together over her breasts and crisscrossed her arms at her waist, hugging herself.

All her life she had been different from other people, unlike the girls she knew. Some saw her as a freak; others envied her because of her unique talents. Many of the townspeople either accepted her or ignored her, a lot of them referring to her as the old witch woman's successor. She supposed that's exactly what she was. As long as her grandmother had lived, Granny had shielded her as best she could. And only Granny had truly understood what it meant to possess abilities few others had. But, then, those talents seemed to be hereditary, passed down from grandmothers to granddaughters, similar to the way certain genes passed on to her from her parents had given her black hair and brown eyes.

Genny sighed as she woke Drudwyn from his nap and herded him toward the back door. Before following him outside, she slipped on her heavy coat, hat, and gloves. The night sky glimmered with starlight, twinkling beacons from millions of miles away. The temperature had already dropped below freezing, but the wind was calm, making it feel less cold. While Drudwyn went about his business, Genny checked the greenhouses.

A barn owl flew overhead and lit in a nearby tree, then began an eerily mournful hooting chant. On the edge of the woods a pair of gray wolves watched, their eyes like amber crystals.

Once Genny had completed her nightly check and made her way toward the back porch, a sudden feeling of unrest came over her. She paused, breathed deeply, and waited. Her eyelids closed of their own accord. *No, not now. Not here.* She tried to make her feet cooperate, tried to walk, but she stood frozen to the spot as dark shadows crept into her mind. Wide awake, standing in the middle of the backyard, Genny gave herself over to the darkness, and the vision consumed her. And as with all the visions she'd experienced in the past, she had no control over this one.

The woman in Genny's vision lay quietly, her eyes wide with fear. When he touched her, she cringed, but she couldn't cry out or make any protest. She was gagged. Gagged and bound. He lifted her off the bed and carried her toward a door. Genny couldn't see the room, couldn't identify the woman or the man.

"Soon, my little lamb, very soon," he whispered in the woman's ear.

Genny did not recognize the voice, which wasn't really audible. The words seemed to be echoing inside her head as if she heard them through a filter. She dropped to her knees, but the vision didn't end, the images simply faded and then reformed at another time and place.

The woman lay on a slab of wood balanced by two wooden

sawhorses. A makeshift altar. A glove-covered hand held an impressive, ornately decorated sword. Daybreak fought the darkness within a large empty space. Genny heard two distinctive heartbeats. The man removed the gag from the woman's mouth. Her terrifying scream rent the deadly quiet.

Suddenly, all Genny could see was the woman. Her mouth. Her blond hair. Her tear-filled blue eyes.

Genny cried out. The owl swooped low and lit on a nearby tree branch. Drudwyn bounded toward her. The two wolves crept out of the woods, moving slowly in her direction.

Genny knew who the killer's next victim would be. She had seen her face. Clearly.

At dawn, Misty Harte would die.

Jacob glanced up from his desk and looked through the open doorway when Tewanda Hardy entered. She removed her hat and jacket and headed straight for his office.

"Any problems?" Jacob asked.

She shook her head. "All quiet on the western front."

"Any sign of Misty?"

"None," Tewanda replied. "No one has seen her today. Looks like you're the last person who saw her."

Jacob didn't like having to share information about his personal life with other people, certainly not with any of his deputies. Even if Misty wasn't Bobby Joe's sister, ordinarily he wouldn't have mentioned Misty spending the night with him. He wasn't the type to brag about his sexual exploits. But with Misty apparently missing and Bobby Joe half out of his mind with worry, Jacob hadn't had much choice but to tell the deputies searching for Misty that she'd been alive and well when she'd left his apartment early this morning.

"Has Bobby Joe been in touch with all her friends?" Tewanda asked, and Jacob heard the unspoken accusation that Misty had so many male friends it might take a week to question them all.

"The ones he thinks she might have contacted. But he's

come up with nothing. It's as if Misty vanished without a trace."

"You don't think . . . well, I mean, what with a killer on the loose and all—"

"I haven't been thinking of much else," Jacob admitted.

"No point in our jumping to conclusions. As flighty as Misty is, there's no telling where she might be. She could have just up and decided to take off somewhere and she'll call Bobby Joe tomorrow. She's done it before."

"Yeah, that's possible."

The phone on Jacob's desk rang. Tewanda jumped. Jacob tensed. He lifted the receiver and identified himself.

"This here's Jimmy Lewey, out on Pike's Gap. You remember me, don't you? Your old man and mine were hunting buddies. Anyhow, I heard you'ens been looking for Misty Harte."

"That's right. Do you know anything about Misty?"

Tewanda's eyes opened wide, her gaze questioning Jacob. When she started to speak, Jacob held up his index finger as a signal for her to wait.

"Ain't got no idea where she is, but I can tell you where her car is."

"What kind of car?" Jacob asked.

"Yellow Vega."

"Where is it?"

"Parked out back of the old filling station on Pike's Gap. I still own the building even though I ain't been in business for years. But I got me a sixty-five Mustang inside the garage there that I been working on. I go over a couple of nights a week, usually pretty late. Like tonight."

"Look, Jimmy, don't bother anything. Leave everything just like it is."

"You're thinking that killer's got hold of Misty, ain't you?"

"I'm not thinking anything in particular," Jacob said. "So don't go around telling folks that the sheriff thinks Misty is the third victim."

"Sure thing. I'll keep my trap shut."

"Wait around out there, will you? We're heading out that way right now," Jacob said.

He hung up the receiver and turned to Tewanda. "Misty's car is parked behind Jimmy Lewey's old service station out on Pike's Gap. Make a couple of calls. I want a wrecker out there to bring the car in and I need a search warrant issued ASAP. Call Judge Tubbs at home. And apologize for waking him."

"I'll contact Bobby Joe, too, and let him know."

"Yeah, you do that. And call Chief Watson."

"And tell him what?"

"I want some of his people on the job. I need all the help I can get. Tell the chief what we need to do is coordinate our efforts. It's time we form a task force to find this killer."

"You do think the killer's got Misty, don't you?"

"I think it's a damn good possibility."

The room was lit solely by candlelight, golden, glistening illumination that cast gloomy shadows and doomed every corner to darkness. A low, repetitive hum droned in his head as he listened to the chants reminiscent of the ones he'd heard so often as a child. Wherever he went, he sought people such as these, the children of the night who petitioned the spirit world for magical powers. Tonight was an auspicious time because, as all good witches knew, when the moon is in its crescent period, any and all things can be accomplished. But to have every aspect in perfect alignment, the experiments must be made by true believers, faithful, and diligent concerning the task at hand.

Wearing hooded dark robes, members of the cult formed a circle around the pentagram drawn on the concrete floor. He pulled his hood up over his head and took his place in the circle. Even though he knew where the greatest power came from, old habits died hard. Besides, he needed all the strength he could acquire, from whatever source, before the ultimate fifth victim gave him what he had longed to possess all his life.

The high priestess of this little band of occultists conducted the ceremony, her eyes glazed as if in a trance while her body swayed to some inaudible music that she and she alone could hear.

"I conjure thee, Emperor Lucifer, Prince of Darkness, Divine Master of Rebel Spirits," the priestess commanded. "Leave thine abode and come hither. I have great need of thee. Come, great lord, and communicate with thy lowly servant."

He could feel the sweet, sick blackness swirling all around him, caressing him, licking at his skin like a tongue of fire, whispering to him that all he desired would soon be his. He closed his eyes and joined the others in a murmured chant that would aid the high priestess with her summoning spell.

"I beseech thee to appear before me, Beelzebub, without harm to me and those here gathered to worship thee."

All the times his mother had beseeched the Devil to appear, he'd never seen the Master. Not once. But he had felt his presence on many occasions, especially when his mother had made sacrifices. The mesmerizing smell of fresh blood always excited him, even as a child. His mother and the cult which she led had been true craftsmen, knowing the ancient ways and practicing black magic as occultists had done for thousands of years. This little group here in Cherokee Pointe were rank amateurs in comparison.

"If thy presence be not possible, then I ask for thee to pluck a messenger from the bottomless abyss and send it in thy stead. Choose a demon and allow him to appear before us in human form and through him we will glorify thee."

A hushed stillness filled the room. They waited. The candles flickered.

"Bring forth the sacrifice," the high priestess shouted.

A robed figure came forward, a bound goat in his arms, and laid the animal on a shiny metal altar.

His heartbeat accelerated, his body tightened with arousal. Excitement zinged through his veins.

"We make this offering to you, Divine Lucifer, Lord Abaddon. Come to us and imbue us with thy power."

His mouth watered, thirsting for the taste of the animal's blood as he closely watched the knife that performed the sacrificial deed. Once he had garnered all the strength he could from this ceremony and these Devil worshipers, he would return to his little victim, sleeping in his basement, waiting for him. At daybreak he could drink his fill of her life's blood. In only a few more hours, he would be one step closer to his ultimate goal.

Jazzy stood with Caleb McCord on the second-story stoop outside her apartment and smiled seductively at the stranger who had rescued her from Jamie. She couldn't remember ever being so immediately attracted to a man. Only common sense stopped her from making an utter fool of herself by inviting him to come in for a nightcap. She was pretty sure that if she invited Caleb in, he would wind up staying the night. God knew she wasn't ready for an affair, especially not with someone she'd just met. But offering the man a job at Jazzy's Joint was another matter entirely.

"If you're planning on staying in town for a while, I can give you a job," she said.

"What sort of job?" He leaned closer to her, his tall, lean frame blocking out everything else from her view.

"I'm going to fire my bouncer, if he ever shows up. I had planned to run an ad in the paper, but if you're interested—"

"I'll think about it."

"I'll need an answer by tomorrow."

"How about high noon? I'll stop by Jasmine's for lunch."

He was too close, his masculinity almost threatening. When he lowered his head, she held her breath, expecting a hard, possessive kiss. But instead he pressed his lips against her forehead. Tenderly. Then he ran the back of his hand gently over her cheek before he turned and walked down the stairs, leaving her in a state of sexual arousal.

Totally mystified by Caleb McCord, she unlocked the dead bolt and opened her front door. Suddenly she realized her phone was ringing. She hoped it wasn't Jamie! Damn.

She needed to get Caller ID on her home phone. After closing and locking the door, she hurried to the telephone and lifted the receiver. The dial tone trilled loudly in her ear.

Genny lay on the kitchen floor, the telephone gripped in her hand. It had taken every ounce of her strength, as well as assistance from Drudwyn, to make her way from the backyard and into the house. This latest vision had been more powerful than any she'd ever experienced, and the trauma of recognizing the killer's third victim had taken a severe toll on her, emotionally and physically.

She had placed a call to Jacob's apartment first and left a message on his answering machine, then she'd dialed the sheriff's office and was told by Tewanda that Jacob was out on a call.

"Tell him . . . tell him Misty is the next victim. I saw her."

"Lord have mercy," Tewanda had said. "I knew it. Misty's car has been found and—I'll radio Jacob right now and tell him you saw Misty."

"Tell him to come . . ." The telephone, too heavy for her to hold another minute, dropped from her grasp.

"Genny . . . Genny. Genny!"

Slightly addled and weak as a newborn kitten, she regained consciousness several minutes later. She managed to call Jazzy. She needed help. Now. But there was no answer.

Oh, God, what am I going to do?

Having used all her strength to make the phone call, Genny slumped to the floor. Holding on to the telephone, she stared at the touch-tone numbers. She wiggled her fingers, then tried her best to punch just one number. The moment she hit the first digit, she felt the black shadows swirling inside her head.

A robed figure carried Misty into a dark cavernous space and laid her on the ground. Genny felt Misty's fear. She also sensed the killer's excitement. A dim light came on, a flashlight to banish the darkness and illuminate the interior of an old barn.

The vision ended as quickly as it had begun, leaving Genny all but paralyzed there on her kitchen floor. She could barely move, so there was no way she could dial the phone again. Not for a while.

She closed her eyes and lay quietly, reserving what little strength she had to send a telepathic message.

Dallas. Dallas, I need you. Please, open up your heart and hear me. Come to me. Come to me now.

Chapter 14

Dallas left his rental car parked on the asphalt strip in front of the cabin, got out and headed for the front door. On the drive from Genny's house, he had tried to put her out of his mind. He was not going to become involved with a woman who claimed she possessed psychic abilities. During the remainder of his stay here in Cherokee Pointe, he planned to avoid Genny Madoc. That was the only sensible course of action. Being anywhere near her was far too tempting.

He unlocked the car door and just as he started to get out, an odd sensation made the hairs on the back of his neck stand up. Tensing, he waited a couple of seconds, then glanced in every direction, searching for any sign of another person or an animal that might have set off his inner radar. Nothing. Only a wintry breeze skimming over the treetops.

Once he opened his coat and jacket to make the gun in his hip holster easily accessible, he got out of the car. As he made his way to the front door, he kept a lookout for anything unusual. After unlocking the front door, he walked into the combination living room/kitchen of the one-bedroom, one-bath cabin that was within walking distance of downtown. No sooner had he closed and locked the door when another jolt of uneasiness pounded him.

What the hell is going on?

He always listened to his gut instincts because they seldom steered him wrong. And he often followed hunches that were actually educated guesses born from years of experience. But these vibes had nothing to do with gut instincts or hunches.

All of a sudden Dallas knew something was wrong with Genny. He didn't know how he knew—he just knew.

Get real, he told himself. How could you possibly know something like that?

A cold chill settled over Dallas when he heard Genny's voice inside his mind. He shook his head, trying to dislodge the words that kept repeating themselves over and over again. *I need you. Come to me.*

"You're losing your freaking mind," Dallas said aloud.

What he needed was a stiff drink and then a good night's sleep. He removed his overcoat and tossed it onto a nearby chair. Doing his best to disregard the sound of Genny's weak, whispered plea, he went into the bathroom, relieved himself, and washed his hands. Inadvertently he caught a glimpse of someone in the mirror over the sink. Snapping around, he looked behind him but saw no one. Then he looked back into the mirror and saw only his own reflection.

His heartbeat rumbled. He *was* losing his mind. For a split second he'd thought he saw Genny's face in the mirror.

Dallas went into the bedroom, sat on the side of the bed, and removed his boots. Try as he might, he couldn't shake the notion that something was wrong with Genny. She was in trouble and needed him.

Hell, just call her and check on her. If you don't, you won't get any sleep tonight.

He picked up the extension phone on the nightstand, then realized he didn't know Genny's number. Surely there was a phone book around here somewhere. He opened the nightstand drawer and found the only contents were a Bible and a phone book. He flipped through the pages and quickly zeroed in on the name Genevieve Madoc. After memorizing the number, he tossed the phone book aside and punched the correct digits.

For his effort he was rewarded with a singsong busy signal. Damn! Who was she talking to at this time of night?

Maybe she wasn't talking to anyone. Maybe the phone was off the hook. What if the killer had broken into Genny's house and when she tried to call for help, he'd knocked the telephone from her hand? Or what if she'd had another one of those nightmares that left her totally drained? If that was the case, then she might have tried to call for help and didn't have the strength to complete the call.

Dallas stuffed his feet into his boots, tromped into the living room, grabbed his coat, and headed out the door. On his way to his car, he managed to put on his coat and fish his keys out of his pants pocket.

Against his better judgment, against good common sense, he was going to drive back up the mountain tonight to make sure Genny was all right.

He gave her another injection, just a half dose this time, enough to keep her compliant until dawn. Moving her to the location he'd chosen for the sacrifice would be much easier with her unconscious. Besides, he didn't need her cooperation in order to derive pleasure from using her.

He had already placed the flashlights, his robe, and the sword in the trunk of his car, so all that was left to be done was transport Misty from the basement to the backseat.

When he lifted her and carried her across the room to where the unzipped body bag lay on the floor, he noticed her eyelashes flutter and knew she was semiconscious. Perhaps she was vaguely aware of what he was doing to her; perhaps not. All that mattered was that she be awake and alert at the moment of sacrifice.

He stuffed Misty into the bag and zipped it up, leaving only her face uncovered.

''Soon, my little lamb.''

In only a few hours she would become the third sacrifice, her blood strengthening him and adding to his power. Before the supreme moment of glory arrived, he had to energize himself to his fullest potential. Only by being at his optimum best could he hope to transfer the fifth victim's power into himself.

The lights were on in Genny's kitchen. Dallas wasn't sure if that was a good sign or a bad sign. After parking the car in the driveway, he bounded out the door and hit the ground running, toward the back of the house. The sight of the animals stopped him cold. Hovering near the back porch were two wolves. They stared at him as if they were deciding whether he was friend or foe. A barn owl flew over his head and perched on the porch roof.

From inside the house, Drudwyn howled. For a split second Dallas's heartbeat stilled.

Disregarding the wolves, Dallas raced onto the porch and through the partially open kitchen door. All he could think about was getting to Genny. If anything had happened to her . . .

She lay on the floor, curled in a fetal ball. Resting only inches from her, the telephone whined an off-the-hook warning. Dallas rushed to her, dropped to his knees, and lifted her in his arms. Drudwyn rose from where he lay beside Genny and moved out of the way. He watched and waited.

Genny opened her eyes and looked up at Dallas. ''You heard me. You listened to your heart.''

''Genny, what's wrong? Are you hurt?''

''Another vision,'' she told him. ''Must call Jacob. Now.'' Her fingers twitched.

''Damn!'' Dallas carried her through the house to her bedroom. All the while she kept telling him to call Jacob. Once he settled her on the bed, he sat down beside her, yanked his digital phone from its holder on his belt, and punched in the number for the Sheriff's Department.

Deputy Hardy answered. Dallas quickly informed her who

he was and that there was an emergency with Butler's cousin Genny.

"He's already on his way there now," Tewanda Hardy said. "How's Genny doing? I know how badly those visions drain her."

"Genny will be all right."

"You take good care of her, you hear."

"I intend to do just that."

Dallas replaced the receiver, then turned to Genny. He smoothed the flyaway strands of her jet black hair from her face and caressed her cheek.

"Is Jacob coming?" she asked.

"He's on his way." Dallas cupped Genny's chin between his thumb and forefinger. "How did Jacob know you needed him?"

"I'd called earlier and he wasn't there. I told . . ." Genny took several deep breaths. "I told Tewanda that I knew Misty Harte was the next victim." She lifted her hand as if it weighed a hundred pounds, then grasped the lapel of Dallas's overcoat. "If we can find her, we can save her."

Dallas put his hands on Genny's shoulders. "You lie here and rest. Can I get you anything? Water? Tea? Coffee? Something to eat."

A fragile smile formed on her lips. "I don't need anything . . . except you."

Her comment affected him in a way he didn't like. Hell, his actions tonight were totally out of character for him. Somehow he'd gotten swept up in all this craziness about Genny's visions. He wanted to help her, but in doing so, he didn't dare release his hold on reality. He had to continue thinking logically.

But for the time being, he simply sat beside Genny as she closed her eyes and rested. In what seemed like only minutes, he heard the roar of Jacob's truck. Then two sets of booted feet tapped through the house.

"Genny!" Jacob called. "Sloan, where are y'all?"

"Back here," Dallas replied. "In Genny's bedroom."

With Bobby Joe Harte on his heels, Jacob burst into the room. "Is she all right?"

"I'm fine," Genny said. "Just weak, as usual. But this time . . . oh, Jacob, I saw her. It was Misty. He has Misty."

Bobby Joe gripped the edge of the footboard of Genny's bed. "You saw Misty in one of your visions? You saw that the killer has her?"

Genny nodded. "If we can find her before dawn, we can save her."

"But how can we find her if we have no idea where he's taken her?" Bobby Joe asked.

Sitting on the opposite side of the bed from Dallas, Jacob reached out and took Genny's hand. "Is there more you can tell us? Anything that might give us a clue as to where she is?"

Dallas listened and watched in amazement. Was it possible that Genny really did possess psychic abilities? It seemed that everyone who knew her believed she did.

Genny clung to Jacob's hand. "He has taken her from the place he's been keeping her to an old barn. I couldn't make out much, except the barn is probably very, very old and terribly dilapidated."

"And probably abandoned," Jacob said.

"Do you know how many ramshackle old barns there are still standing in Cherokee County?" Bobby Joe asked. "There's got to be at least a dozen. Maybe more. And they're spread out all over the county."

"You're right," Jacob said. "It could take us half a day to make the rounds just to the barns we know about."

"You need to form a search party," Dallas suggested.

"Yeah, you're right." Jacob turned to Bobby Joe. "You think you can handle this, what with Misty being—"

"Just tell me what you want me to do."

"Have Tewanda call in all the deputies," Jacob said. "And have her phone Chief Watson and ask him to bring in all his people. Then tell her we need the Highway Patrol involved."

"I'll take care of it right now." Bobby Joe headed out

of the bedroom, but halted in the doorway. "What are you fixing to do, Sheriff?"

Jacob squeezed Genny's hand. "Do you think you've got the strength to come with me?"

She nodded. "If you'll carry me to your truck."

"What the hell's going on here?" Dallas asked. "She shouldn't be going anywhere. Look at her. Dammit, she needs a doctor."

"I don't need a doctor. I'll be all right in a few hours, but we can't wait that long before we start looking for Misty," Genny explained. "If I go with Jacob, I might be able to help him."

"How can you help him?" Dallas asked, but, God damn it, he knew her answer before she replied.

"With my gift of sight," she told him quite matter-of-factly.

"You aren't strong enough to—"

Genny cut Dallas off midsentence. "If you're concerned about me, then come with us." She turned her hand palm up and lifted it slowly toward him in a beseeching manner. "I need you. I can draw from your strength."

· Allowing himself a moment of sanity, Dallas inhaled and exhaled deeply. He had to make an immediate decision. Looking at Jacob, he said, "We'll ride with you." He reached down and lifted Genny up in his arms.

She laid her head on his chest so trustingly, then whispered, "Thank you."

As they made their way through the house, Jacob gave Bobby Joe last-minute instructions. "Contact Tewanda on your way back into town; she can get the ball rolling. Once she's gotten in touch with everyone, I want you to help her coordinate the search party. I'll let you know where we are and where the searchers should start."

"Want me to pick up Sally, or will you do that?" Bobby Joe asked.

"I'll stop by her place and get her and her hounds," Jacob replied.

Bobby Joe hurried outside, just ahead of the others, then

jumped into the patrol car and immediately made radio contact with Tewanda.

On the way out the back door, Dallas snatched Genny's black coat off the rack and tossed it over her. Within a couple of minutes, Jacob was behind the wheel of the big, brawny Dodge Ram, and Dallas held Genny in his arms on the passenger side.

Jacob leaned over, placed his hand on Genny's shoulder, and said, "Okay, *i gi do,* where do we begin?"

Genny closed her eyes. No one spoke. No one moved. The only sounds were three people breathing. And then somewhere off in the distance a wolf howled. Genny's eyelids flew open.

"He's moving her right now," Genny said as she lifted her head from Dallas's chest. "I see a long stretch of winding road. He's bringing her up the mountain." Genny sighed softly, then wilted against Dallas, seemingly exhausted.

Jacob rolled down his window and called out to Bobby Joe, "We need some roadblocks set up immediately. All the roads leading up the mountain." He rolled up the window and turned to Genny. "Anything else?"

"Dammit, can't you see she's totally worn out." Dallas glared at Jacob. "She can't take any more of this. Whatever goes on with her when she's doing whatever it is she does, it's sapping every ounce of her energy."

"East," Genny whispered. "Go east."

Ignoring Dallas's protective outburst, Jacob backed up, turned the truck around, and headed down the driveway directly behind Bobby Joe. The deputy went southwest, toward town. Jacob went in the opposite direction.

After a few minutes, Jacob cleared his throat. "We'll stop by Sally's. If we get anywhere close to Misty, those hounds of Sally's will pick up her scent."

"You'll need something that—" Dallas said.

"Got one of her blouses in a sack back there." Jacob nodded toward the backseat. "Bobby Joe picked it up at her house while he was there this evening. That boy's always thinking ahead."

Genny's small, delicate body lay cocooned in Dallas's arms. She was a delicious weight against him. Her heat seeped through their clothing to warm him. Hadn't it been less than an hour ago that he had promised himself he'd steer clear of this woman?

But he could no more stay away from her than he could stop breathing. And for the life of him he couldn't figure out why she had such a hold over him. Maybe it was because he was beginning to buy into her psychic hoodoo. If Genny was right, if her predictions were accurate, they might catch a killer tonight. Possibly Brooke's killer.

But for the first time in eight months—since Brooke's death—something else had suddenly become as important to him as finding the man who had killed his niece. Protecting Genny. If he had to choose between Genny's safety and apprehending Brooke's murderer, what would he do? A few days ago there would have been no choice to make. But that was before Genevieve Madoc cast her spell on him.

Chapter 15

He parked on the dirt road and turned off his headlights. There was little chance that anyone would come along this time of the morning and spot his vehicle, but it paid not to take chances. The barn was a good fifty feet from the over-grown lane. One day while driving around the area last autumn, he'd found this place and mentally marked it down for future reference. An abandoned building out in the middle of nowhere. A perfect place for the ceremony.

It would help if there was more moonlight, but he would make do with the flashlights. At dawn he would open the barn doors to let in the morning sunshine. Anticipation zinged through his veins, giving him an adrenaline rush. Victim three. He was getting closer and closer. The very thought of what was to come exhilarated him. He popped the trunk, checked on Misty to make sure she was still unconscious, then lifted his black hooded robe and slipped it on. He took out the wooden box containing the sword, stuck it under his arm, and picked up the large flashlight he'd need to make his way to the barn.

Although it was a cold night and remnants of ice and snow still lingered in various spots, he barely felt the frigid night air. He was strong . . . and growing stronger with each new sacrifice. It was only a matter of time until he became invincible.

He took the vinyl boots from the trunk and slipped them over his shoes. Next he pulled on a pair of thick gloves. The shoes he wore were Italian leather and he had no intention of ruining them in the night dampness that coated the earth or in any muddy slush lingering after the snow melted.

Making his way slowly but surely, he crossed the open field. When he reached the barn, he opened the rickety wooden doors. As they parted to reveal the murky interior, their hinges creaked and moaned. But who would hear the mournful wail? He shined the flashlight right and left, back and front. The vast space was mostly empty, except for a set of weathered wooden sawhorses that he'd found in the loft the first time he'd explored the old barn. He placed the box containing his sword on a rotting wooden trough. Shining the flashlight down at the ground, he found it moist beneath his feet. He shined the light upward and noted that part of the ceiling was missing and the rest looked as if it might come tumbling down at any time.

He moved first one sawhorse, then the other into place directly in front of the two large doors, then retrieved the half-inch piece of plywood that he'd left here yesterday. Laying the plywood atop the two sawhorses, he created a perfectly functional altar.

After checking his watch and noting that it was nearly four o'clock, he trudged back to the car to retrieve the most necessary item for this morning's ceremony—the sacrifice.

Jacob wasn't a religious man, but he'd been doing his share of praying tonight. Everything that could be done was being done, but it might not be enough. City, county, and state law enforcement officers were spread out over the mountain, which covered countless miles and endless acres. All the local members of the search party tried to remember every old barn in the area. Jacob knew it could take a couple of days to check out all the barns in Cherokee County. Genny and Jacob agreed that the barn where the killer had taken Misty was empty, probably abandoned, yet they also knew they could be wrong. Genny would be the first to admit that her visions weren't always one hundred percent accurate, that she was not infallible.

Their group now consisted of not only Genny, Dallas, and himself, but Sally and her hounds, Peter and Paul, as well as half a dozen lawmen—Bobby Joe and Tim Willingham, two of his deputies; three Cherokee Pointe policemen; and one highway patrolman. During the past few hours, they had found and searched three barns east of Genny's house. Two were unused and empty; one belonged to a retired farmer who stored his old tractor inside.

They kept in radio contact with the other groups—five in all—and so far they'd come up empty-handed. As they pulled off the road alongside the fence that skirted the old Wells farm and the two other vehicles parked behind his truck, Jacob checked his watch. Four-fifty. Time was running out. It would be dawn in less than two hours. If they didn't find Misty soon, it would be too late.

He tried not to think about Misty as his lover, tried not to remember that she was Bobby Joe's sister, but the fact that she meant something to both of them wouldn't leave his mind. Twenty-four hours ago they'd had sex. Rollicking, raunchy, good-time sex. He didn't love Misty, and sometimes she got on his last nerve. But she was a good ole gal who'd never hurt a living soul. The very thought that some maniac planned to slit her wide open and drink her blood enraged Jacob. But he didn't have time to waste on emotions.

Jacob got out and met the other team members who gathered around near the hood of his truck. Sally Talbot opened the back door and dragged herself out of the backseat, then whistled for Peter and Paul. Both hundred-pound dogs bounded from the truck bed and came straight to their mistress. After grabbing hold of their leashes, she scanned the area with her aged but still sharp eyes. She puckered her lips, spit, and wiped her mouth. Dallas emerged from the cab, then lifted Genny out and onto her feet. He kept his arm securely around her waist and when, after she'd taken a few steps, she faltered, he swung her up into his arms.

Jacob turned to Genny. "Are you picking up on anything?"

With her arm around Dallas Sloan's neck, she stared out into the darkness, at the shadowy outline of the old barn. "There's someone inside."

"God Almighty," Bobby Joe cried out. "Is it Misty? Have we found her?"

"I-I don't know. I can't be sure." Genny's voice quivered.

Jacob looked right at Dallas. "Put her back in the truck and stay here with her."

Dallas nodded.

"We're going in," Jacob said. "Sally, you wait here. Keep Peter and Paul quiet for the time being. The rest of you spread out. I want the barn surrounded. I'll go in alone. Does everyone understand?" When no one contradicted him, he added, "And whatever the hell y'all do, be careful."

Jacob had lost track of how many rescue missions he'd been a part of during his years as a SEAL. He might lack training as a sheriff, but he was an expert when it came to going in after a hostage.

As he drew close to the barn, he motioned his team into place. He leaned his back against the north wall and listened. Silence. While the others secured the perimeter, Jacob circled the barn, and he found the doors at the back of the barn missing. Silently, he crept inside. With his weapon drawn and his flashlight in his hand, he kept his back to the wall. He switched on the flashlight and searched the interior, moving the beam slowly as he checked things out.

When the beam of light hit a bundle on the ground, Jacob moved in. Cautiously. The bundle grunted and rolled over. When the light hit the man's face, his eyelids flew open and he yelped as if in pain. Jacob didn't recognize the man, but he could tell from his ragged clothes, matted hair, and dirty face that he was probably a bum, a drifter who had sought shelter for the night.

"I ain't done nothing wrong," the man hollered as he rose to his feet and put his hands over his head. "Don't shoot, mister. I'm harmless. I swear."

"Keep your hands over your head," Jacob instructed.

"Yes sir." The man placed both hands on top of his head.

"Come on in," Jacob called to the others. "It's not Misty. It's just a drifter." Jacob focused on the trembling man. "What's your name?"

"Curry Hovater."

"Where are you from, Curry?"

"I move around a lot. I've lived in Kingsport and Bristol and Johnson City."

"Have you been here alone all night?"

"Yes sir, I sure have. Just me and the mice."

"Willingham," Jacob called to his deputy. "Take Mr. Hovater with you. And when we go back into town, get him some breakfast from Jasmine's and then put him on the next bus out of town."

While the others stood around watching Jacob, waiting for his orders, he turned his back on them and shut his eyes for just a minute. He wanted to pound his fists against the walls and tear this ramshackle barn to pieces. Hell! He had thought maybe they'd find Misty alive in this old barn.

He turned toward the men and barked out a command: "Let's get moving. We've still got a lot of territory to cover."

As they made their way around a sharp curve in the winding mountain road, every nerve in Genny's body came to full alert, but she couldn't manage to open her eyes. She had spent endless hours concentrating on finding Misty, using every ounce of her strength to keep her senses alert and active. This was the first time in her life she had forced herself to remain connected for so many hours to the forces that powered her sixth sense. The darkness kept trying to suck her in, but she fought tirelessly to keep herself safe.

Great evil lurked nearby. She sensed its presence. Cruel and malevolent. Close. So close.

"Stop the truck!" Genny cried as she opened her eyes and lifted her head from Dallas's shoulder.

Jacob skidded to an abrupt halt in the middle of the road. Bobby Joe came within inches of ramming into the back end of the truck as he slammed on his brakes.

"What's wrong? Are you all right?" Dallas clamped his hand down on her shoulder.

"Are you sensing something?" Jacob asked.

"He's somewhere close by."

"Misty and the killer?" Dallas asked.

Genny nodded.

Jacob glanced through the windshield at the surrounding area. "This is the opposite end of the county from where I grew up, and I'm not as familiar with it so I don't know if there might be an abandoned barn around here or not. Genny, can you tell us if they're still inside a barn?"

Genny's breath caught in her throat when she noticed a faint glow in the eastern horizon. Dawn was fast approaching. "I don't know. I can't see." Genny grasped Jacob's arm. "Find them. Find them now or it will be too late."

Once again the entire entourage gathered at Jacob's truck, but this time Genny insisted on going with them. Dallas supported her with his arm around her waist.

"Anybody know of an old barn around here anywhere?" Jacob asked.

No one responded for a couple of minutes, then finally Jess Whitaker, a Cherokee Pointe police officer said, "If I remember right, from when my brothers and I used to go hunting on this side of the county, there was a really old barn that was falling apart twenty years ago somewhere around here. I can't remember where exactly."

"Okay. Sally, it's time to let Peter and Paul see if they can pick up Misty's scent."

Sally pulled Misty's blouse out of the sack Jacob had

given her earlier. She let the bloodhounds get a good sniff, then released them.

"We'll follow the dogs," Jacob said. "The rest of you spread out and start searching for that damn barn."

Genny tried to keep up, but she simply couldn't. When she halted, totally exhausted, she turned to Dallas.

"Y'all go on without us," Dallas called to Jacob and Sally, who were already a good piece ahead of them, following Peter and Paul. "I'll take care of Genny."

"The dogs picked up Misty's scent, didn't they?" she asked.

"Yeah, I think they might have."

She glanced toward the east. The first tentative glimmer of daylight colored the dark sky. "Oh, Dallas. It's already dawn." She slumped against him, needing his comfort, seeking his strength.

Off in the distance she heard Sally's hounds howling. Mournful cries that sent cold chills up her spine. And then the sound of car and truck doors slamming and loud voices—numerous voices—echoed through the open fields. As if coming from out of nowhere a band of men appeared, marching up the road, their lanterns and flashlights illuminating the area like fireflies on a warm summer night.

Genny realized that these men had emerged from their parked vehicles and were headed toward her. In the dawn light and at a distance, she couldn't make out any faces. "What's going on? Who are all those people?"

"Hell if I know, but none of them are in uniform."

As the group of boisterous men approached, Genny immediately recognized the one leading the pack—Jerry Lee Todd. He was shouting loud enough to be heard in the next county.

"There they are!" Jerry Lee broke into a run, coming straight toward Genny and Dallas. "We're at the right place. Jacob's gotta be around here somewhere."

"Hell!" Dallas murmured a few choice curses under his breath. "Looks like a lynch mob to me. Who's the idiot leading them?"

"That idiot is our beloved mayor, Jerry Lee Todd. His wife was Cindy Todd, the second victim."

"Then he's not thinking straight," Dallas said. "He's probably half out of his mind. And one thing's for sure— he doesn't have the slightest idea that what he's doing could jeopardize Jacob's chances of capturing the killer."

Before Genny could respond, Jerry Lee reached them, and his army of vigilante citizens halted only a few feet behind him.

Jerry Lee glanced from Genny to Dallas. "When I heard about Misty, I formed a group of locals to help in the search. Is Jacob here? Have y'all found Misty?"

"How did y'all get past the roadblocks?" Dallas asked.

"I'm the mayor of Cherokee Pointe," Jerry Lee said as if that was explanation enough.

"Get these men quiet," Dallas said. "If you're in charge of this pack of yapping morons, then take control of them. Jacob and his men are handling the situation and don't need your assistance." When Jerry Lee stared at Dallas, eyes wide and mouth agape, Dallas added in a deadly calm voice, "Do it now."

"Hey, fellows, quiet down," Jerry Lee called to the others, then turned back to Dallas. "Well, have they or have they not found Misty?"

Although so weak she could barely walk, Genny took several steps toward Jerry Lee, then reached out and laid her hand on his arm. "You shouldn't be here. You know that, don't you?"

"I've got a right to help track down Cindy's killer. I've got every right—"

Genny squeezed Jerry Lee's arm. "Let Jacob and the other lawmen handle this."

Jerry Lee jerked away from Genny. "Where's Jacob?"

Dallas gripped Jerry Lee's shoulder. "Jacob and the men with him are doing their job."

"There's a deserted old barn around here somewhere," a voice called out. "I'll bet that's where Misty is. And wherever she is, that's where we'll find our killer!"

Recognizing the voice, Genny snapped her gaze around to seek out the speaker. Jamie Upton, looking rakishly handsome in his designer jeans, expensive leather coat, and Italian loafers, made his way through the rumbling posse.

"I say we follow the sound of those howling dogs," Jamie said. He eyed Genny. "Those are Sally's bloodhounds, aren't they?"

"What all of you need to do is go home and let the law handle this," Dallas said.

"And who are you?" Jamie inquired.

Dallas glared at Jamie.

Another familiar voice rang out loud and clear. "He's FBI Special Agent Dallas Sloan," Royce Pierpont said.

Genny's gaze connected with Royce's. He smiled at her. She couldn't understand what Jamie Upton was doing with this group, but seeing Royce with them surprised her even more. Apparently Royce had been dragged from bed to join in, because despite his impeccable attire—from cashmere overcoat to a pair of Italian loafers similar to Jamie's—his hair was mussed and he needed a shave.

Genny supposed Jerry Lee must have contacted every man in Cherokee Pointe and probably implied that anyone who didn't join his little search party would have his masculinity called into question.

"If you're a Fed, why aren't you with Jacob and the others?" Jerry Lee asked Dallas.

"Because I know Sheriff Butler and his men can handle this job without any interference from me . . . or from anyone else."

Genny's gaze traveled over the entire group of men, one man at a time. There wasn't a face in the crowd of about twenty-five that she didn't recognize. Farmers, mechanics, and truck drivers. Mail carriers, sanitation workers, and teachers. Dillon Carson; Reverend Stowe; Dr. MacNair; and even Brian MacKinnon.

Had the entire male population of Cherokee County simultaneously gone crazy? The local citizens were in a panic now that they knew a third victim had been kidnapped; and

God only knew how this pack would react if Misty was found dead.

Genny caught a glimpse of Brian just as he moved away from the others, took his cell phone out of his pocket, and began talking rapidly. She suspected what he was doing. Calling in a story to his newspaper. And probably sending for a news crew from WMMK.

Jacob knew time had run out, but he tried not to think about it; tried to hang on to the possibility that they weren't too late to save Misty. As they reached the barn, the sun peeked over the mountain crest. Surrounded by brilliant pink and purple offshoots spreading across the eastern horizon like floating liquid, the upper curve of the fiery ball banished the darkness. Jacob's gut knotted painfully as he approached the crumbling structure that had once been a barn. The others spread out around the site, circling the weathered wooden bones of the building. Sally's dogs had found what they'd been sent to find. Howling their success, they stood alongside their prey. The double barn doors hung open, like a mouth frozen in a dying scream. With his gun drawn, Jacob moved closer to the entrance. What he saw stopped him immediately. He shut his eyes for an instant, praying that he hadn't seen what he thought he had.

He opened his eyes. Misty Harte's naked body lay sprawled out on top of a makeshift altar that was nothing more than a couple of sawhorses topped with a piece of plywood. Even from ten feet away, he could see the blood and gore. Hell, he could smell the blood. Fresh blood.

God damn it! Bile rose to his throat. He took several tentative steps forward, then paused. Think straight, he told himself. There's nothing you can do for Misty now. The killer might still be here. Don't forget your training just because the woman lying there ripped apart from breasts to pubic bone is someone you screwed only hours before she was abducted.

After making a clean sweep inside the dilapidated structure and finding no one else there, Jacob called his men. When Bobby Joe approached the open barn doors, Jacob grabbed his arm to stop him.

"You don't want to see," Jacob said.

"Yes, I do. I gotta see." Bobby Joe pulled free and rushed into the barn.

Tim Willingham came over to Jacob. "Is it Misty?"

Jacob nodded.

Bobby Joe let out a piercing yell and dropped to his knees beside the altar. Every man in their group stood perfectly still and remained silent, each one knowing how he'd feel if the victim had been his sister.

Jacob forced himself to do what had to be done. He radioed the other units to notify them Misty had been found. Found too late. And he had to tell them that the killer had escaped. Then he ordered a forensics team to get to the site ASAP.

He'd have to keep the crime scene as pure as possible, but before he secured the site, he had to take care of Bobby Joe.

Just as he put his hand on his deputy's shoulder, Sally called out to him. "The boys have picked up a scent."

Jacob snapped his head around and looked directly at the old woman. "The killer's scent?"

"Could be," she said. "They're heading out the other side of the barn. Best we follow them before they get too far ahead of us."

Chapter 16

Erin Mercer roused from sleep and wondered what had awakened her. Then she heard someone pounding on the door of her rental cabin. Who in the world would be out and about at this time of the morning? She opened her eyes, turned her head, and, without her glasses, tried to make out the numbers on her digital clock. Farsightedness was a curse of people over forty-five and she had passed that birthday four years ago. The insistent pounding continued. Erin forced herself into a sitting position, dragged the clock closer so she could see the face, and realized it was almost seven o'clock. An ungodly hour for a woman who seldom rose before eleven.

By the time she dragged herself out of bed, donned her robe, and made it into the living room, she heard a deep male voice bellowing.

"Erin, dammit, woman, are you in there?" Big Jim Upton shouted loud enough to wake the dead.

What was Jim doing here? Why was he so upset? Since the beginning of their affair, he'd seldom visited her more than a few times each week, and never in the mornings.

"Are you in there? Are you all right?" Fright deepened Jim's already robust baritone voice.

Hurrying across the room, she called, "I'm here, Jim. And I'm just fine."

She undid the lock and jerked open the door. Without saying another word, Jim lifted her off her feet in a bear hug and kissed her so soundly that he cut off her breath for several seconds. When he ended the kiss, he set her on her feet, and, keeping a tight hold about her waist, walked her backward into the cabin. Lifting his big booted foot, he slammed the door shut.

He cupped her face with his large, weathered hands. "The killer has struck again. He kidnapped Misty Harte, a waitress at Jasmine's. Jerry Lee gathered up a group of men to help the lawmen scour the countryside looking for her."

Erin placed her hands over his. "And you came to check on me because you were worried about me. Afraid I might be next."

He flung off her hands and released his tender hold on her face, then grabbed her hand and gazed into her eyes. "I just found you, honey. I couldn't bear it if I lost you so soon."

She squeezed his hand. "You aren't going to lose me."

"Yeah, I will. One of these days you'll look at me and see an old man, then move on to greener pastures."

"You're being ridiculous." She stood on tiptoe to plant a quick kiss on his lips. "I happen to be in love with you, Jim Upton. Haven't you figured that out yet?"

Jim shook his head, then speared his fingers through his thick white hair. "I'm too damn old for you. I'm old enough to be your daddy."

"If people knew about us, they'd think you're my sugar daddy."

Jim grinned. "Shows you what people know."

"How'd you get away from the house so early in the morning? Won't Reba wonder where you are?"

"I left a note. Explained that I would probably join up with the search team Jerry Lee had put together."

"You said another woman has come up missing. Does the killer have her? Is—is she dead?"

Jim nodded. Erin could tell something else was bothering her lover, something more than his concern about her safety. From the first moment she met him—in, of all places, church—she'd felt drawn to the big, gruff man with the beautiful blue eyes. He was twenty-five years older than she and married. She'd never fooled around with a married man. Not ever. And if she had waited for him to make the first move, she'd still be waiting. She had immediately decided to learn everything she could about him, and deliberately set about running into him wherever he went. She couldn't explain exactly why, but she'd wanted him in a way she hadn't wanted anything or anyone in a long time. People might think she was after his money, but she wasn't. She didn't need Big Jim's fortune. She had a sizable fortune of her own, a trust fund from her grandfather since she was twenty-one. That wealth had allowed her to pursue her dream of being a painter. But here she was, nearly fifty, and success in her chosen field still eluded her.

"Come on in and sit down." Erin led the way to the sofa. She sat, then patted the cushion beside her. Jim eased his big frame down on the plaid couch. "What's wrong?" she asked.

"I told you—with a killer on the loose, I'm worried about you living here all alone." He reached out and lifted a strand of her hair and curved it around her ear.

She loved the way he couldn't keep his hands off her. Whenever they were together, he was always touching her, as if that simple act gave him immeasurable pleasure. He'd touch her hair, her face, her hands. And when he made love to her, he didn't leave an inch of her body untouched. He was the most considerate, caring lover she'd ever had.

"Jim, we might not have known each other for very long, but I've become acquainted with your moods well enough to know when something is bothering you." She caressed his cheek. "If you need someone to talk to, I'm here. Talk to me."

He closed his eyes, and a look of pure agony strained his features. Erin's heart jumped into overdrive. That terrible look of pain on his face scared her.

"My Lord, Jim, what is it?"

He slumped forward, braced his elbows on his thighs and rested his chin against his cupped hands. "I want you to tell me that I'm crazy for even suspecting . . . I feel that just thinking what I'm thinking is wrong. How can I believe him capable of anything so horrible?"

She laid her hand on Jim's back and rubbed comfortingly. "You aren't making any sense. What are you talking about? Who do you suspect of what?"

"Jamie." Jim bounded up off the sofa, turned, and looked right at Erin. "He didn't come home again last night. I have no idea where the hell he was. I figured he was with Jazzy or with some other woman. But now I'm not so sure."

"Your grandson didn't come home last night, so you suspect he might have been doing what?"

Jim grabbed her hands and jerked her to her feet, then looked pointedly into her eyes. "Tell me I'm wrong. Tell me . . . Jamie didn't come home last night, and a woman was killed. I heard the news on the radio just as I drove up out front that they'd found her dead."

"The waitress was murdered just like the other two women?"

Jim nodded. "When Susie Richards was killed, Jamie wasn't at the house that night, and he'd been home less than forty-eight hours. And he wasn't at home the night Cindy Todd was murdered. And now—"

"Oh, Lord, Jim, you aren't saying . . . you can't believe—"

"God knows I don't want to think what I'm thinking, but I've known for a long time that that boy is no good. But I never dreamed he was capable of . . . I can't believe he could kill those women, but . . . what if he is the killer?"

Erin wrapped her arms around Big Jim and whispered soothingly, "Jamie didn't kill those women. Good or bad, he's your grandson. He wouldn't be capable of cold-blooded murder.''

When Jim trembled, she knew he was weeping silently. She held him all the tighter and loved him all the more.

By the time the forensics team arrived and began going over the crime scene, at least a hundred people, other than the citizens' search party Jerry Lee had formed, lined the road and congregated in the field. Reporters from the *Cherokee Pointe Herald* were hurling questions right and left; and a news crew from WMMK kept trying to get closer to the old barn. Jacob had sent Tim Willingham to take Bobby Joe home. He could only imagine how difficult it would be for him to tell their mama that Misty was dead.

As much as he wanted to send Genny home—God, she looked totally beat—he needed her here for as long as she could endure delving into that secret place she went when she used her gift of sight. Sally's old bloodhounds had tracked the killer's scent several yards behind the barn, then suddenly started acting peculiar. Immediately Sally had realized they were sick, and it hadn't taken her long to figure out why.

''Our killer's a damn clever boy.'' Sally bent down and rubbed first Peter's head and shoulders, then Paul's. ''He's tried to poison my dogs. I'll need some help getting them to Doc Swain.'' She shook her head. ''They ain't gonna be of no more use to you this morning.''

While Jacob and a couple of deputies helped load the two dogs into the back of a deputy's SUV, Sally explained that the killer had probably mixed arsenic with some chemical fertilizer, more than likely some old stuff left over in the barn, then added water—more than enough melted snow puddles all around—and produced a slow yielding gas. He'd spread the mixture along his path a few yards from the barn.

''My guess is he heard Peter and Paul howling and had to think quick on his feet,'' Sally had said. ''He's smart enough to know that sniffing that gas would mess up the boys' sense of smell and stop them from following him.''

With Peter and Paul out of commission, he had no choice but to rely completely on Genny.

"I want to see Misty's body," Genny requested.

"No way," Jacob told her.

"Please. I need to see the body. I'm sensing something very strong coming from nearby."

Reluctantly, Jacob agreed to her request. He and Dallas escorted her to within twenty feet of Misty's body. She looked on while the forensics team went about their job. With a pained expression on her face, Genny studied the murder scene, taking special note of Misty's mutilated corpse.

"No . . . no . . . oh, no . . ." Dallas caught Genny when she collapsed. Cushioned in Dallas's arms, she opened her eyes, looked at Jacob and said, "He's still here. Close by. Watching."

"How can you be sure?" Dallas asked.

"He's communicating with me."

"What?"

Jacob placed his hand over her mouth. "Don't," he said. "It's too dangerous."

"Tell me what the hell is going on?" Dallas demanded.

Jacob lifted his hand from Genny's mouth. "She's purposely making telepathic contact with the killer," Jacob said, then focused on Genny. "Stop it. Right now. It's too dangerous for you."

"He's laughing," she said. "Laughing at you, at everyone, because he knows you can't catch him." She grasped Jacob's arm. "He's singing—inside his mind. He keeps singing, 'you can't catch me.' He's so . . . happy."

"Get her the hell away from here," Jacob told Dallas. "Take her home. Call Jazzy to come help you. And make sure she doesn't try to contact the killer again."

Jacob could tell by the concerned look on Dallas Sloan's face that he would take good care of Genny, but Jacob could also tell that Dallas was confused. He was still an unbeliever. But not for long.

"You need me here," Genny whispered, so weak she could barely talk.

"Go. Now." Jacob barked out the order. He tossed Dallas his keys. "Take my truck. I'll catch a ride later."

Dallas didn't hesitate. He carried Genny across the open field and straight toward Jacob's Dodge Ram.

With Genny out of harm's way, Jacob called over several of his deputies and told them to collect every lawman still on the scene and begin a thorough search of the woods surrounding the barn. He hesitated a moment, then added, "And make a sweep through the crowd. Anybody who looks suspicious, I want to talk to him."

Dallas slid Genny onto the front seat and started to close the passenger door, but Royce Pierpont suddenly appeared and before Dallas could stop him, he peered into the truck cab and spoke to Genny.

"Sweetheart, are you all right?" Royce asked.

"She's tired and I'm taking her home," Dallas said.

"Yes, yes, you must take her home so she can rest." Royce sighed. "Using her abilities drains her terribly. Poor little darling."

"Move, please." Dallas forced himself to be polite for Genny's sake. "I need to close the door."

"Oh, sorry." He didn't budge an inch. "I was wondering, if it wouldn't be too much trouble, could y'all give me a lift?"

"We're not going into town," Dallas replied.

"Oh, just take me down the road a bit. My car's parked along the roadside about a mile from here."

Dallas eyed Pierpont quizzically.

"I left it there when I met up with a couple of other men in their vehicle. We didn't see any need to take two cars."

"Of course, you may go with us," Genny said.

Dallas bristled. Royce Pierpont opened the back door and hopped into the truck.

Several minutes later they reached Pierpont's Lexus on the roadside. He thanked them for the ride, got out of the truck, and hurried to his car. Dallas started to leave, but when he didn't hear the Lexus's motor come to life, he glanced out the window and noticed the car's headlights were on. Had that idiot gone off and left his lights on? If so, his battery was probably dead.

After several minutes Pierpont emerged from his car, tossed up his arms in a what-do-you-think-about-that? gesture and came back to the truck.

"Guess my battery's dead," he said. "Mind if I go on with y'all to Genny's place?"

Before Dallas could reply, Genny said, "No, we don't mind at all."

"I could give you a jump-start," Dallas suggested. "I'm sure Jacob's got some jumper cables somewhere here in the truck."

"No, no, don't bother," Royce said. "You need to get Genny home as soon as possible. I'll catch a ride into town with Jacob later. I'm sure he'll stop by to check on Genny."

Dallas grimaced, but didn't respond. Once again, for Genny's sake, he'd force himself to be polite. Even if it killed him.

Genny slept all the way home, so when they arrived at her house, she awoke the minute Dallas lifted her out of Jacob's truck and the cold air hit her in the face.

Dallas smiled at her. "Feeling better?"

"Some."

"I'm taking you inside, putting you to bed, and then fixing you some breakfast." He slammed the passenger door. "Do you want me to call Jazzy?"

"If you'll stay with me, I won't need her."

Royce leapt out of the backseat and slammed the door.

"I'll be happy to stay here with Genny if you need to go back and help Jacob."

"I don't think the sheriff needs my help," Dallas said. Ignoring Royce, he headed for the back porch.

Genny called out to Royce, "Please come in and stay until Jacob stops by for his truck."

Dallas growled.

"I'm sure it won't be that long until Jacob comes by," she whispered to Dallas.

"It had better not be."

Genny cuddled closer to the warmth of Dallas's big, strong body. "I can't be inhospitable," she murmured softly.

Dallas grunted.

"If Jacob doesn't come by in a bit, I'll call into town to Pilkington's Garage as soon as they open," Royce said, following closely behind. He had to walk fast to keep up with Dallas's long-legged gait. "I must admit that I'm pretty unnerved myself by all these killings."

Dallas tromped onto the porch, unlocked the door, and carried Genny into the kitchen. Drudwyn lumbered toward them. He sniffed Dallas and licked Genny's hand that she held down to him.

"Go on out, boy," Genny said.

Drudwyn headed to the open back door, then halted when he saw Royce. The bristles on his back raised and he growled.

"That dog doesn't like me," Royce said. "He growls at me every time I visit Genny."

"Behave yourself," Genny warned Drudwyn. "Royce is a guest in our house."

Royce gave Drudwyn a wide path, staying in a corner of the porch until after Drudwyn raced out into the yard; then he entered the kitchen.

Dallas didn't say anything. He simply carried Genny through the house and straight to her bedroom. When he laid her on her bed, he stacked one pillow on top of the other and helped her into a semi-sitting position.

"You stay here and rest while I get us some breakfast. What would you like to eat?" he asked.

"I'm really not very hungry. Maybe just some tea . . . or coffee, if you prefer."

"You're eating something."

"Then just a slice of toast."

"If you need anything—"

"I'll be fine."

Dallas turned to leave her bedroom and nearly bumped into Royce, who stood in the doorway.

"You go right on in the kitchen and get Genny's toast and tea," Royce said. "I'll keep her company."

"Genny needs to rest," Dallas told him.

"I won't disturb her." Royce looked to her for confirmation. "Will I, Genny?"

"No, of course not," she said, when what she really wanted was for Royce to leave. She didn't need or want anyone—except Dallas.

"Go on," Royce said. "You're leaving her in good hands."

Dallas grumbled under his breath. Genny thought she picked up on a couple of less than gentlemanly comments.

The moment Dallas disappeared down the hall, Royce pulled the cane-bottom, ladder-back chair from her dressing table and placed it beside her bed. He plopped down in the chair, then leaned closer.

"Special Agent Sloan is acting quite proprietorial around you," Royce said. "Should I be jealous?"

"You and I are friends. Brian and I are friends. And Dallas and I are—"

"More than friends."

"No, not exactly. We're not really even friends, but I'm not sure how I would define our relationship." Genny sighed. "I am not going to discuss how I feel about Dallas with you."

Genny burrowed her head and shoulders deeper into the soft goose-down pillows. She desperately needed rest. At this precise moment she felt as if she could sleep for days. She yawned. Her eyelids drooped.

"I'm bothering you, aren't I?" Royce gazed longingly at Genny.

"No, of course not. But you understand how tired I am after one of my visions or after I've used the other powers that I inherited from Granny. I used my gift repeatedly while we were searching for Misty."

"That poor woman."

"We came so close to saving her."

"And catching the killer."

"He was out there, you know," Genny said. "Afterward. Watching Jacob and the others. Watching me."

"Yes, I know."

Genny's gaze locked with Royce's. "What do you mean, you know?" she asked.

"You're aware that my sixth-sense abilities are very limited. Nothing to compare to yours," Royce said. "I've told you about how I've always had a keen intuition and sometimes I sense things are going to happen before they do. And I've had a few very unclear visions in my life. But this morning—"

"What are you trying to tell me?" Genny rose to a sitting position.

"I—I think I had a vision. Early this morning, not long before I heard about Jerry Lee putting together a team to help search for Misty Harte," Royce explained. "It was either a powerful dream or a real vision. I saw you out in an open field. You were with Jacob and Agent Sloan. And I saw a man's dark figure lurking in the woods. He was watching . . . watching you, Genny."

Genny held out her hand to Royce, who rose from the chair, took her hand, and sat down on the edge of the bed.

"The dream . . . the vision frightened me because . . . because I sensed that this man wanted you, Genny. He wanted to harm you."

Tears gathered in Royce's eyes. Genny put her arms around him and hugged him to her. "It's all right. I'm fine. Nothing's going to happen to me. I have Jacob and Dallas to look out for me."

Dallas burst into the room, a cup of hot tea in one hand. "What the hell's going on here?"

Royce jumped straight up on his feet and all but trembled in front of Dallas.

"Royce was upset and I was comforting him."

"What's he upset about?" Dallas asked, his voice a husky growl.

"Royce has possessed some mild sixth-sense abilities since he was a child," Genny said. "It's something we have in common, one of the things that helped form our friendship."

"And?" Dallas glowered at Royce as he bent down and handed Genny her tea.

Smiling at Dallas, she accepted the mug. "Royce had a dream vision early this morning. He saw the killer's shadow. And saw the killer watching me while I stood in an open field with you and Jacob."

"A dream vision, huh?" Dallas grunted. "Nice that you two have something in common."

"Look, I think maybe I should go. I can call around and see if there's another service station besides Pilkington's that might already be open and can send someone by here to pick me up and take me to my car and get it running." Royce edged his way around the room, avoiding getting anywhere near Dallas.

Dallas slid his hand into his pants pocket and scooped out a set of car keys, which he tossed to Royce. "Here, take my rental car and drive yourself into town. Just leave the car parked in front of Jasmine's and give Jazzy the keys. I'll pick it up later."

Royce clutched the keys in his hand. "Sure thing. And thanks." He carefully steered closer and closer to the bedroom door. "I'll just let myself out. Genny, you rest. I'll call later and check on you."

"You don't have to go," Genny told him.

Royce looked at Dallas. Dallas frowned.

"Yes, I think I do have to go." He avoided eye contact with Dallas as he all but ran from Genny's bedroom.

"You scared him," Genny said. "You shouldn't have intimidated Royce that way."

"Drink your tea. I have bacon frying and eggs to scramble."

"Don't change the subject."

"That guy is a phony. He's faking it. He isn't any more psychic than I am. He's fed you a line of bull because he wants to get in your pants."

Genny gasped, then laughed. "Dallas Sloan, you're jealous."

"So, maybe I am." Dallas shrugged. "I've got to check on the bacon before it burns."

When he headed for the door, Genny called, "You think Royce is a phony. Do you think I'm a phony, too?"

He paused in the doorway, his back to her. "No, I don't think you're a phony. I'm beginning to believe that, maybe, just maybe, you're the real thing."

Chapter 17

Dallas's cell phone rang. He bolted out of the chair in the corner of Genny's bedroom, immediately snatched the phone from the holder on his belt, and rushed out of the room. Since Genny had fallen asleep a couple of hours ago, he had notified Wallace to take the day off, fed Drudwyn, cleaned up the kitchen, and then returned to her room to sit quietly and watch over her while she rested. It was damn strange the way he felt about Genny, a woman he'd known only a few days. Protective to the extreme. And totally possessive.

Keeping his voice low, Dallas said, "Sloan here."

"Are you all right?" Teri Nash asked. "You sound sort of strange."

Dallas cleared his throat. "I was up all night." Dallas closed the bedroom door and walked down the hall. "The killer struck again. At dawn this morning. We came awfully close to getting to the scene in time to stop him."

"My God, you mean y'all figured out where he'd taken the woman to sacrifice her?"

"Yeah, the sheriff had a lead he followed and it turned out to be right on the money."

"So if your theory is correct about this guy being the same one who committed the murders in Mobile, it means there'll be two more victims in Cherokee County before he moves on."

Dallas grunted.

"Look, I'm actually calling for a reason, other than to check up on you," Teri said.

"Has Linc finished the profile for us?"

"Not yet, but he said to tell you that he should have it ready for you soon and that at this point he'd say the Mobile murders were organized murders." Teri paused. "You know that means most likely the perpetrator has average to above average intelligence and is socially and sexually competent."

"That covers all six guys on our suspects list."

"Speaking of which— I've run a check on the names on the list you sent. I've just started, so all I've got is information about their whereabouts in the past year, from the time the first murder occurred in Mobile."

Dallas clenched his teeth and steeled his nerves, preparing himself for whatever news Teri had. "And?"

"Okay. There are two men who weren't anywhere near Mobile in the past year. There's no record of any kind that shows Brian MacKinnon traveled to Mobile or anyplace within five hundred miles of the city during the time the murders occurred. And Dr. MacNair lived and worked in Bowling Green, Kentucky, for two years before moving to Cherokee Pointe. He hasn't had a vacation in all that time."

"Okay, that seems to rule out MacKinnon and the doc. What about the other four?"

"It's almost unbelievable, but all four were living within easy driving distance of Mobile around the time of the murders."

"All four?"

"Yep. Dillon Carson worked for the Pascagoula little theater group last year. And Pascagoula, Mississippi, is just a hop, skip, and a jump from Mobile."

"Does Carson have a criminal record?"

"Several arrests," Teri said. "No convictions. Mostly petty stuff. A couple of DUIs; resisting arrest; a shoplifting charge that was dropped. And one assault charge. But the woman who accused him of beating her up changed her mind and withdrew the charges."

"Is that it on Carson?"

"That's all I have so far."

"Who's next?" Dallas asked.

"Royce Pierpont worked in an antique shop in Pass Christian, on the Mississippi gulf coast. That's an easy drive to Mobile."

"What about his record?" For his own perverse reasons, Dallas hoped the guy had a rap sheet as long as his arm.

"He's clean as a whistle. Not even a speeding ticket."

"Figures."

"I take it you've met the man."

"Actually, I've met all six men, as of this morning. They were all part of a search party the mayor of Cherokee Pointe formed."

"Ah, the second victim's husband put together his own little lynch party, huh."

"Luckily, they were easily managed, so they didn't turn into a mob."

"Okay, on to the next suspect. Reverend Haden Stowe. Seems he was preaching at a Congregational Church in Atmore, Alabama. It's a quick trip down I-sixty-five from Atmore to Mobile."

"I suppose the good reverend doesn't have any priors?"

"Not a one."

"What about Jamie Upton?"

"Upton's family owns a beach house in the Gulf Shores area. He was living there with a lady friend last year at the time of the five Mobile murders. Gulf Shores is practically a suburb of Mobile." Teri paused for an instant, then went on. "Before you ask, Jamie Upton has never been convicted of anything, but he's been arrested numerous time. DUIs, drugs, brawling, and a couple of rape charges that were dropped. Seems his family's money has been able to smooth over all of his crimes.''

''Looks like Upton and Carson are the two primary suspects, but our killer could be any one of these four. No way to rule out any of them.'' Dallas concentrated on what he knew about the four men, trying to recall everything and anything that had been said about them.

''They could all be innocent,'' Teri reminded him.

''I know.'' Dallas didn't want to think that they were batting zero in the search for this killer, but knew it was a possibility.

''I'll start digging deeper, as soon as I can. I'll go back to three years ago in Hilton Head and see if any of our guys were in that area at the time of the murders there.''

''I can't thank you enough for what you've done,'' Dallas said.

''Chet Morris called Rutherford. You did a good job of talking Sheriff Butler into asking for help. And now that there's been a third murder, I don't think Rutherford will deny approving agents to join the sheriff's task force.''

''Rutherford hasn't wanted to see what was right under his nose because the guy doesn't like me. He never has. But despite his personal feelings about me, I have to admit he's been halfway decent about letting me bend the rules.''

Teri chuckled. ''Never let him hear you say that. Despite his good qualities, the guy can sometimes be a prick and we all know it.''

''Look, I wanted to tell you before I call Rutherford— I'm going to take a leave of absence. I've used up all my vacation and sick days.''

''I understand. You think you're on the trail of Brooke's killer. You're doing what you have to do.''

''Tell Linc to get that profile to us as soon as he can. If we could narrow down our four suspects to just one. . . .'' Dallas huffed loudly. ''Dammit, we came so close to catching this guy. If we'd gotten there just thirty minutes sooner, we could have saved a woman's life and apprehended a monster. And because we have absolutely no evidence against any of our suspects, Butler didn't have any grounds to even question them, let alone check out their cars and homes. Besides, the last thing we want is to scare the killer off.''

''Where did the sheriff get his information about the killer's whereabouts? If he has a source, someone who—''

''You aren't going to believe me when I tell you.''

''I might. Give it a try.''

Dallas took a deep breath. ''Butler has a psychic who's helping him. She's worked with the Sheriff's Department and the Police Department around here before, but never to catch a serial killer.''

''Are you kidding me? A psychic? Hell, Dallas, I thought you said all psychics were phonies.''

''Yeah, that's what I believed, until . . . Genny's different.''

''Genny?''

Damn, he'd said too much; Teri would want to know more. ''Genevieve Madoc. She's Butler's cousin. Everyone who's known her all her life swears she possesses powerful sixth-sense abilities.''

''What do you believe?''

''I'm not sure.'' Why was he lying to Teri? Or was he simply lying to himself? ''Genny's unique. She's definitely got something special going for her. Hell, she could actually be psychic.''

''Will wonders never cease.''

Dallas hated the humor in Teri's voice. She was having a good mental laugh—at his expense.

''Is she pretty?'' Teri asked.

''What's that got to do with—''

''She's not just pretty, is she? She's beautiful, this woman named Genevieve who you think might really be psychic.''

''It's not what you're thinking.''

''Oh, yes, my old friend, it's exactly what I'm thinking. You've gone and fallen for a woman who claims she's psychic.''

''I haven't fallen for anybody.''

"If you say so."

"We're changing the subject right now," Dallas informed her.

"No problem. Look, I'll see if I can get Linc to work all night on that profile. And I'll start digging into info on your four suspects that will take us back to the time frame of the Hilton Head murders."

"Thanks, Teri."

"Take care of yourself."

"Yeah, you too."

Dallas slipped his phone back into its holder and walked down the hall. He paused outside Genny's room, then eased open the door and checked on her. She was still sleeping.

He stood there watching her for several minutes. *Admit the truth,* he told himself. *You have fallen for Genny. You're confused and bewildered. You've gotten yourself so tangled up in Genny's life, in her mystic powers, in your desire for her, that you don't know whether you're coming or going. You came to Cherokee Pointe in search of Brooke's killer, and somewhere along the way Genny has become a major part of that scenario.*

A peculiar thought formed in Dallas's mind. A thought he couldn't seem to shake. It was as if fate had sent him to Cherokee County specifically because Genny was here, because Genny needed him, needed his protection.

All three televisions in Jasmine's were tuned to the local station, WMMK. The noon news had just come on, but during the entire morning the news team had broken into regularly scheduled programming to issue updated bulletins about the murders in Cherokee County. And all the customers who had come in, from breakfast to lunchtime, had talked of nothing else.

Being one waitress short, and with the others in shock about Misty's brutal death, Jazzy took over the hostess duties during the lunchtime hours. And since one of her waitresses, Sandie, had gone home in a nearly hysterical emotional state, Jazzy would, if necessary, wait on tables as well as bus them.

After hearing on the early morning news that local psychic Genevieve Madoc had been on hand when Misty Harte's body had been found, Jazzy knew Genny had used her talent to help locate Misty. That meant Genny was totally wiped out. Jazzy had called twice to check on Genny, and Dallas had reassured her both times that Genny was sleeping. She couldn't say exactly why, but she trusted Dallas to take care of her best friend. There had been something in his voice that told her plainer than any words how much Genny meant to him.

As she cleared away dirty dishes from one of the front booths, Jazzy heard the newscaster mention an interview with Sheriff Butler. Her gaze traveled to the nearest television just in time to see a taped segment, showing Jacob at the scene of the third murder. The reporter, Matt Newton, stuck a microphone right up in Jacob's face. Good God, Jazzy thought, Newton must have a death wish. If the guy only knew how dangerous it was to prod a raging bull, he'd have steered clear of Jacob.

"Sheriff, what can you tell us about your department's failure to save Misty Harte's life? And why is it that with three horrific murders in our county, you have been unable to come up with even one suspect?"

Jacob glared at Newton but didn't reply. Undaunted by Jacob's evil glare, Newton continued. "We understand that not only was the third victim, Misty Harte, the sister of one of your deputies—Bobby Joe Harte—but that you had a personal relationship with her. Is that true? Were you and Misty Harte lovers?"

Jacob walked away from Newton. The idiot followed him, harassing the hell out of him.

"Sheriff, the good people of Cherokee County, who elected you, want some answers. If you don't respond to my questions, people will think you have something to hide," Newton said, all but running to keep up with Jacob as he strode toward a sheriff's car parked along the roadside.

Jazzy held her breath, knowing what was about to happen. And knowing as surely as she knew her name that Brian MacKinnon had ordered Matt Newton to lean hard on the sheriff.

Jacob paused by the car, but didn't turn to face Newton. Not until the reporter asked, "How did it feel, Sheriff, to see your lover sliced open like a ripe watermelon?"

Holy shit!

Jazzy focused on the TV screen, watching Jacob Butler whip around like a flash of lightning and land a hard blow to the side of Matt Newton's face. The microphone the reporter held sailed up in the air, then nose-dived and came down beside Newton as he hit the ground with a resounding thud.

The cameraman who'd been filming the entire incident had apparently fled at that precise moment, because the taped interview with the sheriff ended abruptly.

The noon news anchor commented, "We've heard that our sheriff has been accused of having a short fuse. I'd say after witnessing this incident, we can all verify that Jacob Butler's temper has, in all likelihood, gained him and the Sheriff's Department a lawsuit. And in my opinion, Butler should be brought up on charges."

"Butler should receive an award for not killing that idiot reporter," Caleb McCord said.

Not having heard Caleb approaching, Jazzy gasped and jumped when he spoke. "Damn, you should have let me know you were there. You scared the shit out of me."

"Ooh . . . just what I like—a woman who talks dirty."

"Put a sock in it, McCord."

"You seemed mesmerized by the noon news."

"The whole town is mesmerized," Jazzy said as she finished cleaning the tabletop, then lifted the square metal pail that held the dirty dishes. "There have been three murders in only a few days. People are scared and confused. And having our local TV, radio, and newspaper all ridiculing Jacob isn't helping any. He's doing his very best. Nobody is more determined to find and stop this killer."

"Sounds like you and Sheriff Butler are good friends."

Jazzy lifted the metal pail onto her hip. "We're damn good friends. You won't find a more honorable man anywhere."

"Lovers?" Caleb asked.

"That's none of your business." Jazzy shoved past him and headed toward the kitchen.

When she thumped the swinging door open with her hip, then moved into the kitchen, the door stayed open. She glanced over her shoulder and saw Caleb following her. She set the pail of dirty dishes down on a countertop, turned, put her hand on her hip and glared at him.

"What?" she asked.

"We had a date for noon today, didn't we?"

"A date? No, I don't think so." She jerked a paper towel from an overhead rack, wiped her hands, and tossed the crumpled towel into the garbage. "I offered you a job and gave you until noon today to accept it."

"Ah, so we're keeping this all business, huh?"

"Strictly business." She wasn't going to fall for this man's easy charm. She'd learned her lesson—the hard way—with Jamie Upton.

"I'll take the job," he said.

"Before you know any details? Like hours, salary, benefits—"

"I don't have a job. I need one to pay my bills. You're offering me what I need. Hours don't matter to me. I figure you have to pay at least minimum wage, and any benefits will be a bonus."

"How long can I count on you staying in Cherokee Pointe?"

"Depends."

"Depends on what?"

"On how well I like it here."

"Then I suppose we should both consider this a temporary arrangement. Right?"

He nodded. "So, boss lady, do I have the job?"

"I'll give you a trial run, starting tonight. Come by here around five and fill out the paperwork. And free supper comes with the job. You'll work from six till midnight weeknights and from six till two on Friday and Saturday nights. You're off on Sundays.''

"I take it that the "blue law" is still alive and well in Cherokee County?"

"That's right. No liquor served on Sundays.''

"Anything else I need to know?'' Caleb asked.

"Not that I can think of, but if you have any questions, just ask Lacy tonight.''

"Lacy's the bartender, right?''

Jazzy nodded.

Caleb grinned.

"That's it. You can go now,'' Jazzy told him. "We're finished.''

Caleb's grin broadened. "That's where you're wrong.'' Leaning into her, but not close enough for their bodies to actually touch, he placed both palms flat on the wall, flanking Jazzy's head. "You and I, Miss Jasmine, are just getting started.''

His nearness took her breath away. Before she was able to actually speak, Caleb winked at her, then turned around and walked out of the kitchen.

Jazzy released a relieved breath. Damn, that guy was lethal, even in small doses. She started to run after him and tell him she'd changed her mind about giving him the bouncer's job at Jazzy's. But she didn't. She needed a bouncer. Caleb needed a job. He'd certainly handled Jamie Upton with expert ease last night. Obviously Caleb wasn't easily intimidated, a quality that came in handy if you were a bouncer at a juke joint. So, she'd give him his trial run and see what happened.

Who knows, maybe he was right. Maybe things were just getting started between them.

Dillon Carson arrived at the Congregational Church at precisely two-thirty, the time Esther Stowe had set for them to meet.

"Come to the side door," she'd told him. "I'll leave it open for you. Be sure to lock it from the inside after you come in. I'll be waiting for you in the sanctuary."

Dillon had been interested in the minister's wife for quite some time, and from the sidelong glances she'd given him for the past month or so whenever they happened to meet, he'd figured it was only a matter of time before he had the woman flat on her back. So he hadn't been all that surprised when she'd telephoned yesterday to set up this afternoon's little rendezvous. What he hadn't expected was that she'd want them to meet at the church.

He was glad he'd gotten a chance for a nap. He'd been up most of the night. After returning to his apartment at ten this morning, he'd showered, shaved, and dropped onto his bed, dead on his feet. He'd wakened at one, in time to eat a bite before getting ready for his rendezvous with Esther. The lovely, fascinating Esther.

As he walked down the hallway toward the sanctuary, he wondered if she would actually want them to do it right there on one of the red velvet pews or maybe even on the pulpit floor where her husband bellowed out hellfire-and-brimstone sermons every Sunday. Just the thought aroused him. He liked kinky. Actually he liked sex in any form. He'd been into S&M for a while and found it satisfying, as long as he was on the master's side of the whip. But if Esther was into the rough stuff, his bet would be that she'd want to be the one inflicting the pain.

When he arrived at the sanctuary, he found it empty. What the hell? Where was she?

"Esther?"

The lights dimmed suddenly, throwing the room into semi-darkness. Dillon swallowed hard. What sort of game was she playing?

The lights above the baptismal flashed on, and the velvet curtains swung open simultaneously. Water splashed upward and outward as a body rose from the depths. With arms spreading wide, Esther Stowe emerged from the baptismal like Aphrodite rising from the ocean. Dillon's mouth gaped as he watched the naked woman step out and onto the red carpeted area behind the pulpit. She laughed bawdily and shook her head, whipping the long, wet strands of her white-blond hair about her face and sending a shower of moisture whirling all around her.

Good God, she was beautiful. Voluptuous. Large, round breasts with tight nipples. Long, slender legs. Tiny waist. He watched her every movement, stirred to excitement by her sensuality. She opened her arms and beckoned him to come to her. His sex swelled and throbbed.

"Oh, baby, am I going to give you what you're asking for." As he approached her, he noticed that her pubic area was shaved clean, and just above the pubic bone a black tattoo glistened. He couldn't seem to take his eyes off the emblem.

Following his line of vision, she glanced down at the tattoo. "Don't you recognize the Seal of Zepar?" She fondled herself with the tip of her middle finger. "Zepar, one of the great Spirits of the Firmament, inflames women with love for men. He has the power to transform a woman into any shape for the pleasure of her lover."

"The shape you're in right now pleases me just fine," Dillon said, still transfixed by the small tattoo.

Within seconds he reached out and dragged her up against him. Her wide mouth opened and she licked him from chin to ear, then she delved between them, grabbed his hand and shoved it between her legs.

"I want the first time to be very fast and very hard," she told him. "And I want it now!"

He stuck a couple of fingers up inside her and found her gushing with moisture. She was ready; more than ready. She was hot and wet and panting.

When she unbuttoned his slacks and undid the zipper, he stood still and let her handle everything. Within minutes she had his penis free from his briefs and was leading him toward one of the large golden chairs on the pulpit podium. She shoved him down onto the red velvet seat, then straddled him. Positioning herself just right, she slid down over him in one quick fluid move that implanted his sex to the hilt within her.

Damn, she was so hot and so tight and . . . She bit his neck, then raked her fingers over his shirt, popping a couple of buttons in the process.

Dillon grasped her hips and pumped her up and down. The friction of her tight, milking body brought him closer and closer to the edge. He was more than half gone already and hadn't been inside more than a couple of minutes.

Panting and gasping, she tossed back her head as she rode him. The world closed in around them. He couldn't see. Couldn't think. All he could do was feel.

His climax hit him hard. The minute he groaned with release, Esther went wild. She grabbed his shoulders and rode him like a madwoman. She screamed when she came, then fell limp against him. Sitting beneath her, his heartbeat drumming in his ears, he lifted her head from his shoulder, grabbed her face with one hand, and gave her a tongue-thrusting kiss.

When she came up for air, she smiled wickedly. "I knew you'd be good at this. I can always tell by just looking at a man."

"He was good, wasn't he, my dear," the Reverend Mr. Stowe said.

Dillon gulped. God damn it, when had Esther's husband walked in? Hell, he should have known fucking in the church was bound to get them into trouble.

When Dillon started to shove Esther off him, she wrapped her arms around his neck and laughed. "Don't get upset. Everything's all right."

"How is that possible? Your husband just walked in and caught us—"

"He didn't just walk in," Esther said. "Haden's been watching us the whole time." She sneaked a glance over her shoulder, then held out a hand and wriggled her fingers. "Come here, darling, and tell Dillon how much you enjoy watching other men fuck your wife."

Chapter 18

Genny roused from her semi-asleep state, stretched languidly, and sat up in bed. The room lay in cool, gray shadows, a minimum of sunlight penetrating the windows. Before even glancing at the bedside clock, she surmised it was quite late in the day, probably after four in the afternoon. Undoubtedly she had slept the day away; but the rest had revived her. The last thing she remembered was a sleepy glance at Dallas sitting across the room in the corner chair. He'd been watching her—watching over her. But he was no longer here. The room was empty. Not even Drudwyn was anywhere to be seen. Only when she rose from the bed and placed her feet on the cold floor did she realize she was in her sock feet. Her boots had been placed neatly at the foot of the bed. She picked up the boots and put them on.

Wonder where Dallas is? She knew he hadn't left her alone. His protective instincts toward her had become too strong for him to leave her unguarded. When she opened her bedroom door and went out into the hall, she heard voices coming from the kitchen. Female voices. Arguing voices. Mercy, it was Sally and Ludie.

Genny hurried into the kitchen, then paused just inside

the doorway, realizing that neither old lady was aware of her presence.

"I say we wake her if she's not up by five," Sally said. "The gal needs to eat. Dallas said she barely touched her breakfast. She's skinny enough as it is. A strong wind would blow her away."

"Let her sleep. She'll wake up when she's good and ready. Dallas said the poor little thing was totally exhausted."

"You know she always gets like that whenever she uses her witchy ways. Melva Mae was the same." Sally went about setting the kitchen table, paying no heed to Ludie. "I'm waking her at five and we can all eat together before Dallas goes back into town."

"Genny's talents aren't witchy ways and you damn well know it," Ludie corrected. "Ain't nothing but pure goodness in that child."

"You think I don't know that." Sally's face hardened as she glared at her best friend. "Genny practices white magic, same as Melva Mae did."

"You're a crazy old woman," Ludie said quietly, but loud enough to be easily heard.

"Who're you calling crazy?"

"You," Ludie replied. "Melva Mae had the sight, same as both her grandmas. She knew what was going to happen before it happened, and she had visions. She could find things that were lost, and she could talk to all them animals in the woods, as well as cats and dogs."

"Yeah, and she could talk to folks, too, without saying a word. She could sneak right into a person's mind." Sally planted her big, bony hands on her hips. "I call that magic. And 'cause Melva Mae never used her magic against nobody, then it was white magic."

"It weren't magic at all. It was a gift from the Good Lord. You know Melva Mae was a God-fearing woman."

"Did I say she wasn't?"

"You said—"

Genny cleared her throat. Startled, Sally and Ludie hushed immediately and turned to face Genny.

"What are you doing up?" Ludie asked.

"She's up because she's had plenty of rest," Sally said. "Can't you see that? Now, who's the crazy old woman?"

"I'm feeling much better," Genny told them. "I guess I've slept all day, haven't I?"

"Purt' near all day," Sally said.

"How long have y'all been here?" Genny asked.

"Since noon," Sally replied. "Doc Swain's keeping the boys overnight. He says they'll be right as rain in no time, that they didn't breathe enough of that damn gas to do any permanent damage. So, when Jacob stopped by to check on us and he said he was headed up here to see about you, I caught a ride with him."

"I came by to check on you when I heard on the TV what had happened this morning, that the killer had murdered Misty and that you were helping the law," Ludie said. "I got here about an hour before Sally." Ludie glanced at the stove. "I been fixing us a real good supper. Fried chicken, green beans, mashed potatoes, deviled eggs, cornbread, and a sweet potato pie for dessert."

"Smells delicious." Genny eyed the table set for four. "Where's Dallas?"

When Ludie smiled, her cheeks rounded and the fine lines in her soft face deepened. "He went for a walk. Said he needed to clear his head."

"That man's been hovering around you like a drone buzzing around a queen bee," Sally said. "He's worried himself sick about you, child."

"Do you know which way he went?" Genny headed toward the back door.

"Just down the road a piece." Sally came over and placed her hand on Genny's shoulder. "Don't you go running off after him. He'll be back soon enough."

Ludie lifted the lid on the pot of boiling potatoes, then slammed it down hard, making a crashing noise. "A little fresh air and exercise might do you good. Drudwyn's outside. Take him with you and go for a little walk. Dallas headed west. Tell him that supper's not quite ready."

Sally huffed, then glared at Ludie.

Genny opened the back door. ''I won't be gone long. And I'll take Drudwyn as my bodyguard.''

As she slipped on her coat and headed off the porch and into the backyard, she heard Sally and Ludie resuming their never-ending quarrel. Jazzy and she had laughed many times about the peculiar friendship between the old women. Anybody who didn't know them would swear they didn't even like each other.

Drudwyn came running the moment he sensed Genny's presence. She knelt to give him a loving hug, then silently ordered Drudwyn to follow her.

After descending the steps coming down off the hill, Genny headed west. A fairly straight, even road lay ahead of her for at least a mile. With the sun quickly descending, the evening air had turned cold. Genny retrieved her hat and gloves from her coat pockets and put them on. She and Drudwyn traipsed along for about a fourth of a mile before they came upon Dallas, who was headed back toward the house. With a good twenty-five feet between them, he stopped and stared at her. She lifted her hand and waved. He returned her wave. They walked toward each other at an average pace at first, then each increased speed until, when they came together, they practically ran into each other. Dallas reached out and grabbed her by the shoulders. Breathing hard, her warm breath vaporizing as it rushed from her mouth, she looked up at Dallas and smiled.

''What are you doing out here?'' he asked.

''I came to tell you that supper will be ready soon.''

''How do you feel?''

''I feel just fine.''

''No lingering aftereffects?''

She shook her head.

Dallas's left hand slid down her shoulder, over her arm, and grasped her wrist. His right hand lifted to her head; his fingers speared into her hair, knocking her knit hat lopsided.

''You have no idea how worried I've been.''

''I'm sorry you worried.''

"I'm sorry you had to go through—"

She placed her fingers over his mouth. "Thank you for taking such good care of me."

"Genny . . ."

She saw an odd look in his eyes. Primitive. Proprietary. A primeval craving. He wanted her—in the most basic, fundamental way a man can want a woman. That kind of need he understood. But she realized he knew nothing about the greater need that was overwhelming his senses. A passion of the spirit. A desire for eternal bonding.

She waited, knowing what was to come. Wanting it. Needing it. As much as he did.

His mouth came down on hers as he enveloped her in his strong embrace. A hungry, devouring possession, and yet gentled by the tenderness he felt toward her. She responded with equal abandon.

The kiss went on and on; and when they came up for air, Dallas moved his lips up the side of her face to her ear, then down her neck and over to her throat. She rubbed herself against him, her breasts against his chest, her legs against his. And then he kissed her again. Deeper. More intense.

I love you, Genny told him telepathically, knowing he wasn't ready to hear the words aloud.

Drudwyn whimpered. Dallas slowly ended the kiss and lifted his head. Genny sighed.

"What are you, our chaperone?" Dallas looked squarely at the wolf-dog.

Genny laughed. "I think he's just hungry. He knows Ludie has fixed fried chicken for supper."

"Then maybe we should head back to the house." Dallas wrapped his arm about her waist.

"You aren't staying the night with me, are you?" she asked as they turned and faced the east.

"Sally told me she planned to stay with you tonight," Dallas replied. "And when Ludie found out Sally was staying, then she decided she'd stay, too."

Genny reached down and took Dallas's big hand into her

small one. "I have an idea how I can help you find the killer. I'll come into town tomorrow and—"

"What have you got in mind?" Dallas slowed his gait and reversed their hands so that he enclosed her hand in his.

"I can try to link with the killer's mind again. I did it for a few brief moments this morning."

"Hell, no!" Dallas stopped in the middle of the road. "It's too dangerous for you. Isn't it?"

Genny couldn't look him in the eye and lie to him. She kept her gaze focused on the road ahead. "There might be some danger, but you'd be there. And Jacob would be there, too. If I got sucked in too deep, I'd have a lifeline. You could pull me back—"

"Forget it." Dallas squeezed her hand and resumed walking.

She had to increase her speed just to keep up with him.

"Don't be angry with me. I just want to help you . . . and help Jacob. This terrible man has already murdered so many women."

"We'll find him." Dallas slowed to a normal gait. "But we'll do it without endangering your life."

She knew better than to argue the point with him right now. But she was well aware of what she had to do, what she must do, to stop the killings. If she could connect with the killer's mind again, she might be able to discover his identity.

He sat curled up in his chair by the fireplace and happily recalled recent events as he watched and rewatched the taped newscasts that had been playing on and off all day on WMMK. He was becoming quite famous in Cherokee Pointe, and he had them all stumped. Every stupid lawman working on the case.

He licked his lips. Ah, Misty Harte's blood had been delicious. And empowering. And the unexpected mind-meld with Genny Madoc had been exhilarating. He didn't know which he looked forward to more—satisfying his sexual needs with the fourth victim or playing head games with Genny. Of course he couldn't tap into her mind; he didn't possess that ability. He'd have to wait for her to initiate the next contact, just as she'd done this morning. But once they were linked, he thought he'd be able to communicate with her without any problems.

He smiled as delicious images of success filled his mind. He was so close to achieving all that he desired.

Only one more sacrifice to build his strength before he claimed his prize. He had been waiting a lifetime for her. All the other transfers had been only partly successful because the women he'd chosen had been too weak, too powerless. But this time, he had found the perfect woman. This fifth victim would give him everything he had longed for all his life. Strength. Power. Perfection.

When Linc Hughes held out his mug, Teri Nash refilled it with coffee. Regular, high-octane java. They had spent the past four nights at BSU headquarters in Quantico pooling their efforts. Both had other cases they were working during the day, but they were determined to help Dallas and Sheriff Butler. With only ten full-time profilers working with the Behavioral Science Unit, each of those agents often worked on fifty cases at once.

Linc, the most experienced profiler, had already given the Mobile murderer and the Cherokee Pointe murderer an ''organized offender'' status based on the organized and disorganized dichotomy involved in five basic aspects of the interaction between the victims and the offender: interpersonal coherence, significance of time and place, criminal characteristics, criminal career, and forensic awareness. A man who fell into this category would in all likelihood be fairly intelligent, possibly highly intelligent. He'd be socially and sexually competent and skilled at whatever work he chose, but would often change jobs or leave town after one or more of the murders. More than likely he would be mobile, with a vehicle in good condition. And this type liked to follow his crimes in the news media.

"You know Dallas will be in your debt the rest of his life," Teri said as she leaned over to kiss Linc on the forehead.

"The initial report is ready for you to send him. It's incomplete, but it'll give Dallas and the sheriff something to work with." Linc checked his watch. "It's nearly four o'clock. I'll fax it to the sheriff's office, and you can call Dallas whenever you think he'll be up."

"I'll give him until five-thirty," Teri replied. "If I know him, he's not getting much sleep these days." She yawned. "Speaking of sleep. Maybe we should try to catch a few zees."

Linc glanced at the file folders spread out across the desk in his office. "How's your research into the victims coming along?"

"I don't have all the data I need, but so far I've come up with a big fat zero."

"It doesn't make sense that none of the victims have anything in common, other than all five in each series of murders lived and died in their home area."

"The ages range from teens to forties. Different races. Different physical descriptions. Various backgrounds and occupations. It's as if this guy simply chooses his victims at random."

"Possible," Linc said. "But my instincts and my training tell me that there is some significance to the fact that in each case there are exactly five murders, all occurring around daybreak, all sacrificed in the same manner."

"And he drinks blood from the first four."

"But he cuts the heart out of each fifth victim."

"And eats it?" Teri asked. "Isn't that what you and Dallas surmised?"

Linc nodded. "Yeah, so maybe the first four victims are chosen at random simply because they're easily accessible. But there's something special about the fifth victim. If we can discover what that special thing is, then I'll bet we'll find a connection that links each of the fifth victims."

"Makes sense," Teri said. "So, what I need to do is gather all the info I can on each of the fifth victims."

"I think that may prove to be our missing link."

Teri poured herself another cup of coffee, then sat down in front of Linc's computer and quickly zipped through the basic information on victims number 5.

"Four women, all the fifth victim. Hmmm." Teri bit down on the side of her lower lip and clicked her tongue as she scanned the information. "Our first number five was Kim Johnson, twenty-seven, a TV reporter from Texas. Next was Daphne Alaire, thirty-eight, a novelties and bookshop owner who lived in Louisiana. The third number five, Lori Wright, was from Hilton Head, South Carolina. She was a twenty-year-old college student home for spring break when she was murdered."

"I'm not picking up on any similarities."

"That's because there aren't any." Teri shook her head and clicked her tongue again. "The fifth victim in the Mobile murders was a housewife, Barbara James, thirty, with two kids, who did volunteer work with troubled children."

"What's the marital status on those four women?"

Teri skimmed the info in the computer files. "James was married, Wright was single, Alaire widowed, and Johnson divorced."

"Physical descriptions?"

Scrolling through each woman's file, Teri made a mental note of each description. "One blonde, one redhead, two brunettes. One fat, one skinny, two average. One short, one tall, two average height." She spun the swivel chair around and confronted Linc. "And before you ask—one black, three white."

Linc shrugged. "You'll have to dig deeper. Check into things like religion, clubs and organizations they belonged to, hobbies, things like that."

"You do know how long that could take."

"We're narrowing the search from twenty women to four. If there is a link, a common thread—and I'm sure there is—it will be among those fifth victims."

"Then what you're saying is that if we can hurry up and find that common denominator, we still probably won't be able to save the fourth victim, but we might be able to figure out who the fifth victim is going to be and hopefully save her."

"That's right."

"Brooke was the fourth victim in Mobile," Teri said. "I know Dallas would like to save number four in Cherokee County."

"That might not be possible. He may have to settle for saving the fifth victim."

Chapter 19

Tension was running high in Cherokee County and the fact that the local media was enjoying a feeding frenzy at Sheriff Butler's and Chief Watson's expense only added to the problem. Dallas had seen this happen before—a town panicking when it began to question the competency of its local lawmen. The *Cherokee Pointe Herald* and WMMK TV and radio stations, owned by the MacKinnon family, continued giving a one-sided view of events, thanks to the animosity between Jacob and Brian MacKinnon. But unbeknownst to the media, during the past week, some progress was being made in solving the sacrificial murder cases. With a task force in place, and the FBI officially, as well as unofficially, working in conjunction with local and state law enforcement, they now had a streamlined suspects list that might lead them to the killer.

Neither Matt Newton, the reporter Jacob had coldcocked, nor MacKinnon Media had instigated a lawsuit against Jacob or filed assault charges against him. Dallas figured Newton would do whatever the MacKinnons told him to do, and Brian MacKinnon was enjoying making Jacob wait. Dallas believed MacKinnon was the type who derived pleasure from toying with a man he thought he held any kind of power over.

The majority of public opinion still remained on Jacob's side, despite the media blitz against the local lawman. People tended to like and trust Jacob Butler whereas most intensely disliked and distrusted Brian MacKinnon. What Dallas couldn't figure out was why MacKinnon would deliberately attack Jacob if MacKinnon really was in love with Genny.

Dallas lifted his legs and placed his feet atop the edge of Jacob's desk, then reared back and gripped his hands together behind his head. He hadn't slept well since arriving in Cherokee County. Too much happening too fast to waste time getting eight hours every night. Hell, he'd settle for five good hours. But once the killer was caught, he could rest.

The initial profile that Linc Hughes had faxed them six days ago had reinforced Dallas's conviction that one of their original four suspects was the serial killer who had murdered Brooke and the three Cherokee County women. Even though they had no other evidence against any of the men, they also had no other suspects.

Only yesterday Teri had called Dallas to report her findings from the five murders in Hilton Head, which had taken place eighteen months prior to the Mobile murders. Her findings had narrowed the suspects down to three—that is, if they were on the right track. If they were barking up the wrong tree, then heaven help them, because only a higher power could save the final two victims.

"Dillon Carson was working with a dinner theater in Savannah at the time of the five murders," Teri had said. "That's a forty-five-minute drive to Hilton Head."

Royce Pierpont had been employed at an antique shop in Charleston, an hour and a half drive from Hilton Head. And Jamie Upton had spent that spring with friends at Hilton Head, playing golf, fishing, kayaking, and getting picked up twice for being drunk and disorderly. The Reverend and Mrs. Stowe had been living in Whiteville, North Carolina, during the time of the Hilton Head murders. With the distance between the two cities, it was highly unlikely that

Haden Stowe had been the perpetrator in those five killings. Unlikely, but not out of the realm of possibility. With time running out, Jacob and Dallas had agreed to concentrate on Carson, Pierpont, and Upton, the three most likely suspects. Each man fit the profile Linc had compiled.

Carson and Pierpont had cooperated fully when Jacob asked them to come in for questioning, but neither had alibis for the time of the first two Cherokee County murders, only for the third. They had both joined in Jerry Lee Todd's manhunt that morning, and dozens of other men could swear to their whereabouts. But Dallas knew, considering the mob mentality of the mayor's vigilantes that morning, no one could be one hundred percent certain when any one particular member had joined the group.

Carson had claimed he couldn't remember exactly where he was living at the time of the Louisiana and Texas murders, but did know he'd never lived or worked in Texas. But yes, he had lived in the border state of Oklahoma and had vacationed in neighboring New Mexico. He just couldn't remember when. Nor could he remember when he'd last been in Louisiana. Pierpont said he'd never even been to Texas, but he had worked in Baton Rouge, Louisiana, which was within easy driving distance of Lafayette, where the second set of murders had occurred. However, he wasn't sure about the exact dates. A few years back? Yes. At least four? Yes, at least four. Pierpont had seemed quite calm and controlled, answering without hesitation. Dillon's replies were often vague, but he seemed more aggravated about wasting his time than having to answer questions.

Both men had refused to give DNA samples. But even an innocent man might object to that request.

Jamie Upton had been another matter altogether. He had refused to answer any questions without his lawyer present. And his grandfather's local attorney advised him that he didn't have to answer any questions unless he was being charged with a crime.

"Charge Jamie with something or let him go," Tyson

Baines had demanded, with a smirking smile that accentu-
ated his fat jowls.

Did Jamie have something to hide or was Big Jim Upton
simply throwing his weight around? Possibly both. Only
this morning, Jacob had told Dallas he'd heard that the old
man had put the infamous trial lawyer from Texas, Quinn
Cortez, on retainer. Did that mean Jamie's grandfather suspected he might be a killer?

Dallas spent most of his waking hours at the Sheriff's
Department, which had become command central for the
task force. But he had managed to slip away for a while to
drive up the mountain on the days that Genny couldn't make
it into town. Knowing Jacob would agree with him and nix
her plan, he'd told Jacob about Genny's idea of trying to
telepathically connect with the killer's mind. Jacob had gone
ballistic; and only then had Dallas understood the true danger
to Genny if she tried such a feat.

"We can't allow her to even try," Jacob had said. "If
she were to go in too far, we might not be able to get her
back."

Fortunately, Genny hadn't mentioned it again, not once
in the past six days. The way Dallas felt about Genny, he
found it difficult to believe he'd known her only a little over
a week. This was the first time in his life that a woman had
become so important to him. He wasn't calling it love. Love
was just a word. An overused word. He wanted Genny.
Wanted her desperately. But there was something more to
his feelings, something he couldn't quite define. And it was
that other element that worried him.

A booted foot kicked Dallas's legs where he had them
propped up on the desk. He eased his feet onto the floor
and glanced up at Jacob.

"Daydreaming?" Jacob asked.

"Not exactly. Why?"

"You didn't hear what I said, did you?"

"Was it something important?"

Jacob grunted. "I wish there was a legal way for us to
get hold of Jamie Upton's DNA."

"What brought this on?"

"I just talked to Jazzy. She's thinking about taking out a restraining order on Jamie. Her new bouncer over at Jazzy's Joint has had to get rid of Jamie twice this week. His actions are coming pretty damn close to being harassment, but if she tries to bring him up on charges, he'll walk and she knows it."

"You think Upton is our killer?"

"I think it's highly possible."

Dallas shook his head. "I disagree."

"So, G-man," Jacob said jokingly, "who do you think it is?"

"Carson or Pierpont."

"Carson is a jerk and Pierpont is a wimp, but being either of those things isn't a crime."

"Upton is too obvious. He's an in-your-face type, not caring how much attention he draws to himself."

"Jamie is an amoral bastard who's never thought of anyone other than himself. Our killer has no conscience. That trait fits Jamie to a tee."

"I'm not ruling him out," Dallas said. "Just going by gut instinct and experience."

"In my experience if it quacks like duck, waddles like a duck, and looks like a duck, it's a duck."

Dallas grinned, but before he could counter with a witty response, Tim Willingham knocked on the office door and stuck his head in.

"There's a call on line two I think you'll want to take," Tim said.

"Who is it?" Jacob asked.

"Dr. MacNair. He says his wife is missing."

Genny opened the door to Brian MacKinnon and invited him in, maintaining a polite if somewhat cool expression. She was glad Drudwyn was off in the woods right now; otherwise her dog would pick up on the hostility she felt. And although she could control Drudwyn, she wasn't sure she could stop herself from letting him frighten Brian just a little.

When she'd first heard Brian's car in the driveway, she'd thought Dallas and Jacob had arrived. She was expecting them for supper tonight. She planned to approach them once again about her idea to try a telepathic link to the killer's mind.

"I wasn't sure you'd see me," Brian said as he entered the living room.

"And why would I refuse to see you?"

Brian smiled, but there was no humor in his eyes, only a watchful curiosity. "You're upset with me, aren't you?"

"Would you care for coffee or tea?" Genny asked.

"You have every right to be dissatisfied with the way WMMK and the *Cherokee Pointe Herald* has treated Jacob's part in the murder investigations."

Genny kept her facial expression placid. Brian had no idea just how dissatisfied she really was. She had given him the benefit of the doubt, given him every opportunity to prove himself a good man, and had overlooked several lapses in his behavior. But not this time. She was willing to admit she'd been wrong about Brian. The man was not redeemable.

Brian cleared his throat as he stood with his back to the fireplace. "Jacob doesn't like me. He's made that abundantly clear on more than one occasion. He disapproves of my pursuing a relationship with you." He paused as if he expected some type of response from her. She gave him none. He continued. "Until recently I've given him no cause to dislike me."

"Are you saying that crucifying Jacob in the media is some sort of payback?"

"No, of course not." Sweat popped out on Brian's forehead. "In my opinion Jacob and Roddy are doing a pitiful job with these murders. As a matter of fact, the entire task force has accomplished very little. It's the job of WMMK and the *Herald* to report the news as we see it."

"You could have told me all of this over the telephone

and saved yourself a trip up the mountain." Genny criss-crossed her arms over her chest.

Brian pulled a handkerchief from his coat pocket, wiped the perspiration from his face and moved away from the fireplace. "I've tried calling several times, but you haven't been answering your phone."

Not when your number came up on my Caller ID, Genny thought. She had wanted to avoid Brian, but she should have known he would force a face-to-face confrontation.

"Jacob is like a brother to me. He's one of the finest men I've ever known. If you'd had any feelings for me whatsoever, you would have taken another tactic in reporting what you call the truth."

"That's just it, Genny . . ." He held out his hands beseechingly, but dropped his arms to either side when Genny eased farther away from him. "I do have feelings for you. Strong feelings. And I've come here to prove to you just how much you mean to me."

"How do you propose to do that?"

"You're aware of the fact that Jacob attacked Matt Newton, a WMMK reporter, when the man was simply doing his job."

Genny breathed in deeply, then slowly exhaled. She seldom lost her temper; in fact, most people who knew her would say she never lost her temper. Only Jazzy and Jacob knew better. When pushed to the limit, she reacted. Brian had pushed her almost to her personal limit.

Brian took a hesitant step in her direction, then paused when she glared at him. "If we choose to, we can sue Jacob personally, as well as file assault charges against him."

"And is that what you intend to do? I'm sure you're pulling Matt Newton's strings, so—"

"Genny, Genny . . ."

When Brian moved toward her again, she held up a restraining hand. He stopped immediately.

"Because of my high regard for you, my deep feelings for you, I will see to it that neither Matt Newton nor MacKinnon

Media brings charges against Jacob or files a lawsuit against him.''

''And what do you expect in return for this grand gesture?''

Why had it taken her so long to accept the truth that had been staring her in the face all along? Brian MacKinnon was evil. She sensed that evil all around her. In the past, had he been able to mask his true nature when around her, or had she simply been unwilling to probe too deeply into his psyche for fear her hopes for his reformation would be dashed?

''You suspect an ulterior motive?'' Brian asked. ''Genny, my dearest, I'm willing to give you Jacob's career, which is in my hands, as a gift. To show you how very much you mean to me.''

Truck doors slammed. Drudwyn barked. Feet tramped up the front steps and across the porch.

Brian gazed into the foyer, toward the front door. ''Are you expecting someone?''

''Jacob and Dallas are coming to supper,'' she replied.

''I see.''

''Brian, if you truly mean what you've said, that you'll do this for Jacob . . . for me . . . I'm grateful. But—''

The front door burst open. Dallas came through first, with Jacob directly behind him. Drudwyn rushed past both men and galloped over to Genny. Jacob paused in the living room doorway, but Dallas charged in, not stopping until he was at Genny's side.

''Brian, I don't believe you've met FBI Special Agent Dallas Sloan,'' Genny said. ''Dallas, this is Brian MacKinnon, of MacKinnon Media.''

Brian glanced from the man to the dog, the two flanking Genny, then tentatively held out his hand to the man. Dallas eyed Brian's hand speculatively, then grasped it, and the two exchanged a quick shake. By the way Brian grimaced, Genny figured Dallas had used a macho tactic of superior physical strength to intimidate Brian.

Jacob sauntered into the room, his movements slow and cautious. "What are you doing here, MacKinnon?"

"I came to give Genny a gift." Brian smiled at Genny.

She forced herself to return a watered-down version of her usual smile. "I would ask you to stay for dinner, but—"

Drudwyn's growl almost drowned out Jacob's blatant snarl.

"Some other time," Brian said. "I'll telephone you tomorrow."

Genny moved toward Brian, intending to walk him to the door. Before she'd taken the second step, Dallas clamped his hand on her waist and held her in place. Jacob jumped into action and walked with Brian out of the living room, into the foyer, and through the front door. When the two men disappeared onto the porch, Genny turned to Dallas.

"Brian told me that Matt Newton isn't going to bring charges against Jacob, and they're not going to sue Jacob, either."

"I see." Dallas gripped her waist with both hands and turned her to face him. "What brought about this miracle? Exactly what did MacKinnon want from you in return?"

"He said he's doing it as a gesture to prove to me how much he cares about me." Genny glanced over her shoulder at the closed front door, wondering what Jacob was saying to Brian. "I hope Jacob doesn't—"

"MacKinnon isn't going to get what he wants—because he wants you."

"Yes, he does, but for now he's willing to settle for my good opinion of him."

"Which he doesn't have, does he?"

Genny shook her head. "I've wasted a lot of time believing Brian could change, that he wanted to change. Even poor Wallace thought he saw signs of improvement in Brian's behavior."

Jacob came back into the house, removed his coat, and hung it on the hall tree. "Looks like I can quit worrying about getting sued or having Matt Newton press charges against me."

"I think I can be nice to Brian for a bit longer," Genny said. "It won't be easy, but it's necessary."

"If nothing else good comes out of the media torture I've been going through, your realizing that MacKinnon is beyond redemption is enough."

"I don't want you to be too nice to him," Dallas said.

"I've never been too nice to him," Genny replied. "Not the kind of nice you mean."

Suddenly Jacob's cell phone rang. He paused a couple of seconds before reaching over and lifting it from his coat pocket. "Could be news about Nina MacNair."

Genny looked at Dallas. "What's this about Nina Mac-Nair?"

"Her husband reported her missing. It seems when he woke up this morning, she was gone. No note. All of her things still there at the house. She had taken her purse with her, but that's all. The doctor thinks she might have walked to the grocery store, but no one at Shop Rite has seen her."

"Do you think—"

"Maybe. Our killer hasn't made a move in six days."

Jacob returned his phone to his coat pocket and walked into the living room. "No sign of Mrs. MacNair. Nobody in town has seen her. Roddy and I are in agreement that considering we have a serial killer loose in our county, we're waiving the waiting period on filing a missing person's report."

"Do you have to go now or can you stay for supper?" Genny asked.

"I'll grab a quick bite, then head back into town." Jacob turned to Dallas. "If you decide to stay a while, I can send one of my deputies to pick you up later."

"Thanks," Dallas replied, never taking his eyes off Genny, "but I think I should go back into town with you."

"While y'all eat, I could see if I can pick up anything on Nina MacNair," Genny said. "Since I don't know her and have seen her only a couple of times, I'm not sure—"

"Go ahead and see if you can sense anything about her,"

Jacob said. "But do not go anywhere near the killer's mind. Do you hear me?"

"I hear you loud and clear." Genny ushered the two men into the kitchen, served up plates of chicken and dumplings, along with several vegetables, and tea cakes made from Granny's recipe for dessert.

While they ate, Genny ventured off into the living room and sat alone by the fireplace. Gazing into the flames, she relaxed and let her mind open up and fly away. She kept repeating the name Nina MacNair over and over again. Dark shadows swirled and then vanished. Soft gray light floated through her consciousness. She sensed a desperate need to escape, but no real fear. Laughter bubbled up. A great sense of relief. Keep running. Don't look back. A man's hand reached out. Still no fear. A woman's hand. A man's hand. Together. Touching tenderly.

Genny's eyelids flew open. How odd, she thought. How very odd. She joined Dallas and Jacob in the kitchen, poured herself a glass of milk and sat down at the table. She picked up a tea cake and broke the rich, buttery cookie in half.

"I don't think the killer has Nina MacNair," Genny said, then took a bite of tea cake.

"Then you picked up on something?" Dallas asked.

Genny nodded and wondered if Dallas realized what an about-face he'd done since they first met. A little over a week ago, Dallas Sloan had been a skeptic, believing in nothing beyond his five senses; now he accepted her psychic abilities without question. Or at least with very few questions.

"I think Mrs. MacNair ran off with another man," Genny said.

Jacob snorted. "She didn't happen to leave a forwarding address, did she?" he asked flippantly.

"I'm afraid not," Genny replied, then finished off her tea cake and washed it down with half a glass of milk.

Several minutes later, just as Dallas was helping her clear away the dishes and Jacob was dumping the scraps from their plates into Drudwyn's bowl, a telephone rang. Three sets of eyes glanced at the wall phone, then realized it was the distinctive ring of Dallas's digital phone.

He released it from his belt clip, punched the ON button, and said, "Sloan here."

Dallas listened, while Jacob and Genny watched and waited.

"What's up, Teri?" Dallas asked. He remained silent while she responded. "What?" There was a short pause when Agent Teri Nash spoke again. "My God! Are you sure about this?"

Dallas's gaze met Genny's; she sensed that whatever Teri Nash was telling him had something to do with her.

"You know what this means, don't you?" Dallas spoke into the phone. "Finding out the four women who were the fifth victims actually had something that distinctive in common tells us who he's chosen for his final victim here in Cherokee County."

Chapter 20

Dallas thanked Teri, then returned his phone to its holder, all the while not breaking eye contact with Genny. Of the various things he might have expected Teri to tell him, he'd never expected that her discovery would bring his life full circle. He had spent eight months feeling guilty for not having been able to save Brooke, no matter how irrational that guilt might be. Realistically he knew there wasn't anything he could have done to have prevented his niece's death; but he could do something to find her killer. God damn it, he was a federal agent. He'd spent most of his adult life in a job he thought meant something. He had believed when he'd begun his pursuit of this elusive, diabolical murderer that catching the man and bringing him to justice would bring Dallas and his family some sort of closure. How wrong he'd been. Not in his worst nightmare had he envisioned facing the loss of someone else he loved at the hands of the same madman.

And God help him, he loved Genny Madoc.

"What is it?" Genny asked. "What did Teri tell you about me?"

Jacob snapped his head around and stared at Genny.

"What do you mean, what did she tell Dallas about you? What could she possibly—"

"Teri has searched through every bit of information she could find about the fifth victim in each series of murders," Dallas said. "Linc Hughes believes that all the other victims, the first four in each case, might have simply been chosen at random, but that the fifth victim was somehow different."

"Different in what way?" Genny reached out and placed her hand on Dallas's chest, right over his heart.

"We know he doesn't just drink the fifth victim's blood," Jacob said. "He removes her heart and . . . well, he probably eats it."

"Through some intensive research, Teri has found something that all four of the fifth victims had in common." Dallas laid his hand over Genny's where it rested against him.

"At last, a real breakthrough." Jacob narrowed his gaze to pinpoint where Dallas's hand lay atop Genny's. "Why is it that I get the feeling I'm not going to like what you're about to tell us?"

"Barbara James, who was the fifth victim in Mobile, had a rare talent," Dallas said. "According to her family and close friends, Barbara was clairvoyant."

Genny shut her eyes. Dallas closed his fingers over Genny's hand tightly, holding it over his heart.

Jacob laid the empty plate in the sink. "What about the other three?"

"The first fifth victim, Kim Johnson, entertained her friends with telekinetic tricks. Several of her friends told Teri that Kim could move objects with her mind and . . ." Dallas sucked in a deep breath, then released it slowly. "Daphne Alaire worked part-time as a medium. She claimed to have the ability to converse with the dead. And Lori Wright was telepathic. Her sister told Teri that Lori didn't want any of her college friends to know about her ability because the kids she'd grown up with considered her a freak."

"Good God!" Jacob clenched his jaw. "Why is this information just now surfacing?"

"Because Teri dug pretty deep," Dallas said. "Apparently the friends and families of the fifth victims hadn't bothered mentioning their unique talents to the authorities because they hadn't thought that information had anything to do with their murders."

"How the hell did this guy find these women? And why is he killing them?" Jacob balled his hands into tight fists.

"We don't know," Dallas replied. "But if he's true to form, then his fifth victim will be someone who has a sixth-sense ability."

"I'm the reason he's come to Cherokee County," Genny said, certainty in her voice. "He intends for me to be his fifth victim."

"It won't happen," Dallas told her with absolute conviction.

"You're damn right it won't," Jacob added. "We'll keep you under guard twenty-four seven. I'll move back in here to protect you."

"Jacob, you have a job to do. Let me take care of Genny," Dallas said. "I'll move in here with her tonight."

"Yes, of course," Genny replied. "But, Dallas, you can't stay with me all the time. Jacob needs you to help him find this man before he kills the fourth victim."

"Whenever Dallas can't be with you, I'll make sure a deputy is," Jacob said. "And in the meantime, we're going to do whatever it takes to find the killer."

Dallas grasped Genny's shoulders tenderly. "We will keep you safe. I swear to you that this man isn't going to—"

"You must let me help you discover his identity," Genny said. "With my life at stake, I have every right to take a risk and try to telepathically connect to the killer's mind."

"No!" Jacob shouted.

"Yes," Genny told him. "I'll get plenty of rest tonight and tomorrow morning, and then tomorrow afternoon, with you and Dallas here with me, I want to try."

"She's going to do it whether you agree or not," Dallas said. "I'll be here with her when she does try. Will you?"

Jacob huffed. "Damn it, yes!"

Laura tossed back her blond curls and lifted her snooty little nose into the air. "As your fiancée, I have every right to know what's going on. Ever since we came to Cherokee Pointe to visit your grandparents, you've been gone more than you've been here. You stay out all night and tell me you've been with old high school buddies. How many old buddies can you possibly have?"

"Now, don't go getting your panties in a wad, lover." Jamie tried to wrap his arm around her, but she outmaneuvered him so that he grasped thin air.

"Are you seeing other women?" Laura demanded. "Is that where you're going tonight, to see someone else?"

"Now, why would I be seeing other women when I have you?" Jamie grinned sheepishly at her. "Baby doll, you're more than enough woman for me."

"You're lying! I may not be all that experienced, but I know when a man finds me boring."

Jamie lunged toward her and this time was able to catch her before she sidestepped him. When he pulled her into his arms, she struggled to free herself.

"Calm down and let me show you how easily you can satisfy me." He tried to kiss her, but she turned her head.

He bit her earlobe. She yelped in pain.

He licked her ear, then whispered, "I don't find ass-fucking boring." He rubbed his hand over her buttocks. "Take your panties off and bend over and I promise I won't be going anywhere else tonight."

Laura's eyes widened in shock. "Are you seriously asking me to participate in such a depraved act?"

"I could force you," he told her. "Would you like it better that way? You could cry and whimper and beg me to stop and act as if you didn't like it."

"No, Jamie. I don't want to—"

He silenced her with a kiss. A tongue-down-her-throat kiss. Laura was a good-looking girl. Not really pretty, but cute. And she had perky tits and a first-class ass. Unfortunately, she wasn't very adventurous in the bedroom. He'd figured out after the first time he'd screwed her that she didn't know much about sex. Later, she'd admitted that he was only her third lover. Hell, he couldn't even remember who his third lover had been ... or his thirtieth. His first had been one of the maids who had worked for his grandmother. He'd been fourteen and enjoyed the twenty-five-year-old's body for quite some time. Until she'd up and quit. The next memorable partner had been Jazzy Talbot. Now there was one hot piece of ass. But for the life of him he didn't recall if she was lover number five, six, or seven. Certainly not number three.

The kiss quieted Laura momentarily, but the minute he released her mouth, she groaned. "I love you, Jamie, but I won't put up with your having other women after we're married." She stuck out her lower lip in an adorable pout.

He grinned, then planted a quick kiss on her pouting mouth. "I promise that once we're married, I'll be as faithful as an old dog." He wasn't lying to her. Not really. What she didn't know was that he had no intention of ever marrying her.

"I wish I could believe you."

When she relaxed in his arms, he knew he had her. She was succumbing to her love for him. He preferred it when a woman loved him. Women in love were always easier to handle.

"I love you, Laura. You know that. I've never loved another woman the way I love you."

God, how gullible women were. They fell for that old line every time. He'd lost track of how many times he'd used those exact words. Hell, all he did was tell Laura what she wanted to hear, what every woman wanted to believe.

Putty in his hands, she melted into him. "Will it hurt?" she asked.

"Will what hurt?"

"You know." She grasped his hands and dragged them down from her waist to cup her buttocks.

Jamie laughed. "Oh, that. Lover, it won't hurt me a bit, but . . . it could be a little uncomfortable for you."

"How uncomfortable?" She looked directly into his eyes, her gaze filled with anticipation.

"You're dying to find out, aren't you?" He grabbed her hand and dragged her across the room toward the bed. "Just take off your robe and remove your panties and I'll satisfy your curiosity."

He released his hold on her. She hesitated for a second, then eased her robe from her shoulders and let it pool at her feet. Beneath the robe she was naked. He sucked in his breath. Just looking at her gave him a hard-on.

"I love you, Jamie." She turned her back to him and bent over, bracing herself with her open palms flattened on the foot of the bed. "I wouldn't let you do this if I didn't love you so much."

Jamie ran his hand over her smooth, firm butt, then unzipped his pants and freed his sex.

Jacob spent the night in his office. Again. Since Susie Richards's murder, he'd spent as many nights at the Sheriff's Department as he had his own apartment. With each passing day, he came to regret having run for sheriff more and more. Logically he knew the only way to become a top-notch lawman was with experience, but right now he sure as hell would like to find a quick way to bypass those years of on-the-job-training and move right on up to seasoned sheriff.

Hell, man, what more could you do than you've already done? he asked himself as he looked through the stack of crime-scene photos for what seemed like the millionth time. Was there something he was missing? Was Dallas's personal experience clouding his expert vision? Why hadn't the task force helped them solve these crimes?

With frustration and lack of sleep added to his normal quick temper, Jacob swept his hand across the top of his desk, a motion that sent the photos flying into the air and then dropping haphazardly onto the floor. He shot up so quickly that he accidentally flipped his swivel chair onto its side. He kicked the back of the overturned chair and cursed a blue streak.

The killer wanted Genny. He had chosen her as his fifth victim because she had psychic abilities, because she had inherited *the sight* from Granny.

He had to protect Genny at all costs. She was the dearest person on earth to him. He loved her like a sister.

And Dallas Sloan loved her, too. Instinct alone told Jacob that Dallas would lay down his life for Genny.

Tewanda Hardy called out through the closed office door. "Sheriff Butler, Dr. MacNair is here to see you."

Jacob checked his watch. Ten-fifteen. "Yeah, Tewanda, tell him to come on in." Jacob righted his chair and bent to hurriedly pick up the scattered photos.

The door opened and the town's newest doctor crept in. Crept was the only way Jacob knew how to describe the man's demeanor. Head bowed. Eyes downcast. Acting like a whipped dog. MacNair was one of those soft-looking men, stocky in build but not muscular, with a ruddy face, washed-out blue eyes, and small, almost feminine features.

"I've made a terrible mistake," MacNair said.

"How's that?" Jacob had a feeling he already knew what the doctor was going to say. Genny had probably guessed right—Nina MacNair had run off with another man.

"My wife isn't missing."

"Have you heard from her?"

He shook his head. "Not directly. But her mother called me about thirty minutes ago. It seems Nina contacted her because she didn't want her mother to worry about her. Nina knew I'd call Mrs. Grant."

"And your mother-in-law told you that your wife is all right?"

"Nina has left me. Mrs. Grant told me that Nina had her old boyfriend come to Cherokee Pointe and pick her up early this morning. She walked from our house into town.

She's going to move in with her mother until after we get a divorce, then she's going to marry. . . . She didn't take anything with her this morning. She didn't want to risk getting caught. She was afraid I'd beg her to stay."

Jacob didn't need to hear this, didn't want to hear it. He hated seeing a man humbled and humiliated by a woman he loved.

Jacob crossed the room, planted his hand on the doctor's shoulder, and said, "I'll take care of the missing person's report. I can explain that Mrs. MacNair's gone home to visit her mother."

"I'm sorry about all this. I honestly thought . . . ." MacNair gulped down a sob. "Thank God I was wrong about the killer having her."

Jacob walked the doctor outside to his car, all the while very grateful that he'd never allowed any woman to emotionally castrate him.

Genny lifted a quilt down from a high shelf in the hall closet and carried it into Dallas's bedroom. She'd given him Jacob's old room, which was directly across the hall from hers. When Dallas heard her approaching, he turned to face her.

"Here's an extra quilt." She held out the last patchwork creation Granny had put together before her death. "Is there anything else you need?"

Her heartbeat accelerated when she noticed the way he was looking at her. As if she was everything he wanted, all that he would ever need.

Dallas took the quilt and tossed it onto the foot of the bed. "You need a security system."

"All right. Should I call someone tomorrow?"

"I'll do it."

"Thank you."

"No need to thank me. I'm here to take care of you, and getting a security system installed is part of keeping you safe."

"Your being here makes me feel safe."

Dallas studied her, his gaze moving rapidly from her face to her feet and then coming back up again in slow motion. "When we first met, I was surprised by how strongly you affected me. I told myself you'd cast a spell on me."

"Now what do you think?" she asked.

"Now I know you've cast a spell over me."

"You're aware that it works both ways. We're caught up in the same magic spell."

Dallas lifted his hand. Genny came to him as if drawn by an unseen force. He skimmed the back of his hand down her cheek. She closed her eyes, experiencing his touch to the fullest.

"You must know how much I want you." He let his hand drop to his side.

"Yes, I know. You want me as much as I want you."

"More," he said, his voice low and rich with longing.

She had waited her entire life for this man and this night. She sensed danger all around her, drawing closer and closer with each passing day. Soon—very soon—she would come face-to-face with death. And the only thing that could save her was this man's love.

Chapter 21

Genny had wondered what it would be like to fall in love. Now she knew. The sensations were exhilarating. The thoughts swirling through her mind enticed her. She wanted to know Dallas in every sense of the word. Mentally, emotionally, physically. Tonight they would form those bonds, connecting on levels that would bind them together for a lifetime. The spiritual bonding would come later, when Dallas accepted her for who and what she was—accepted her completely and without reservations. Once they were spiritually linked, it would be for all eternity.

Dallas reached for her, his hand sliding over her waist as he draped his arm around her. "Are you sure?" he asked. "I don't want you to regret it later."

"I'll have no regrets," she told him.

"I . . . uh . . . I should get a . . . I have protection in my shave kit."

Standing on tiptoe, she kissed his cheek. "Take a shower and shave, while I soak in my tub. When you're ready, I'll be waiting for you in my room."

"It'll be the quickest shower and shave on record."

She smiled. "Don't rush. We have all night."

Sucking in a deep breath, he released her. As she walked away, she could feel his gaze on her, all the way to the door.

Once in her bedroom, she built a fire in the fireplace, then opened a bottom dresser drawer and removed a dozen fat, homemade, white candles and their clear glass holders. She placed the candles throughout the room and lit each one before turning off the lights.

Her bed was an antique, like most of the furniture in the house, a large mahogany sleigh bed that had belonged to her mother and to Granny before she married. Genny turned back the quilt of colorful hand-embroidered birds and flowers on what had once been a solid white background, now aged to a pale ecru. Beneath lay a white down comforter and white sheets of thick woven cotton. The cases on the four fat feather pillows were edged with delicate aged lace, hand-crocheted by Great-Grandmother Butler. Almost everything in Genny's room had a connection to the past, to ancestresses who had lived and loved and died in these Tennessee hills.

Genny had long ago accepted the fact that she was not a modern woman, not an aggressive go-getter like Jazzy. Genny's world was confined by her unique personality and by her rare psychic gifts. She would never leave this house, this land, these hills of home. The familiar kept her centered, helped her balance reality with the supernatural. Perhaps Dallas would be unable to accept a simple life here in Cherokee County. If that turned out to be the case, then she would have no choice but to let him go. She could not leave with him, but she would not force him to stay.

She was willing to accept whatever the future held. In her mind's eye she envisioned a future with Dallas, free from fear and filled with love. But she knew, better than anyone, that all predictions were subject to change. Life altered moment to moment, depending upon billions of actions and reactions. Each person's life touched others, affecting the outcome of Genny's glimpses into the future.

Some things, however, did seem to be set in stone. Some things could not be changed without miracles occurring.

Genny believed in miracles, especially the profound yet subtle miracles that happened in people's lives every day. An infant's birth. Falling in love. A child's beautiful laughter. Inner peace. Sweet dreams coming true.

Tonight was her miracle.

She knelt before the cedar chest at the foot of her bed. Her great-grandfather had made this chest and given it to his only daughter, Melva Mae, to use as a hope chest. During the years in which she grew to womanhood, Granny had filled this chest with the items she would need when she became a bride. After Genny lifted the lid, she reached out and ran her hand over the cotton gown that lay on top of the neatly packed goods beneath. The white gown was semi-sheer, simple in design and adorned with tiny pearl buttons. Fragile lace graced the bodice and the hem. It was a virginal garment, created for a night of initiation. Genny lifted the gossamer-light nightgown and placed it over her arm, then hurried into the bathroom.

After shaving, Dallas stripped out of his clothes, left them lying in a pile on the bathroom floor, and stepped beneath the lukewarm water jetting from the shower. While he lathered his body, he tried not to think about how it would feel to have Genny's small hands touching him. But he could not control the images in his mind. What would it feel like for her to caress him, arouse him? Just the thought created an instant erection. His sex jutted forward. He washed himself, and the touch of his own fingertips almost sent him over the edge. Genny's presence was everywhere, all around him. Her scent lingered in every room of this house. Flowery. Subtle. Barely discernable.

Having sex wasn't a new experience for him. He'd been sexually active since he was sixteen and had lost his virginity to one of his sister Alexandria's college roommates. Jillian had given him a night he'd never forgotten.

Wonder whatever happened to Jillian?

During his late teens and early twenties, he'd "gone

steady'' several times. In his midtwenties he'd even lived with a woman—Shannon—for nearly a year. He usually gave as good as he got, but he'd always been honest about not wanting a commitment. He knew there were happy marriages; his parents had spent twenty great years together. But he was also well aware of marriages made in hell. His father's second marriage reeked of fire and brimstone.

Of course, the bottom line was simple. He'd never loved any woman enough to want to spend the rest of his life with her.

So how do you feel about Genny?

Dallas turned off the shower, stepped out onto the tile floor and grabbed a thick, fluffy towel from the nearby rack. While he dried himself, he mulled over the question. How did he feel about Genny? He wanted her. And yeah, if he was completely honest with himself, he had to admit that he was in love with her. The initial feelings had hit him the moment he first saw her and had been expanding like a summer wildfire ever since.

As corny as it sounded, he'd never felt this way about another woman.

After drying off, Dallas picked up his bundle of dirty clothes and carried them with him into the bedroom. He stuffed them into a black plastic bag, then looked through the items in his suitcase, searching for something to wear. He didn't even own a pair of pajamas. He'd slept in his skivvies since he'd been a kid. After searching through his limited wardrobe, Dallas decided on a pair of well-worn jeans. Since the house was comfortably warm, he left off his shirt. After all, he'd be stripping out of his clothes soon anyway.

Standing alone in his bedroom, barefoot and bare-chested, he considered what he was about to do. He was going to make love to Genny. All night long. Once wouldn't be enough. Hell, two or three times wouldn't be enough.

Usually he didn't put this much thought into a night of sex, but, then, he'd never made love to someone like Genny.

He had no idea how experienced she was. She was a sexy, sensual woman. There had to have been other men.

Hell! For some absurd, purely irrational, macho reason, Dallas didn't want to think about those other men.

Tonight wouldn't be an isolated incident. He had moved into Genny's house and would be living here until the killer was caught. Whatever they started tonight would continue for as long as he was here in Cherokee County. Would a brief affair be enough for Genny? Would it be enough for him?

Just what are you thinking? he asked himself. The kind of love he felt for Genny was new to him. He wasn't sure how to deal with it. Was marriage out of the question? Would she leave her mountain, her way of life, to go to the big city with him? Or on the flip side, would he be willing to leave the Bureau and settle for a bucolic life in the hills?

Hell, why was he letting himself get all worked up over the future? All that mattered was tonight. The here and now. Tomorrow would take care of itself. It always did. Live for the moment. That was his philosophy.

Pushing aside all his concerns, Dallas walked down the hall to Genny's room. The door stood ajar, giving him a full view of the candlelit interior. His stomach knotted. He'd never seen anything so damn romantic in his entire life. A fire flickered in the stone fireplace. The covers had been turned down on the bed. Pale, wavering shadows danced across the wooden floor.

The bathroom door opened. Genny flipped off the bathroom light and walked into her bedroom. Her beauty took his breath away. Her jet black hair hung loosely down to her waist. The silhouette of her slender curves showed plainly through her floor-length gown when she moved toward him in the candlelight.

"Please, come in," she said, her voice low and soft.

He took several steps beyond the threshold, then paused, unable to take his eyes off Genny. Every masculine urge within him wanted to lay claim to her. Now.

But he couldn't rush things. Not with this woman. There

would be only one first time for them. He wanted to make it memorable.

"I don't have any champagne in the house," she said. "All I have is some apple cider."

"We don't need champagne." He glanced around the room, before focusing on her. "We have everything we need."

"If I have you, I have everything." She glided toward him, like an angel in a woman's body.

"Genny, honey . . . God, I don't know what to say."

"Words aren't necessary, are they? We don't need words to communicate. Our hearts can speak for us."

And his body could speak for him. It could tell her how much he wanted her, how desperately he needed her.

When he held out his hand, she came to him. He eased his fingers beneath her hair and clasped the back of her neck. She tilted her chin and looked up at him. And that one look was his undoing. She was right—they didn't need words. Everything she felt was there in her eyes. All the love and longing.

"Genny." Her name reverberated in the hushed stillness of the room.

Her mouth parted on a gentle sigh.

He urged her face upward as he lowered his mouth to hers. He kissed her. And in that one moment he knew his life would never be the same again.

Genny surrendered to the kiss, giving herself to him now, without reservation. Her body leaned into his. Oh, the feelings that washed over her. The ache between her legs. The heaviness of her breasts. The pulsating desire that spiraled through her.

Her fingers inched up his arms to his shoulders, then tightened fiercely, clamping down on his hard muscles. When she stood on tiptoe, trying to get closer to him, Dallas slid his hands down her back, cupped her buttocks and lifted her off the floor. And all the while he kept kissing her.

She could smell his heat. His hot masculine scent aroused her unbearably. The throbbing between her legs intensified. Moisture gathered inside her, preparing her body for mating.

Dallas ended the kiss, then swept her up into his arms and carried her across the room. He laid her on the bed; then hovering over her, bracing his knees on either side of her hips, he began undoing the row of small pearl buttons that ran the length of her gown. Each time he slipped a pearl through a buttonhole and exposed another tiny bit of flesh, he lingered over the newly visible area. Caressing, kissing, licking. Inch by slow torturous inch, he opened her gown. By the time he reached her navel, she was writhing and whimpering, the passion within her winding tighter and tighter.

When he reached the last button, he spread the gown apart and looked at her. She felt his gaze burning into her, branding her.

He kissed each breast, then laved the nipple of one before moving to the other. Her hips lifted off the bed, her body seeking closer contact with his. He sucked greedily at one breast. His fingers plucked and pinched at the other.

While he licked a trail from her collarbone to her navel, his right hand slipped between her thighs, parting them. His fingers skimmed over her mound, dipped between her pubic lips and then thrust up inside her.

She felt his whole body tense. He realized she was ready for him. He lifted himself off the bed, removed his jeans, then pulled a condom from a pocket before tossing his pants on the floor. Genny watched in fascination as he worked the condom up and over his large, erect penis.

Then he did the unexpected. He pulled her to the edge of the bed, lifted and separated her legs to rest on his shoulders and covered her with his mouth. She cried out when he sucked, then licked. The tension inside her intensified as his tongue rubbed and pushed and stroked, bringing her to the very brink several times before he withdrew and kissed the inside of each thigh. When she thought she would go mad unless he gave her the relief her body craved, he increased the pressure and the pace.

Tighter. Tighter.

Explosion.

She sprang loose, her orgasm splintering through her, shaking her from head to toe. Just as the last trembling spasm hit her, Dallas shoved her up into the bed, came down over her, lifted her hips and rammed into her.

When he ripped away her virginity, the pain sliced through her like a dull knife. He froze the minute he realized what he'd done.

"My God, Genny, why didn't you tell me?"

She reached up, put her arms around his neck and drew his face to hers. She kissed him, then slowly began moving her hips, taking him deeper into her body.

"Are you sure?" he asked. "If it hurts too much—"

She silenced him with another kiss, while her body moved to an undulating rhythm, encouraging him to continue.

"Genny . . . Genny . . ."

Smothering her with kisses, he eased deeper and deeper inside her, until he was buried to the hilt. He stilled his movements, then carefully withdrew. He lunged again. Slowly. Gently. Ever so gradually he increased the tempo. And when she sighed with pleasure, he stopped holding back and began pumping into her harder and faster.

She couldn't believe she was going to come again, but she was. She did. And seconds after she cried out with release, Dallas gasped. He climaxed. His big body shivered. He moaned, then collapsed on top of her.

Dallas awoke with a hard-on. He felt Genny's slender arms and legs wrapped around him beneath the waist-high covers, and her head rested on his chest. He tenderly cradled the back of her head with his hand. Lying here in his arms, totally trusting, completely abandoned, Genevieve Madoc was the living, breathing embodiment of his male fantasies. A virgin who'd never been with another man. An innocent who'd responded to him passionately, eager to please him, willing to do anything he asked. A lover who came to life every time he touched her, climaxing twice, despite being a novice.

He noticed that the candles were still glowing and the fire still burned brightly. It had been only a couple of hours since they'd fallen asleep after the first loving, but he already wanted her again.

He kissed her forehead. She stirred, but didn't awaken. He ran his hand over her back and down her hip, then cupped one rounded buttock. She moved against him . . . silkily, sensually . . . like a spoiled little cat wanting attention; and when he heard her purr, he knew she was awake.

"How sore are you?" he asked quietly.

She lifted her head from his chest, slid up his body and kissed his neck. "Not very sore."

He caressed her belly in a circular motion, then plunged his hand between her thighs. She tightened around him, trapping his inquisitive fingers.

"I want you again," he told her.

She kicked the covers to the foot of the bed, then crawled on top of him, aligning her body perfectly for a quick, smooth joining. Gripping her waist, he lifted her just enough to settle her over his erection. Only after he was deep inside her did he remember he'd taken her raw, without any protection. But when he started to withdraw, she clung to him.

"No, not this time," she murmured. "This time I want all of you. Everything."

"But Genny . . ."

"You want this, too. I know you do."

She was right. He did want it like this. No barriers between them. Only with Genny would he throw caution to the wind; because only with Genny did the consequences seem unimportant.

She rode him as if she'd sat astride him a hundred times. They moved together in perfect unison. They kissed. They caressed. She sighed and cried. He groaned and whispered earthy, erotic words that seemed to ignite a fire inside her.

As passion built inside them, their movements became wilder. They tumbled about on the bed, reversing dominate positions several times before they rolled off the bed and onto the floor in front of the fireplace. Dallas lifted her from the large oval rug and placed her on top of him again. She sat there, her head tossed back, her breasts begging for his lips, and suddenly he knew what she'd meant when she'd said she wanted all of him. Everything.

He could feel what Genny was feeling, could hear what she was thinking, could sense his own body through her. Whatever the hell was happening to him, it was unlike anything he'd ever experienced. He couldn't explain it, but somewhere in his dazed mind he knew that Genny had made a connection to him. But not just telepathically. This was more.

Without saying a word, she begged him to love her, to never stop loving her, to be a part of her forever. And in that moment, when fulfillment claimed them both simultaneously, Dallas knew that Genny was all he needed. All he'd ever need.

Chapter 22

"We'd better get out of bed and put on some clothes." Dallas ran his hand down Genny's back and caressed her hip. "Jacob will be here in less than an hour."

"I'll need to bring Drudwyn inside and feed him again," Genny said.

"When I let him out earlier, he headed straight for the woods."

"Well, he has a girlfriend, and I'm sure he was eager to see her."

"I know the feeling."

Genny lifted her arms above her head and stretched like a feline basking in the sun. "I've never felt so wonderful in my entire life." She flung her arms around Dallas and spread kisses from his ear to his shoulder. "Dallas Sloan, I think you're very good for me."

He reached out and lifted her just enough so that the front of her body rested along his right side, her head on his chest; then he kissed the top of her head. "That works both ways. You're definitely good for me. As a matter of fact, you're the best thing that's ever happened to me."

Genny snuggled closer, loving the feel of their naked

bodies pressing intimately against each other. "I feel the same." As she rubbed one leg up and down his, she curled her fingers around several strands of his chest hair.

"Genny, about what happened . . ." He cleared his throat. "I don't mean the great sex. I mean the other . . . I don't know quite how to describe it."

"You mean the connection." She lifted her head and gazed down into his blue eyes. "We can feel what the other is feeling, sense what the other is thinking."

"Yeah, I guess that's it." Dallas continued fondling her, as if he had no choice but to touch her. "After the first time, each time we made love, it happened. I was experiencing what you were experiencing and—"

"And I was feeling . . . sensing . . . everything that you did."

"How?" he asked. "How is that possible?"

"I don't know. It's never happened to me before." She laughed softly. "But Granny told me that it would. It happened with her and Papa Butler. She called it *the connection.*"

"This connection—you feel it even when we aren't making love, don't you?" He grasped her chin. "Tell me the truth. Can you always read my mind?"

She smiled and shook her head. "I can't read your mind. Not even when we're making love. Not really. It's more of a bonding, a physical, mental and emotional joining . . . becoming one."

"Yeah, that's how it felt." He eased his big hand down over her neck and across each breast. Genny sucked in a deep breath when her nipples peaked. "But you can't read my mind right now?" he asked.

"No, but I can send you a telepathic message," she told him. "And if you'll listen, you can hear me."

"The night I swore I'd never come back up here to see you again, when I returned to my cabin, I got this overwhelming feeling that you needed me." Dallas shot straight up in bed, inadvertently shoving her aside. Turning sharply, he glared at her. "I thought I saw your image in the mirror over the sink. . . . My God, you sent me a telepathic message that night, didn't you?''

''You didn't actually hear me,'' she said as she rose from the bed. ''You only sensed what I was saying to you.'' She picked up her gown off the floor and put it on, hurriedly working the tiny pearl buttons through the buttonholes. ''Now that we've bonded in a physical way, you should be able to hear me talking to you . . . inside your mind. If you're willing to listen.''

''That will certainly make telephones unnecessary.'' Dallas got up, grabbed his jeans off the floor, and slipped them up over his legs and hips.

''But not until you're able to communicate with me in the same way—''

He snapped his head around; their gazes locked. ''Oh, okay. Yeah, I see what you mean. You can send me a message, but I don't have the ability to respond to you telepathically.''

''You do have the ability within you,'' she told him. ''You just haven't found a way to use it.''

How could she tell Dallas that only by believing wholeheartedly in his own sixth sense, as well as hers, could they become truly connected, in every way, as Granny and Papa Butler had been? He would have to discover that fact for himself. Once his love for her was strong enough, his faith in their union powerful enough, the boundaries between them would disappear completely. And when that happened, they could go away any time they wanted to, just the two of them, to their secret place. A place within themselves that no one else could ever share.

Dallas continued staring at her for several minutes, then he nodded his head. ''I guess I'll have to get used to having a girlfriend who possesses all these psychic abilities.''

Genny went to him, lifted her arms up around his neck, stood on tiptoe and kissed him. Responding immediately, he deepened the kiss, then swung her up into his arms and carried her to the bathroom. He turned on the shower, then stripped her out of her gown and took off his jeans.

"If we shower together, we'll save time," he told her, then lifted her by her waist and set her into the stall.

"Maybe we should wash each other and save more time."

"I like the idea," he said. "But I'm warning you—if you touch me, I'll have to make love to you."

Her hand hovered over his chest. Without touching him, she eased her hand lower . . . and lower. Then she reached out and circled his erect penis.

"I warned you, didn't I?"

Dallas grabbed her. She laughed when he picked her up, then slid her down onto his sex. She wrapped her legs around his hips and surrendered to the pleasure ripening inside her.

Dallas and Jacob stood just inside the doorway of Melva Mae Butler's bedroom and watched while Genny drew the curtains and lit all the white candles situated throughout the room.

"She prefers Granny's room when she does readings or uses her sight for a particular purpose," Jacob said. "She might not admit it, but I think she believes Granny's soul protects her in some way if she's in this room."

"You know, a couple of weeks ago I'd have thought you were crazy to believe in her the way you do," Dallas admitted. "At first, I thought Genny was just a very beautiful nutcase."

"Now you know different." Jacob looked right at Dallas. "Don't hurt her. Don't break her heart. If you do . . . I'll have to break your damn neck."

Dallas nodded. "I swear to you that I would do anything for her." Dallas added silently, I'd kill to protect her. I'd even die for her."

"Yeah, I figured as much."

Genny moved three chairs around the small table at the side of the room, then motioned to Dallas and Jacob. "Come here, please, and sit down. Both of you."

They did as she requested. After they took their seats, she, too, sat. "This may work. It might not. But if it does,

I'll go very deep into another realm. And if I venture in too far, I may need help coming back.'' She looked at Jacob. ''We've done this before, so you know what to expect.''

''Just be very careful,'' Jacob told her. ''I remember another time when I almost didn't get you back.''

''You won't be doing it alone. You'll have help this time.'' Genny smiled at Dallas, then reached over and clasped his hand. ''To pull me back, you can use verbal words, but you must use mental words, too. Use your mind to draw me back to you. Do you understand?''

Dallas swallowed. ''I think so.'' He squeezed her hand. ''If you believe you have to do this . . . be careful. Be damn careful.''

Genny released his hand, sat straight up in her chair, and shut her eyes. Dallas watched her closely. She appeared to relax completely. Minutes seemed like hours. He could hear his own heartbeat, could sense each second ticking away inside his mind. The silence in the room was almost unbearable. Then he began to hear the subtle little sounds he ordinarily wouldn't notice. The gentle wind outside the windows murmured softly. The bedside clock's ticking grew louder and louder. Ice cubes chinking as they dropped from the ice machine in the refrigerator echoed down the hall. The repetitive pounding of his own heartbeat drummed in his ears.

Suddenly Genny's breathing became heavy and rapid. Her mouth gaped as she sucked in air. Her eyelids flickered. She moaned softly.

''What's happening?'' Dallas whispered.

''She's made a connection,'' Jacob replied in a low voice.

''Is she in pain?''

''No.''

Genny made odd noises. Gasps. Whimpers. Groans. All the while she sat with her eyes closed, her body barely moving.

And then as Dallas and Jacob watched her, she tossed back her head and a look of sheer agony appeared on her face.

"No, please, no!" Genny cried.

"What is it, Genny? What's happened?" Dallas reached for her, but Jacob grabbed Dallas's arm and shook his head.

"Can you talk to us?" Jacob asked.

"Blood. Blood on her face. Blood on her arms . . . the knife. No, don't!"

Darkness all around. Swirling mists of malevolence surrounded the bare feet standing inside the pentagram painted on the floor—painted in blood. The woman's own blood. It dripped from the small incisions in her arms. She held the crimson-stained knife over her head as she swayed slowly and hummed. Her white blond hair fell in wild array around her naked shoulders.

"Prince Beelzebub, I beseech thee," the woman shouted. "I desire to make a pact with thee, and request that thou protect me and bless me."

Genny could see the woman's face plainly. A face etched with pleasurable pain. She stood, totally naked, in the center of a dark room. Alone.

"I command thee, Great Lucifer, to send an emissary to receive my offerings, and if these gifts please thee, then do my bidding on this day. I desire thy instruction in the ways of the ancients."

This isn't right, Genny's mind cried out. *Do not ask favors from the dark powers. Evil will take your soul.*

Startled when she heard Genny's voice inside her head, the woman dropped the knife to the concrete floor. She stopped abruptly and looked all around her.

"Who is speaking to me?" She stepped out of the unholy circle and began searching the room.

I'm not in the room with you. I'm in your mind. I see what you're trying to do. I know what you hope to accomplish. You must stop now. No good can come of this. Not for you or for others.

The woman shook her head, as if trying to dislodge the voice inside her. When she found nothing in her search, she reached for a switch on the wall, flipped the lever and flooded the room with overhead lighting.

Genny realized the woman was in a large room in a basement. She saw cinder-block walls and a concrete floor, both in their natural state. Weathered gray. Cold. Damp.

"Are you a witch?" the woman asked.

I am no witch, Genny told her.

"Who are you? What do you want? How did you contact me? Please, answer me. I want to learn. I must—"

Genny began backing away, knowing that she had connected with evil, but not the monstrous mind of the killer she sought.

"Answer me, damn you!"

Genny tried to free herself from the mental connection she'd made with Esther Stowe, but the minister's wife held tight, refusing to release her.

"I must know who you are!"

I am one who wishes you no harm.

"Are you a messenger from my Lord Satan?"

No, Esther, I am not. My powers come from a kind and loving God.

Suddenly as if what she'd heard startled her, Esther's grip on Genny snapped like a rotten twig in the wind. Genny's mind swirled through endless clouds of darkness. Black. Poisonous. A dangerous vortex of unholiness threatened. Genny fought valiantly to escape.

Gray mists curled all around her, then disappeared, leaving only a clean, pure white light. She heaved a deep sigh, knowing she was free and once again in total control.

She opened her eyes and looked first at Dallas and then at Jacob. Both men were leaning toward her, concerned expressions on their faces.

"I didn't reach the killer," Genny said in a weak voice. "I made contact with a woman who proclaims herself a witch, someone who practices black magic."

"How did that happen?" Jacob asked. "If you were concentrating on Cherokee County, then that must mean—"

"She lives in Cherokee Pointe," Genny told them. "It's Esther Stowe, the minister's wife."

Esther ran upstairs to her bathroom, showered hurriedly, washing the blood from her body; then she covered her cuts with antiseptic cream. She couldn't believe what had happened. Didn't really understand what it meant. But she knew, without a doubt, that she had telepathically linked with another mind. But it had not been a believer in the occult, not someone such as herself.

The voice had said she wasn't a witch, but Esther believed otherwise. Whoever possessed such incredible power had to be no less than a high priestess, albeit a high priestess in the art of white magic. If only she could connect with this person again.

Esther opened her closet door, jerked a set of gray sweats from a hanger and slipped into them. She put on socks and shoes, then headed for the front door. After grabbing her black-and-white wool tweed coat from the hall tree, she rushed out of the house, leaving the front door unlocked. She raced along the sidewalk, bursting into a run several times, then slowing her pace back to a fast walk. She made it from the parsonage to the church, half a block away, in record time.

She hoped Haden was alone. He spent much too much time working with, consoling, and comforting the members of his church. At heart, Haden was a do-gooder, despite his odd behavior quirks. When she'd first met him at seventeen, he'd been the minister at the church her aunt Theda attended back in Abilene, Texas. They'd started screwing around within a month of meeting, and as soon as she turned eighteen, they'd gotten married. Hell, she would have married just about anybody to have gotten away from Aunt Theda and Abilene. At first the sex had been good and Haden had doted on her, giving her whatever her heart desired. But it hadn't been long until he revealed his little sexual oddities.

He was a voyeur. He liked to watch. And nothing turned him on more than watching her fuck another man.

Marty Gannon had become her lover and her teacher. He had introduced her to satanism, and she quickly discovered her true calling. For the past five years she had worked diligently at her trade, at first seeking out other covens when she and Haden moved from one parish to another, then eventually forming her own covens and anointing herself as the high priestess.

Haden had strenuously objected to her practicing black magic, but when she threatened to end the fun and games he couldn't live without, he became more tolerant. At first he had refused to join her in the rituals, but when sexual orgies were added to the coven's list of practices, Haden had been unable to stay away. He never participated himself, but he watched with lascivious pleasure.

Esther knocked on the office door and waited. She'd learned not to flounce in on her husband while he was at work.

"Yes, please come in," Haden said.

She opened the door and peeked inside. "Are you alone?"

"Yes, I'm working on my Sunday sermon."

"I have something wonderful to tell you. Something you aren't going to believe."

She burst into the room and ran straight to him. She threw her arms around him as she flopped down on his lap. Stunned, he drew back tensely and stared at her.

"I made a telepathic connection to someone this afternoon," Esther said.

"My God!" Haden's eyes widened in shock. "Who . . . ?"

"Calm yourself. I didn't speak personally to Old Scratch." Esther laughed. "I linked with a woman who says she's not a witch, but I know she is. She's a white witch, though, and—"

Haden grabbed Esther's chin. She yelped when his long, thin fingers bit into her cheeks.

"You've allowed someone to learn your identity, someone you don't know and trust?" Haden glowered at her. "You little fool, do you know what you've done?"

"What's wrong with you? Why are you so upset?"

"Do you know who this woman is?"

Esther shook her head.

"Does she know who you are?" he asked.

"I don't think she knows—" Esther gasped.

"What?"

"She called me Esther."

"You're an idiot. You've exposed yourself. Exposed us. This woman who is capable of telepathy knows you're a practicing witch. Our lives will be ruined if that truth is revealed."

"But . . . but . . . why would she . . . what would she have to . . . oh, Haden, who do you think she is?"

When he shoved her off his lap, she almost lost her balance, but managed to grab hold of the desk. He paced the room. Esther stood silently by and waited until he'd worked off some of the anger-fed energy.

"Genevieve Madoc!" Haden cried. "The girl who lives on the mountain. The people here in Cherokee Pointe say her grandmother was a witch woman. Supposedly she has strong psychic talents. It has to be her. I don't think there's anyone else it could be."

"Isn't the sheriff her cousin or her brother or something?"

"Her cousin. And if she tells him about you and he starts poking into our business—"

"I'll hide everything," Esther said. "I'll gather up all my books and potions and . . . I promise I won't—"

He grabbed her shoulders. "If he connects us to the animal sacrifices that were done in the woods last fall, then it will be only a short leap to suspecting us of murder."

"Murder? But who—"

"There have been three women sacrificed in Cherokee County. Don't you think people are going to believe that someone who sacrifices animals as part of their devil-worship rituals might easily sacrifice human beings?"

"Maybe it wasn't Genevieve Madoc that I contacted. Maybe it—"

Haden shook her soundly. "You didn't contact her, you fool. You have no powers. She contacted you. Now she knows who you are."

"What—what are we going to do?"

"You're going to get rid of everything connected to your black magic. I don't care what you do with it, just make sure it can't be linked back to us."

"But what about the Madoc woman?"

"Don't worry. I'll take care of her."

Chapter 23

With his strong arm firmly placed around her waist, Dallas walked with Genny from her grandmother's room to her own. She had depended on Granny for most of her life, whenever she'd recuperated after using her gift of sight. But during the past six years, she'd had no choice but to rely on Jacob and Jazzy and occasionally Sally and Ludie. They were the only people she trusted implicitly, the ones who truly understood her situation. But now she had Dallas, for however long he chose to remain in her life. He gave her strength, as no one else could, the bond between them unique.

As Dallas helped her into her bed, Jacob stood in the doorway. Genny held out her hand to him and called his name.

Jacob went to her and took her hand in his. "I'm here, *i gi do*. What is it?"

"Esther Stowe is practicing witchcraft. She is the high priestess of a coven in Cherokee Pointe," Genny said. "While I was inside her mind, I drew images from her thoughts, images of animal sacrifices and wild orgies." Genny paused, took several shallow breaths and then continued. "She yearns for magical powers and is calling on the devil with incantations that she actually believes will work."

"Did you get a sense that she is in any way connected to the sacrificial murders?"

"No, but . . ." Genny's eyelids drooped, then closed.

"Genny?" Dallas called to her.

"She's asleep." Jacob released her hand and turned to Dallas. "You'll stay here with her?"

Dallas nodded and the two men walked out into the hall.

"I think I'll pay a friendly visit to the Reverend and Mrs. Stowe," Jacob said. "I can't accuse them of anything since I have no evidence of any kind. And no judge is going to issue a search warrant so we can inspect the church and the parsonage just because Genny had a vision. But I can shake the Stowes up a little simply by dropping by to see them."

"Genny didn't seem to sense that Esther Stowe was connected to the murders, but what if Reverend Stowe is? Or maybe one of the members of Esther's coven. Could be our guy has a past history with witchcraft."

"I'll call—"

"Let me contact Teri. We'll get quicker results that way."

"You'll have her check out Carson, Pierpont, and Jamie Upton, as well as Haden and Esther Stowe?"

"Most definitely," Dallas said. "Call me after you talk to the Stowes."

"Yeah, I'd planned to call you to check on Genny, anyway."

"Don't worry about her. I'll be here to keep watch over her."

Esther Stowe was a delicious creature, lithe and supple, her body made for fucking. When she'd asked a favor of him, he'd readily agreed, knowing she would repay him with sex. Since he was a faithful member of her inept little coven, she believed she could trust him. And she could— up to a point. If he gave away her secrets, he'd also be admitting that he belonged to a devil-worshipping cult. Not something he wanted made public. But if she ever betrayed him by naming him as a follower of Satan, he would punish her severely.

"You'll have to keep everything in your basement," Esther told him. "I know it'll be safe with you. And we won't be able to meet for a while. Haden said not until we're sure the sheriff isn't watching us."

"There's no need to worry," he told her. "We'll find a way to get around Sheriff Butler. In a few weeks, we can use my basement, if we're very discreet."

"Yes, of course. What a wonderful idea, since all my things will be here—"

He clutched the back of her neck and drew her to him. "If for any reason the sheriff questions you and Haden, you mustn't reveal the names of the members of your cult."

With fear in her eyes and tension tightening her body, Esther shook her head. "No, of course not. I'd never do that."

He smiled at her; she relaxed and returned his smile.

"Does Haden know you've brought your things here to store them for safekeeping?"

"He was still at the church when I packed everything up and put it in the car," she said. "I left him a note on the refrigerator telling him I was stopping by here. If he came home and found me gone, he'd worry."

"I would prefer for Haden not to know about my helping you. At least not for now. When you return home, destroy the note you left."

"Sure, I'll do that. Unless Haden's already seen it."

He tightened his hold on her neck, yanked her up against him, and put his mouth to hers. She trembled. He laughed.

With their lips just barely touching, he said, "I want to fuck your mouth."

She sighed deeply.

He released his tenacious hold on her neck. She dropped to her knees in front of him and hurriedly undid his zipper. When she started to reach inside his shorts, he grabbed her hand.

"I'll do the rest," he told her. "Just open your mouth wide."

She did as he requested. Some high priestess she was. His mother would never have allowed a man—any man—to tell her what to do. Mother had been a true high priestess. She gave the orders. She inflicted the pain.

He freed his penis, cupped the back of Esther's head and slid his sex into her mouth. When the tip reached the back of her throat, she gagged, but he held her in place, withdrew, and repeated the process.

Such an obedient little whore. If she hadn't left her husband that damn note, she could become his fourth victim.

The sheriff's big truck was parked in their wide driveway. Esther cursed, wishing damnation on the man. What was he doing here? Had his cousin, that Madoc woman, already called him and told him about their telepathic conversation? What if the sheriff asked her if she was a witch?

Oh, God, what if Haden was entertaining him in the kitchen? What if the sheriff had seen the note?

Esther eased her older model BMW Mini Cooper past the sheriff's truck and parked it beside the church's Sedona minivan that Haden drove. When she tried the back door, she found it still locked. Good. That meant Haden had come in through the front when he'd returned from his church office. She unlocked the door and rushed into the kitchen. She heard voices coming from the living room. Haden and the sheriff. After dumping her shoulder bag and keys on the counter, she looked at the refrigerator. Her note to Haden was still there. She breathed a sigh of relief.

She lifted the magnet and snatched away the note, then tore it into tiny pieces and threw them into the trash.

His smell was still on her, his taste still in her mouth. She couldn't walk into the living room and greet the sheriff until she'd removed the evidence of her recent sexual encounter. First she rinsed her mouth out with water, then took a bottle of lemon juice from the refrigerator and squirted some into her mouth. After she washed her hands and face with liquid soap, she reached under the sink, took out the Lysol canister and sprayed a heavy mist of the deodorizer all around her. That's as much as she could do without going to the bathroom, and she couldn't go to the bathroom from the kitchen without being seen from the living room.

Esther squared her shoulders, forced a warm, welcoming smile, and went into the living room to greet their guest.

"Esther, my dear," Haden said the moment he saw her. "Come in and say hello to Sheriff Butler."

Esther and the sheriff exchanged pleasant greetings.

"You'll never believe what the sheriff and I have been discussing," Haden said, his nose crinkling as he sniffed. Esther faked a puzzled expression. "He's been telling me that he suspects there's a satanic cult here in Cherokee Pointe. Devil-worshiping witches. Isn't that unbelievable?"

"Yes," she replied. "Quite unbelievable."

"I thought your husband should be aware of our suspicions," Sheriff Butler said. "I'm contacting all the ministers in Cherokee County. I think it's something our God-fearing preachers should concern themselves with."

"Of course. Of course." Haden nodded.

"We appreciate your sharing this news with us," Esther said. "Do you have any idea who these people are?"

"I'd rather not say, ma'am. But you can be sure we'll do our best to find out. Folks around here won't put up with any more animal sacrifices."

Haden rubbed his hands together nervously. Damn him! Esther could slap the man. Now wasn't the time to weaken. Earlier today when he'd warned her to get rid of anything that linked them to the coven, he'd been quite masterful. She preferred the harsh, demanding Haden to the simpering, weak creature he often was.

"You—you don't believe there's a connection between the animal sacrifices and the sacrificial murders, do you?" Haden asked, his voice quivering ever so slightly.

The sheriff looked directly at Esther. "We think there's a possibility a member of the coven is our murderer."

"How awful." Esther shook her head in a mock show of sadness.

"I'll be checking in with you from time to time." Sheriff Butler held out his hand to Haden, and the two shared a quick handshake. "I have a few more stops to make, so I need to get going."

Haden walked the sheriff out to the sidewalk, then as soon as he got in his truck, Haden rushed back into the house. The minute the sheriff backed out of the driveway, Haden turned on her.

"See what your insanity has done?" he yelled. "He knows. I tell you, he knows."

"He doesn't know anything except what Genny Madoc told him, and believe me, anything she said isn't something that will hold up in court."

"Court? Do you think being arrested is my only concern? If the truth about your being a witch ever came to light, I'd lose my job. I'd never be allowed to preach ever again."

"I can't say that would be so bad. I hate being a minister's wife. I always have."

"Yes, I know." The look Haden gave her told her that he loathed her every bit as much as she despised him. "We have a great deal to concern us. A great deal. What if Genevieve Madoc tries to contact you again?"

"I hope she does. She's very powerful and she could—"

Haden slapped Esther. She reeled backward, rubbed her cheek, and glared at him.

"I won't allow it," he told her. "Do you hear me? You must know how dangerous that woman is to us."

She laughed at her husband. "I did as you asked. I've made sure all the items that could connect us to the coven are well hidden. I intend to do my part to protect us. But understand this—I'm not afraid of you, Haden. You can't control me." She walked right up to him and smiled. "And no matter what you think, you can't control Genny Madoc. But maybe I can. I can put a curse on her. I can—"

"You're a fool if you think you can cast spells or put curses on people. You don't have any magical powers." He looked at her, running his gaze from her head to her feet. "The only talent you have is using your body to pleasure men. You can't handle Genny Madoc, but I can. I know a way."

Wallace MacKinnon had called late in the afternoon to ask if he should come to work the following day. Dallas had told him he should, unless he heard otherwise from Genny. There was no reason to assume Genny wouldn't be able to continue her life in a fairly normal way, despite her knowing she was the final target for a madman. Dallas felt reluctant to leave her alone, even if Jacob could provide adequate protection. But as it was, Jacob's deputies were limited in number, and each was needed, so it would cause a hardship to the Sheriff's Department to post one officer to guard Genny. And Dallas wasn't sure if he would trust her safety to anyone else.

While Genny rested, Dallas inspected the greenhouses for her as she had requested when she'd awakened briefly. He'd left Drudwyn at her bedside and had double-checked all the doors and made sure they were locked before he'd gone outside.

The sun had already set, and twilight shadows crept across the hills. Night was fast approaching. Standing near the back porch, Dallas gazed skyward. Overhead storm clouds swirled. Off in the distance, thunder rumbled. They'd probably get rain before morning. And if the temperatures dropped into the low thirties tonight, they might get some sleet.

Dallas entered the screened porch, wiped his feet on the mat, and removed his coat. He should put on water for tea. When Genny woke, she'd want something warm to drink. And he'd fix sandwiches for supper. She probably wouldn't want anything to eat, but he'd encourage her to put a little something in her stomach.

After hanging his coat on the rack on the porch, he went into the kitchen and began preparations for their evening meal. Before the teakettle whistled, he heard Drudwyn yowl-

ing and knew Genny was awake and playing with the wolf-
dog. Quickly, he prepared a cup of tea. As he carried the
mug down the hall, he thought about how unlike him it was
to be smothering a woman with tender, loving care. In his
relationships, the TLC was usually directed at him. Women
tended to chase him, and when they thought they had even
the slightest chance of catching him, they'd smother him
with attention. This was the first time in his life that he'd
been the giver and not the taker.

He grunted as he paused outside Genny's bedroom. Funny
thing was, he'd never cared enough about a woman before
to concern himself with her needs beyond sexual satisfaction.
Genny was different.

God, what an understatement!

When he entered the bedroom, he found her sitting on
the floor in front of the fireplace. She had her arm draped
around Drudwyn's neck and was stroking him lovingly.

"Feeling better?" he asked.

She looked up at him and smiled. "I'm feeling fine."
She eyed the mug he held. "Is that for me?"

"Hot tea." He brought the mug to her.

"Thank you." She accepted his offering, then lifted the
mug to her lips and took several tiny sips.

He reached down and skimmed his hand over her hair,
from earlobe to shoulder. "Drink your tea while I go back
in the kitchen and put together a couple of sandwiches for
us."

"I'm really not very hungry."

"Then you'll eat what you can," he told her. "But you're
going to eat."

"Yes, *yu ne ga,* I will obey," Genny said teasingly.

"What did you call me?" he asked.

Genny laughed. "I called you a white man."

"Well, I am a white man, so I guess that wasn't an insult."
He grinned. "What is it that Jacob calls you? *I gi go?*"

"I gi do," Genny corrected. "It means sister in the Cherokee language."

Suddenly Dallas felt a twinge of jealousy that she shared

so much with her cousin Jacob, that he even had a pet name for her. "Maybe I should learn the Cherokee language," Dallas told her as he started to leave.

"Do you want to know a name I would like for you to call me?" she asked.

He paused when he reached the doorway, then glanced over his shoulder. "What would you like for me to call you?"

"A qua da li i."

Dallas repeated the words. "What does it mean?"

"I'll tell you . . . someday."

Genny's smile brightened the whole room. Hell, it brightened his whole world.

"I could ask Jacob."

"You could. But you won't."

"Drink your tea," he told her. "I'll be back in a little while with your supper."

"I can come to the kitchen."

"All right, if you feel up to it."

"I'll come with you now. I need to put out feed for the birds and other animals. They'll be expecting it."

"Tell me where you keep the feed sacks and—"

"They won't take food if anyone else has touched it."

Dallas grimaced. "I should have known."

When Genny rose to her feet and followed Dallas, Drudwyn galloped after her. Once in the kitchen, Dallas set about preparing their sandwiches while Genny went out onto the back porch. She removed a huge feed sack from a wooden storage box near the stack of firewood; then she filled four bowls and stacked them one on top of the other and set them on the floor. After removing her coat from the wall rack and putting it on, she picked up the bowls.

When she swung open the screen door with her hip, Drudwyn dashed outside. Balancing the bowls with both hands, Genny walked out into the backyard. The screen door flopped shut with a loud bang. Dallas dropped the butter knife he was using to spread mustard on the bread slices and ran after her.

"Genny, wait," he called. "I don't want you—"

The shot rang out in the hushed stillness of twilight. Dallas yelled her name. Suddenly he felt as if heavy weights were attached to his ankles. Everything seemed to be happening in slow motion. He heard the shot. He heard his own voice echoing inside his head. He saw Genny balk, then grab her shoulder and lean to one side. He saw Drudwyn take off like a rocket, chasing something—or someone.

Genny crumpled into a heap on the ground. When Dallas reached her, she lay still and unmoving. He knelt beside her, saw the blood staining the back of her coat, and was forced to accept the fact that she'd been shot. Someone had shot her. In her own backyard. With a big, brave FBI agent guarding her.

He held her in his arms for several seconds before his training kicked in. He checked her vital signs. Weak. But she was still alive. He had two choices: get Genny to the hospital immediately or follow Drudwyn's lead and chase after the person who had shot her.

Dallas scooped Genny up off the ground. As far as he was concerned there was really only one choice. The only thing that mattered right now was Genny.

Chapter 24

Jazzy placed her hand on Dallas Sloan's back. He tensed immediately but didn't turn to face her. Ever since she'd arrived at Cherokee County General last night, she hadn't heard Dallas utter a single word. The small waiting room was filled to capacity with people who loved Genny. Jacob. Sally and Ludie. Royce. Wallace. Brian. And dozens of people had come and gone during the long night, offering prayers and assistance. Numerous Cherokee County folks had telephoned, as had ministers from the Baptist church and the Methodist church, even though Genny wasn't a member of either denomination. The nurse's aides had brought out coffee several times and offered to bring food up from the snack bar. Anyone who knew Genny thought she was special. The entire county cared what happened to her.

And no one, absolutely no one, could understand why anybody would want to harm such a kind, gentle, and loving soul.

When Jacob called her last night, Jazzy had rushed to the ER, but too late to see Genny before they carried her to surgery. She'd found Jacob sitting quietly, his head bowed and his eyes closed, in the surgery waiting area on the second floor. Dallas had been pacing outside in the hall. When she'd spoken to him, he hadn't even noticed her.

Jacob had explained what had happened, at least what little he'd been able to get out of Dallas. "I've got a team up there at the house now searching for evidence all around," he'd said. "This wasn't what we were expecting. There's no way we could have known. Dallas is blaming himself and nothing I've said to him has convinced him otherwise."

After endless hours of waiting and praying, they'd heard good news. Genny had come through surgery with flying colors, and the doctor assured them she would recover fully. The bullet had entered her back and exited her shoulder, but hadn't struck anything vital. Jazzy had expected Dallas to react the way she and Jacob had—with happy relief. Instead, he'd fled. She didn't know where he'd gone, but she suspected he had sought a place of solitude where he could be alone. The bathroom? The chapel? He'd probably puked. Or cried. Or offered a prayer of thanks. Maybe all three.

Now, at four-fifty in the morning, Jazzy stood behind Dallas at the end of the hallway where he stared out the window into the darkness. She patted his back. "They're going to let us go in to see her in a few minutes."

He nodded, but still didn't turn around.

"Genny is going to be all right."

Silence.

"You've got to snap out of it before you go in to see her," Jazzy told him. "She'll sense something's wrong the minute she sees you. You look like a man who's been to hell and back."

He glanced over his shoulder; his bloodshot eyes glared at Jazzy.

"All this guilt you're wallowing in won't help Genny," Jazzy said. "So take off your hair shirt and accept the fact that you're not Superman, that you're just human like the rest of us."

When he looked away from her, she grabbed his arm. "Damn it, you had no way of knowing some nut was outside waiting for a chance to shoot Genny. She's the one who is psychic, not you, and she probably didn't realize she was in danger until it was too late.''

"I should have stopped her from going outside!'' The words rumbled from his chest like a cannon blast.

Jazzy tightened her hold on his arm and shook him, then moved around to stand in front of him. "If this person planned to shoot Genny, he could have shot her through a window. You couldn't have prevented it. If Jacob had been there, he couldn't have, either.''

Dallas didn't respond.

Jazzy released her tight grip on his arm, turned, and walked away. She had sense enough to know when to back off. Dallas wasn't ready to listen to reason. He was still too consumed by guilt and remorse. She'd been to that particular hell a few times herself.

She met Jacob coming out of the waiting room. "How's he doing?'' Jacob nodded toward the end of the hall.

"Is there something going on that I don't know about?'' Jazzy asked. "He's acting like he was the one who shot her. His guilt isn't reasonable.''

Jacob hesitated, then motioned for her to follow him, which she did. He pulled her around the corner where two halls crisscrossed.

"Nobody else is to know about this. Understand?''

Jazzy nodded.

"Only Genny, Dallas, and I know.'' Jacob looked as if what he was about to say caused him great pain. "Dallas has been tracking a serial killer, a guy he thinks killed his niece in Mobile last year.''

"Yeah, I know. So?''

"This guy kills in fives. Dallas has discovered four sets of practically identical murders occurring over the past few years. None of the victims had anything in common—except that the fifth victim in each case was gifted. The way Genny is gifted.''

Jazzy's mind spun around and around, trying to absorb the implication of Jacob's statement. "The sacrificial murders here in Cherokee County—'' Jazzy gasped. ''My God, he came here because of Genny. She's his fifth victim.''

''Dallas volunteered to act as Genny's bodyguard, and I'd planned to keep a deputy there at the house with her whenever Dallas couldn't be.''

''Do you think the serial killer changed his MO and shot Genny instead of—''

''It wasn't him,'' Jacob said. ''But I have a good idea who it might have been. All I need is one tiny scrap of evidence and I'll haul his ass into jail.''

''Who are you talking about?''

Before Jacob could reply, a nurse walked down the hall toward them, calling Jacob's name.

''Sheriff Butler, you can go in to see Genny now.''

Jacob whispered to Jazzy, ''I'll explain later.''

When Genny regained consciousness, Jazzy was at her side. She tried to lift her head, but the dizziness quickly aborted the effort.

''Hello, sleepy girl,'' Jazzy said. ''How do you feel? Pretty rough, huh?''

''I feel like I've been shot.'' Genny tried to smile, but even that simple action seemed impossible.

''Ah, sweetie. You're going to be all right. Good as new in a few weeks.''

Genny glanced from side to side, then forward, and caught a glimpse of Jacob standing in the doorway. He came toward her, his movements unnaturally hurried. When he reached the bedside, he smoothed his hand over her cheek.

''You gave us a real scare, *i gi do.*''

''Where's Dallas?''

Tense silence.

''Is he all right? He wasn't shot, too, was he?'' The thought that Dallas might be dead flashed through her mind.

''He's fine. He wasn't shot,'' Jacob replied. ''He's been here all night and he's still here somewhere. He's been in awfully bad shape. He blames himself for what happened.''

"What did happen?" Genny asked.

"You went outside to feed the animals before Dallas could stop you and somebody hiding in the woods shot you," Jacob said.

"Who—? Oh, Lord, Jacob, do you think it was—?"

"Either Esther or Reverend Stowe. You got too close to their wicked little secret."

"Find Dallas," Genny said. "I want to see him."

"Hey, girl, there are a few other people out there dying to see you. Aunt Sally and Ludie. Wallace. Royce and Brian. And—"

"I want Dallas!"

"Calm down," Jazzy told her. "I'll go find Dallas and bring him to you if I have to hog-tie him and drag him in here."

"No, you stay with Genny." Jacob leaned over and kissed Genny's forehead. "You rest and stop worrying. I'll find Dallas."

It took Jacob over thirty minutes to find Dallas, and in the meantime he'd gotten a call from Tim Willingham telling him they had found shell casings, footprints, and a piece of material snagged on a bush in the woods near Genny's house. Evidence. Proof that the shooter was a rank amateur, someone who'd been very sloppy. The sacrificial killer was an overconfident pro, who covered his tracks and left behind nothing. Nothing but his DNA. But the really good news about the shooter was that Tommy Patrick, Genny's neighbor who lived on a farm half a mile up the road, had been hunting down a stray cow that had wandered off into the woods at sunset, right about the time Genny was shot. Tommy had heard the rifle fire and had seen a man running through the woods to a car parked on a dirt path leading to the main road. The tall, thin, dark-haired man had been driving a older model BMW that fit the description of the one belonging to Esther Stowe.

Bingo! Got 'em!

Jacob paused before approaching Dallas and tried to put himself in the guy's shoes. What would be the best way to handle him? *Hell, man, what would be the best way for somebody to handle you if you were in this situation?*

Dallas sat alone in the empty snack bar. Hunched over, his arms crossed and resting on the tabletop, he stared off into space. Not much traffic in the snack bar at five-thirty in the morning. When Dallas heard Jacob approach, he lifted his head and looked straight across the room.

"Has something happened to Genny?" Dallas asked.

"Yeah, something's happened. She's awake and asking for you."

Dallas's shoulders slumped.

"I want you to go upstairs and see her before we drive over to the Stowes and bring them in for questioning," Jacob said.

"Then your team found some sort of evidence against them?" Dallas's eyes brightened, and his shoulders lifted.

"Yeah, the best kind—an eyewitness who places a man fitting the reverend's description in the woods near Genny's house. And he saw this man get into a car identical to the one Esther Stowe drives."

Strain marred Dallas's features as he shut his eyes for a moment. Jacob knew he was thanking God, thanking the Good Lord that Genny was all right and that they probably had enough evidence to arrest Haden Stowe for attempted murder.

Jacob moved closer to the table where Dallas sat. "I'm sure you want to be there when I question them."

"You know it." Dallas rose from his chair.

"We'll head over to the courthouse just as soon as you go upstairs and see Genny."

"I can't." Dallas avoided direct eye contact with Jacob.

"You can and you will. She's up there waiting for you. She didn't understand why you weren't there when she woke up."

Jacob clamped his hand down on Dallas's shoulder. Their

gazes locked and held, two fierce combatants, neither giving an inch.

"How do I face her after what happened?" Dallas glanced away first.

Jacob released his tenacious hold on Dallas's shoulder. "She's not going to blame you. Nobody holds you responsible for what happened, except you."

"How would you feel if you'd been the one who was supposed to be guarding her?"

"I'd feel just like you do. But I'd suck it up and go on with what had to be done. I'd face my worst fear. I'd walk into that ICU unit and let Genny know that I hadn't deserted her, that I never would."

Five minutes later, Dallas stood outside Genny's ICU cubicle, his hands sweating and his stomach tied in knots. Jazzy glanced up from where she sat by Genny's bed, smiled at him, and motioned for him to come on in. He hesitated, his heart hammering in his ears. Jazzy said something to Genny, then got up and walked toward him.

She paused beside him and said quietly, "It's about time you showed up. Genny's been about to fret herself to death about you. Now get your ass in there and tell that woman you love her and you're sorry you worried her."

Dallas let out a pent-up breath, nodded, and forced his legs into action. When he was halfway across the cubicle, Genny saw him. For the rest of his life he'd remember the look on her face. Joy. No other word could describe her expression.

"Dallas." Her soft voice was terribly weak.

He all but ran the last few feet to her bedside.

"I've been so worried about you," she said and lifted her trembling hand.

Dallas grabbed that small, delicate hand and brought it to his mouth, kissed it, then held it to his cheek. She was the one who'd been shot—because he'd been lax in his attention for a couple of minutes—yet she was the one worried about him.

"I thought I'd die," he said, choking on his emotions.

"I would have felt the same if you'd been hurt. But you can stop hurting now. Release the pain. Let it go. I'm going to be all right. What happened wasn't your fault."

He swallowed hard, then kissed her hand again several times before he leaned over and kissed her mouth tenderly. "I love you, Genny Madoc."

"I know. I love you, too."

Dallas sat across the room in the corner while Jacob questioned Esther Stowe. Her husband was cooling his heels in another room, waiting for his lawyer. Esther had waived her rights to have an attorney present, telling them that she hadn't done anything wrong.

"I didn't have anything to do with shooting your cousin," Esther said. "Why would I want to hurt her?"

"You tell me," Jacob said. "Why would you or your husband want to kill Genny?"

Esther shrugged.

"We have a witness who saw your husband leaving the scene of the crime," Jacob said, stretching the truth slightly. "And that witness saw Reverend Stowe get into your car. Were you with him? Did you sit there and wait for him while he staked out Genny's house and shot her the minute she walked outside?"

"I didn't go anywhere with him. He drove off like a madman after we had an argument. How am I supposed to know what he was doing out in the woods? Besides, maybe your witness was wrong, maybe—"

"Does your husband own a rifle?"

"He has several rifles. Haden likes to hunt."

"If the bullet the doctor dug out of Genny's back matches one of your husband's rifles, then we'll have all the evidence the district attorney will need to prosecute the reverend for attempted murder."

"Okay, let's say he did try to kill her." Esther glanced at Dallas standing beside the window, then looked right at Jacob. "It's nothing to do with me. I wasn't with him. I'm not a part of it."

Jacob continued questioning Esther for a good thirty minutes, then took a break. Dallas figured he realized he wasn't going to break Mrs. Stowe. She was as tough as nails.

Jacob called Tewanda, who'd skipped her classes today just so she could pull a double shift and help out. The young deputy came to the office door and waited.

"Take Mrs. Stowe with you," Jacob said. "Get her something to drink and find her a place to relax for a few minutes."

After Tewanda escorted Esther from the room, Jacob shut the door and turned to Dallas. "I didn't do a very good job with her."

"You did fine. She's not going to tell you anything. As long as you don't have anything on her, she isn't worried. Even if people find out that she practices some form of devil worship and claims to be a witch, neither is actually a crime, not unless you can prove she's responsible for the animal sacrifices. As for her husband—she doesn't give a rat's ass if you nail his hide to the wall."

Dallas went over to the coffeemaker and poured two mugs full of the dark brew, handed one to Jacob, then took a sip from his.

"Tim's bringing Tommy Patrick in. They should be here soon. If Tommy can ID Haden Stowe, we won't have to wait any longer to arrest the bastard."

"Even if your guy can't positively ID Stowe, you should be able to get a search warrant for the parsonage. My bet is you'll find the gun Stowe used, as well as the shoes and coat he wore. It's only a matter of a little lab work and you'll have this case sewed up."

Someone knocked on the door. Dallas and Jacob turned just in time to see a stout, middle-aged man in a three-piece suit ease the door open and poke his head in to test the waters.

"Come on in, Maxie," Jacob said, then made an introduction. "Special Agent Dallas Sloan, let me introduce you to Maxwell Fennel, Reverend Stowe's attorney."

"May I come in?" Maxwell asked.

Jacob motioned him in. "Have you seen your client yet?"

"Just talked to him. He's a sorry sight. Pretty busted up about what happened. The man's on the verge of a nervous breakdown."

Jacob harrumphed. "You aren't planning on trying to use an insanity plea, are you?"

"Look, Jacob," Maxwell said, "the thing is, the good reverend has instructed me to tell you that he's ready to sign a confession. He says he shot Genny."

Chapter 25

Esther Stowe had become a liability since her husband's arrest five days ago. He couldn't allow her to live. She had deserted her husband without blinking an eye. The little witch could betray him just as easily. By now Sloan and Butler had probably figured out that their killer was a member of Esther's coven, so it was only a matter of time before they asked her for names. When they did, she might hold out for a while, but not for long. Not if she thought helping the law would work to her advantage. He knew she'd wind up giving them the names of the other satanists. He couldn't risk more suspicion falling on him. At this point they had no real evidence against him. He wanted to keep it that way.

Once again Fate had decreed who the next victim would be. He smiled to himself, thinking how shocked the high priestess would be when she realized she had become the sacrificial lamb. He considered it simply poetic justice that someone who had slaughtered so many animals in her quest to do the devil's bidding would in the end die in a similar manner.

He picked up the telephone receiver and dialed her number. She answered on the third ring. "Esther, my little lamb, I want to see you."

"So, come on over," she said. "Haden's still in jail. I'm sure as hell not posting his bond."

"Why don't you come here instead? I'll fix dinner, open a bottle of wine, and we can . . . enjoy ourselves."

"Sure, why not? It'll give me something to do. I've been told not to leave town."

"I look forward to our evening together."

"Right. Me, too. I could use a diversion, something wild and funky to take my mind off my problems."

Just the thought of her naked body aroused him. He licked his lips. He could almost taste her blood.

"I promise you the wildest night of your life."

After she'd been placed in a private room three days ago, Genny had asked the nurses not to give her any more pain medication, but Jacob had instructed them to disregard her protests. If only she had some of Granny's healing herbs, she could discontinue the narcotics. Sally had told her she'd go to the house, get her whatever she needed, and slip it in to her room. But Jazzy, knowing both her aunt and Genny quite well, had figured out what they were up to and had intercepted the contraband herbs.

Although she'd been in the hospital only five days, she felt as if it had been five weeks. The drugs induced odd, meaningless dreams and somehow made her more aware of colors and light. Everything seemed too bright, too vivid. But her usual sixth-sense abilities were dulled by the pain-killers. She picked up on things, bits and pieces of thoughts and feelings, but it was all fragmented. Her gift of sight had become cloudy, as if she were looking through muddy water instead of sparkling clean spring water.

Thankfully, just this morning the doctor had agreed to lower the dosage of her medication. Already she felt better, more like herself, although her psychic abilities remained subdued.

Since she'd been moved from ICU, she had received so many flowers that her room was beginning to look like a florist shop. Dallas alone kept The Cherokee Flower Box busy. Every day a new bouquet of roses arrived from him. Red roses. Pink roses. Yellow roses. Peach roses. White roses. And every day Dallas visited her at mealtimes and bullied her into eating. Dallas, Jazzy, and Jacob were the only three people allowed to come and go at all hours. So many friends and acquaintances had paraded in and out of her hospital room that the nurses had been forced to limit her visitors. Although allowed to visit only once a day, Brian and Royce called several times daily to check on her. And Ludie and Sally had been caught sneaking into her room more than once for a second daily visit. The nurses had nabbed the old ladies; whichever deputy was on guard duty outside her door at any given time knew both women and apparently didn't have the heart to turn them away.

Jazzy cracked the door and poked her head in. When she saw that Genny was awake, she smiled and walked into the room.

"How's it going this evening? You're looking even better than you did this morning."

"The doctors finally put me on a lower dosage of pain medication, so I'm feeling much better. More like myself."

"Do you think you're doing well enough to hear a news update?"

Genny nodded, then braced herself, uncertain what Jazzy might tell her.

Jazzy removed her coat, folded it, and laid it at the foot of the bed. "Maxwell Fennel has gotten two psychiatrists to swear Haden Stowe is crazy."

"I see. So that means he probably won't be sent to prison."

"Yeah, if the court-appointed psychiatrist agrees. If not, things could drag on for a while."

"How are Dallas and Jacob taking this latest turn of events?"

Jazzy clenched her teeth as she grimaced. "They don't

think he's nuts. They think he's faking it. And believe me, both of them would like to personally rip Reverend Stowe from limb to limb.''

"Neither of them will tell me anything about the murder cases,'' Genny said. "And they've made sure I don't see any local news. Would you please tell me, have there been any new developments?''

"You want to know if he's killed the fourth victim, don't you?''

"Since we're all ninety-nine percent sure I'm his intended fifth victim, yes, I'd like to know if I'm now next in line.''

"There haven't been any more murders.'' Jazzy sat on the edge of the bed and squeezed Genny's hand. "Now that you know, let's change the subject.''

"Thanks for telling me at least that much.'' Genny had to admit that spending day after day in a hospital bed, relying on others for her needs, gave her much too much time to think. And to worry. "How's the new bouncer working out? Has he kicked Jamie's butt again?''

"Everything in my life is just fine, except for the fact that my best friend got herself shot. As for the new bouncer—he's working out all right. Nobody's even tried to give him any trouble.'' Jazzy grinned. "Not even Jamie.''

"That's good.''

"Yeah.'' Jazzy glanced at her watch.

"You really don't have to stay with me until Dallas gets here. I'm perfectly fine by myself. After all, there's a deputy outside all the time.''

"I'm not going anywhere until Dallas gets here at eight o'clock.''

"It's ridiculous that he thinks he has to stay all night, every night.''

"Let the guy do what he wants to do.'' Jazzy got up, walked across the room, and dragged a chair next to the bed. "Believe me, he's sleeping better here curled up in a chair than he would back at his cabin. Honey, that guy is so crazy in love with you he can't see straight.''

"And I'm crazy in love with him, too.'' Genny burrowed

the back of her head deeper into the pillow, closed her eyes, and smiled.

"Want to watch *An Affair to Remember*? It's on the movie channel at six-thirty." Jazzy tapped the face of her chunky silver watch. "Five minutes till show time."

"Sounds great." Over the years, Genny had watched many an old movie with her best friend. One of Jazzy's passions was classic movies. Especially romances.

Jazzy turned on the TV, kicked off her shoes, and flopped into the chair. Genny relaxed and waited for the movie to start. They chitchatted for several more minutes, but once Cary Grant appeared on screen, Jazzy didn't say another word.

About an hour into the movie, Genny began to feel drowsy. She did her best to fight the grogginess, but finally she couldn't resist. She closed her eyes.

Dark swirling mists appeared in her mind. Deep purple fog grew darker and darker until black clouds swept away the mist. A woman was weeping, pleading for mercy. She didn't want to die. Tears streamed down her face. Genny saw the silhouette of a face blurred by some sort of veil. She tried to see the face, but something held the veil in place.

She heard the woman's thoughts. *Help me! Oh, Divine Lucifer, I am your devoted servant. Do not forsake me.*

Esther Stowe!

Genny didn't need to see the face to know who the woman was. Why was she having a vision about Esther? Would Esther actually become the killer's fourth victim? Could Genny trust her eschewed senses?

Clear your mind, Genny told herself. *Don't focus on Esther. You tried focusing on Misty Harte, but it didn't lead you to her in time to save her. You know who you must contact. If you can get inside his head, there's a chance you can save Esther and yourself.*

The darkness returned, but this was a different obsidian realm. More evil. And the presence she sensed was far more diabolical. He was as wicked and perverse as the devil Esther Stowe had tried to summon.

Who are you? Genny asked.

Genevieve Madoc, is that you?

She'd made the connection! Heaven help her.

I've wondered how long it would take you to visit me, he said, but Genny didn't recognize his voice because he spoke to her without a voice. Mind to mind. Thought waves.

Do you have Esther Stowe with you right now? Genny asked.

That isn't what you really want to ask me, is it?

Are you going to kill Esther? Will she be your fourth victim?

At dawn tomorrow, she will be sacrificed. And then, I will come for you.

Fear ate away at Genny's mind like a burning acid. And that fear broke the link to the killer's mind.

Genny cried out, "No, no. Come back."

Suddenly strong arms grabbed Genny and held her. Somewhere outside herself, in a reality far removed from the inner struggle tormenting her, she heard people talking.

"What the hell happened?" Dallas asked in an angry voice.

"I don't know," Jazzy replied. "She fell asleep while we were watching the movie. I thought she was resting until she started twisting and turning and mumbling. I tried to wake her, but she didn't respond."

Dallas shook Genny very gently. "Genny, sweetheart, wake up. Do you hear me? Come back to me right now."

Genny's eyelids fluttered. She tried her best to leave the depths of her subconscious, but something held her there.

"Get a nurse," Dallas said.

"She doesn't need a nurse," Jazzy told him. "I've seen her like this before. Many times. She's having a problem returning to reality, to true consciousness. Keep talking to her."

Jazzy moved to the other side of the bed and sat, then began patting Genny's cheeks. "Open your eyes. I know it's not easy, but you can do it. Come on. Work at it. Listen to my voice and to Dallas's voice.''

"Genny, you've got to come back to me," Dallas said. "Jazzy's right. You can do it.''

She could feel Jazzy's hands on her face, could hear their voices, sense their concern. She felt as if she were drowning in a pool of darkness, and the harder she tried to make her way to the surface, the stronger the stygian force became, pulling her deeper and deeper into a terrifying abyss.

Dallas, please help me. Pull me out of this darkness. I can't do it alone. She felt his strength and understood how desperately she needed it. If he connected with her, she could absorb the power coursing through him and free herself.

She sensed his surprise at being able to hear her. *Genny, you need to open your eyes and look at me.* Communicating to her without talking, Dallas's thoughts reached her subconscious. *I'm waiting here for you and I won't leave you. Whatever is holding you there isn't as strong as we are. Together we can fight and conquer any foe. Leave the darkness and come into the light.*

The minute she responded, he telepathically connected to her again. His thoughts and feelings surrounded her. Protected her. Together they fought the darkness.

Genny's eyelids fluttered again, and this time they slowly eased open. She blinked repeatedly. Then, after several tries, she managed to open her eyes fully and look up at two concerned faces.

"Thank God." Jazzy gave Genny a hug. "You had us scared to death.''

Genny stared directly at Dallas. "Esther," she said in a barely audible voice. She cleared her throat, then placed her hand atop Dallas's hand, which rested on her shoulder. "He's got Esther Stowe. He—he's going to kill her at dawn.''

"Did you get inside his head?" Dallas asked

Genny nodded.

"Damn, I thought you promised us not to—''

"Don't be angry." Tears gathered in Genny's eyes.

Dallas rubbed Genny's shoulders tenderly. "Don't cry. Please, don't cry. I'm not angry, just concerned."

"He told me that after he kills Esther, he's coming for me."

Dallas uttered a string of obscenities. He shot off the side of the bed and stormed out of the room.

"Dallas?" Genny called.

Jazzy grabbed Genny's hand. "Calm down. He just went out into the hall to cool off. You've got to understand how frustrating it is for him, and for Jacob, to know you're in danger and they can't get their hands on the killer who's threatening you."

"I have to help them find Esther." Genny tossed back the sheet and light blanket covering her and tried to sit up.

"What do you think you're doing? Don't you dare try to get out of that bed."

"Go get Dallas. Tell him I want to try to connect with the killer again. And I might be able to locate him, if—"

"I'm not going to say any such thing to Dallas. He'll go ballistic."

On her second attempt, Genny managed to sit up in bed, then she turned and dropped her legs over the side.

Jazzy rushed out of the room to get Dallas. Good. Genny had to make them understand that if they didn't find Esther before dawn, the minister's wife would become the fourth victim.

Just as Genny got to her feet, Dallas barreled into the room. Before she could slip into her house shoes, he lifted her in his arms and put her back in bed.

"Stay put." He pointed his index finger at her.

"I want to leave the hospital. Right now," Genny told him. "I think I can find Esther. I can sense that she's right here in Cherokee Pointe. Somewhere in town."

"You aren't strong enough to go anywhere," Dallas said.

"Dr. Rawlins plans to release me tomorrow afternoon. What difference is it going to make if I—"

"You came close to dying the other night." Jazzy sat on the foot of the bed and stared pleadingly at Genny. "You've barely recovered from a gunshot wound. And to make matters worse, you're wiped out from another visit to la-la land. Dallas is right—you aren't strong enough to go off on a psychic search for Esther Stowe.''

Genny glanced from Jazzy to Dallas. They weren't going to allow her to leave the hospital. So be it. She knew what she had to do. Genny lay down, closed her eyes, and placed her hands on top of her stomach.

''Damn it, she's fixing to try to go under again,'' Jazzy shouted.

Dallas grabbed Genny and shook her gently. He called her name repeatedly. She didn't reply. Then he tried to talk to her telepathically, but she wouldn't respond. She shut him out.

Genny knew it would be more difficult to locate Esther staying here in one spot. Not being mobile, she would be unable to feel her way closer and closer to where the killer was keeping his next victim. It would be more difficult, but she could locate Esther without leaving the hospital. It was the only way to save the woman's life.

Genny focused her thoughts on Esther. Every fiber of her being concentrated on locating the woman. Darkness swirled and parted, leaving cool gray shadows. *Where are you Esther? Where are you?*

No response.

Genny kept trying to make the connection. The power within her struggled to renew itself, but she soon comprehended the fact that her power was depleted. Being physically wounded, undergoing surgery, and then using her sight to connect to the killer tonight had rendered her psychic powers temporarily inert.

Emotion lodged in her throat. Tears trickled from her eyes. She reached up and wiped the moisture from her cheeks.

''She's crying,'' Jazzy said.

''Genny?'' Dallas brushed his hand across her damp cheek.

She opened her eyes and looked at him with her blurred vision. ''Tell Jacob about Esther. And tell him that I can't help him. I'm much too weak to . . ." Her voice trailed off. Weariness overpowered her.

"Thank God." Jazzy looked at Dallas. "Call Jacob, then go meet up with him and see what y'all can do to find Esther Stowe. I'll stay here with Genny."

"She'll be all right, won't she?"

Jazzy nodded. "After a good night's sleep, she should be fine."

When Genny realized Dallas was leaving, she tried to call out to him, but she couldn't even open her mouth. Her eyelids grew heavy and suddenly closed of their own volition.

Sleep claimed her for the night.

Chapter 26

Dallas appreciated the fact that Jacob had no qualms about letting him take part in his questioning of the three suspects that topped their list: Carson, Pierpont, and Upton. If just one of the three came up missing tonight, they would be able to narrow that list down to one suspect. And if all three were accounted for, then that meant one of two things— either the killer had Esther hidden away and he would return to her before morning or someone other than one of those three was the killer. If the latter was the case, then God help them, they'd be starting from scratch.

Dallas stood at Jacob's side when he rang the doorbell at the Upton mansion. The housekeeper came to the door in her robe and slippers.

When she recognized Jacob, she gasped. "Lord have mercy, what's wrong, Sheriff Butler?"

"Nothing's wrong, Dori," Jacob replied. "At least we hope not. But we need to see Mr. Jamie. Would you please tell him the sheriff needs a word with him."

"Land's sakes, do you know what time it is?" She gave Jacob a stern glare.

"It's not much after ten," Jacob told her.

"I'm not even sure Mr. Jamie is here. He's out and about so much since he came home. But I'll go see, so y'all might as well come on in. You can wait right in here, in the foyer."

Jacob removed his Stetson when he entered the house. "Thanks."

Before Dori reached the stairs, Big Jim Upton emerged from his study. "What the hell's going on?" He glanced from Jacob to Dallas. "Hold up, Dori."

The housekeeper stopped immediately.

"You go on back to bed," Jim said. "I'll speak to Sheriff Butler."

"We need to see Jamie," Jacob said.

"The boy's under the weather," Jim replied. "Think he might have a touch of food poisoning."

"Sorry to hear that, but all I need to do is see him for a couple of minutes."

"About what?"

Jacob huffed.

Dallas wondered what the odds were of their finding out if Jamie Upton was actually upstairs resting after a bout of vomiting and diarrhea, or if he was, as Dori had put it, out and about.

"We've got another woman missing," Jacob explained. "If Jamie's here, then we'll know he probably wasn't the one who abducted her."

Jim Upton narrowed his gaze and glowered at Jacob. "Come on. You can look in on him, but that's all. Not one damn word. Do you hear me? You harass that boy while he's sick and I'll press charges against you for police brutality."

Five minutes later, Jacob and Dallas got back in Jacob's truck and headed toward Dillon Carson's apartment.

"Well, if Jamie Upton wasn't sick, he deserves an Academy Award for his performance," Dallas said.

"He could still be the one. He could have kidnapped Esther Stowe earlier, stashed her somewhere, then gotten sick."

"Anything is possible."

Heading straight for town, Jacob pressed his foot on the

accelerator and the truck sped along the practically deserted road. When they arrived in Cherokee Pointe, they drove directly to Dillon Carson's place. Jacob whipped into the parking area of the apartment building where Carson lived, then killed the motor and got out. Dallas followed him upstairs and down a dimly lit corridor, right to their next suspect's front door.

Jacob rang the bell. No response. He rang it again. They waited. Nothing. Dallas looked at Jacob, who shook his head.

"He could be at Jazzy's Joint," Jacob said. "I think he's there nearly every night."

"Want me to call over there and find out?" Dallas asked.

Jacob punched the doorbell again. "Yeah, might as well. Apparently he's not here."

Just as they started to leave, the door swung open and a half-naked woman, wearing nothing but a sheer teddy that left nothing to the imagination, said, "What y'all want?" Her words were slightly slurred, and a rather dazed expression flattened her broad, full face.

Both Jacob and Dallas tried not to look at her large breasts or the black triangle of curly hair between her thighs. Practically simultaneously, they both swallowed, then cleared their throats. Obviously drunk, the big-boobed brunette swayed back and forth in the doorway.

"We're here to see Dillon Carson," Jacob told her.

"He's busy." Giggling, she put a finger to her lips. "Busy sleeping. I wore the poor guy out."

"Then he's here, in his bedroom?"

"He's not in the bedroom." She flung the door open all the way and pointed toward the sofa. "He's right over there."

Dillon Carson lay with his head and upper torso on the floor and his hips braced against the front of the sofa. His legs gaped apart and one foot rested atop a cushion and the other under it. He was buck naked.

"How long have you been with him?" Jacob asked.

"Not sure. A couple of hours . . . maybe," she said. "We

met up over at Jazzy's Joint, had a few drinks and then came back here.''

While Jacob spoke to the woman, Dallas walked across the living room and inspected Carson. He reached down and lifted the guy's arm. When he let go, the arm dropped to Carson's side like a lead weight.

''He's out cold,'' Dallas said.

''Sorry to have bothered you, ma'am.'' Jacob tipped his Stetson.

Dallas nodded to her as he followed Jacob. Neither man said a word until they reached the truck. Dallas paused and glanced across the hood at Jacob.

''We're batting zero,'' Dallas said.

''One more strike and we'll be out.'' Jacob frowned. ''Pierpont's place isn't far from here. He's got an apartment over his antique shop.''

''Let's head out.'' As soon as Jacob unlocked the truck, Dallas got in. ''You drive, I'll contact Chief Watson and get an update from the task force. With a dozen men out scouring the town for Esther, maybe somebody's come up with a lead.''

Within a few minutes Jacob parked in front of the antique shop. He kept the motor running to provide heat while Dallas finished his conversation with Chief Watson. Damn, Jacob had been right about that guy—he was an idiot. Instead of being at the police station heading up the investigation for his department, Watson was home watching a basketball game on TV.

''Haven't heard a word,'' Watson said. ''So I guess nobody's come up with anything on that Stowe woman's whereabouts. You and Jacob having any luck?''

''Not so far. Sorry to have interrupted your ball game.'' Dallas hit the OFF button on his cell phone.

''Ball game?'' Jacob lifted his eyebrows. ''Let me guess—he's home watching TV.''

''A trained orangutan would make a better police chief.''

''Ever thought about changing jobs, moving to a small

town, and settling down with a good woman?" Jacob asked as he killed the truck's motor.

"Since meeting Genny, I've had lots of odd notions," Dallas admitted. "I don't think she'd want to leave Cherokee County."

"Nope. You could never take her away from these hills."

"So, do you think the chief's job might come open anytime soon?" Dallas opened the truck door.

Jacob and Dallas got out, then Jacob locked the doors and stepped up on the sidewalk. "After the way he's mishandled his part of the murder investigations, I don't think even Big Jim Upton will be able to help him keep his job. I'd say there will be an opening for police chief before too long."

Once again Jacob led and Dallas followed. The apartment upstairs was reached by a long narrow hallway hidden behind an exterior door between the antique shop and the lawyer's offices next door. Dallas waited several steps down from the apartment entrance since there was barely enough room for Jacob on the narrow landing.

"I don't see any sign of a doorbell, but it's so damn dark up here, I can barely see my hand in front of my face." Jacob lifted his hand and knocked loudly.

Silence.

Jacob knocked again. Louder and longer.

No answer.

Maybe Pierpont was their man. Maybe he had Esther Stowe bound and gagged in his bedroom right now. Or perhaps he'd already moved her to the altar site.

Jacob tried a third time. Nothing. Then just as they turned around and were headed downstairs, they heard the sound of footsteps. The door creaked open and a ceiling light came on.

A bleary-eyed Royce Pierpont asked, "Who's there?"

"Royce, it's Sheriff Butler."

"Jacob, what's wrong? Has anything happened to Genny?"

Dallas stayed put while Jacob climbed back up to where Pierpont waited in the doorway.

"Genny's fine. But Esther Stowe is missing, and Genny's sure Esther is the next victim."

"Then why are you here to see me?" Pierpont gasped and clutched the lapels of his silk robe. "My God, you still suspect me of being the killer, don't you?"

"We're just checking around town," Jacob replied. "We have to do everything we can to find Esther."

"Yes, yes, of course you do." Pierpont nodded. "I understand. If it will ease your mind, feel free to come inside and search my apartment. I assure you that Esther Stowe isn't here."

Jacob hesitated a moment. Dallas cleared his throat, then said, "Go ahead and take a look. I'll wait right here for you."

"Yes, yes, come in." Pierpont waved his hand in a welcoming gesture. "I apologize for taking so long to come to the door. I haven't been sleeping well lately. Not since Genny was shot. I finally gave in to my desperate need for rest and took a sleeping pill about an hour ago."

"Yeah. Okay." Jacob entered the apartment.

Dallas waited. He could hear Pierpont's incessant chatter as he followed Jacob from room to room during his inspection. In three minutes flat, Jacob returned, said good night, and motioned for Dallas to head downstairs. Pierpont politely left the light on for them.

"So where do we go from here?" Jacob asked.

"We join up with the task force and pray we can find Esther before daybreak." Dallas paused on the sidewalk in front of the antique store. "Put a tail on Pierpont, Carson, and Upton until morning. If any one of them decides to take a midnight ride, we want to know about it."

Butler and Sloan suspected him, but he wasn't the only one they suspected. There were others on their list. Both men were smart, but he was smarter. In the end, he'd out-

smart them all. Now that the two lawmen had paid him a
visit and he'd allowed a few hours to pass, he knew what
he had to do. He'd never sacrificed a victim anywhere near
where he lived, but in this case he'd have little choice. Esther
was in the basement, bound, gagged, drugged, and waiting
for his return. He didn't dare try to move her. If Butler was
as smart as he thought, then he'd have sent out watchdogs
to keep an eye on his three main suspects. That probably
being the case, he had no choice but to sacrifice Esther in
the basement. The dawn sunlight could be seen through the
two small, high windows in the area where he had erected
the altar.

It might take weeks, even months for someone to discover
Esther's body in the basement. By then it wouldn't matter.
By then he would be invincible, powerful beyond his wildest
dreams. Once he had taken Genevieve Madoc's heart and
consumed it, her powers would belong to him. He would
have no equal here on earth. Only divine spirits would be
his equals.

*You would be so proud of me, Mother. Your bad, bad
little boy is going to be the most powerful creature in the
world. If only you were still alive to see the glorious day.*

Genny screamed. Jazzy shot up out of the chair where
she'd been sleeping and rushed to Genny's side. Genny lay
there, her eyes closed, her body stiff as a poker. And she
kept screaming and screaming. A plump, blond nurse rushed
into the room almost immediately and tried to waken Genny,
but without any luck. The screams woke everyone on the
floor. Over Jazzy's protests, the nurse gave Genny an injection.

"Just a sedative to calm her," the nurse explained.

"She doesn't need a sedative, damn it," Jazzy said. "She
needs to wake up."

The screaming continued for several minutes, then Genny
started crying and moaning. She thrashed about in the bed
as if she were fighting a demon.

"I've never seen anything like it," the young nurse said.

"I have," Jazzy murmured.

"I'll put in a call to Dr. Rawlins."

"He won't be able to help her."

Jazzy sat on the bed, grabbed Genny by the shoulders and held her as she struggled. "Come back, Genny. You've gone in too deep. Wherever you are, it's dangerous for you there. Don't let him win. Don't you dare let him win!"

Genny continued fighting for several minutes, then she stilled and began breathing normally. Her eyelids fluttered, then opened.

"Call Jacob," Genny whispered. "He's already killed Esther. I could see her plainly. She was lying on a tattered chaise longue. And the sword . . . the sword ripped through her flesh. Blood. So much blood."

Jazzy glanced at the closed blinds covering the window in Genny's room. She walked over to the window and opened the blinds. The faint pink glow of morning light brightened the dark sky.

Chapter 27

He had waited until the officer watching his home drove away at seven o'clock. Apparently his orders had been to stay until well after daybreak. What no one knew, not the officer who'd kept watch all night nor the sheriff and the members of his task force, was that he had already sacrificed Esther Stowe, down in the basement. Everything had gone according to plan. His only regret was that he hadn't dared allow Esther to scream. Someone might have heard her.

He kept his coat and hat on and a scarf wrapped around the lower part of his face as he entered the hospital through the ER entrance. Earlier in the week, he had taken the time to scope out the entrances, determine where the guards were located, and discover what doors were locked at night and exactly when they opened each morning. The only entrance that was open twenty-four hours a day was the automatic double doors leading from the ambulance delivery area to the ER's waiting room.

There were only two people in the waiting room, but neither paid much attention to him as he walked through and headed toward the long hallway that would take him to the elevators. He checked his watch. He had to get to Genny's room and take her from the hospital before Dallas Sloan arrived for breakfast. Or perhaps Sloan wouldn't show up this morning, since the federal agent had probably joined the task force in the massive manhunt for Esther Stowe. They wouldn't find her, of course. At least not any time soon.

He kept a close lookout all around him; it wouldn't do for him to run into someone he knew. Of course, if necessary, he could just say he'd stopped by to see Genny. After all, it wouldn't be a lie. He really was here to see her. To see her, drug her, and take her away.

After entering the elevator and finding himself alone, he smiled as he punched the UP button. So far so good. With a little luck his plan would work. When he arrived on the second floor, he went directly to the storage room he'd spotted when he'd been checking out Genny's floor. He closed the door behind him, then flipped the light switch. He removed his scarf, coat, and hat, folded them neatly, and stuffed them in the garbage can. Then he took off his trousers and added them to the other clothing. Placing his hands on either side of his head, he adjusted the wig he wore.

Too bad there wasn't a mirror in here, he thought. He'd really like to check his nurse's attire, to make sure he looked just right. But he'd put together this costume as meticulously as he did everything else. And he had applied his makeup carefully. Lipstick, blush, and eyeliner. Thankfully, no one would suspect he wasn't female, not with his pretty face. Mother had always said he was too pretty to be a boy.

Hustle, hustle, he told himself. Time's a-wasting. Luckily he didn't encounter any of the nurses as he made his way down the hall. In his peripheral vision, he spotted a cafeteria staffer rolling the five-tier breakfast cart from the elevator. The young woman brought the cart to a halt several feet from the nurses' station, then went over and began talking to the LPN on duty.

He eased up behind the cart, slid a tray off the top, and, whistling inside his mind, headed toward Genny's room. He recognized the guard outside her door.

"Good morning, Deputy Willingham," he said in his best alto voice. He could mimic his mother's voice so well that sometimes he spooked himself just hearing the sound.

"Morning," the deputy replied.

"May I take Genny's breakfast in to her?"

"Sure. Go on in."

He slipped right past the stupid deputy. The man hadn't bothered to ask why Genny's breakfast was early, and he hadn't even noticed that no one else on the floor had received a tray yet. And Genny's room was near the end of the hall, so she should have been one of the last patients served.

When he entered Genny's room, he kept his head down. He had to work fast if his plan was to come off without a hitch. Being as astute as she was, Genny might pick up on his true identity, so it was best if she didn't get a close look at his face before he subdued her. There would be time enough to reveal himself later.

He glanced at the bed. Empty. Suddenly he heard water running in the bathroom. He set the tray on the portable table, then removed one of the two hypodermics in his pocket. He popped off the plastic cap to expose the needle and opened the door very quietly. Deputy Willingham had his back to the door.

Thanks for being so cooperative.

He eased up behind the deputy and shoved the needle into his buttock, right through his pants. Willingham yelped and grabbed his butt, but before he could do more than glance over his shoulder, he slumped to the floor. He clutched the guy by his shoulders and dragged him straight into Genny's room. Just as he positioned the deputy halfway under the bed and only partially out of view, Genny emerged from the bathroom.

"Morning, dear," he said to her in Mother's sweetest voice. "Breakfast's here."

Genny stopped just outside the bathroom. She stared at him. Hell, was his wig on crooked? he wondered. Had she recognized his voice even though he'd disguised it?

''Need some help getting back into bed?'' he asked and scurried toward her.

She held up a hand, motioning him to stop. He paused, then moved toward the bed. He fluffed the pillow and straightened the cover. Genny crept around the foot of the bed and headed toward the door. He grabbed her just as she caught hold of the door handle. When she opened her mouth to cry out, he covered her mouth with one hand and dragged her to the bed. She fought him, but luckily she was a small woman who wasn't fully recovered from surgery. He threw her onto the bed and with his one free hand jerked the other hypodermic from his pocket. Using his teeth, he removed the plastic cap covering the needle. Genny's eyes widened in fear when she realized what he was going to do. When she squirmed and tried again to fight him, he flattened one of his knees atop her chest, then took the syringe and aimed it at her hip. Within seconds, she passed out.

The door to the stairs was at the end of the hall, only two rooms down from Genny's room. All he had to do was wrap her in a blanket, carry her less than fifteen feet, and he'd be almost home free. There was little chance anyone would see him. Few people used the stairs, especially not this early in the morning. And he'd parked his car in the employee's lot, near the back entrance. Since the day shift had already come on and the night shift had left, there shouldn't be any activity in that area. Once he had her safely in the trunk of his car, he would take the back road from the hospital out of town.

He had chosen the perfect place for her sacrifice. A place worthy of a Druid priestess or a Cherokee shaman. The blood of both ran through Genevieve Madoc's veins. She'd told him so herself.

Dallas arrived at the hospital at precisely eight-twenty. Genny would have showered by now and would be waiting for him. For the past thirty minutes or so he'd had the oddest feeling. He couldn't quite put his finger on it, but he sensed something was wrong. Of course, the problem could be that he'd been up all last night, working with Jacob and the task force, trying their best to track down Esther Stowe. But she was still out there somewhere. Either dead or alive.

When he came out of the elevator on the second floor, he immediately realized the staff was in a frenzy. He'd never seen so many hospital personnel running up and down the halls. The minute he reached the nurses' station, the nurse on duty recognized him.

"Oh, Agent Sloan, thank God you're here." The nurse wrung her hands nervously. "I called Sheriff Butler and he's on his way to the hospital right now."

Fear grabbed Dallas by the gut and squeezed tight. "Is Genny all right?"

"I don't know how it happened. None of us saw a thing."

Dallas broke into a run. As he neared Genny's room, he noticed a hospital security officer talking to several white-clad women. When he tried to shove past them to get into Genny's room, the security officer grabbed his arm.

"Deputy Willingham is unconscious. One of the nurses found him under Miss Madoc's bed."

Dallas grabbed the officer by his shirtfront and glared directly into his eyes. "Where is Genny?"

"We don't know. She's gone."

Dallas released the officer, then shoved past him and into Genny's room. The first thing he spotted was the used syringe lying on the bed.

God damn it to hell! The killer had Genny!

When Genny regained consciousness, she didn't know where she was or what had happened; then her eyelids flew open and everything came back to her all at once. A frigid chill racked her body. She was cold. Terribly cold.

She glanced around, trying to see if she recognized her

surroundings. She was in a cave. A campfire sparkled golden orange in the shadowy darkness within the cave, but was too far away to warm her. When she tried to move, she discovered her hands and feet were bound. She tried to open her mouth, but couldn't because she'd been gagged. Looking down at herself, she realized she was still wearing the same flimsy hospital gown, and a blanket covered her from her waist to her feet.

She searched all around as best she could, but saw no sign of another human being. *Where is he?* Had he brought her here and left her? If so, he would come back before dawn tomorrow morning.

She had to contact Dallas. *And tell him what?* she asked herself. *You don't know where you are.*

Genny rolled over, flipping the blanket off, and continued rolling across the cold, damp ground inside the cave. Like a baby unable to walk and undecided about crawling, she rolled over repeatedly until she reached the cave's entrance. Gazing up at the sky, she realized it was already noon. The sun shone high overhead. As she lay flat on her back, she scanned the area outside. Trees. Trees. And more trees. She was in the middle of the woods somewhere, probably on the mountain, since the hills were pocked with caves. Off in the distance, toward the east, she noticed a clearing. *Think, Genny, think. Does anything look familiar?*

The town was overrun with panicked folks being filmed by local and out-of-town TV cameramen. What appeared to be law enforcement officers from nearby towns and from the state merged half a block away at the courthouse. Jazzy tried to make her way through the horde that lined the streets. She'd heard that not only was Esther Stowe still missing, but that Genny Madoc had been kidnapped from her hospital bed. If Genny was missing, why hadn't Jacob called her? She had tried to call him, but the lines were busy and his voice mail had responded when she'd tried his cell phone.

As she walked up the street, she noticed the mass of

people all around the courthouse. She thought she caught a glimpse of Jamie, but when she looked again, he was gone.

After fighting her way through the crush of people, she saw Bobby Joe Harte in the parking lot at the rear of the courthouse, guarding the back entrance that led directly to the sheriff's office. She jumped several times to lift herself above the milling crowd and shouted his name. Bobby Joe waved her forward as he ordered the people blocking her path to let her through.

Before she reached her destination, a TV reporter thrust a microphone in her face. "Miss, may I ask your name?"

"Get out of my way," Jazzy warned him.

"Why is it that the deputy over there is going to let you through when he's holding everyone else at bay?" the reporter asked.

"Who the hell are you and what are you doing in Cherokee Pointe?" Jazzy asked him.

"Whit Conners from WHRB in Chattanooga."

"Well, Whit, get the hell away from me and tell your cameraman"—she pointed her index finger at the burly six-footer who had the camera aimed directly at her—"to stop filming me or I'll take his toy away from him and stomp it to pieces."

"Are you a witness of some sort?" Whit just wouldn't give up. "People all over eastern Tennessee are interested in what's happening here in your little town. We understand there have been three gruesome murders recently and now two more women are missing."

"She's Jazzy Talbot," a voice in the crowd shouted. "Her best friend is our local psychic, the one who was kidnapped right out of her hospital room this morning."

Jazzy managed to break through a line of newspaper reporters stationed in front of Bobby Joe and successfully managed to leave Whit Conners behind.

"What's going on?" Jazzy asked Bobby Joe, shouting to be heard over the din of voices.

"Go on inside and talk to Jacob," Bobby Joe said. "We

haven't had time to get in touch with you. This all came down so fast.''

''Just tell me this—is Genny missing? Was she kidnapped from the hospital?''

Bobby Joe nodded.

Jazzy felt as if she were going to throw up. The killer had Genny! Oh, God! Oh, God!

Chapter 28

"Going somewhere, my precious?"

Genny gazed up at the man towering over her, a sick smile on his handsome face. Her stomach knotted painfully. Even when Dallas and Jacob had put him on their suspects list, she hadn't seriously considered the possibility that he was the killer. She thought she knew him, thought he was her friend, and had actually believed he loved her. Using his own psychic skills, though they were limited, he had apparently been able to block any negativity coming from his mind and thus made it even more difficult for her to read him correctly. And as a general rule, she tried not to delve into other people's minds without their permission. If only she had gone against her principles and looked beyond the gentle, sweet facade he presented to the world.

He reached down and removed the gag from her mouth. "Scream all you want up here; no one will hear you."

"Why?" she asked. "Tell me why?"

Holding the back of her gown, he dragged her across the ground and into the cave. Tiny shards of sharp pebbles and jagged edges of windblown twigs scratched her back, buttocks, and legs. Clamping her mouth closed, she endured the pain, determined not to cry out, not to give him the satisfaction of hearing her weep. He hauled her toward the campfire, then released her.

"You, Genevieve Madoc, are my crowning achievement," he told her. "After Mother died, I set out to prove to her—and to the world—that I was not a weakling, that although my own psychic powers were limited, I would find a way to become the most powerful of all earthly spirits. I've searched for years, choosing my victims carefully, picking the ones who possessed special powers."

Genny swallowed hard. "All of your victims weren't gifted. Only the fifth victims."

His smile widened. His pale crystal blue eyes sparkled with wicked delight. "Very astute observation. Your lover is a smart man, but not smart enough to catch me."

"Dallas will get you, even if he has to spend the rest of his life tracking you down. You'll never be free from him."

"Once I obtain your power, I will be beyond any man-made law. No one can touch me then."

"And just how do you intend to obtain my power?" she asked, knowing all along that he intended to kill her, sacrifice her as he had all the other poor women.

"You must be sacrificed, of course." He reached down and ran his fingertips from her neck to her belly.

She cringed, hating his touch, fearing his next move. "And after I'm sacrificed?"

"Mother taught me that a person's power lies in the heart, and that those unique gifts given to only a special few— such as she—can be transferred to another if you consume their heart."

Genny closed her eyes. *Do not let the fear overtake you. Concentrate on finding a way to escape and on making a telepathic link with Dallas. If you panic, if you allow the sheer horror of his intentions to paralyze you, he will win— and you will lose your life.*

"Tell me more about your mother." Whatever demons plagued him, they had come to life at his mother's knee.

"Mother was a powerful witch." He knelt beside Genny.

"She was a true high priestess." He laughed, the sound deceptively soft. "Nothing like Esther Stowe, who was a phony. That stupid little witch was nothing than a whore trying to pass herself off as a priestess."

"Your mother was—" When he pulled a knife from his pants pocket, she tensed. "Your mother was very important to you. You must have loved her a great deal."

He grabbed the top edge of Genny's hospital gown, lowered the knife and sliced the thin material from neck to hem. Genny shivered, more from aversion and foreboding than from the wintry cold.

"Loved her?" He cocked his head to one side as if listening to someone speaking. "Yes, Mother, I should tell her, shouldn't I?"

"Tell me what?"

"I was afraid of her. I feared her power. I was a great disappointment to her, you see, because my talents paled in comparison to hers. She thought I would be a great sorcerer, but alas, I was not, but I proved myself useful to her. I assisted her with the sacrifices and learned from her the importance of the fifth victim. She always sacrificed five animals, the fifth with the greatest power. And sometimes, if I was a very good little boy, she would allow me a bite of the fifth animal's heart."

"But your mother didn't kill people, did she? She didn't do what you're doing."

He knelt over her until his face was up against hers. "That's why I will be more powerful than she ever was. I'll give her what she always wanted." He licked Genny's face. "I sacrificed four animals when Mother died, and then when I cut out her heart and ate it, I thought her power would transfer to me, but it didn't. I realized then that the first four had to be humans also. Otherwise it wouldn't work."

He was completely insane!

Dallas, can you hear me. Please, hear me. I'm in a cave somewhere in the mountains. Open your heart, and listen.

I need you. Come to me. Follow my thoughts and you'll find me.

He ran his fingertips over her breasts. She tried to block out the feel of his hands on her body. Summoning her ability to remove herself from reality, she went farther inside herself.

Dallas . . . Dallas . . . please, respond to me. She tried to concentrate solely on making contact with the only person with whom she shared the rarest of all connections. He would be able to track her through her thoughts and find her. But only if he believed. Only if his love was strong enough.

When her captor's warm, vile semen hit the valley between her breasts, she turned her head and emptied her stomach.

Checking out the whereabouts of their three primary suspects, Jacob and Dallas found Dillon Carson still at home, sporting a massive hangover, the results of his drunken binge the night before. And Jamie Upton was resting in bed, with his grandmother and fiancée catering to his every whim. But Royce Pierpont's antique shop was closed, and he didn't respond when they knocked on his door. Going against the law and not giving a damn, Dallas broke into Pierpont's apartment. He and Jacob searched the place from top to bottom, but found nothing that might link him to Genny.

"Does this place have a basement?" Dallas asked.

"Yeah, I think so. Almost all these old buildings have basements."

"Got any idea how to find the entrance?"

Jacob shook his head. "Not really, but my guess is we'll find it somewhere in one of the back rooms of the antique shop."

"We'll try the back door. No need for anyone to see us breaking and entering." Dallas headed down the apartment stairs. By the time his feet hit the sidewalk outside, Jacob came up behind him.

"You don't have a problem breaking and entering, do you?" Jacob asked.

"I've never been a by-the-rules kind of guy," Dallas said. "And when it comes to saving Genny, I'd break every law in the books, if that's what it took."

"Then what are we waiting for?"

The two men exchanged a meaningful look, then Dallas ran down the block, rounded the corner, and headed up the alley. When Jacob caught up with him, Dallas already had the back door to the antique shop open and was going inside. As luck would have it, the stairs to the basement were in the storage room directly off the alleyway.

Groping in the dark, Dallas sought and found a light switch. Several high-wattage bulbs came on instantly, lighting the stairs and brightening the dark, dank basement. When he reached the foot of the rickety, wooden stairs, Dallas sniffed the air.

"I smell it too. Blood and . . ." Jacob's jaw clenched.

"The scent of death."

Jacob nodded.

They found Esther Stowe on an antique chaise longue that had been used as an altar. Her body had been sliced open, just like the other victims.

"It's Pierpont," Dallas said. "And he has Genny."

Leaving everything just as they'd found it, Dallas and Jacob returned to Jacob's truck. Esther Stowe wasn't going anywhere. No one would be disturbing the scene of the crime. With saving Genny their top priority, they headed out of town, following the massive manhunt for Genny that had moved from Cherokee Pointe into the surrounding county.

They knew who the killer was. Unfortunately, that knowledge wouldn't help them find Genny. He could have taken her anywhere in the whole county.

Leaning his head back against the leather seat, Dallas closed his eyes. *Genny, where are you?*

Jacob turned to Dallas, a somber expression on his face.

''We're going to find her. And when we do, I want Pierpont. Do you hear me? Pierpont's mine.''

''No,'' Dallas replied, his eyes still closed, his heartbeat humming in his ears. ''He's mine.''

Jacob didn't respond. He had to understand that as much as he loved Genny, she was no longer his responsibility. She belonged to Dallas now, as he belonged to her. He was her protector.

Genny, reach out to me, connect with me. Help me find you.

Dallas's mind began floating free, off into another realm. Dark, swirling clouds filled his mind.

I'm here, Dallas. I'm here.

''Genny!'' Dallas's eyelids popped open as he shouted her name aloud.

Jacob slammed on the brakes. ''What is it? What's wrong?''

''I don't know. Nothing.'' Dallas gulped several times. ''I think Genny just contacted me.''

''Then by God, you'd better listen to her.''

Dallas closed his eyes. *Genny, I'm listening. Talk to me.*

Come to me. He heard the words that weren't spoken, only felt with the heart. *If we stay together and don't break the bond, you can find me. You'll know where I am.*

Can't you tell me where he's taken you? Dallas asked her.

High in the mountains. Deep in the woods.

Has he harmed you?

When she didn't respond, a horrific ache began in Dallas's gut and spread through his entire body.

If he's hurt you, I'll—

Concentrate all your energy on staying linked to me so you can find me. Don't waste your strength on anger.

Dallas tried to banish every thought from his mind except Genny. As he focused on her and her alone, a sensation of unbelievable power encompassed him. And then he knew.

''Go northeast, up the mountain, to the very top,'' Dallas said.

Without questioning him, Jacob headed the Dodge Ram northeastward.

"Only a few more hours to wait," Royce told her. "I've prepared the altar in the grove. Here atop the mountain is a perfect setting for you, my precious Genevieve. Your blood will spill onto the earth you love so dearly."

Genny heard the drone of Royce's voice, but she didn't even try to listen to his undistinguishable words. She kept her mind linked with Dallas's as she had for endless hours. Time had ceased to exist. All she felt was Dallas's love. All she heard was Dallas's thoughts. All she knew was that with each breath she took Dallas was drawing closer and closer.

Suddenly she felt other thoughts intruding, other minds trying to link with hers. She fought the intruders, but their voices became so strong they forced her to hear them. Precariously hanging on to her bond with Dallas, she listened and responded.

Yes, yes. Come to me. Help me. Lead Dallas to me.

The search party had combed the mountaintop, with Sally and her fully recovered bloodhounds tracking, hoping for a scent to lead them to Genny. Still linked to Genny, Dallas knew she was in this area and not far from him. But where was she? Her signals had grown weaker during the past couple of hours, as if her strength was depleted and she was struggling to hang on.

"Is this the highest point on the mountain?" Dallas asked Jacob.

"Yeah." His eyes widened with revelation. "No! Oocumma Mount is the highest elevation."

"Is it east of here?"

Jacob pointed the direction. East. "Straight up there, right into the clouds."

"That's where Genny is," Dallas said.

"There are no roads up there. He would have had to park his car and carry her."

"Then that's what he did." Dallas grabbed Jacob's shoulders. "I'm telling you she's up there. I need you to show me the way."

"Let's tell the others," Jacob said. "They can follow us."

"Time to leave our cave," Royce said. "It will be dawn shortly. I don't want to wait until the last minute and not have everything prepared perfectly." He ran his gaze over her from face to feet. "It should be a consolation to you to know your great psychic gifts will live on after you, that when you die, your power will transfer to me."

"You're wrong," Genny told him. "You will never possess my power. Do you hear me, Royce? If I die, my special gifts die with me. My talents are hereditary. They can't be transferred to anyone."

He lifted her off the ground and carried her out of the cave. She wriggled and squirmed with what little strength she had left, trying to make it as difficult as possible for him to hold her. He paused, set her on her feet, and grabbed her by the neck.

"Why aren't you afraid?" he asked her. "You're going to die, and no one can save you."

Genny could sense them nearby. They were coming to her, dozens of them, showing Dallas the way.

"You will be the one to die," Genny said, her voice utterly calm.

He tried lifting her again, but Genny dropped to her knees. *Come to me. You're close. So very close.*

Royce glared at her. "Either cooperate or I'll drag you from here to the altar."

Genny considered her options. Royce lifted her to her feet, then hoisted her over his shoulder. She lay there quietly, all the while summoning her rescuers.

*   *   *

After removing a couple of rifles from Jacob's truck and slinging the weapons over their shoulders, Dallas followed Jacob up the winding path leading to Oocumma Mount. Sally had let Peter and Paul loose as soon as they cleared the mountain spring that created a wild, flowing brook criss-crossing their path.

"I can't make it to the top," Sally said, then spit out a stream of tobacco juice. "I'll wait here and show the others the way." Suddenly Sally looked overhead at the starry night. "What the hell?"

"What is it?" Jacob's gaze followed Sally's. "I'm be damned."

Dallas looked up. Dozens of owls filled the sky.

The mournful wail of a wolf echoed through the hills, then several reciprocal cries began an animal chorus. A rumble of hooves was added to the whoosh of winged creatures. All around them the forest awakened, bursting into life. As if being herded in one direction—or summoned to one place—deer and elk joined bobcats, mountain lions, coyotes and red wolves.

"It's Genny," Dallas said, more certain than he'd ever been in his life.

"Yeah, it's Genny." Jacob slapped Dallas on the back. "Follow them. They'll lead us straight to her."

Royce had constructed a crude altar of stones and covered it with a folded white sheet. He laid Genny on the altar and pulled her bound hands over her head so that her breasts lifted. After checking the sky, he knelt down and picked up a wooden box from the ground beside the altar.

The frigid air chilled Genny. She was so cold she was almost numb. Raised off the ground, with the winter wind tormenting her naked body, she prayed.

She could feel her prayer leaving the earthly realm and entering the spiritual region. She gave herself over completely to the power of goodness. Love surrounded her. Dallas's passionate love. Jacob's brotherly love. Jazzy's sisterly love. The love of all the kind souls who knew her. And the pure, devoted love of God's creatures.

A dog's howl blended with those of the wolves. Genny continued praying, sending out positive energy into the world.

Royce removed the sword from its velvet bed and brandished it over Genny's head.

He bent down and whispered in her ear, "Soon, my little lamb. Soon."

"Yes, soon."

He dipped the sword toward her, letting it almost touch her as he slid the blade along the chosen path. "Why aren't you screaming, Genny? They always scream in the end. You will, too."

"You will be the one screaming," she told him.

Genny glanced to the east. A hint of pale pink crept over the dark horizon.

"The moment the sun touches this sword, everything I've ever wanted will be mine," Royce said triumphantly.

"Look around you," Genny said. "See the fate that awaits you."

"What are you talking—" Royce squinted, trying to make out the shadows surrounding them. "What's going on? What are they—"

The sky grew lighter as dawn arrived. Royce stared at the array of wild animals that formed a circle around the altar, only a few feet away. A pack of wolves formed the inner circle. Genny's Drudwyn was with them, along with Sally's Peter and Paul. At least a dozen deer stood off in the distance, watching and waiting. And enormous wolves lumbered toward the altar from east, west, north, and south. Owls and various birds filled the trees and circled overhead.

"What's happening?" Royce's voice quivered with fear.

"Don't you know?"

Royce shook his head.

"Can't you guess?" Genny taunted him. "I called Drudwyn and he summoned the mountain's predators and woodland creatures to protect me."

Royce lifted his sword into the air. The first faint rays of sunlight reflected off the metal.

"You will die. Your power will be mine," Royce shouted. "Then I will control these beasts!"

He swung the sword backward, then brought it forward, but before it could touch Genny, a rifle shot rang out. The bullet from Dallas's weapon whizzed past the congregation of animals to hit its mark—Royce Pierpont. He screamed with pain, then fell to the ground.

Dallas and Jacob rushed toward the altar. Tears of thankfulness filled Genny's eyes. Working fast and furious, they untied Genny's bound hands and feet, then Dallas lifted her into a sitting position, removed his coat and wrapped it around her.

"I knew you would come to me," Genny told him, her voice barely audible.

"Don't try to talk, sweetheart," Dallas said. "We need to get you to the hospital right away."

"I'll be fine. Don't worry." She glanced toward the ground where Royce had fallen, but he wasn't there. "Where's—" Her heart stopped beating for an instant when she realized that two wolves—under Drudwyn's directions—were dragging Royce's body by his arms.

"I'm not shooting any wolves just to retrieve that monster's body," Jacob said.

"Let them have him." Dallas cocooned Genny in his strong embrace and headed away from the clearing on Oocumma Mount.

While the wolves provided nature's justice, the woodland animals dispersed, disappearing into the forest, and the owls and other birds flew away, clearing the morning sky.

Epilogue

Springtime in the mountains was just around the corner. The winter-dead world was already showing signs of new life. Crocus flowers poked their small, colorful heads through the hard, cold ground to announce the annual renewal of Mother Earth. And with each passing day, Genevieve Madoc healed. Physically. Mentally. Emotionally. But more importantly, she was healing spiritually. Dallas's love and devotion enveloped her with the strength she needed to not only survive, but to regenerate.

What was left of Royce Pierpont's body when the *wolves* finished with him, was sent through the proper channels and as far as everyone knew had received a Christian burial. Jazzy, for one, hoped they tossed his remains in the river for fish food.

Cherokee Pointe and the entire county had begun to bounce back and return to normal. In a few weeks the spring tourist season would begin, and the little town's numbers would triple. Jazzy could hear the cash registers ringing already. She smiled to herself.

"Everything's ready," Tiffany said.

Startled, Jazzy gasped.

"Sorry." Tiffany laughed. "We're all set. When do you expect them to get here?"

"Any minute now."

"Do you want to do a quick inspection?"

"Yes, I'd—"

The front doors to Jasmine's swung open, and Dallas escorted Genny inside. Jazzy rushed to meet them.

"You look absolutely gorgeous." Jazzy clutched Genny's hands and surveyed her from head to toe. Genny wore a black satin dress in a simple design, topped with a hand-embroidered black cashmere sweater.

"What about me?" Dallas asked teasingly.

Jazzy gave him a quick glance. He was decked out in a black suit, white shirt, and solid red tie. "You look gorgeous, too." Jazzy lifted Genny's left hand. "Let me see it."

"See what?" Genny smiled.

"Hey, half the town knows that Dallas was giving you a ring tonight."

"Everybody knew except me," Genny said.

Jazzy studied the diamond solitaire on the third finger of Genny's left hand. "Wow, what a rock." She glanced at Dallas. "That must have set you back a pretty penny." She winked at him. "Are you sure you can afford it now that you don't have a job?"

"I've got a sizable nest egg, Ms. Mother Hen," Dallas replied. "Shrewd investments and wise financial planning."

"That's good to know." With a sweep of her hand, she invited the couple into the empty restaurant.

Genny glanced around at the beautiful roses on every table and the white candles shimmering in crystal holders. "Are you having a private party here at Jasmine's tonight?"

"Yep. Sure am."

"Oh, Jazzy, did you—?"

"What a perfect intro." Jazzy let out a long, loud whistle.

Dozens of people streamed out of the kitchen and into the restaurant, Jacob leading the pack. Sally and Ludie, along with Wallace, followed Jacob. Countless other friends and acquaintances filled Jasmine's, each offering Genny and

Dallas their best wishes. Then the crowd parted to allow Dallas's family to come forward. His eyes widened in surprise as he watched his sisters, Savannah and Alexandria, come rushing to him. He opened his arms to embrace them. His brother-in-law, niece, and nephew hovered in the background; then when the sisters finished hugging and kissing him, his brother-in-law shook his hand and slapped him on the back. His nephew, Mark, shook hands, following his father's lead. But ten-year-old Amy jumped up into his arms and gave him a sloppy kiss on the cheek.

"It's a surprise engagement party," Jazzy said. "In case you haven't figured it out yet."

Genny turned to Dallas. "Did you know about this?"

When he grinned sheepishly, Genny punched his arm.

"I swear, I didn't know." Dallas tapped the tip of her nose with his index finger. "But why didn't you know, my little sorceress?"

"Because someone has been keeping me so occupied with physical matters that I haven't had time to think, let alone use my clairvoyance."

While Dallas introduced Genny to his family, Tiffany came over with a silver tray laden with champagne flutes. Jazzy removed two glasses and handed one each to the happy couple.

A violinist strolled down the hall from Jazzy's office, already playing a romantic melody.

"Ain't life grand?" Jazzy hugged Genny. "I don't know anyone who deserves to be happy more than you do."

Genny hugged Jazzy fiercely. "Your time will come. I promise."

Jazzy pulled away. "There are presents, you know. Lots of presents. But don't think this takes the place of a bridal shower. And I've got the bachelorette party all planned."

Dallas slipped his arm around Genny's waist. "Come on, *a qua da li i.* Let's mix and mingle. Now that I've been offered Roddy Watson's old job, I should get better acquainted with my constituents."

"Calling me your wife is a bit premature since we're not

making it legal until June.'' Suddenly comprehending what
he'd said about the position as chief of police, Genny gasped.
''Oh, Dallas, you didn't tell me. When did—''

''I got the phone call today, while you were taking a nap.
I wanted to wait until our dinner tonight to tell you.''

''Congratulations, Chief Sloan!'' Jazzy laid her hand on
Dallas's back.

''What's this?'' Jacob asked as he joined the threesome.

''Dallas has been offered Roddy Watson's old job,'' Jazzy
said. ''Imagine that.''

''Let's keep that news to ourselves for now,'' Dallas said.
''Tonight is all about Genny accepting my proposal and
making me the happiest man in the world.''

''How the mighty have fallen.'' Jacob chuckled.

''You just wait,'' Dallas told him. ''Your time is coming.
One of these days some sexy little thing is going to come
along and you won't know what hit you. Not until after she
has you on your knees begging her to put you out of your
misery.''

''Not going to happen,'' Jacob assured him.

Jazzy sashayed over to Jacob and slipped her arm through
his. ''Since you're going to be the best man and I'm going
to be the maid of honor come June, we should make the
first toasts tonight. Try to say something romantic, something
from the heart.''

''I don't do romantic,'' Jacob grumbled.

''For Genny's sake, you could try.'' Jazzy tugged on
Jacob's arm and he responded, allowing her to lead him
toward the bar.

''She gets enough romantic mush from Dallas.''

''You, Jacob Butler, are hopeless. I pity the poor woman
who winds up with you.''

''Jazzy Talbot, the guy who gets stuck with you will be
the most henpecked, dominated poor soul on earth.''

''Since we know each other so well, warts and all, maybe
we should just get married. That way we wouldn't ever have
to concern ourselves with romance.''

Jacob chuckled. "We've already tried dating and found out there just aren't any sparks between us."

"Maybe we'd be better off without sparks. It would make things less complicated."

"Less complicated, but not worth the effort."

Jacob and Jazzy lifted glasses from the bar and raised them in honor of the engaged couple. Jazzy clinked her long nails against the side of her glass, hoping to gain the guests' attention. But the noise level was so loud that no one heard her.

Jazzy hoisted herself up and onto the bar, then shouted, "Listen up, everybody."

The room grew quiet. Jazzy smiled.

She hoisted her champagne flute higher. "Here's to Genny and Dallas." She looked at the couple and smiled. "May you always be as deeply in love as you are tonight."

The partygoers cheered. Jazzy nodded to Jacob.

He cleared his throat and saluted the couple with his glass. "Here's to you, Dallas. And all I can say is—better you than me."

Everyone laughed.

Dallas pulled Genny into his arms and kissed her, right there in front of their families, friends, acquaintances—and before God. A preliminary for their wedding day.

Jazzy had never envied anyone so much in her entire life.

Dear Reader,

I'm sure when you finished reading THE FIFTH VICTIM, you were left wondering what the future held for several important secondary characters, especially Jazzy Talbot and Jacob Butler. From the conception of Genny's and Dallas's story, I visualized a trilogy set in Cherokee County, Tennessee, with Jazzy as the heroine of the second novel and Jacob the hero of the third. I'm pleased to tell you that both books are available. First look for THE LAST TO DIE. Jazzy will be accused of murder and no one suspects that the real killer has plans for Jazzy to be the last to die in a string of brutal murders. Be sure to read the brief excerpt in the back of this book. The final book of the trilogy is AS GOOD AS DEAD.

I love hearing from readers, so please write to me in care of Kensington. Check out my website at www.beverly barton.com where you can enter my contests, find my e-mail address and a list of all my books. And don't forget to sign up for my e-mail newsletter.

Warmest regards,
Beverly Barton

Turn the page for a
sneak peek at
The Last to Die by Beverly Barton.

Prologue

He pounded on her door and shouted her name. *Go away,* she wanted to scream. *Leave me the hell alone.* But she knew he wouldn't go. Not unless someone came and dragged him away. Maybe she should call Jacob and tell him that Jamie was harassing her again. As the county sheriff, he could hold Jamie in jail overnight. Or she could phone Caleb and ask for his help in getting rid of an unwanted midnight visitor. Caleb had gotten plenty of practice lately as the bouncer at Jazzy's Joint. He'd thrown Jamie out of the place several times recently. But for some reason, she just couldn't bring herself to pick up the telephone. It wasn't that she wanted to see Jamie. Not tonight of all nights. But she'd been expecting him, had known somewhere deep down inside her that he would pay her a visit after his engagement party ended.

"Jazzy . . . lover, please, let me in."

His voice was slightly slurred, no doubt the result of numerous glasses of champagne, and not the twenty-dollars-a-bottle stuff either. Probably Moet's Dom Perignon or Taittinger Comtes des Champagnes. Or possibly Roederer Cristal or Pommery Cuvee Louise. Something that cost no less than eighty bucks a bottle. In hosting the big bash celebrating their only grandchild's upcoming nuptials, Big Jim and Reba Upton had spared no expense. Everybody in Cherokee Pointe had been talking of nothing else. The Uptons had hired a catering service out of Knoxville for the engagement party and the rehearsal dinner, the same service the bride's parents had chosen to cater the wedding reception next month.

While Jamie continued banging on the door and pleading with her to talk to him, Jazzy curled up tightly on the sofa and placed her hands over her ears. Jamie had been engaged twice before and hadn't followed through with wedding plans either time. But it looked as if his engagement to Laura Willis might actually end in marriage. If for one minute she believed Jamie's marrying another woman would put an end to his obsession with her, she'd be the first in line to offer them congratulations.

Sure, there had been a time when she'd dreamed of becoming Jamie's wife, but that had been years ago, when she'd been young and foolish. That stupid dream had died a slow, painful death as maturity had given her a firm grip on reality. No way would Jamie's rich and socially prominent family ever accept her; they still saw her as nothing but a white trash tramp who'd gotten pregnant at sixteen. Did she still care about Jamie? Yeah, somewhere in her heart remnants of that passionate first love still existed. Only a few years ago, she had still been as obsessed with Jamie as he was with her. For the past ten years he had floated in and out of her life, just as he had floated in and out of town. But this time, when he'd returned a few months ago with a new fiancée in tow, Jazzy had turned him away when he'd come to her. And one night, when he hadn't taken no for an answer, she had threatened his life. Or, to be more precise, she'd threatened his manhood. And what truly frightened her was the realization that she would have shot him—shot his balls off—if he'd come after her again.

"Jazzy . . . don't be mean. Please, doll baby, let me come in. Just one last time. Don't you know how much I love you?"

No, damn you, no! You don't love me! You never did. You're not capable of loving anyone except yourself.

While she sat on the sofa, hugging herself, wishing she could block out the sound of Jamie's pleading, memories washed over her, flooding her senses. The first time Jamie had kissed her. The junior/senior prom, when she'd given him her virginity and had known she would love Jamie forever. The day he'd cried when he told her he couldn't marry her even though she was carrying his child. The night he had returned to Cherokee Pointe after his first year of college. They'd made love repeatedly for forty-eight hours, leaving bed only when necessary. The first return visit, years ago, when he'd brought home his first fiancée—and Jazzy had welcomed him into her arms, into her bed, not caring about his bride to be.

How many times had she forgiven Jamie? How many times had she given him just one more chance? Time had run out for them. She knew it, even if he didn't. She'd turn thirty soon; she had wasted enough of her life waiting for Jamie Upton to give her what she wanted, what she'd always wanted from him. Marriage.

"Jazzy . . . Jazzy . . . baby, please, talk to me. Even if I marry Laura, it doesn't mean we can't still be together."

A cold, deadly calm settled over her heart. She stood, squared her shoulders and walked to the door. Her hand hovered over the knob. *You're the only one who can end this thing once and for all,* she told herself. *Do what you have to do to free yourself from Jamie.*

Simultaneously Jazzy unlocked the deadbolt and turned the knob. When she eased open the door, Jamie took full advantage and shoved his way into her apartment. Before she could say a word, he grabbed her and kissed her. Impatiently. Brutally. His tongue thrust inside her mouth. For a split second, she savored his savage possession. Then common sense took charge. She broke away from him, her breathing ragged. He reached out for her, but she sidestepped his grasp.

"I need you, Jazzy. I'm aching, I want you so bad."

"What we once had is over," she told him. "It's been over for a long time. I've accepted that fact. It's time you did."

"I don't love her. I'm marrying her because Big Mama is giving me no other choice. She expects me to marry Laura."

Jazzy laughed, mirthless chuckles. "And God forbid you ever go against what Big Mama wants."

"I'm sorry." His shoulders slumped. "I know I'm a spineless bastard. But if I don't keep Big Mama happy, I could lose everything. Big Daddy's done told me this is my last chance. If I screw things up with Laura, he'll write me out of his will."

Jazzy almost felt sorry for him. Almost. "You know I'll never be your mistress. I draw the line at fooling around with a married man."

Lifting his sedate gaze from where he'd been staring at the floor, he looked directly at her. "Would you let me stay tonight? Just for a little while. A couple of hours." He held up his arms in an "I surrender" gesture. "Just let me hold you. I swear, I won't do anything you don't want me to do. I need you, Jazzy. One last time. Please, lover. Please."

Against her better judgment, she nodded. "You can stay an hour. That's all." When he opened his arms to her, she shook her head. "Sit down on the sofa. I'll fix us some coffee. I think you could use some. You should sober up before you head home and try to explain to your fiancée where you've been."

"Hey, honey, if you're planning on getting your gun while the coffee is brewing, there's no need. Believe it or not, I want us to be friends. I'd prefer lovers, but I'll settle for friends. I just can't imagine my life without you in it."

Oh, hell. Why had he said that? *Don't go soft. Not now. You've heard Jamie's line of bull before. You know the guy can sweet talk his way out of any jam—or into any woman's bed.* But not her bed. Not ever again.

"You aren't going to get to me," she told him. "Remember, I've heard it all before. I'm the girl you honed your persuasion skills on."

"You may not believe me, Jazzy, but . . ." He came up behind her, but didn't touch her, just stood very close, his
breath warm on her neck. "In my own selfish way, I do
love you. I always have. And I always will."

Odd how a part of her wanted to believe him, maybe even
needed to believe him. When she turned to him, he reached
out and caressed her cheek. She sucked in her breath.

"Please, Jazzy." He looked at her with those sexy hazel
eyes, his expression one of intense longing. "Baby . . .
please."

She didn't protest when he pulled her close. Gently. And
kissed her. Tenderly. All the old feelings resurfaced and for
a moment—just a moment—she wanted him in the same
old way. He allowed her to end the kiss. Then he stood there
staring at her, waiting for her judgment call.

"I can offer you coffee and conversation for an hour,"
she told him. "That's it. Take it or leave it."

"I'll take it." A sly, seductive grin curved the corners
of his lips as he turned and walked over to the sofa, then
sat and crossed one leg over the other knee.

You're a fool, Jazzy told herself as she rushed into the
kitchen and prepared the coffeemaker. Being nice to Jamie
wasn't the answer. But God in heaven, old habits died hard.

Tonight she would say good-bye to Jamie. This time
would be the last time. And if he ever came to her again,
she knew what she'd have to do. She'd have no choice, not
if she wanted to save herself.

The man had to die! It wasn't that she wanted to kill him
or anyone else, but he had left her no other choice. Not only
would he have to die, but she feared others would have to
forfeit their lives, also, if they interfered. Of course, it wasn't
entirely his fault; after all, he was only human, a mere man,
with all the weaknesses inherent to his sex. But he was the
worst of his kind, spineless and weak. He gave in to his
baser instincts without regard to how his actions might harm

others. He reveled in the depravity that plagued most men and many women.

Her hand settled over her belly. In order to protect herself—and her baby—she needed to plan a strategy that would put suspicion on someone else. But not just anyone. She wanted that woman to pay with her life, and what better justice than to have her executed for murdering her lover? After all, the whole town knew she'd threatened to kill him.

She stood in the shadows, waiting and watching, knowing where he was and what he was doing. He was with that woman, making love to her. How could he do this? He had sworn his love was true. Lies. All lies! They were fornicators. Sinners. Evil to the core. Both of them deserved to die. To be punished.

She shouldn't act hastily, in the heat of the moment. That was the way mistakes were made. She had made mistakes in the past, but not this time. She had trusted when she shouldn't have, but never again. She needed to be calm and in control when she ended the son of a bitch's life. There was no need for her to kill him tonight. As long as she eliminated him before his wedding day, everything would be all right.

She would not kill him quickly. A quick death was too good for him. He needed to die slowly, painfully, tortured and tormented. The thought of listening to his agonizing screams excited her. Her mind filled with vividly gruesome impressions of his last hours on earth.

"Everything I do, I do for you, my sweet baby. I won't let anyone hurt you. They think we aren't good enough for them. They think they can sweep us out the door and pretend we don't exist. But I won't let that happen. You don't have anything to worry about. Not now. Not ever. Mother's here . . . Mother's here."

NEW GAME

The game is simple—he is the Hunter. They are the Prey. He gives them a chance to escape. To run. To hide. To outsmart him. But eventually, he catches them. And that's when the game gets really terrifying . . .

NEW RULES

Private investigator Griffin Powell and FBI agent Nicole Baxter know a lot about serial killers—they took one down together. But this new killer is as sadistic as they've ever seen. He likes his little games, and he especially likes forcing Nic and Griff to play along. Every unsolvable clue, every posed victim, every taunting phone call—it's all part of his twisted, elaborate plan. And then the Hunter calls, wanting to know if they're *really* ready to play . . .

BUT WINNER STILL KILLS ALL . . .

There's a new game now, and it's much more deadly than the first. A brutal psychopath needs a worthy adversary. He won't stop until he can hunt the most precious prey of all—Nicole. And with his partner in a killer's sights, Griff is playing for the biggest stakes of his life.

Please read on for an exciting sneak peek of Beverly Barton's THE MURDER GAME, coming in February 2008!

Prologue

I am not going to die! Damn it, I refuse to give up, to let him win this evil competition.

Kendall Moore pulled herself up off the ground where she had fallen, face-down as she ran from her tormentor. Breathless and exhausted, she managed to bring herself to her knees. Every muscle ached. Her head throbbed. Fresh blood trickled from the cuts on her legs and the gashes in the bottoms of her calloused feet.

The blistering August sun beat down on her like hot heavy tendrils reaching out from a relentless monster in the sky. The sun was her enemy, blistering her skin, parching her lips, dehydrating her tired, weak body.

Garnering what little strength she had left, Kendall forced herself to stand. She had to find cover, a place where she had an advantage over her pursuer. If he caught up with her while she was out in the open, he would kill her. The game would be over. He would win.

He's not going to win! Her mind screamed orders—run, hide, live to fight another day. But her legs managed only a few trembling steps before she faltered and fell again. She needed food and water. She hadn't eaten in three days and hadn't had any water since the day before yesterday. He had been pursuing her from sunup to sunset for the past few days, apparently moving in for the kill. After weeks of tormenting her.

The roar of his dirt bike alerted her to the fact that he was nearby, on the narrow, rutted path to the west of her present location. Soon, he would come deeper into the woods on foot, tracking her as he would track an animal.

At first she had been puzzled by the fact that he had kidnapped her, then set her free in the middle of nowhere. But it hadn't taken her long—only a matter of hours—before she realized that she wasn't free, no more than a captive animal in a game reserve was actually free.

Day after day, he stalked her, hunted her down, and taught her how to play the game by his rules. He'd had more than one opportunity to kill her, but he had allowed her to live, and he'd even given her an occasional day of rest. But she never knew what day, so she was forced to stay alert at all times, to be prepared for yet another long, tiring match in what seemed like a neverending game.